MW00335886

NOBODY'S SAFE HERE

BILL PERCY

BLACK ROSE
writing™

© 2016 by Bill Percy
All rights reserved. No part of this book may be reproduced, stored in a retrieval
system or transmitted in any form or by any means without the prior written
permission of the publishers, except by a reviewer who may quote brief passages in a
review to be printed in a newspaper, magazine or journal.

The final approval for this literary material is granted by the author.

First printing

This is a work of fiction. Names, characters, businesses, places, events and incidents
are either the products of the author's imagination or used in a fictitious manner.
Any resemblance to actual persons, living or dead, or actual events is purely
coincidental.

ISBN: 978-1-61296-787-5
Library of Congress Control Number: 2016956751
PUBLISHED BY BLACK ROSE WRITING
www.blackrosewriting.com

Printed in the United States of America
Suggested retail price $20.95

Nobody's Safe Here is printed in Adobe Caslon Pro
Cover design by David Levine at https://www.linkedin.com/in/david-levine-a094b110.

MONDAY, DAY ONE

1

A candle, sputtering on a darkened shelf, cast twisted shadows onto the wall. The boy sat against the opposite wall, only five feet away. On the floor in front of him, he saw a black shape, darker than a shadow. It terrified him. He hunched inside the storage unit, curled into himself, hugging a rifle against his chest, the barrel's hard steel caressing his cheek. The black shape, like a chasm, pulled him. He clamped shut his eyes. *No.* He forced himself to open them, to look, though he felt paralyzed. *Try to understand.* Sudden waves of rage buffeted him, then fear, then rage again, storm-tossed waves, billowing, battering. As each surge ebbed, a new crush of panic, fury, confusion rolled over him. He felt tossed. Hanging on, he pressed the rifle harder against his chest, his cheek harder against the cold steel barrel, as if it were a stanchion on a capsizing ship.

If I move, I'll kill them.

He closed his eyes to escape the flickering, jerking shadows. Had he seen blood spattered on the wall behind the shadows? Were the screams in his ears real?

Have I killed them already? He pressed his cheek harder against the barrel, hoping pain would block the terror and the fury. But no. He sank beneath this storm. He struggled, panted, panted again, then held his breath. Went under.

Perhaps he fell asleep.

Perhaps he died.

He opened his eyes. The room was black. The candle had guttered. For a few moments, its death comforted him. The storm of hate and horror seemed to have subsided, leaving an emptiness laced with confusion. How long had he been away? And where? His chest ached from the hard steel.

Painfully, he untangled himself, tried to stand. Stiff, dizzy. He braced a hand against the wall. After a moment, he searched, his hands blind, for the electric lantern. Knocked over the dead candle. Found the lamp, flicked it on.

Dazed by the sudden light, he squinted, but saw no blood on the wall, no black hole in the floor. His head, filled with screams before, was silent. *Maybe I haven't done it yet.* As his eyes adjusted to the light, he counted the rifles stacked in the corner beside the ammunition boxes. *No, all here. Not yet, thank God.* Eight weapons, plus the one lying at his feet. His chest throbbed. From embracing the rifle? From terror?

Groggy, he aligned his lone weapon with the others lining the wall and arranged the boxes, neatly re-stacking the ammunition as his grandfather had taught him. He rubbed his chest as he doused the lantern and opened the shed door. Morning sunlight stunned him; he retreated into the darker space, letting his eyes come to terms with the bright air streaming in. A last burst of anger lurked behind his heart.

When his eyes were ready for the sun, he stepped through the door. Turning back to lock the door, he thought, *I'll be late for school.* That last anger boiled. He slammed his fist against the wooden wall.

When will this shit end?

2

From across the street, Loretta Tweedy, eighty-nine years and a month, watched the boy lock the shed door, then strike it with his fist.

She stage-whispered toward the kitchen, as if the boy could hear, "Ardyss! Come quick! He's coming out!"

Ardyss Conley, Loretta's friend and roommate, herself only seventy-four, came into the living room, wiping her hands on a flowered apron. "Breakfast is almost ready." She stooped and peered over Loretta's shoulder through the window. "Awfully early in the morning to be doing whatever he does in there."

"I tell you," Loretta snapped, "I've seen him at all hours." She pulled the curtain wider. "There, see?" The boy was climbing into his green pickup truck. "Isn't that the Hansen boy?"

Ardyss chuckled. "Aren't you the nosiest old lady on the block?"

"Humph. I'm the *only* old lady on the block. What's he doing in there?"

Ardyss shrugged. "Why don't you go out there and ask him?"

Loretta dropped the curtain. "It's not right, a young man like that spending hours in a storage unit. Believe me, he's up to no good."

Ardyss turned back to the kitchen. "I'll have breakfast on in five minutes. If you're so worried, call the sheriff's office."

"They'll think I'm an old busy-body, for heaven's sake."

"You *are* an old busy-body. Call that Deputy Pelton. She's a nice girl. Get it out of your system."

Loretta grumped, "My system." But when Ardyss went into the kitchen, she reached for the telephone.

3

"April's the cruelest month, but I'm damned if this one ain't a killer," groused Sheriff Ben Stewart.

His deputy, Andi Pelton, grinned. "Shakespeare, right?"

Ben grunted. "Might be." He liked to hide his erudition. "First we get us the flood, then this heat." Standing beside him outside the open storage unit, Andi heard a raw catch of anger in his voice, a stifled rage against the violations in his valley. Two weeks ago, eleven unforecast inches of rain had drowned half the town. Now, this, whatever this was.

Ben glared into the open storage unit. Inside, Deputy Pete Peterson scribbled on a clipboard, inventorying a stack of weapons and ammunition boxes. Beside him, Deputy Brad Ordrew was opening cardboard boxes.

"Crap on toast," Ben muttered. "Makes a guy think there ain't nobody safe here anymore."

Ordrew, his eyes narrow, called from inside, "We got us a mass shooter in full prep mode, folks."

Andi peered over Ben's shoulder. Visible in the dim unit, beside the rifles, stood a carefully stacked pile of ammunition boxes. She grimaced. "Maybe. Could be another explanation. But thank God for Loretta's tip. Never saw this coming."

Pete nodded. "Old Loretta's got the eagle eye, all right." He chuckled. "Even if she does piss off the neighbors."

The sheriff pulled off his cap and roughly rubbed his graying, curly hair. "Overtime budget's already shot to hell, and this'll put a big dent in what's left—and it ain't even wildfire season yet." He put his cap back on, patted it tight.

Andi stepped around him, her hand resting briefly on Ben's arm, as if comforting him. She leaned into the storage unit. "Pete, can you tell if anyone else beside the Hansen boy is involved?" After Loretta's call, when they'd phoned the building's owner to meet them and unlock the storage room, he'd told them it had been rented by Jared Hanson, a local teen, seven weeks ago.

Pete straightened up and shook his head. "No sign of that yet. Just Jared, best I can tell." He stepped out into the sunlight and removed his cap; sweat beaded his forehead. "Damn hot in there. Strangest weather."

Andi looked up at the iron-blue sky and nodded. Ordrew followed Pete out; he too mopped sweat off his face. "Must be a hundred-ten degrees in there," he said.

Pete nodded. "At least." He fanned himself with his cap, then gestured with it toward the unit. "This looks wrong as hell."

"Meanin'?" Ben asked.

"The Hansens belong to our church. I've known Jared since he was seven. Always been a great kid."

"So, what do you make of it?"

"Beats me. Nine rifles, two hundred rounds of ammunition. A pressure cooker. Jesus." He shook his head. "This doesn't square with anything I know about him."

Ordrew said, "Isn't it obvious? Pressure cookers? He's prepping for a mass shooting or a bombing."

Pete frowned. "Just one pressure cooker. If I didn't know Jared, I'd think it's possible, but he's just not right for that."

Andi asked, "How old is he?"

"Seventeen, maybe eighteen. He's a senior." Pete turned to Ben. "I know I'm up to catch this case, but..."

Ben stopped him. "I'm puttin' Andi in the lead on this one, Pete; you're too close. Brad, you'll work second with her."

Ordrew's eyes darkened, but he shrugged.

Ben ignored the look, said to Pete, "That good for you?"

"Thanks, boss. I like Jared too much."

Andi looked in at the pile of weapons in the shadows. "You said nine rifles? They're not semi-automatics."

"Nope, not one. They're all single-shots, take 30-06 Springfield cartridges. He's got a couple hundred extra rounds in the boxes."

DEDICATION

This one's for Aaron, Cary, Jason, Jen, John, and Melissa—
no author could be as proud of a book as I am of my powerhouse offspring
and their beloveds. As long as I have you guys,
I don't need to write another word.
Well, okay, maybe another novel, or three.

ACKNOWLEDGMENTS

I seldom feel really safe asking for help with my books, but my expert crew not only made *Nobody's Safe Here* much better than I could by myself, their feedback and advice were given so safely that I was always left wanting more.

My first and finest reader, Michele, read the rawest draft (actually the fifth—who feels safe exposing the first draft, for heaven's sake!) and so skillfully sandwiched her "Oh my, this has to go" between such hearty "Wow, this stays!" moments that I gladly killed the darlings she marked in red.

My editors, Lorna Lynch and Kim Cheeley, tightened and cleaned the manuscript until its aim was true and its action smooth. Lorna and Kim have mastered the editorial art of saying, "This could be so much better..." without alarming the authorial "unsafe-index." Brilliant, and so affirming.

I owe a thousand thanks to David Levine for the stunning cover design and to book designer Patti Frazee for the interior design and preparation of the book for printing. Both were easy to work with and kept the process safe and straightforward.

My beta readers, Mark Cherniak, Ken Stewart, Sandy Kostere, and Sara Wright, each found their own unique, gentle, and safety-generating ways to deliver remarkably astute and intuitive suggestions to improve the book.

Finally, profound thanks to Scott Edelstein for his canny, professional, and off-the-charts useful advice about publishing and marketing, about which I remained—until I met Scott—a wide-eyed rookie, ripe for the picking. I'm still a rookie, but not so wide-eyed. Especially, thanks to Scott for his amazing tweak of the title, from *Nobody's Savior* to *Nobody's Safe Here*. In this season of Trump, terrorists, and tribulation, when none of us feels very safe, he persuaded me that the title—and the book—nails the moment.

NOBODY'S
SAFE HERE

MONDAY, DAY ONE

1

A candle, sputtering on a darkened shelf, cast twisted shadows onto the wall. The boy sat against the opposite wall, only five feet away. On the floor in front of him, he saw a black shape, darker than a shadow. It terrified him. He hunched inside the storage unit, curled into himself, hugging a rifle against his chest, the barrel's hard steel caressing his cheek. The black shape, like a chasm, pulled him. He clamped shut his eyes. *No.* He forced himself to open them, to look, though he felt paralyzed. *Try to understand.* Sudden waves of rage buffeted him, then fear, then rage again, storm-tossed waves, billowing, battering. As each surge ebbed, a new crush of panic, fury, confusion rolled over him. He felt tossed. Hanging on, he pressed the rifle harder against his chest, his cheek harder against the cold steel barrel, as if it were a stanchion on a capsizing ship.

If I move, I'll kill them.

He closed his eyes to escape the flickering, jerking shadows. Had he seen blood spattered on the wall behind the shadows? Were the screams in his ears real?

Have I killed them already? He pressed his cheek harder against the barrel, hoping pain would block the terror and the fury. But no. He sank beneath this storm. He struggled, panted, panted again, then held his breath. Went under.

Perhaps he fell asleep.

Perhaps he died.

He opened his eyes. The room was black. The candle had guttered. For a few moments, its death comforted him. The storm of hate and horror seemed to have subsided, leaving an emptiness laced with confusion. How long had he been away? And where? His chest ached from the hard steel.

Painfully, he untangled himself, tried to stand. Stiff, dizzy. He braced a hand against the wall. After a moment, he searched, his hands blind, for the electric lantern. Knocked over the dead candle. Found the lamp, flicked it on.

Dazed by the sudden light, he squinted, but saw no blood on the wall, no black hole in the floor. His head, filled with screams before, was silent. *Maybe I haven't done it yet.* As his eyes adjusted to the light, he counted the rifles stacked in the corner beside the ammunition boxes. *No, all here. Not yet, thank God.* Eight weapons, plus the one lying at his feet. His chest throbbed. From embracing the rifle? From terror?

Groggy, he aligned his lone weapon with the others lining the wall and arranged the boxes, neatly re-stacking the ammunition as his grandfather had taught him. He rubbed his chest as he doused the lantern and opened the shed door. Morning sunlight stunned him; he retreated into the darker space, letting his eyes come to terms with the bright air streaming in. A last burst of anger lurked behind his heart.

When his eyes were ready for the sun, he stepped through the door. Turning back to lock the door, he thought, *I'll be late for school.* That last anger boiled. He slammed his fist against the wooden wall.

When will this shit end?

2

From across the street, Loretta Tweedy, eighty-nine years and a month, watched the boy lock the shed door, then strike it with his fist.

She stage-whispered toward the kitchen, as if the boy could hear, "Ardyss! Come quick! He's coming out!"

Ardyss Conley, Loretta's friend and roommate, herself only seventy-four, came into the living room, wiping her hands on a flowered apron. "Breakfast is almost ready." She stooped and peered over Loretta's shoulder through the window. "Awfully early in the morning to be doing whatever he does in there."

"I tell you," Loretta snapped, "I've seen him at all hours." She pulled the curtain wider. "There, see?" The boy was climbing into his green pickup truck. "Isn't that the Hansen boy?"

Ardyss chuckled. "Aren't you the nosiest old lady on the block?"

"Humph. I'm the *only* old lady on the block. What's he doing in there?"

Ardyss shrugged. "Why don't you go out there and ask him?"

Loretta dropped the curtain. "It's not right, a young man like that spending hours in a storage unit. Believe me, he's up to no good."

Ardyss turned back to the kitchen. "I'll have breakfast on in five minutes. If you're so worried, call the sheriff's office."

"They'll think I'm an old busy-body, for heaven's sake."

"You *are* an old busy-body. Call that Deputy Pelton. She's a nice girl. Get it out of your system."

Loretta grumped, "My system." But when Ardyss went into the kitchen, she reached for the telephone.

3

"April's the cruelest month, but I'm damned if this one ain't a killer," groused Sheriff Ben Stewart.

His deputy, Andi Pelton, grinned. "Shakespeare, right?"

Ben grunted. "Might be." He liked to hide his erudition. "First we get us the flood, then this heat." Standing beside him outside the open storage unit, Andi heard a raw catch of anger in his voice, a stifled rage against the violations in his valley. Two weeks ago, eleven unforecast inches of rain had drowned half the town. Now, this, whatever this was.

Ben glared into the open storage unit. Inside, Deputy Pete Peterson scribbled on a clipboard, inventorying a stack of weapons and ammunition boxes. Beside him, Deputy Brad Ordrew was opening cardboard boxes.

"Crap on toast," Ben muttered. "Makes a guy think there ain't nobody safe here anymore."

Ordrew, his eyes narrow, called from inside, "We got us a mass shooter in full prep mode, folks."

Andi peered over Ben's shoulder. Visible in the dim unit, beside the rifles, stood a carefully stacked pile of ammunition boxes. She grimaced. "Maybe. Could be another explanation. But thank God for Loretta's tip. Never saw this coming."

Pete nodded. "Old Loretta's got the eagle eye, all right." He chuckled. "Even if she does piss off the neighbors."

The sheriff pulled off his cap and roughly rubbed his graying, curly hair. "Overtime budget's already shot to hell, and this'll put a big dent in what's left—and it ain't even wildfire season yet." He put his cap back on, patted it tight.

Andi stepped around him, her hand resting briefly on Ben's arm, as if comforting him. She leaned into the storage unit. "Pete, can you tell if anyone else beside the Hansen boy is involved?" After Loretta's call, when they'd phoned the building's owner to meet them and unlock the storage room, he'd told them it had been rented by Jared Hanson, a local teen, seven weeks ago.

Pete straightened up and shook his head. "No sign of that yet. Just Jared, best I can tell." He stepped out into the sunlight and removed his cap; sweat beaded his forehead. "Damn hot in there. Strangest weather."

Andi looked up at the iron-blue sky and nodded. Ordrew followed Pete out; he too mopped sweat off his face. "Must be a hundred-ten degrees in there," he said.

Pete nodded. "At least." He fanned himself with his cap, then gestured with it toward the unit. "This looks wrong as hell."

"Meanin'?" Ben asked.

"The Hansens belong to our church. I've known Jared since he was seven. Always been a great kid."

"So, what do you make of it?"

"Beats me. Nine rifles, two hundred rounds of ammunition. A pressure cooker. Jesus." He shook his head. "This doesn't square with anything I know about him."

Ordrew said, "Isn't it obvious? Pressure cookers? He's prepping for a mass shooting or a bombing."

Pete frowned. "Just one pressure cooker. If I didn't know Jared, I'd think it's possible, but he's just not right for that."

Andi asked, "How old is he?"

"Seventeen, maybe eighteen. He's a senior." Pete turned to Ben. "I know I'm up to catch this case, but..."

Ben stopped him. "I'm puttin' Andi in the lead on this one, Pete; you're too close. Brad, you'll work second with her."

Ordrew's eyes darkened, but he shrugged.

Ben ignored the look, said to Pete, "That good for you?"

"Thanks, boss. I like Jared too much."

Andi looked in at the pile of weapons in the shadows. "You said nine rifles? They're not semi-automatics."

"Nope, not one. They're all single-shots, take 30-06 Springfield cartridges. He's got a couple hundred extra rounds in the boxes."

"Well, he's not going to shoot anybody very fast using single-shots. Why nine?"

"Good question."

Andi stepped inside the unit, felt the immediate heat, already thirty degrees hotter than morning air outside. "And why a pressure cooker?"

Pete followed her inside, shaking his head. "There's no shrapnel or explosives, so maybe it's just a pressure cooker."

Ben, from the doorway, said, "What's the kid plannin'?"

Ordrew frowned. "Think of those assholes in Boston. Seems pretty clear to me."

Pete said, "Maybe, but like I said, he's got nothing to turn them into bombs."

"Collecting things a bit at a time. Avoiding notice," Ordrew said.

"Could be. But look at these." Pete squeezed around Andi and reached into a cardboard carton on the shelf. "Weird as hell," he muttered. "Check these out," he said, handing a couple of small books, covers tattered, to Andi. "Books on Buddhism, for God's sake."

Ordrew stepped inside, looking annoyed. "Yeah? Check these out." He pulled some books from a second box, the one he'd opened earlier. "Jesus," he muttered, looking at the spines. "Library books." He read. "*Columbine.*" Then, pulling out a second book. "How's this? *Hunting Humans: The Rise of Modern Multiple Murder.*" He pulled out a third. "*Give a Boy a Gun.*"

Andi checked the title of the book in her hand: *Living Buddha, Living Christ.* "Buddhism and mass murder? What's that mean?" She riffled the book's dry pages, her forehead wrinkling. Maybe there was a note, a photo, something to give her a clue about the boy's thinking. Nothing inside. She handed the book back to Pete and said, "Check the pages of the other books," and to Ordrew, she said, "You too." The contrast among the books disturbed her. She opened a third cardboard box. "What's this stuff?"

Inside was a Mason jar filled with black seeds, a can of Zippo lighter fluid, another jar marked "ethanol," some slices of what smelled like ginger, and on a small plate, a tarry residue.

Pete looked into the box. "Weird. No idea what this crap is."

Andi took the jar and examined the seeds; she opened the jar and sniffed. "This gets stranger. I don't recognize the smell." She turned to Ben standing just outside the door. "I want to send all this stuff to DCI up in Helena."

The sheriff nodded. "Do it."

Ordrew said, "DCI?"

Andi said, "Division of Criminal Investigation. They help us with cases we don't have resources for."

Ordrew nodded. "Roger. Back in LA, they're the DLE. Division of Law Enforcement."

Andi, tired of hearing Ordrew's references to the LAPD, thought, *Homesick.* She turned to Ben. "We probably should call and warn Monica. Once this gets out, she'll have a tidal wave of upset students banging down her door." Monica Sergeant was the high school principal, a year from retirement.

"Her and one part-time school counselor." He snapped his cell phone off his belt. "I'll call the school, give her a heads-up." As he scrolled to the principal's number, he said to Andi, "Give your boyfriend a call and tell him we'll pay him to help the counselor."

"Ed won't like that," she said. "His practice has been crazy busy."

"Ain't nobody's gonna like none of this," Ben growled. "Call him. That counselor's only here two half-days a week. Ain't no way she handles a flood of scared kids on her own."

Andi nodded, reaching for her own phone. "I'm thinking I'd better go find young Mr. Hansen and invite him in for a little talk. He's probably at school now."

Ben, already dialing, stopped for a moment. "Good point. I'll tell Monica to pull the boy out of class and keep him in her office till you get there." He looked at Ordrew. "Brad, you finish up here, seal off the damn unit, and log-in the evidence back at the station. We're callin' this suspicion."

Ordrew frowned. "Suspicion of what?"

Ben frowned back. "Suspicion. We'll figure out the what later." He resumed dialing.

Andi touched Ben's arm. "Once I pick Jared up, this'll be all over the valley. Do you think...?"

Ben hit the *End* button, nodded. "Jesus in a sidecar, you're right." He rubbed his face. "Look, I'll hightail it back and work out a statement, run it by Irv." As he looked at his phone and hit *Speed-dial*, he caught Ordrew's puzzled look and said to him, "Irv's the DA."

After a moment, he spoke into the phone. "Callie, do me a favor. Find Irv Jackson and set up a meetin'." He listened. "On the phone's better, and we gotta do it no more'n fifteen, twenty minutes from now. Don't take no for an answer." He waited. "Whatever. Tell him we got us real trouble." He ended the call and started dialing again. While he waited for the principal to pick up, he said to Andi, "Irv and I'll write a statement and Callie can read it when the calls start comin' in." He walked toward his SUV, the black-and-tan colors of Adams County, consulting his watch, phone against his ear, then turned back and lifted his voice. "People," he said, "we got us maybe thirty minutes before word gets out and Bud Groh starts prowlin' around. Let's get movin'."

Ordrew said to Andi, "Who's Bud Groh?"

"Radio station manager, reporter, radio engineer, you name it." They watched as Ben continued toward his vehicle, and they heard him say, "Monica? Ben Stewart here. Sorry to say it, but you got some major crap about to hit your fan."

4

Just as Ed Northrup stuck his head into the waiting room, his cell phone buzzed. His patient, a new one, hadn't arrived yet. Ed wondered how many first sessions in his career had started late. *Nobody likes seeing a shrink.* The phone screen told him it was his friend Magnus Anderssen calling. Ed gave another quick glance into the waiting room—still empty. He punched *Talk* and said, "Morning, Mack. How's it going?"

"Ed, it is Luisa. Please, I need you to come out to the Anderhold. For Magnus." Like a monk puzzling out a Latin verse, Ed worked it over. Why wasn't Magnus himself calling? They were old friends and Mack had never had Luisa call for him before. Why the urgency in Luisa's voice?

"What's going on?"

"I cannot say more over the telephone." Ed enjoyed Luisa's formal English; growing up in Mexico, she'd learned the language from the nuns. "He says he will talk only to you." She cleared her throat. "He, ah, needs you, Ed."

Ed squinted. Her tone was urgent, almost frightened. Of what? It couldn't be Magnus, whose love for her was steady and deep. He pulled close his appointment book, scanned the page. "Boy, today's tough, Luisa. I'm scheduled tight. Can it wait till evening?"

"It is necessary. Please, look in your calendar again."

He hated cancelling sessions with anyone. Well, Magnus Anderssen had been a good friend, not only to Ed, but to the valley people, all his life. He decided to move his five o'clock—who needed the session—to two, then reschedule the three and four to...what? Tomorrow morning early? Tomorrow evening? "Luisa? I can be out there around four, but if it's urgent, maybe Mack can come to my office and we can talk right at three o'clock."

"No, I am sorry, *amigo*. You must come to the Anderhold." When he didn't answer immediately, she added, her voice husky. "If it were unnecessary, I would not ask."

It was true. Luisa's generosity was known across the valley; she had never wasted his time, nor anyone else's. *Something's very wrong*, he thought. He said, "Sure, Luisa. I'll be out there as soon as I can, right around four."

"We, ah, need you, Ed." Her voice cracked.

That catch in her voice disturbed him as much as that word *need*. Magnus and Luisa Anderssen seldom needed anyone in the valley, except perhaps each other. Truth to tell, the valley people needed the Anderssens. The entire southern half of Monastery Valley and the lower flanks of the surrounding mountains belonged to the Anderssen's *Double-A* brand; and Magnus's cowhands and foremen, his farmers, his miners, his loggers, and the men and women working in his outfitting business all spent their wages in town. Not everyone may have loved Magnus, but they needed him.

The waiting room door squeaked. Probably Art Masters, his new patient. Ed leaned into the waiting room and saw Art closing the outer door. He held up a finger, mouthed *One minute?* Art smiled and nodded. Ed, thinking Art's smile looked strained, went back into his office, pulling the door closed as he thought about his friend, Magnus Anderssen.

Last November, a stroke had felled old John Trimble while elk hunting in the Washington Mountains. Magnus had called Ed. "You've heard about Jack Trimble?"

"I have. How is he?"

"Bad. You still on the hospital board?"

"Sure."

"Do me a favor. When he goes home, let me know what his bill is."

"You going to help Jack out?" It wouldn't be the first time Magnus had privately paid someone's hospital bill.

"Somebody will," was all he'd said. Ed knew of many such anonymous gifts, but most people didn't. To the valley folks, Mack Anderssen was a good man, important, and like many important people, remote. Wealthy, calm, a leader, but hard to know. His open love for Luisa was perhaps the warmest thing they saw in him. But Ed cared deeply about his friend, and knew him well.

"Ed? Are you there?" Luisa's voice in his ear, urgent, brought him back.

He pulled out of the reverie. "I'm sorry, Luisa. I'll be there a little before four."

Luisa said, "Thank you, Ed. We will be waiting."

Ending the call, he felt a tremor in his chest. What could be wrong with Magnus, a bull of a man?

He went out to the waiting room. Art Masters stood looking out the south window, toward the Coliseum, the towering cirque at the southern end of the valley. Ed said, "Art."

The old man turned stiffly, his eyes squinted, taut. Ed could sense that he was in pain. Art's smile was tight, but he nodded. "Let's do this."

5

Art had made this appointment just last Friday. Ed watched him move painfully toward the inner office. He felt a tight hollow form in his stomach.

"Can I get you a coffee, Art?"

The old man shook his head. "Thank you, no. Don't need any more heartburn." He chuckled, seemed to be about to say something, then shook his head a little. "Funny. Thought I'd make a joke of this whole business, but it isn't..." His voice faded; a shadow passed over his face. He winced.

Ed saw the wince, and that Art's face had gone pale. He waited while Art settled himself; when Art looked at him expectantly, Ed said, "What can I do for you?"

Art smiled crookedly. "Ever help an old cowboy die?"

Startled, Ed couldn't respond for a moment. Die? He collected himself. "Can't say that I have. You the old cowboy?"

The old man nodded, then roughly cleared his throat. Ed heard the thick congestion. "The big C. Pancreas. Spread to my lungs, too." He paused a moment, looking out the window. "They tell me I got me a few weeks, maybe." He gave a small shrug, then coughed. "Way I feel, I'm guessing that *few* means two. Maybe three."

"Ah, man." Ed felt his throat swell. "That's shit." Ed liked Art. Everybody liked Art. Monastery Valley people, ranch wives, bachelors, cowboys shopping for their bunkhouse mates, all shopped at *Art's Fine Foods*, the grocery-pharmacy-hardware store he'd opened when arthritis had ended his cowboy days.

Art shrugged. "I've had me a good run. Some ways, going out quick doesn't seem such a bad thing. But I reckon I need to sort some things out before..." He paused. "Before I can't." He smiled. "You game?"

"Of course. What needs sorting—?"

His cell phone, sitting on the desk, vibrated loudly. Ed ignored it. Art pointed at the phone. "Go ahead, pick 'er up."

"Sorry. I usually turn it off during sessions."

" 'Sessions' we call this, huh?" He chuckled, then coughed. "Take your call, Ed." He gasped a moment. "I'm not going any place. Leastways, not today."

Ed picked up the phone and looked at the screen. *Andi*. Andi Pelton. Ed knew she was on duty. Andi never called during work hours. Something was wrong.

"I'll make this quick, Art," he said.

"Take your time. Reckon the big C's teaching me I'm not in charge." His smile didn't conceal the shimmer of pain washing across his face.

Ed nodded and pressed *Talk*. "Hey, Andi. What's up?"

"Look, we've got a serious situation out here." Her voice was tense, curt. "A kid's been collecting weapons and ammunition, maybe building a bomb. We don't know what his plan is, but it looks like it could be a mass shooting. There's going to be a flood of upset kids at the high school, and the counselor can't handle it alone. Ben wants you to clear your schedule this week to help her. Either the county or the school district'll pay your regular rate, of course. Which one hasn't been figured out."

Ed's palms went damp. *First Luisa and Magnus, then Art, now this.* He crinkled his eyes apologetically at Art. To Andi, he said, "My afternoon's booked, kid. I can start tomorrow, but nothing's open today."

"We need you *now*, Ed. The media's going to be involved, and the dam's bursting. Nobody's going to feel safe here."

Her peremptory tone annoyed him. "Tomorrow morning, Andi. It's the best I can do. I'll need time to cancel the week's patients." He softened his tone. "Look, I've got someone here with me. I'll call you back in an hour."

Silence. Then, "An hour, then." The line clicked dead.

He turned to Art. "Sorry, man." He considered what to say. News like this could easily spread all over the valley before Art's session was done, and within an hour or so, no doubt it'll be on the radio. It wasn't confidential information, but Art didn't deserve to have his session pre-empted. He decided not to say anything, but Art said, "Sorry for eavesdropping. You said *cancelling the week's patients*, so I figure something bad's going on. It's my town too, Ed. What's up?"

He nodded. "Seems the sheriff's department found weapons and they think there may be a threat of a school shooting. Good news is they found the stuff before it went down."

"Damn," said Art, his faded, pain-creased face going gray. "Was hoping I'd be gone before that nonsense came to Monastery Valley."

6

Andi waited for Ordrew in the corridor outside the interrogation room. She didn't know him very well yet, so she cut him some slack: No doubt, he had a reason for being late. He'd only joined the department five or six weeks ago. His former job, with the LAPD, had sent a good reference letter—which of course probably meant he'd left under some cloud. Reading the letter, Ben had growled, "This damn thing glows so much it's radioactive." Still, short-handed was short-handed, and when nobody else answered the ad in *Sheriff* magazine, Ben had hired the only deputy he could get.

Andi paced impatiently. Ordrew was taking too long in the evidence room—logging in the material from the storage unit wasn't that complicated. She'd put Jared Hansen in the interrogation room, waiting for her new partner. She debated knocking on the evidence room door, but as she approached it, it opened.

Ordrew came out. Stifling her annoyance, Andi said, "Let's go. Jared's in here. We need to talk with him."

"You up to this?"

Andi, hand resting on the doorknob, stopped, her eyes narrowing. "What's that mean?"

He shrugged. "This kid's a mass shooter. I doubt you people have much experience with shit like that."

Andi ignored the challenge. " 'Mass shooter'? That's a little premature, don't you think?"

He shook his head. "Not at all. Guns and bomb materials? We could be talking terrorism, Andi. Wake up."

Andi put up her hand. "Whoa! You're too far out ahead of the evidence. We haven't got any information about this boy yet, and until we do, I don't want preconceptions interfering with the investigation. Am I clear?"

His face darkened, angry, but he smiled through it. "Clear as a bell, honey. Total neutrality from now on. My mind's a *tabula rasa*."

Andi smiled. "Blank slate, my ass."

Ordrew let his eyes wander down her body. "Not a bad ass, either. For a small-town girl."

She shook her head. "Cool off, Romeo. We've got work to do."

7

Jared Hansen, seventeen, sat still as stone behind the metal table bolted to the floor in the cement block interrogation room. His eyes were red, his hands bunched in fists on the table. Andi entered the room first; Ordrew followed, slamming the door. Jared didn't flinch at the sound, only looked angrily at them, but it startled Andi and she glanced sharply at her partner.

Collecting herself, she took a seat across from Jared and, as she opened her file, noticed scars on the backs of his hands. Jared saw her looking at them and lowered his fists to his lap. She smiled at the boy, and said, "Jared, I'm Deputy Andi Pelton. This is my partner, Deputy Brad Ordrew. Before we talk, I want you to know that this interview is only informational. You—"

He interrupted. "You didn't read the Miranda warning when you arrested me."

"You haven't been arrested, that's what I'm saying. We just want to talk with you about the storage unit."

"But then why did you bring me here? What am I charged with?"

Either he's not paying attention, she thought, *or he's smart.* "Jared, you're not charged with anything." Ordrew interjected, "Yet."

Andi ignored him. "We brought you here to talk about your storage unit, and we didn't want to do that at school. We'd like to know more about what you're doing there. Are you willing to talk with us?"

He shrugged, his face dark. "Makes no difference."

Andi looked at him a long moment, considering her path. Friendly or aggressive? Beside her, Ordrew shifted restlessly. She decided on friendly. "Thanks. Let's just get some facts on the record first. You rented the storage unit on..." She consulted her notes. "Uh, on—"

"You're going to kill me."

She looked up, fast, searched his face. It was hard. "No, we aren't, Jared. What makes you say that?"

He gestured around the room, his hands fisted. "I'm powerless here. I'm nobody, you're the government. You'll kill me."

"Why would we want to kill you, Jared?"

Ordrew grunted. She glanced at him; his face was reddening. *Stay cool, partner*, she thought.

Jared turned toward Ordrew. "You're playing bad cop, and she's the good one."

Ordrew snarled, "You have no idea, asshole. Shit you can't imagine will land on you any minute if you keep playing games with us."

Andi stood up, trying to appear casual. "We have something to attend to, Jared. We'll be back in a few minutes." She tapped Ordrew's shoulder and nodded toward the door.

Outside, after she clicked the door shut, Andi pitched her voice just above a furious whisper, "Drop the attitude, Brad. This isn't Los Angeles. Either you back me up in there and keep it light, or stay the hell out. This is no case for the good-cop-bad-cop routine."

Ordrew looked disgusted and turned away from her, looked through the one-way at Jared for a moment, then swung back. "The kid's a terrorist. Or a mass shooter. Ladylike won't get us what we need."

"Screw *ladylike*. We don't know what we need yet, and your anger won't help us find out." She considered it for a moment. "On second thought, observe through the mirror. Stay out of the room." She moved toward the interrogation door.

Ordrew stepped back, his face flaring now. But after a moment, he shrugged, muttered, "Whatever." As he turned, she heard him mutter, "Bitch."

She stopped. "Wrong word. Try 'boss.' You'll be better off."

"Ben made you lead, but you're no boss." He faced away from her, staring through the one-way.

Andi paused at the door to calm herself, then stepped back into the room. Jared leered at her. "Good guy won, eh?"

She ignored that. "We're not interested in harming you, Jared, only in understanding what's going on. Let's talk about why you have those rifles."

"To kill my classmates."

Andi caught her breath at the baldness of it. Was Ordrew right? She looked Jared in the eye. "Why do you want to kill your friends?"

He glared back. "The government's watching us. They want to disarm and kill us, and schools are government agencies. I'm fighting back." He folded his arms tightly against his chest. For a moment, his eyes clouded, but his face quickly hardened with anger.

Smart, she thought, *but listens to too much talk radio.* He was taking half-truths and driving them straight off the cliff. "But your friends aren't the government," she said. "Why kill *them*?"

He hesitated, then looked hard at her. "I've got to."

"You *have to*? Why?" She could sense Ordrew's satisfaction on the other side of the window.

Some emotion she couldn't read flickered across his face. "Compassion. I'm evil. I need to protect them." He seemed to shiver. "Or, I guess I do." For a moment he looked unsure, but after a moment, his eyes hardened again.

She tried to make some sense of it, but the dots wouldn't connect. "You need to kill your friends to protect them? Out of compassion? Protect them from...what?"

"When they realize how evil I am, they'll be hurt. They'll suffer. I can't allow that. It's to protect them from the revelation."

The revelation? Then it clicked. "The revelation that you're evil?"

He nodded.

Andi paused. "So what makes you think you're evil?"

"Didn't you listen?" His voice rasped.

"I did. But I don't understand."

"I'm going to kill people. That's evil."

The crazy irrationality stunned her. She stood and walked across the room, buying time. Was he gaming her? She decided to push him, go after the facts later. She sat back down. "You said you'd kill your friends to protect them. Isn't compassion a sign of good?"

The boy sat silent for a few beats, staring into her eyes. She held his gaze. For a moment, she thought he might cry, but the moment passed and his eyes steeled, hard and bitter, and she saw paranoid zeal glowing in them. "You don't understand. None of you will ever understand."

8

Andi knocked on Ben's office door; Ordrew waited sullenly beside her.

"Ain't locked," boomed Ben's voice inside.

Ordrew pushed ahead of her, and didn't wait for Andi to speak. "She's going to tell you the kid's crazy, but he's crazy like a fox."

"Meanin'?"

"Meaning he isn't crazy at all."

Ben frowned. "You got a fact or two to back that up?"

"He says schools are 'government agencies.' He says he has to kill his friends to protect them from finding out he's evil, and he knows he's evil because he intends to kill his friends. It's crazy *talk*, but there's nothing crazy about it—he's setting up his defense. The kid's a shooter, or a terrorist, and he's making himself sound crazy so some hot-shot lawyer can shut us down."

Andi bristled at her partner's prejudgments, but Jared's paranoia disturbed her. Ordrew might be right.

"Well," Ben said, "talkin' crazy ain't no crime, and ownin' a bunch of rifles and a pressure cooker ain't crimes in Montana, neither."

Ordrew interrupted him. "Put them together, Sheriff. Give me one damn reason he'd keep nine guns and the pressure cooker."

Ben gave a weak smile. "Who knows? The kid wants to be a wild game chef: He kills his meat, then cooks it."

"Give me a fucking break."

Ben shrugged. "Sure, it's weak. And watch your language: This here's a professional conversation." He turned to Andi. "Your thoughts?"

"I'm stunned, actually. He sounds paranoid, and totally illogical, but Brad's right, he could be playing us. He seems smart to me. And talk radio's full of crap about the government threatening us, lots of people talk like that." She heard Ordrew grunt. "I'm not sure what to think, but we need more facts before I'm ready to draw any conclusions." She looked directly at her partner. He glared back, eyes hard. *Man's got a problem*, she thought.

Ben rotated a pencil. "Still, there's the threat. We'll hold him, at least till we talk to more people."

Andi nodded. "It occurs to me that Gracie—" She turned to Ordrew. "Grace is Ed's adopted daughter."

He frowned. "Who's Ed?"

"Ed's my...boyfriend." She stopped. It seemed a silly term to use, and she felt a moment's embarrassment. She was forty-eight, Ed ten years older. She shook off the feeling. "I think Grace knows Jared pretty well. I'll get her take on him tonight."

Ordrew shook his head and turned to Ben. "We can't wait till tonight. The kid's a mass murder waiting to happen." He glared at Andi, then turned back to Ben. "Don't stick your head in the sand about this, Sheriff. He was going to build a pressure cooker bomb and he was going to kill people with it. Or shoot people. Or both. He blames the government. That's terrorism. I say charge him."

"Well, he ain't doin' mass murder from a jail cell. But you might be right—somethin' don't add up here."

Ordrew snorted. "No shit, Sherlock, something's wrong, all right. Don't let it be us."

Ben stood up, eyes flashing. He glared at Ordrew for a moment, but he only said, "Noted." He looked at the clock. "Law lets us hold the boy forty-eight hours before we charge him, so get to work. After you talk with the parents, then talk to everybody in town. I called the mom. She's willin' to come in now, but dad's over in Missoula and won't get back till four, four-thirty." His rotating pencil flipped out of his fingers onto the floor. He bent down for it. "I'm thinkin' you'll want 'em together."

Andi nodded, but Ordrew shook his head. "Do the mom now, before dad gets back and they cook up some bullshit story."

Ben shook his head. "Ain't how we think about citizens around here, Brad." The two men's eyes locked, until Ordrew looked away. Ben turned to Andi. "You got an opinion about the parents? Alone or together?"

Back in Chicago, they'd have separated the parents, just as Ordrew said, but things worked differently here in the valley. Much less us-against-them. Citizens generally shared what they knew with the sheriff's department. She shook her head. "We'll interview them together, the first time." She glanced at Ordrew, who shook his head. She added, "If anything doesn't add up, we'll separate them."

Ben nodded, reached for his phone. "Right, then. So while you wait for the husband, start door-knockin'."

Ordrew stood up, facing off with Ben. "All due respect, Sheriff, but we have a terrorist on our hands and you're saying to wait?"

Ben stopped dialing and narrowed his eyes. "How 'bout we cool the drama, son? We ain't got enough yet to call the kid a terrorist. He ain't likely to hurt nobody sittin' in a cell, so get your butt out and find me some evidence to back up your theory." He resumed dialing.

Ordrew stood abruptly. They turned to leave. As they closed Ben's door, he muttered to Andi, "That fat old man's going to get people killed."

9

Jared stared stonily at the wall while Andi explained that he'd have to stay in the jail while they investigated, and Mirandized him.

"Do you understand, Jared?"

He remained utterly still; she felt cold on the back of her neck.

Ordrew grabbed Jared's arm and yanked him out of his chair. "Let's move it, kid. We've got a cell with your name on it."

Jared resisted for a moment, then Andi saw his face collapse, its hard refusal crumbling into a look of terror. But as Ordrew pulled on his arm, the angry, rejecting glare returned as suddenly as it had gone. "I know what you're going to do. I'll die in there."

Andi opened the door. "This way, Jared."

As Ordrew walked the boy into the cell, Andi said, "If you want to talk to us more about the weapons, just tell one of the officers."

Jared glared at her. "I already told you what they're for." He turned his eyes away, but his head was unmoving. "There's nothing else to say."

As he came out, Ordrew slammed the cell door hard. But Jared just stared, unflinching, his eyes dark.

As they came out of the cellblock, Bud Groh, the general manager of the radio station, was standing at Callie's desk with Ben. The sheriff was waving his hand. "You'll get your statement when it's ready, Bud. How the hell'd you hear about this?"

"So there is something going on? There'll be a statement? What do you know so far?"

"What I know is I ain't talkin' to media till we get us a statement, which oughta be within a few minutes." Ben scowled. "Still would like to know how you knew about this."

Bud shrugged. "Scanner. I heard Callie call for deputies to the storage units. Went there myself soon as I could call my night DJ back in to cover the station. You folks had skedaddled."

Ben nodded. "Didn't tell anybody else, did you?"

"No, but once you issue a statement, if it's big enough, we'll do a live exclusive on the radio and once that happens, the Missoula media'll be swarming like teen girls on Justin Bieber."

Ben blew out a long breath. "Christ on a crutch. It'll be big enough, don't worry."

10

A little past three o'clock, Ed drove south toward the Anderssen's massive ranch house, the Anderhold. Named for the ranch's founder, Magnus's great-great-grandfather Anders, the house sat on a terrace carved out of a high bench of granite above the river. Halfway down the valley, Ed was pondering what Magnus could need from him when his cell phone buzzed.

"Northrup, it's me."

His daughter, adopted two years ago, had always used his last name, the only person in his life who did. He liked it. But her voice sounded disturbed. He glanced in the rear-view—all alone on the highway. He decided not to pull over.

"Hey, Grace. What's up?" He slowed down a bit.

"You heard about Jared Hansen?"

Ed grimaced. "I did." He reconsidered. "Wait a minute. I have to pull off the road." As he did, he waited to see how Grace was taking the news.

"I don't believe it."

"You don't believe what?"

"Everybody's saying he's planning a school shooting, but I say no way. Jared's always been good. It just makes me sick, everybody being so ready to turn their back on him." She was quiet a moment. "Could it be true, Northrup?" This time, her voice sounded scared.

"Well, I don't know. I just heard about it from Andi. She didn't know what his plan was, but—" He hesitated. *Don't sugar-coat. She's sixteen.* "What you've heard is a possibility they'll have to check out." He glanced again at the rear-view. Nobody coming.

Grace was silent a long moment. "I thought it might be. I still don't believe Jared could be that way. He's just not a bad guy at all."

"Then there'll probably be another explanation. We'll just have to wait till Andi and Ben sort it out."

Another silence. Then, "Yeah, I suppose. Anyway, I have a favor to ask. Though I feel stupid asking at a time like this."

"Shoot."

He heard her gasp. "Bad choice of words, Northrup. Anyway, I need to borrow your truck for a little while. Me and my girls have to pick up some of the prom decorations."

" 'My girls and I.' Sorry, honey. I'm not in the office; I'm on my way out to see someone."

"Darn. Well, maybe I can borrow a truck from Zach Norlander. He's always offering to do something nice for me." Ed smiled. This was Grace's not-so-subtle way of worrying him that the boys were nosing around. And of getting whatever it was she wanted. As in, *If you don't give it to me, Zach will.*

He started to ask what kind of truck Zach drove, but the line went dead. Annoyed, he dialed her number. When she answered, he said, "Look, don't hang up on me."

"Yeah, I shouldn't have. I just hate begging for rides, Northrup. I got passionate there for a minute."

"Passionate?" He chuckled. "Well, you'll catch more flies with—"

"—ice cream than ice cubes. I know, Northrup. I'm sorry I got crabby."

"Accepted. See you later." He ended the call, smiling. He put the phone on the seat and took a long breath, his anxiety returning. *What's going on with Magnus?*

Ed glanced at the dashboard clock: If he upped his speed, he'd make it to the Anderhold by four o'clock. Approaching the bridge where the Monastery River arced west across the valley, mud deposited by the flood lay thick and gray on the fields along the river. No one had expected the heavy rains three weeks ago, and the usual sandbagging operations for spring flooding hadn't held. In town, houses had been ruined, and Magnus had provided lodging for the displaced families in his various bunkhouses and his Streamside Lodge. Besides Marty Bailey, the banker, Ed was the only one who knew that the first anonymous deposit in the emergency fund—twenty-five thousand dollars—had been Magnus's. The rancher had always hidden his generosity.

Ed recalled the first time he'd met Magnus.

He'd moved to the valley a few weeks earlier, after losing his psychologist's license in Minnesota. He'd come to Montana to start over; the state at that time didn't license psychologists. He'd set up his office, but had no patients yet. There was a knock on his door.

The man who came in was Ed's height, about six foot, but larger, broader. His hand, held out for shaking, was rough and surrounded Ed's. "Magnus Anderssen, Doctor. I own the Double-A ranch in the south of the valley."

"Magnus? A great name."

Anderssen looked amused. "You know Latin?"

Ed smiled. "Eight years' worth, high school and college."

"You must be Catholic."

Ed shook his head. "Not any longer. You?"

"Same answer." He suddenly looked uncomfortable and changed the subject. "I understand you're a psychiatrist."

Ed shook his head. "Psychologist. And not a very busy one, at the moment."

"A couple of my cowboys are depressed. Would you take them on, help them through?"

"Of course, gladly." Ed felt a surge of excitement—from what he'd heard, Magnus Anderssen employed half the ranch hands in the valley. Maybe the move to Montana might work out after all.

Magnus hesitated, then rubbed his cheek. "Don't want to step on toes, here, but there's talk you had a little trouble back in Minnesota. I don't need to know what happened, but I have to ask, was it anything that could make you, let's say, not be up to helping my boys?" His face flared red under his blond hair. "I'm sorry, Doctor, but I can't let them be in the wrong hands."

Ed felt his own face warm, and he smiled. "Not to worry, Mr. Anderssen. A girl I was treating committed suicide. The parents sued. When the testimony conflicted, I lost the suit. The psychology board suspended my license for two years. In a big city like Minneapolis, that's close-up-shop time, so I came out here. I'll do a good job with your men."

Magnus looked relieved, smiled. "Send your bills to me directly. I'll pay. They're good men."

He turned to go. With his hand on the doorknob, he said, "And my friends call me Mack."

This had pleased him. He'd liked the man. "Mack. Well, Mack, mine call me Ed."

The big head gate of the Double-A came in sight ahead, and Ed clicked on his turn signal. His cell phone buzzed on the seat beside him. Absorbed in thinking about Magnus, he ignored it. In a moment, it beeped: A message waited. He glanced at the screen. It'd been Andi. *Damn!* Five hours ago, he'd promised to call back in an hour.

Driving up the long road to the Anderhold, he thought about Luisa. When Magnus had brought Luisa home after nine months of international courtship, the valley people had been taken, first, with the soft Mexican lilt of her contralto voice. Luisa's English flowed easy as a river around the occasional boulders of a difficult grammar. After she had hosted parties at the Anderhold—to which no one had been invited during the years Magnus's father, Daryl, had owned the ranch—the valley folks themselves had fallen for this cattle woman from Mexico, who welcomed them into the great house.

Ed drove slowly through the mile of apple orchards lining the driveway on both sides, onto the massive log bridge spanning the Monastery River, tires rumbling over the heavy planks, then up the second mile to the ridge on which the Anderhold presided over the vast Double-A. Nosing his truck to the edge of the greening grass in front of the great house, he sat for a moment looking out across the wide valley, watching the sun caress the summit of Hunter's Peak. Such beauty thrilled him, and for the moment, he stopped worrying about Andi's call and Magnus's need, whatever it might be.

Damn! Andi's call! He grabbed his phone and dialed her number.

11

"Hey," he started. "Sorry I didn't call. I'm out on an emergency. Remind me what you need?"

"We needed you this afternoon, but that's shot to hell." She sounded annoyed, which wasn't like her.

He said, "Look, I'm sorry. I've got a lot going on." He almost told her about Luisa's call, but stopped. Andi would keep it to herself, but better not to say anything until he found out what was going on with Magnus. Far across the valley, he saw a V of geese, black dashes slanting across the sky.

He watched them fly south.

On the phone, Andi expelled a deep breath. "I'm sorry too," she said. "Shit's hitting the fan out here. No reason to take it out on you."

"About Jared Hansen?"

"The same. You know him?"

"Not well. What I do know doesn't fit with weapons and bombs."

"That's what Pete says. My partner's insisting the kid's a mass shooter or a terrorist wannabe, but so far, we've got nothing that fits that scenario. Except nine rifles and a pressure cooker."

"Who's your partner on this?" The department was small, so deputies worked alone, except on serious cases. This one must count as serious.

"Brad Ordrew. He's got a short fuse on him."

"He's the new guy, from LA?"

"Uh-huh."

Ed looked out at the peaks across the valley; the geese were a distant shadow against the high snow. "You'll handle him. So, what do you need, exactly?"

"We need you at the school this week to meet with students who're freaked out, settle them down if you can."

"All week? Man, Andi, my schedule is jammed."

"We put a notice on the radio that there'd be counselors available tomorrow morning. Monica Sergeant's already had twenty or more students come in wanting to talk. She can't handle it alone."

"Damn." He considered: His patients were generally resilient people; Montana winters did that to you. They'd handle it. The few who couldn't put off their session for a week or two he could see in the evenings. "All right. I can start tomorrow morning. I'll need to be informed about what's going on, so I can sort out the rumors."

"Well, I'll tell you what I can, but mostly, just stick to shrink stuff. Calm them down, give them some perspective. If they want news, have them call Callie. Tell them the sheriff's department is on top of it. Blah blah blah. You know."

He felt uneasy. "Not really. You'll keep me posted so I—"

"Later, Ed. I gotta get back on it now. The boy's parents are coming in any minute now."

"Okay, fill me in tonight."

Andi paused, then said, "Yeah." She sounded tense. "Like I said, the shit's flying around here. I gotta go. Tomorrow, though, I need you on hand, okay?"

"And you'll do what with that hand?"

A silence, then she laughed. "Stop. You're a sex maniac."

"Just a healthy fifty-eight-year-old with a hot girlfriend."

"Well, I'm not hot today. I'm fried."

He chuckled and ended the call, then sobered quickly. He looked up at the big house. *Okay, Magnus, your turn.*

12

The ten-foot oaken door swung open as he climbed up to the deep, dim porch, and Luisa Anderssen waited, her hand pale against the black iron handle.

"Welcome, Ed. Come in." Her eyes were puffy, haggard and red, and her sorrow-ridden face shocked him. He'd never seen Luisa, usually so warmly welcoming, so forlorn. *What the hell's going on?* he wondered.

"Mack waits in his den," she said as Ed stepped inside. Her calm voice belied her red eyes and taut lips.

"What's going on, Luisa?"

She shook her head. "He agreed to talk to you alone. I am to say nothing." She hesitated. "I believe he is afraid of something."

Afraid? Ed couldn't remember a time he'd seen Magnus afraid. He touched her arm gently, then climbed the wide, familiar stairs.

Over the years, he and Ben Stewart and Jim Hamilton, their priest buddy who'd since left the valley with his new wife, had often met in Magnus's den. They'd plan hunts or fishing trips or the annual Labor Day fireworks show, charity fundraisers, Ben's re-election campaigns—or just share a drink and talk. Maps or budgets or plans would be spread across the twelve-foot plank table, splits of oak and larch would crackle in the fireplace. Magnus poured good single-malt Scotch for his friends, though he himself seldom touched it. The room resembled the single-malt—amber-colored pine, the sweet fragrance of burning wood, the deep brown chairs redolent of leather, the lamps' tan shades tinting the light toward autumn. Ed knocked on the closed door.

"Come."

Magnus sat in the dark, sagged back in his big chair behind the wide oak desk, his usually strong face gaunt and deep-shadowed by a single small lamp. His jaw and thin lips appeared swollen, his eyes bloodshot and dark. The dirty thatch of white hair was untouched and he had dressed himself only in a frayed bathrobe sloping over wide shoulders that had lost their square. Gray beard stubble caught the dim lamplight.

"I look like hell," he said softly. His eyes were dull and sad.

Ed nodded. "Yes, you do."

Magnus gestured to the leather chairs facing the cold, dead fireplace. He splayed both hands on the desk and pushed himself upright. "Just hung over," he said, coming around the desk and slumping heavily into the chair beside Ed, who reached back and switched on the lamp between them. Magnus squinted but said nothing. He looked worse in the light.

That Magnus had been drinking enough to be hung over stunned Ed: The man almost never took a drink. The valley people spoke in code when they gossiped about someone's drinking, and Ed knew the codes. "He ain't much for the sauce" meant pretty much just that—the fellow doesn't drink. "Old Jim, he likes a taste now and then" signified that Jim drinks every night. "Bill now, that boy sure likes his beer" translated to "Bill's a drunk." And "that fella can't hold his liquor" indicated that the man needs detox and the twelve steps, or maybe twenty. About Magnus, the word was, "The only booze in Mack Anderssen's life is the booze his daddy drank."

"Mack, what's going on? You don't drink."

Magnus held up his big hand. "Ed, this is not easy for me. Before you start with the questions, understand that Luisa insisted on this." He waved his hand between them. "It wasn't my idea." Ed imagined that scene, the big bull against his fiery wife. Such a fight must have cost them both.

"So you ask your questions, Ed, and hear my answers, and that's the end of it."

Ed was struck by the hardness of Magnus's voice, which didn't match the haunted look in his eyes. "That's the end of what, exactly?"

Magnus sagged. Ordinarily, patrician white hair framed his strong, tanned face. Ordinarily, his mouth fell naturally into a quiet smile, as if his strength and presence assured him that whatever drama was playing out would end well. Ordinarily, he looked the strongest man in the room, and often was. This was not ordinarily. For a moment, Magnus looked sadly at Ed, and then shrugged and leaned back in his chair. The leather creaked. He said, "Well, I suppose I answer your questions, then you tell me what I should do." He paused, then added, "Then I decide."

So he wants help, but he needs control. Ed nodded. "Got it."

Magnus pushed his big fingers through his uncombed hair. "I'm sorry, Ed. I forgot your question." His voice quavered.

Luisa's right, Ed thought. *Mack's afraid of something.* He said, "You don't drink, Mack. What's with the hangover?"

"I guess I drink now," he said. "Since the eleventh of March, I've been stone drunk every night." His words were spoken casually, as if they didn't matter, but his tone was strained.

"You looked fine at your Easter party. That was the twenty-sixth, wasn't it? The week before the flood?"

"Fuck it, Ed. I don't lie."

Surprised, Ed looked sharply at his friend, saw a mismatch between the angry words and the sadness or fear in Magnus's eyes. Since he'd married Luisa, Magnus did not swear. Ed apologized, but noted the obscenity.

"You people left the party by midnight. Once you were gone, I drank the whole fucking night." After a moment, he said, "I'm sorry. I've been pretty touchy lately."

That's two more fucks *than I've heard Mack Anderssen use in twenty-seven years,* Ed thought. He nodded. "No problem. So, I'm listening. Why?"

Magnus stared intently at Ed for a long breath, then nodded, as if giving something up. "You want the why." The look on his face told Ed the rancher didn't want to tell it.

Ed noticed the rancher's big hands trembling. *Alcohol withdrawal? Or fear?*

"On March tenth, Junior came home from college and announced he was dropping out for a while." Magnus Jr., Junior to everyone, was his son. "I couldn't stop him and I couldn't bear it. So I took a drink. Didn't stop."

Junior's dropping out of college did this? The Magnus Anderssen Ed knew didn't collapse in the face of difficult situations. During the recent flood, he'd rowed the first rescue boat, and he'd deployed the work crews to swamp out the houses and rip out the mold. Ed recalled people commenting that Magnus had looked haggard, and that his usual gruff good cheer was absent, but despite that, the man had never wavered. Calamities did not break Magnus: Facing them, he took action. Ed said, "During the flood, were you drinking?"

Magnus didn't answer for a moment, then nodded slowly. "Every night.

A few of those days, I doubted I'd make it through." The haunted look returned to his eyes, the sadness to his voice.

"Huh. I don't think anyone knew." He paused, considering what to ask. "I guess I don't see the connection between Junior dropping out of college and your drinking."

"I haven't told it yet," he said roughly, almost rudely. But Ed caught his anxious sideways glance, as if checking to see how Ed was reacting. "No offense, my friend. I'm testy."

"That's not like you. No offense taken. In fact, it'll help me understand things if you just let your feelings show. Don't worry about me." Magnus's rudeness was a sign of something, like the *fucks*.

Magnus said, "That's hard for me, Ed. I'm not one for showing feelings."

Ed smiled. "At least, not one for showing them if they're unpleasant. I remember lots of laughs we've shared."

The rancher nodded, even managed a brief smile "As do I." He shrugged. "Back to the drinking. I couldn't bear Junior's failure. Drinking blocked it out. Even the hangovers kept my mind off it." His voice cracked, and he winced. "I spent his birthday completely drunk. I don't recall if I even came out to wish my son a happy birthday." Moisture showed at the corner of his eye.

His voice thickened. "Sometime in there Luisa blew up. Don't remember too much about that. Then last night, before I got too far along, she told me either I talked to you or she'd take Junior down to her ranch in Mexico."

He stood up, shaken, his broad shoulders slack. For a long time he stared into the dead ashes in the fireplace. "I said terrible things, Ed. Told her to go the hell back to Mexico. I never raise my voice to her." He coughed softly, brushed his hand over his eyes. "I said 'fucking Mexico.'"

Ed leaned out from his chair to get a better look at Magnus. A shine of tears lay down his cheek. "Middle of the night, I went to her and told her I'd talk to you." Ed saw him shiver. "Twenty-four years, Ed, not a harsh word to her. Until last night."

Ed marveled at Luisa's kindness in not calling until office hours. Waiting through that ragged night must have tortured her. And Magnus's tears signaled something deeper than regret. *The man is suffering.*

After a moment, he said, "Mack? A question?"

Magnus said nothing. He stopped staring into the dead fireplace and walked stiffly to the ornate antique Mexican credenza. He poured himself a tall tumbler of Scotch, then tilted his head slightly toward Ed. "Drink?" he asked.

Ed stood, alarmed. He shook his head. "No. And I need you to hold off while we talk."

Magnus slammed the glass on the credenza, splashing the liquor on his hand. He wiped it on his robe. "Fuck that, Ed! You're the shrink, but don't pull rank on me in my own den." Despite the challenge in his words, though, Magnus's eyes were searching, doubtful. Almost afraid.

Another *fuck*, and again that mismatch between his words and his eyes. Ed leaned over and picked up his coat.

"Sit down," Magnus said, returning to his chair. "Please. I'm sorry for my rudeness." The glass remained on the credenza. "We're not done here."

"Yes, we are, Mack. You're right, I'm the shrink and I make the rules for this. Either we talk sober or we don't talk." Ed held his coat and his breath.

Magnus studied him for a moment. Then he attempted a half-smile that did not overcome the sadness in his eyes and dropped into his chair. He tipped his head back toward the glass on the credenza. "I can't drink from a glass ten feet away." But then, his face changed, something sore and very old welling in his eyes. The half-smile had faded. "I'm sorry, Ed. Don't know what's got ahold of me, but it's got a mean grip."

Ed nodded and sat down. Magnus said, "Your question?"

"You called Junior's coming home a failure, but dropping out doesn't have to mean failure. Did he give you a reason?"

Magnus stared at the cold fireplace. "He claimed he wanted a few months off to think about which major to choose."

"That doesn't even sound like dropping out to me, much less failure. Tell me why you think it's failure."

"No." Magnus stared into the darkened fireplace.

Ed waited, but his friend continued staring at the dead ashes.

"I can't do much for you if I'm in the dark, Mack."

"Not asking you to do anything for me, Ed." The man's veering irritability puzzled Ed, although no doubt the drinking and the hangover accounted for it.

"You said when you were done I would tell you what I think you should do. Well, it appears you're done."

"I'm not done." His voice was gruff, but again Ed saw something else in his eyes.

"You said you wouldn't tell me."

Magnus looked at him. "Apologies. Should have said I *can't* tell you why I think he's a failure." His voice, already harsh, thickened. "I gotta work my way to that, my friend." He took a huge breath. "There's stuff...to tell first. You have to let me build this out my own way." He looked away, then back at Ed. "That make sense?"

"Uh-huh. You talk, I listen."

Magnus roughly brushed something from an eyelid. "Yeah."

A wash of sadness for his friend thickened Ed's throat. He cleared it. "Okay. Should we take this fast or slow?"

Seeing the frown on Magnus's face, Ed added, "Fast means we talk...sorry, you talk, every day till you get it built out. Slow means once or twice a week."

"I was thinking one time only." But his voice quavered again.

He's unsure, but he wants to do this. "If we talk all night will you get it built out?"

The white head shook. "Doubt it."

"So either it's one time and you don't finish or we meet a few times, right?"

Magnus was looking at the floor in front of his chair. His body read *defeat.* "And if I don't finish? What then?"

Ed shrugged. "I've no idea, Mack. Maybe you drink yourself into the grave. Maybe Luisa and Junior leave. Maybe you stop drinking on your own and this all blows away. I don't know what happens, because I don't know yet what causes it."

Magnus took a long breath. "Or maybe I kill myself."

Ed sat up straighter, but carefully kept alarm off his face, out of his voice. "Think so?"

Magnus nodded. Ed waited, his heart beating faster, holding his hands still in his lap.

Magnus grunted. "Okay. Let's do it fast."

Ed eased up. "Good. Come into the office tomorrow."

"No! You come out here. The whole damn valley'd know it in an hour if I came to see you."

Ed had never known Magnus to worry about gossip. "They'll know I'm driving out here just the same."

"We'll cover that. We'll make a story. You come here." After a moment, he added, "Please." Again, after a longer pause, he said, his voice almost too soft to hear. "It's rough, Ed. Rough."

"The drinking?"

Magnus shook his head. "Well, yeah, that, but the nightmares are worse."

Nightmares? Ed caught his breath. *Not good.* "Tell me about them."

"Can't remember them. But they terrify me, wake me up. Never felt fear like this."

Nightmares? Physical abuse? Sexual? To Ed's knowledge, Magnus had not served in combat. Ed chanced it. "Mack, a hard question?"

Magnus nodded.

"Were you sexually abused?"

Magnus turned and looked hard at him. "What causes you to ask that?"

"Nightmares sometimes signal problems with sexual or physical abuse. I already know about your father beating you." Ed knew that to Magnus, his father was a sensitive topic.

"Daryl beat me, but nothing sexual." He shook his head. "Don't go down that road."

"Maybe someone else, then, something you've forgotten?"

"I wouldn't forget a thing like that."

"It happens. It's called traumatic amnesia. Not too common, but it's not unheard of. The brain can wall off unacceptable memories. It usually breaks down eventually."

Magnus waved his hand. "There's no sexual abuse."

"You're sure."

Magnus nodded, fiercely.

"Okay," Ed said. He decided to let it go. Time would tell. "Back to building it out. I can't spare the time it'll take for me to drive out here every day." He thought of the sheriff's department needing him at the high school, but decided not to burden Magnus with the trouble in the valley. "I have other obligations."

Magnus's mood shifted again. "I'll pay for your fucking time, Ed. Three hours, one for the talk, two for the round trip. What's your price?"

Ed stifled his irritation, and noted the fourth *fuck*. Another signal. Something sexual? Or the buildup of rage? "We call it a fee, Mack. You make it sound like I'm selling used cars."

Magnus shrugged. "Jury's out on that." He smiled weakly. "No offense.

Just a little humor. What's your *fee?*"

Ed noted again the veering of Magnus's emotions. He said, "Seventy-five for the hour, another seventy-five for the round trip." Magnus offered to double it. Tempted, Ed leaned back in his chair. Three hundred a day would quadruple his income for a while. But he didn't need it. Money wasn't the issue, and Magnus knew it. This was a game within a game: Control. A game Ed needed to win, if he was to be of any help.

"No, Mack," he said. "Thanks, but I'll charge you same as I'd charge anybody. And I can only drive out here at five o'clock in the afternoon. Every day until we finish this." The high school let out at *3:30*; he'd stay till four, drive down to the Anderhold, then reserve seven, eight, and nine o'clock for his own patients. Ugly, long days, a lousy week—but nothing as bad as whatever Magnus was hiding from in his bottle, or that Andi was facing in Jared Hansen. He didn't wait for Magnus's objection, but pressed on. "That work for you?"

The rancher's eyebrows arched. "Look who's thinking he's in charge." But his sorrow-stricken eyes looked grateful.

He's afraid, Ed thought, then nodded. "Okay, then. Between meetings, pay attention to your thoughts and feelings. See if you can maybe make a note or two about those nightmares. They might help you build out what you have to talk about. And no more drinking—for the duration." Here he expected a fight, but his friend merely smiled.

"Whatever," he said. "You're the shrink. No guarantees, though."

Ed knew the drinking wouldn't stop. You take what you can get, he thought.

13

Grace Northrup hopped nimbly out from the passenger seat.

"Thanks, girlfriend," she called to the driver, Jen Fortin. "You don't have to pick me up. I'll walk back to town and Northrup can take me home."

"Yes, my princess."

Jen said it smiling, but Grace frowned. "I'm sorry, man," she said. "Northrup's being a real Nancy Reagan about my car."

"Nancy who?"

"That old president's wife? The one who said 'Just Say No' to drugs? Northrup just says no to my car."

Jen waved her off. "No worries, Gracie. He'll come around. I'll get payback when you get your wheels." She backed around, drove toward town.

Grace pulled a blanket out of her backpack and settled it around her shoulders. She passed under the headgate, enormous logs with the words *Jefferson Memorial Cemetery* carved in the top beam, and walked toward the lone maple tree at the end of the narrow gravel drive bisecting the long lawn. It had no buds yet, but she thought there was a hint of green in the bark. Mara's grave, just west of the tree, in summer lay in shade, in the fall blanketed in red leaves. Now the grass covering her showed spring green.

Grace folded the blanket on the ground and sat down. She pulled a silver flask from her pack and opened it, and spoke to the headstone, which read, *Mara Ellonson, 1960 - 2014.* "Don't tell Northrup I borrowed his hunting flask. I know how much you liked your martinis." She tipped a few drops onto the grave.

She corked the flask, then squared her shoulders. "So, Mara." A deep breath. "It's me again." She thought back to the times since her mom's death that she'd come here to the graveside, seeking something, though she hadn't quite known what. She ran her fingers softly across the grass. "So, how's death?"

She waited a minute or so, then shrugged. "Hello to you, too." Although she liked to come here and pretend to talk with her dead mother, and occasionally learned what she herself was thinking about whatever had brought her here, the silence always made her sad. She sighed. "I heard something awful today. My friend Jared got arrested for planning a mass shooting. Except, I don't believe he'd do that."

Grace waited only a moment; she never liked the long silences. "I know, we didn't talk much when you were here." That was part of the sadness. Mara had been an unreliably loving mother, occasionally doting on Grace, but more often ignoring her while carrying on the latest affair or divorcing the last husband. At the end, when Mara was dying without any living relatives able to take care of Grace, she abandoned the girl here in Monastery Valley, banking that Ed Northrup would take her in. Mara had known her man: Thirty years before, back in Minnesota, Ed had been her first ex-husband, and Mara had recalled his soft spot for helping kids.

Grace stood up. An eagle launched from a tall pine just beyond the cemetery fence. She watched him work his way up into the high sky. She looked down at the headstone. "I don't know what to think about Jared."

After a time, she said, "Okay. I thought maybe you know me better now than before you died." She sank back down onto the blanket. The eagle had caught a thermal, soaring out into a wide arc.

"Help me out here," she whispered.

No response.

After a long moment, she said, "Yeah, I figured you'd keep it to yourself."

She looked west to the Monastery Range, the jagged peaks snow-burdened. The eagle was gliding back, closing its long circle, almost above the cemetery now.

"It's pretty here, Mara. At first, when you left me, I was pissed, but after you died, Northrup said you left me here because you loved me." Grace poured a few more drops of martini on the grave. "I could use a little love just about now. I just can't figure out what to think about Jared."

A breeze touched Grace's cheek.

"Mara? Mom?" She held back a sob. "Is Jared bad?"

Nothing.

A raucous, cawing crow swept out and chased the eagle across the blue northern sky. Grace watched their spiraling, twisting dance. *The crow's protecting her nest.*

She looked down at the grave. "I get it. You want the whole flask." She laughed, and poured the rest of the martini on the grass, then got up. "Okay. Nice to talk with you."

The crow broke off its pursuit, and the eagle swung off in long, sweeping circles toward the peaks. Grace watched it for a minute, thinking about her mother and wishing she'd been more like the crow, then walked down the cemetery drive.

I'll go see Ardy. She'll at least talk back.

14

Loretta Tweedy turned from her window and called into the kitchen, "Ardyss, come quick! It's Gracie Northrup. She's coming up the driveway now." Loretta couldn't keep the excitement out of her voice. Ardyss came into the sunroom, smiling, and opened the door. Loretta whispered, "Ask her about Meals-on-Wheels!"

Ardyss stepped onto the porch. "Well, aren't you a sight for sore eyes!"

she said to Grace, holding out her arms. "In all my seventy-four years, I do think seeing you walk up the drive is one of the nicest things. Second only to my Price, of course." Price was Ardyss's long-dead husband. "You're a blessing to this old woman."

Loretta, still sitting, harrumphed. "You're not old."

Grace hugged them both, then said, "Ardy, I need some advice."

Loretta stood, unwrapping her body from her perch by the window as if every joint had rusted in place. When she got upright, she said, "I'll get some tea started and leave you kids alone."

Ardyss winked at Grace. "Loretta, Grace and my average age is forty-five. We're hardly 'kids.'" Loretta harrumphed again, and holding onto the furniture, limped through the dining room into the kitchen.

Ardyss patted the sofa, and they sat down. "All right, dear, what's this advice you need?"

"Have you heard about Jared Hansen?"

"We certainly saw all the commotion this morning. You know Loretta called Sheriff Stewart about the boy?"

"Uh-uh, I didn't. What commotion?"

Ardyss pointed across the street. "He was in one of those storage units, the second one on the right. When Loretta called, the sheriff and your friend Deputy Pelton and a couple of others came with their squad cars and tore the place apart, it looked like. I don't know what they found, exactly. Loretta told me to go over and ask, but I'm not a gawker." She chuckled, a dry sound deep in her throat.

Grace thought about how to say it. Long ago, she'd confided in Ardyss about her occasional graveside conversations with her mom. When she had first told Ardyss about them, then blushed with embarrassment, the old woman had patted her arm. "I visit my Price every Sunday after church. I tell him about the sermon and the latest gossip in the valley. He always liked to keep up."

Still, Grace plowed ahead, though she was self-conscious about it. "I'm upset Ardy. I left school and went out to the cemetery to talk to Mara."

Ardyss asked, "And what did she say, dear?"

"Nothing, as usual. That's why I need your advice. I just can't believe what they're saying about Jared, and I don't know what to do."

"What are they saying?"

"That he was planning to do a school shooting."

Ardyss paled, her fingers touched her lips. "My dear Lord. Here? In Jefferson?" Her voice cracked.

Loretta hobbled into the sun porch with a tray and two cups of tea.

"Join us, Loretta. I've just had terrible news."

Grace stood. "I'll get you a cup, Loretta," and went into the kitchen. When she returned, Ardyss had filled Loretta in. Both ladies looked terrified.

"I don't believe Jared would do that," Grace said as she sat down. "He's not like that."

Loretta gathered herself. "People always say that, afterwards. 'He was such a nice boy.' How are we to know what gets into people's hearts?"

"I *know*, Loretta. But I don't know what to do."

Ardyss looked at Grace fondly. "You are a remarkable young woman, dear. I know what *your* heart is capable of." Soon after Mara had abandoned Grace in the valley, she'd gone to live with Ardyss while the sheriffs searched for her mother. Ardyss had taken ill, nearly dying, and Grace had nursed her, spending nights in the hospital, even nearly dying in a blizzard trying to reach Ardyss's bedside. Ardyss touched Grace's cheek softly. "What do you think, Gracie? What do you want to do?"

"I don't know," she whispered, close to tears.

Ardyss glanced at Loretta, said, "Trust yourself, child. Trust that heart of yours."

Grace waited, wondering what *trust yourself* meant. She remembered the crow, who must have been protecting her new spring brood from the eagle.

She took a breath. "I'm going to find a way to help Jared, Ardyss. He helped me when I came here."

Ardyss smiled. "You will, child. Where do you get this strength?"

Grace thought about it. "From my mom, I think. When she was dying, she protected me the only way she knew how. She helped me, so I'll help Jared."

Loretta said, "Be careful, Grace. Be very careful. If what they say is true, the boy could be a danger."

"I will, Loretta. But he won't hurt anybody." She stood up to leave.

Loretta smiled, then looked meaningfully at Ardyss. "Before you go, Ardyss has a question to ask you."

Ardyss frowned. "You can ask it."

Loretta's lips went into the sort of straight and hard line that said, *Not one word more from me.*

Ardyss wiped her hands on her apron. "All right. Grace, we—" She emphasized the we. "—have a favor to ask. As you know, I drive Meals-on-Wheels around to some of the older ones here in town. But my eyesight isn't so good, and I'm being told not to drive. I have to, of course, for groceries and the doctor and such, but *we'd*—" She glared at Loretta "—we'd hoped that you might consider taking over my route during summer vacation."

"I don't have a car, Ardy."

"You can drive ours, dear." She pointed to the garage, where Grace knew an ancient heap rusted.

Grace gulped. "How old is your car?"

Ardyss pursed her lips. "Oh, I never thought about it. Loretta, how old's the Plymouth?"

Loretta's loosened her grip on her lips and said, "Not very. Oliver bought it brand-new in 1952."

Grace flinched. "Maybe I can talk Northrup into buying me a newer one."

"So you'll take over the Meals-on-Wheels?"

Grace nodded. "Ardy, if you can drive lunches around when you're really old, I can do it too."

Ardyss patted her arm. "That's sweet, dear. But I'm hardly 'really old.'"

15

Callie Martin, receptionist-dispatcher, poked her head into the evidence room. "Andi. In Ben's office. The boy's folks are on their way."

Andi was inspecting the rifles and the other items, looking for something to follow up. And finding nothing. She nodded. "Got it. Brad's in the squad room starting the investigation book. Could you get him?"

"Already done, darlin'."

Andi laughed.

The only fingerprints on the shed and the stuff in it were Jared's, and a half hour staring at the rifles and the pressure cooker and the books and the strange seeds hadn't enlightened her. Maybe the interview with the parents would turn something up. Tomorrow, they'd tackle the friends and classmates. As she locked the ER door, Ordrew fell in behind her; they walked toward Ben's office.

He murmured to her back, "Wish I had that swing in my back yard."

She felt herself blush angrily, and swung around. "Knock it off, Brad. We're partners, not school kids."

He held up both hands, palms spread, grinning. "Whoa. Just voicing some appreciation."

"Keep it professional."

"Whatever." His smile faded.

Andi hesitated at Ben's door. After she'd confronted Ordrew during the interview with Jared, they'd been tense with each other all day. Had she misread his comment about her ass? Could be he was trying to loosen things up. She turned to say something conciliatory when Ben called out, "Ain't got all day, people!" She led the way into the sheriff's office.

As they walked into his office, Ben said, "Hansens'll be here in fifteen. What've you got?"

Andi shook her head. "Mysteries." After interviews with a few teachers, neighbors, and the staff at the high school, they knew only that Jared was perhaps the most popular, thoughtful, and engaged young man at the school. No one had a single bad word to say about him. Everyone was mystified.

Ordrew said, "Everybody's like nuns talking about Jesus." He looked disgusted. "The kid's a terrorist and nobody gives a damn."

Andi's annoyance flared, the day's tension escaping. "Get past it, Brad. Terrorists don't tell us they're evil. And if he's as good a guy as everybody says, we've got a real mystery here."

Ordrew narrowed his eyes. "Maybe, maybe not." He turned to Ben. "I've got a beef."

"Which is what?"

"Andi called me out in front of the kid during our interview. Partners don't do that, even if they work for a backwoods department."

Ben's bushy brows lifted.

Andi didn't wait for Ben to respond. "Brad, I didn't want you throwing your weight around to scare Jared and shut him up. And when the parents come in, I need you on your game, not feeling sorry for yourself."

She could see the anger playing across Ordrew's face, and realized she was only making the situation worse. If Ordrew's flirtation had been his way of trying to reach out, she'd shut him down. Time to make peace, before the parents arrived. "I'm sorry," she said, touching his shoulder. "Partners hang together. I shouldn't have embarrassed you in front of Jared."

At first, he looked sharply at her, but after a moment, his eyes softened, and he shrugged. "I'm good." His head swiveled to the window. A Honda SUV was pulling into the lot. Ordrew rubbed his hands together. "Showtime. Sheriff, you still want us to take them together?"

Outside, as the SUV parked, two men, one with a video cam, ran up to it. Ben swore. "Damn! Forgot about that TV reporter. You two get out there and escort the Hansens in. Last thing we need is them sayin' somethin' to the nation."

On the way out, Andi said, "We'll interview them together. Keep it informational. If they give us anything to justify separating them, we'll do it then."

The Hansens got out of their sedan and were being accosted by the reporter when Andi reached them. "No comments, please. Mr. and Ms. Hansen, come this way." Ordrew held open the door and they went inside.

As Andi lead the way, she could feel his eyes on her backside.

16

Phil Hansen started objecting even before they sat down at the conference table. "What the hell is this about? Are you people out of your minds?"

Andi stopped him with her hand. "I'm really sorry that we have to do this, sir. It's probably nothing, but your son was found to be renting a storage unit filled with rifles, ammunition, and what could be the makings of a bomb. We don't know what's going on, but it looks very serious. We thought you might be able to help us understand some things." She paused. "By the way, I'm Andi Pelton."

Hansen shook his head. "I know you, Andi, and I respect you. But this is nuts. Jared wouldn't do something like that. I want to see him."

Ordrew said, "I'm sorry, Mr. Hansen. We need to have this conversation first. There could be a very simple explanation, and we'd like you to help us find it."

Marie Hansen put her hand on her husband's arm. "We'll talk." She looked at Ordrew. "I don't know your name, though, officer."

"Sorry, ma'am. I'm Brad Ordrew. I just joined the department a few weeks ago."

The mother nodded. "Thank you."

Ordrew said, "Can I get either of you something to drink?" Andi caught his eye; he smiled serenely.

Hansen shook his head, still impatient. "Let's get going. What do you want to know?"

Andi said, "Well, to start, I'd like your permission to tape this conversation."

This set Hansen off again. "What the hell? Is this an interrogation? We need our lawyer here." He stood up.

His wife touched him again. "Relax, Phil. Let's cooperate. It'll be better for Jared." He took a long breath and sat down. She said, "What do you want to know, Andi?"

Her husband interrupted, still agitated. "Why does this have to be taped?"

Ordrew said, "Like you say, sir, this might be nothing at all. We tape all our interviews when we can, because otherwise, it comes down to he-said, she-said. Taping protects your interests and preserves a good record for the court." He landed hard on court; Phil Hansen flinched. Ordrew paused, then added, "And if at some point you decide to bring in your lawyer, he'll have a transcript to evaluate to make sure we didn't do something wrong. Or did." He smiled.

Hansen had calmed during Ordrew's speech. "I guess that's sensible. I don't build a house without a contract to back me up." He rubbed his jaw. "I'm sorry. This whole thing has thrown me."

"Got it, sir. It would upset me too. May we tape?"

Hansen nodded. "Go ahead. I'd like a copy of the tape."

"We'll see to it," Ordrew said. He looked at Andi, signaling her to go on. She knew he didn't say the rest of what he meant: *When your son's attorney asks for it.*

Despite his half-truth, Andi was impressed. Ordrew had defused the father's anger and brought him to their side, at least for the moment. She nodded to him. *Good job, partner.* "Okay," she said, pressing the *Record* button. "Tape's running. Let's just get the housekeeping done." She named the case and the date and time, and who the participants were. "Mrs. Hansen, shall we start with you?" It wasn't really a question. "Tell us a bit about Jared. What he's like, his interests, how he's been doing in school, that sort of thing."

Marie looked at her husband, then began. She described a normal boy, popular in school, athletic, a good student, a frequent volunteer in his church and the community. "He's always been a happy kid," she finished.

44

Her husband narrowed his eyes, and Ordrew asked, "Something to add, sir?"

"Well, lately he's been a little, oh, quieter than usual. Nothing unusual for a kid who's about to graduate and go off to college, though. Real world, you know." He looked apologetic. "My business is pretty good, but with four kids, I can't afford four college tuitions. I figure he's just worried about money. Growing up, you know? Facing adult things. Normal stuff."

Ordrew nodded. "Any *other* adult things he's facing, other than just growing up?"

Hansen looked uncomfortable. "No, none that I know of." He looked at his wife, who looked away.

Andi noticed that. "So you haven't noticed anything more than some senior anxiety?"

The parents both shook their heads.

"Okay, what can you tell us about the storage unit?"

Hansen's face darkened. "This is the first time we've heard about it. We don't know a damn thing."

Andi nodded. "So he rented it without your knowledge?"

After glancing at one another, both parents nodded.

"Where do you think he got the money?"

Hansen looked bewildered. "I have no idea. We give him a good allowance, so he..." His voice trailed off.

"How much, sir?"

"Twenty-five dollars a week."

Andi jotted the figure in her notebook.

Marie asked, "Are you people sure it was Jared who rented the unit?"

Andi nodded. "Yes, ma'am. We obtained the lease documents from the company."

Ordrew asked, "Has Jared been away from home more than usual lately?"

Andi interrupted. "Before we get into that, has Jared been asking for additional money for the last six, seven weeks?"

Hansen squinted. "Like, is he spending his allowance on the unit and needs something extra?"

"Yeah, exactly."

"No," he said. But Marie took in a quick breath, and her eyes looked frightened.

Andi said, "Ma'am?"

Her eyes were wide. "He came to me. A couple times. Said he'd spent too much on his immigration project at church and could I loan him twenty dollars."

Hansen looked shocked. "And did you?"

She nodded, her face crimson. Andi held up her hand. "There's no law against a kid manipulating his parents for money." She chuckled. "Did it myself."

But Hansen didn't let it go. "How often did this happen, Marie?"

Ordrew held up *his* hand. "What we need to figure is *why* he rented the unit and stored those weapons in it. If he was storing charitable donations for Ebola orphans in Liberia, who'd object, right?"

Hansen took a long breath. "But he wasn't, was he?"

Ordrew shook his head.

Jared's mother said, "He's a senior, which means he's almost never home. If it's not this club or that team, it's girls or friends hanging out. And he's very involved at church, which takes time. So we don't always know what he's doing." Her eyes were suddenly full. "Not like when he was little."

Andi waited a moment. "I know this is hard, Marie. Tell us about what Jared does at church." They could tackle in other ways what Jared did when he wasn't home.

When his wife, working to keep control of her tears, couldn't answer, Hansen said, "He's president of the Young Methodists. They're doing volunteer work with kids of undocumented immigrants who want to go to college. Dreamers, they call them. It takes a lot of time." He sounded proud.

"What kind of volunteer work?"

"They clean basements and garages for ten dollars each, and do other odd jobs. They donate the money to the larger church effort on this cause."

"Got it. So Jared's a pretty good kid, involved in all the stuff kids do, have I got that?"

Hansen nodded, but glanced quickly at his wife. Andi caught it. She turned to the mother, who had composed herself. "Is there anything you can tell us that's been different lately? Something not so positive?"

Marie looked uncomfortable, and looked to her husband for something. He looked away. She shook her head.

Ordrew, glancing at Andi, lifted his eyebrows quickly. He turned to Marie. "Ma'am, I hope you're not keeping something from us that might help us help your son."

Marie looked again at her husband. She waited a moment. "When Ben Stewart called and told me what was happening, I looked in Phil's gun closet. The rifles were gone."

Hansen paled. "Why didn't you tell me?"

She looked stricken. "I'm afraid, Phil." She turned to Andi. "What does it mean?"

"That's what we're trying to find out," Andi said. "How many rifles are missing?"

Marie glanced at her husband. "All of them."

"Jesus," Hansen muttered.

Ordrew said, "How many were there?"

"Nine."

"That's what we found in the storage unit."

Hansen took in a long breath. "I still say, he's no different from any normal seventeen-year-old."

"So why did he take your rifles and hide them in the unit? You saying that's normal behavior?"

Hansen shrugged, but he wavered. "I'm sure he can explain it. Seventeen-year-olds, you know they sometimes aren't completely rational."

Ordrew smiled. "I was a basket case at seventeen." He chuckled. "'Course, I wasn't exactly president of the church youth group." He turned serious. "The way you describe Jared, he seems like a kid who's got a good take on things and feels pretty confident. So can you think of any reason why he would tell us that he's evil and the government is out to kill him?"

The parents looked swiftly at one another, their faces suddenly pale. Marie said, "He said that?"

Andi nodded. "He did. It's different from what we keep hearing about Jared. Help us understand."

Marie looked at her husband, then said, "I don't know that I can. Like Phil said, Jared's been quieter than usual lately, but I haven't seen anything more than that. What else did he say?"

"When you say, 'lately,' what time frame are we talking about?"

The parents looked at each other. "A month," Hansen said. Marie shook her head. "It's more like six, seven weeks."

Hansen said, "What else did he say?"

Ordrew looked at Andi, who nodded. He said, "He told us his friends are deluded. And he told us that he needs to kill his friends before they find out he's evil."

Hansen closed his eyes. Jared's mother began to weep.

17

Andi, with Ordrew again lagging behind her, knocked on Ben's office door. *He's probably ogling my rear again.* She refused to swing around to catch him. *Gonna have to confront this guy. Just now, though, stick to the case.*

"Come."

As they were sitting down, Andi started her report, not giving Ordrew the first word. "His folks didn't give us much. They said they didn't know anything about the unit or the weapons. They were shocked about Jared's paranoid threats. Otherwise, they say he's a good kid, no problems, nothing wrong."

Ordrew shook his head. "They gave us one fact: The rifles belong to the father."

He was going on, but Ben interrupted. "Didn't Phil know they went missing?"

"Uh-uh. Says he got them from his own father, but he doesn't hunt anymore. Hasn't looked in the gun cabinet in years." He paused. "But they're covering up. Parents know when something bad's going on with their kids. It's not just 'quietness,' for Christ's sake."

Ben narrowed his eyes. " 'Quietness?' "

Ordrew said, "They say he's been, and I quote, *quieter than normal* lately. They're hiding something."

Ben rubbed his head. "The three of us ain't got kids, so we ain't no experts on that. Seems to me there's been a pile of shooters whose mamas didn't know."

Ordrew shrugged. "Or whose mamas *pretended* not to know. Hell, this kid's got the perfect cover. He's president of the fucking Young Methodists, for crying out loud. If those Boston bombers could hide in plain sight, this kid could get away with damn near anything and nobody'd give him a second thought."

Andi pursed her lips. "Which one is it? Either he can't hide from his folks or he can hide in plain sight, but he can't do both. Anyway, that isn't the main question."

"Which is what?"

"Is he bad, or is he mentally ill?"

"Bullshit, that's not the question," Ordrew snapped. "The question is, what's he doing? And is it illegal? Arguing about mental illness is the lawyers' job."

Andi nodded. "We have to consider it, though."

"No, we don't. Not our job."

Ben waved them quiet. "Brad, you're right, it ain't our job, but let's not beat the criminal drum too loud, till we get us some evidence."

"For the record, Sheriff, I think a stockpile of weapons and ammunition and a stated threat to kill the senior class is plenty of evidence. Let his lawyer worry about his mental state." He shot a glance at Andi, as if daring her to challenge him.

Ben looked at them both. "Noted. Andi, your thoughts?"

She hesitated; she didn't want to concede the point, not yet—but she didn't know how to counter it. "Brad's right," she said. "We have the weaponry and the other materials, and we've got the threat. Still, Jared's a kid everybody says is an outstanding young man, no problems. We're missing something."

Ordrew laughed, dismissively. "You think the parents are going to tell us their kid's fucked up? You ask me, our only choice is treat him as a shooter-wannabe. If that old lady hadn't gotten suspicious, we'd be facing some god-awful shit." He looked hard at Andi. "I sure as hell don't want to be the cop who lets him grow up to be the real thing."

Andi bristled, but his insinuation touched a nerve. She kept her voice level. "So let's do our job and start digging, and skip the preconceptions."

Ordrew pursed his lips. "In LA, what you call *preconceptions* we call forming a theory of the case. Guess you guys approach police work a little, ah, different."

"LA or here," she retorted, "you need evidence for your theory. Let's go get some."

Ben nodded. "Sounds like a plan." He stretched, looked at a stack of pink message slips. "Got us a pile of media folks arrivin' as we speak. Irv Jackson wants me to do a press conference, issue a statement, stonewall any questions, and shut this down. I want you two there, standin' right behind me.

It went as Ben said. He read the statement he and the county attorney had written; the weaponry was described as "suspicious materials," and

49

nothing else was described at all. An investigation was being undertaken with all the resources of the sheriff's department at its disposal. As information emerged, the media would be informed, and not before then.

"Sheriff, what are the 'suspicious materials'?"

"I ain't ready to answer that question. We got us a new investigation. Hell, you probably know as much about some of this as I do."

Another reporter barked, "Is it true that you've arrested someone? Who is it and what is the charge?"

Ben squared his shoulders. "Well, that's another one I ain't ready to answer. We're talking to a minor, but I can't release his name or any information about him. Like I said, when we know something, you'll know it."

It went like that for ten more minutes, then Ben and the deputies went to his office and shut the door. He called Callie.

"Let me know when the last one leaves."

Only a few minutes later, Callie stuck her head into his office. "Jack What's-his-name said he's booking a room at the Jefferson House. The rest of them are going back over to Missoula. Place is clear."

"Why's he stayin'?"

"Who knows. Wants a scoop, probably."

"He starts hangin' around here, I'll give him a scoop." He looked at his watch. "Hell, nearly seven. Bear of a day." To Andi and Ordrew, he said, "Get some rest tonight and hit 'er hard in the mornin'."

As Andi and Ordrew walked out to the parking lot, she said, "Look, I've been kind of a hard-ass today." She suddenly blushed, immediately regretting her choice of words. "I'm sorry. How about we declare a truce and start fresh tomorrow." She extended her right hand.

Ordrew looked at her hand, then took it. He didn't so much shake it as hold it steadily. For a moment, Andi thought he might not let go, but then he did, starting to smile.

"Love to get fresh with you."

18

Driving out to Ed's, Andi stifled her annoyance. Ordrew's attitude grated on her, like gravel in her shoe. Besides, she was tired and hungry, but she needed to talk with Grace about Jared; she focused on that.

As she pulled into the graveled yard, she saw Grace sitting on the front porch, holding her cell phone against her ear with one hand and gesturing with the other. When she saw Andi's Suburban, she quickly ended the call and jumped down the porch steps toward her.

"Andi! Tell me about Jared! Everybody's talking about him, but the stories are all different. What's going on?"

Andi held up her hand. "Hold on a minute. I'm starving. Is your dad home?"

"No. He called. He's seeing patients tonight. He said he has to be at school tomorrow. So what's the story?"

"Let's talk inside. I'm hungry."

Inside, while Andi heated some soup, she said to Grace, who was sitting at the counter, "What have you heard?"

"That he had a bunch of bombs and assault weapons."

Andi shook her head. "Uh-uh. We're not sure what we found, whether it's trouble or not. He—" The microwave dinged.

"People are saying he had a pressure cooker. Like those Boston guys."

How the hell did that get out? She said, "We don't know, Grace. And we're not forming any conclusions until we learn more." She thought about Ordrew. *At least some of us aren't.* "How well do you know Jared?"

"Oh, real well. Everybody does. And we all like him." Grace looked toward the ceiling for a moment. "I don't think I've ever talked to him when he didn't, like, pay real attention to what I was saying." Her eyes welled; she grunted and turned away from Andi.

Andi noted the tears. She took the soup out of the microwave and said, "Let's talk on the porch. It's nice enough outside."

When they were settled on the swing, Andi said, "Tell me about Jared."

Grace took a long breath. "He's awesome. When I came here, he showed me around school and introduced me to people, even though he was a year older than me."

Andi swallowed some soup. "Maybe he was just—"

"Just trying to get in my pants?" Grace shook her head. "Uh-uh. I know when a boy is horny. Not Jared."

Andi grinned, always amused at Grace's inexperienced sophistication. *I hope it's inexperienced,* she thought. "Jared's not interested in girls?"

"I didn't say that. What I mean is, he's just a nice guy. He always says hi, even to freshmen, and he volunteers for everything, and when you talk to him, you can feel him listening and understanding. He's never crabby. You can always count on him to help. He's been class president all but his freshman year."

"Huh. We're told that he works at his church on some project for immigrant kids."

Grace nodded. "Yeah. You know, a lot of kids criticize him for that. They say illegals should be deported, but he argues with them. I think it's really cool, the way he doesn't let it stop him."

Andi spooned more soup, but said, before eating it, "That's pretty much what everybody's telling us."

"What was he going to do with those guns, Andi?"

"What are the rumors?" She didn't intend to tell Grace what Jared had said. She took another spoonful of soup, which was rapidly cooling.

"That he was going to do a school shooting?"

"What do you think about that?"

Grace's eyes narrowed, deeply serious. "I can't believe it. You should have seen how upset he was about Sandy Hook and all those other shootings."

Andi caught doubt in Grace's voice. "But?"

"He wants to be a Marine. Not that that proves anything."

Andi spoke through a mouthful of soup. "Tell me more about that."

Grace said, "I don't think it means anything. He's talked about joining the Marines since I first met him. He's real patriotic, that's all."

Andi lifted her eyebrows and looked out over the valley, where the last sunlight backlit the peaks, turning the snowpack the color of new copper. "Or it could mean something other than patriotism, couldn't it? Maybe he's got a violent streak and wants an excuse to exercise it?"

Grace's fierce head shake registered her disagreement.

"Why not?"

"Jared and a bunch of us took an elective on Buddhism last year. He told the class his goal was to become a bodhisattva."

"What's a bodhisattva?"

"A person who's almost a Buddha, but he takes a vow not to enter nirvana until all living beings are saved. It's about compassion."

Andi frowned: Jared had said compassion explained his need to kill his friends. "How does that square with joining the Marines?"

"I asked him that. He said he wants to bring Buddhism to the Marine Corps. He says it'll humanize the war machine."

Ah, the idealism of seventeen-year-old boys, Andi thought. *Or the gullibility of sixteen-year-old girls.* "So, if he's a Buddhist and wants to save everyone, what's the gun collection about?"

Grace frowned, said, "That's a hard one. They weren't assault rifles?"

Andi shook her head.

"Everybody owns rifles around here. I think most people, men especially, have a few. Jen's dad has six or seven."

"Your dad hasn't got any."

"He's from Minnesota."

Andi nodded, smiled. She looked out over the dusk-shrouded valley, her eyes roaming the dimming peaks, pondering how many weapons there were here in the valley. She shivered, remembering when she'd been shot. She brushed her eyes. The sky was golden above the mountains. Scattered lights in town were twinkling on. "Too many contradictions," she said, quietly.

"What's going to happen to Jared, Andi?" Grace asked.

Andi shrugged. "Not sure about that. We'll hold him a couple days while we try to find out what's going on. After that, I have no idea, Grace. No idea at all." She stood and gave a last look over the valley, then took her soup bowl back into the kitchen.

Grace followed her inside. "Andi, me and my girls gotta work on a book report, so can I drive your Suburban into town? Northrup's not home yet."

"Sure." She pulled her keys from her pocket and tossed them to Grace. "But be home by ten, okay? I'm sleeping at my place tonight." Andi spent four or five nights a week with Ed and Grace, enjoying the sense of family with them, but tonight she needed quiet and time to think.

"How about ten-thirty? It's already eight."

"Okay."

Grace stood there, looking hesitant. Andi said, "What?"

"Can I ask you a favor."

"Sure."

"I need you to persuade Northrup to buy me a car. I hate being a mooch, always asking my girls or you or him for rides."

"Doesn't he want you to wait till senior year?"

Grace looked like she'd swallowed a bug. "Can you imagine, Andi? It'll be the summer before I'm a senior, everybody'll be going places in their own cars, and Mooch Grace Northrup has to beg for rides. You gotta help me here."

Andi smiled. "I'll talk to Ed about it."

"Do more than *talk*, please! Like, withhold sex or something." When Andi's eyes widened, she added, "Just kidding."

19

In the darkness, the air remained warm, and Andi dozed in the porch swing. An hour after Grace left, Ed's pickup crunched slowly into the graveled yard. She opened her eyes, and watched him. When his door swung open, he rubbed his face under the dome light before getting out. When he came around the truck, she called from the porch, "Long day, big guy?"

In the dark, she could see only his outline, limned by the lights of town below and behind him. His voice came softly out of the night air. "I'm so tired, I won't get an erection till an hour after you kiss me."

"You're in luck. Not in the kissing mood."

He plopped down beside her. "I had to squeeze in three patients and another one at seven tomorrow morning." He yawned. "Lynn tells me the kids are frantic."

"Lynn?"

"The school counselor. She lives over in Missoula and usually comes two half-days a week, but she's staying at the Jeff House till Friday. She said the rumors are crazy and everybody's scared." He yawned again.

Andi rubbed his neck. "Yeah, I was talking to Grace about it. What was your emergency?"

He made a purring noise. "Yeah, rub right there. I wish I could tell you. It's a strange case."

"Confidentiality?"

"Confidentiality." He yawned. "How about yours? What's with Jared?"

She hesitated a moment. "Well, so far it's a mess of contradictions." She told him what they'd found and what Grace had said.

Ed winced. "So, he's a Methodist Buddhist Marine, planning mass murder to protect people from discovering he's evil, out of some twisted kind of compassion."

"Uh-huh. Makes no damn sense," she muttered. "On the one hand, he threatens to kill all his classmates and thinks government agents want to kill him. On the other hand, nothing about him predicts that. He's a good kid, a school leader, smart, active in his church. Everybody likes him." She paused, thinking about the interview with the Hansens. "His parents say lately he's been a little quieter than usual, maybe a bit tense, but they say it's nothing unusual for a senior approaching graduation." She groaned, then muttered, "Damn."

"What's wrong?"

"I forgot to ask Grace about whether he's been quieter or more tense at school lately." She paused. "Speaking of Grace, she wants me to withhold sex so you'll buy her a car before September."

In the darkness, Andi couldn't see his expression, but his voice sounded hesitant. "To which you said?"

She smiled. "I said I'd talk to you."

Ed chuckled, then took her hand. She didn't respond, and after a moment, he let it go and said, "You're on edge about this case."

"Well, nothing makes sense. And I'm nervous about my partner. He's made up his mind that Jared's a terrorist."

"Fuck him." He chuckled, then put his arm around her shoulders. "On second thought, fuck *me*."

"I thought your machinery won't work."

"You used the word *sex*: Little Eddie woke right up."

"Well, put him back to sleep. I need to figure out this damn case. He did say he wanted to kill people."

"Little Eddie?"

She mock-punched his shoulder. "No! Jared."

"Shooters don't tell the cops. They just do it."

"Yeah. That's why Ordrew worries me. He's jumping to conclusions that don't have much support. He's got a big-city attitude, get-them-before-they-get-us."

"He's LA, right?"

She nodded. "From what I've told you, do you have any ideas?"

"Well, LAPD has a pretty violent reputation, so—"

"Not about Ordrew. About Jared Hansen."

Ed sat silent for a while. "From what you say, he sounds paranoid, with the government stuff." He yawned again. "And he's smart? Maybe he's got some variant of Asperger's syndrome. Or drugs or alcohol. They're all possible."

As if answering, Andi yawned too, at the same time shaking her head. She said, "Well, we did the breathalyzer, negative, and the usual tox screen, which we should get back tomorrow." She yawned again. "If he's paranoid or Asperger's, give me some questions to ask."

"Psychology's a baby science. We talk like we know what's going on, but we really don't. Psychosis probably has as many causes as cancer. And nobody knows what causes Asperger's. In other words, who the hell knows?"

"Some questions."

"Okay. Does he have any social skills?"

"In spades. He's popular, elected class president three years running, works for his church's social activities, listens to people well."

"So rule out Asperger's. Paranoia needs a professional examination."

"Can you do it?"

"Not while I'm working for you at the school. Maybe next week."

"Shit." She gave another long yawn. "Well, I gotta wake up and think about this."

He rubbed her neck for a moment, then slid his hand down her arm to her lap. "How about going inside and waking up Little Eddie?"

She removed his hand and stood up. "Soon as Grace gets back with my vehicle, I'm going home. I have to sort out this damn case. No sex tonight."

"Ah." Ed withdrew his hand. "So you're thinking I should buy Grace a car?"

TUESDAY, DAY TWO

20

At four o'clock on a frustrating, fruitless afternoon, Andi and Ordrew filed into Ben's office; she stepped aside to let her partner go first. He smirked and glanced at her ass anyway. Ben, eyes glued to some paperwork, said, "The boy's parents lawyered up, a woman from Missoula. She was here early and told Jared to button his lip unless she's with him. Doubt we'll get much more from him." He handed Andi a paper. "Finally got Dickie Flure to sign the search warrant, so you can tear the kid's room apart. Bring in his computer, all that stuff, too. We'll ship it up to that DCI geek tomorrow to dig into it. So what've you got?"

Andi frowned. "Who's the lawyer?"

Ben consulted a note. "Donna Ratner. I called my buddy Johnny Marks in Missoula. He says she's a ball-buster, but damn good attorney. What've you got?"

Andi shook her head. "Been talking to students all day. He's a great kid, according to everybody we've talked to so far. Even the high school counselor agrees."

Ben frowned. "How's she know? He gettin' some counselin'?"

Andi shook her head. "She helped him connect with some resources in Missoula for his immigration project. His pastor down at First Methodist says he's been late for a couple of meetings lately, and seemed a bit 'preoccupied,' but otherwise, nothing. The kid's everybody's idea of the perfect teenager."

Ordrew shook his head, his frown deepening the lines around his eyes. "St. Jared the fucking Good." He looked like he could spit. "I wonder what the pastor *really* knows."

Ben looked at him. "You ain't thinkin' Pastor Markham's coverin' somethin' up, are you?"

"Can't say. I don't know the man," Ordrew said. "But this kid can't be as good as everybody makes out."

Ben shook his head. "Charlie Markham wouldn't lie to save his mother. If he knows somethin', he'd tell us."

Ordrew's frown deepened. "I still think we go with the worst case. He's planning to shoot some people, God help us if we cut him loose to do it."

"We need to consider the possibility that he's mentally ill. People do have paranoid thoughts, you know. It's a mental illness." She watched Ordrew's face redden.

"And crazy people pull triggers, damn it." He breathed deeply, slowing himself down. Andi thought he wanted to say much more. "Determining mental illness isn't our job."

Andi said, "That reminds me. Ben, can we get Ed to evaluate him?"

"Not yet. We gotta have charges first. Once we charge him, if the DA goes along, then we can eval him." Ben drummed his fingers on the arm of his chair. "You both got your points. But if we ain't got evidence he's actually plannin' to do a crime, he walks tomorrow. Havin' a bunch of rifles ain't no crime in Montana."

Ordrew stood up abruptly, his anger so obvious that Andi flinched. He said, "For the record, Sheriff, I said it before and I'll say it again: Having an arsenal and telling the cops you want to kill your friends is evidence enough."

Ben stood too. "Go search his room. Find me somethin' besides crazy talk I can take to the county attorney. Or the boy goes home."

21

Before meeting with Magnus, Ed parked outside the Anderhold and sat for a moment, his windows rolled down, enjoying the soft afternoon air. Long ribbons of white cloud draped across the northern sky, but threatened nothing. The sweet, warm weather looked to hang around awhile. The sun leaned west, gilding the snowy peaks. Sunset wouldn't be for another three, four hours, and the warm breeze relaxed him. He wouldn't get home till ten—after this meeting with Magnus, when he got back to town, his evening would be jammed with the patients displaced by his day at the high school. He glanced at the dashboard clock: 4:58. He rubbed some color into his face and climbed out of the truck. *Showtime.*

Luisa, today dressed with her customary casual grace, greeted him at the big door. Her dark eyes, though red and tired, were warm, but tinged with anxiety. She extended her hand, and Ed felt in her grip the strength of a woman accustomed to working side by side with her husband. On her father's cattle spread in Mexico, she'd grown into womanhood working beside the men, and when her father died, she'd run the ranch herself, before marrying Magnus and moving to Monastery Valley. Now, she and Magnus owned *Árboles Blancos* jointly with their head foreman, Ernesto Escobar.

To Ed, she said, quietly, "You will help him." In her voice he heard hope, but also a command, and he squeezed her hand gently. Magnus was waiting again in his study, dressed this time in his trademark creased Levis, an elegant flannel shirt, and soft indoor boots. Today his white mane was combed and clean. His eyes, though, were dark, shadowed pools, and his usually ruddy face was pale.

"You look better today," Ed ventured, moving toward the chairs.

Magnus stood. "Don't sit. We're talking in the small study." He took Ed's elbow and guided him down the hall into the back section of the Anderhold. Ed had not been there before. "We call this the Addition," Magnus said. "My grandfather Royal built it onto the main house back in 1914, when he and Eugenie and their kids moved in with Günter and Berit."

Ed traced what he knew of Magnus's genealogy. "Günter was Royal's father, right?" Royal was Magnus's grandfather.

"Yes. Royal's Addition is half-again larger than Gunter's original house."

Magnus led the way through Royal's great-room, and past the second fireplace. Beamed archways beside the fireplaces connected the adjoining living rooms—halls, really. Royal's river rock fireplace alone was a good six feet tall and ten feet wide.

"Competitive, eh?" Ed wondered aloud as Magnus gave the rooms' histories.

"Yes," Magnus stopped and turned toward him. "Royal was a big man, taller and heavier than Günter. Günter was a builder, but Royal had larger appetites. He wanted Eugenie—"

"—His wife?"

"Yes. He was crazy about her and he wanted to give her the world—they had six little ones. So, he built the Addition. Günter had offered him the main bedroom and two smaller bedrooms in the main house, but Royal wanted his own family place, and wanted to live in the Anderhold too. So the Anderhold is really two large homes, connected at nearly every central room."

"Daryl was Royal's only child?" Daryl was Magnus's father.

For a moment, Magnus looked sad. He shook his head. "Only son. There were four girls before him."

"But only he inherited the Double A."

"He did. Three sisters hated the ranch and married wealthy Easterners. The fourth girl died when she was ten. Measles, they say. Royal was heartbroken. It was said he took his grief out on Daryl."

He ushered Ed into a small office, more intimate than his study, at the rear of the Addition, and closed the door. The single Palladian window overlooked the wide acre that in summer would be Luisa's garden. Magnus said, "Luisa agreed to stay in the main house when we meet. I don't want her to overhear anything."

Luisa would not eavesdrop, Ed thought. Magnus's precaution spoke of his distress. The room was snug, companionable, not quite as leather-and-amber as Magnus's study, but still a man's room. Beside the oaken gun closet hung pictures of hunting friends with their elks taken on hunts over the years. For a moment, vanity prodded Ed to look for his image; he found it toward the center, suddenly feeling embarrassed. He scanned the rest of the room. Perhaps the smallest room in the Anderhold, this office was nonetheless twice the size of his in town. He liked it.

They sat. For a moment neither man spoke. Then Magnus said, "I was rude yesterday. My apologies."

"Not necessary, Mack. Whatever you feel while we do this, let it come."

Magnus narrowed his eyes. "Hmm. So how does this go?"

Ed smiled. "You made the rule yesterday: You talk, I listen. When you're done building out your story, I tell you what I think."

"And you want to know why I started drinking."

"Well, only as a means to an end. I want to help you resolve whatever started the drinking."

Magnus frowned, his eyes reddening suddenly. "I doubt there's any dealing with that, Ed."

The room's silence enfolded them. Magnus brushed his eyes and glared at the floor for a moment, then lifted his head. His voice was low. "You knew Daryl."

Ed nodded. *Always at the root, fathers and sons.* "Only in his last years, after his stroke. He wasn't easy to know."

Magnus said, "Even before the stroke he was...hard." He'd selected the word carefully. "He had too much pride. But you've got to understand him and me first."

"All right. Tell me."

Magnus looked away, clearing his throat. "I've never talked about this before. Give me a minute."

Ed settled himself comfortably in his chair.

"Maybe it's not a minute I need," Magnus said softly. "Maybe I'm wrong to try this." He looked away, shame crossing his face.

Ed waited quietly.

Then, almost inaudibly, Magnus began his tale.

In the kitchen of the Main House, he, his father, and his mother, Anne. It's a warm September evening, 1972, Magnus's first week in high school. He grips a book, knuckles white, as if to fling it at his father, who is shouting at his mother.

"Damn it, woman! You're coddling him! He can do chores before he goes to school. Four a.m. never hurt me, and it won't hurt him!"

Anne tries to mollify her husband. "No, Daryl, no, no, you turned out just fine. High school was different then, remember? We didn't have homework every night like they do now."

Daryl shakes his head, disgusted. "I don't care what they do now. Reading his damn books won't make him a man. Work makes men. He's always been weak."

Magnus's voice quivers. "Father, I do the chores. I always have. But just because I don't enjoy the things you do doesn't make me weak."

Daryl glares at his son with contempt. "Not weak? You can't lift half the weight I can, and I'm thirty years older. You can't walk half as fast on a hunt as I do. You can't carry your own meat out when you do get an elk."

Anne lifts her hand. "Daryl, be fair. The boy's fifteen."

Daryl shouts. "Quit defending him, Anne. It's for his own good." He turns back to Magnus. "And that damn papist church you go to. Sissies. Celibates. Queers!"

Anne's voice lifts as well. "Now, Daryl, just stop it. He's just experimenting—"

In a fury, Daryl slaps her, snapping her head to the side. She staggers back against the stove, knocking a pot to the floor. Red tomato sauce spreads slowly over the tiles.

Magnus's voice had turned to gravel. "He'd never hit her before. He hit me plenty, especially after I started going to St. Bernard's on Sundays, instead of our church. But never my mother."

"Why'd you do that?"

"Do what?"

"Start going to St. Bernie's."

"To spite him. The Anderssens are Swede Lutherans. We kept our distance from the Catholics, although Anders, Günter, and Royal did business with the monks up on the mountain." He coughed roughly. Ed wondered why. "Anyway, when I was thirteen, one Sunday morning when we drove in to Pastor McNally's church, I got out of the truck and hung back a minute, then just walked down the street and into St. Bernard's. Never said a word. After the services let out, the old man was so angry he hit me right there on Division Street, in front of God and everybody." Magnus gave a small laugh. "It was worth it."

"He started hitting you after that?"

"He'd been hitting me since I was eight or nine. It just got more frequent." Magnus's voice caught. He looked at the floor.

Ed saw the anguish on his face. He started to say something, but Magnus raised his hand. He looked to Ed like a man wrestling with an invisible urge. While he waited, Ed tried to piece together how Daryl's abuse linked to Magnus's drinking and to Magnus Junior's dropping out of college for a term. The connections weren't clear yet. Hell, they weren't even connections.

Magnus took a long breath, the sound a rasp, or, perhaps, a sob. He started again.

Easter dinner, two years later. Daryl, Anne, and Magnus eat in gloomy silence. The usual holiday guests are absent, the fine holiday china still in the sideboard. There are no Easter lilies in the windows or flowers on the long table. Magnus's brother Calvin's place sits empty. Last November, Calvin, who'd always liked antiques, had borrowed great-grandpa Günter's old elk rifle for a hunt, but it had exploded on the first shot, killing him. Since carrying his son from the hunting ground, Daryl has reeled like a drunken man, moment-to-moment, hour-to-hour, veering wildly between despair and rage. Calvin, his beloved son.

Without lifting his eyes from his plate, Daryl snarls, "You defied me, boy. You went to the papists again this morning. I'd be in my rights to—"

Anne interrupts, "It wasn't defiance, Daryl. We talked about that."

"Shut up, Anne. This is between the boy and me."

Magnus, as unmoored by his brother's death as his parents are, says nothing.

"I don't take to being laughed at, boy. I don't take to having my pastor ask me where my son is on Easter morning. I've my rights to be respected in my own home."

"Pastor McNally didn't ask you that, Daryl. He..."

Daryl slams his fist on the table. Whiskey splashes from his glass. "I told you to be quiet! I won't tolerate your protecting him!"

Magnus looks at his father. Anne gets up and walks to the sideboard. She turns her back to them, hands braced on the sideboard's dark wood, and says, her voice pitched low, intense, "Daryl, I need you to stop this. Magnus can't be Calvin. He can't."

Daryl erupts from his chair and dashes to her, striking her, full-fisted, from behind. Anne's head snaps forward, and she slumps against the sideboard, then slides to the floor. Plates and a brass candlestick crash from the shelf. Magnus leaps onto his father's back, pulling him down. Daryl bucks back and forth like a wild horse, throwing Magnus off, turns on him, begins kicking. Magnus, grounded, sees the boot coming toward his shoulder and rolls, but it catches him in the ribs. Daryl is above him, silent, intent, driving his boot into Magnus's ribs, again, again. Anne screams from the floor. Daryl swings toward her, she lifts the brass candlestick to defend herself, but Daryl grabs it from her hand, throws it across the room, then drives his boot into her face. She crumbles against the cabinets.

Daryl suddenly stops and stalks from the room.

Magnus stopped, exhausted. "No more. No more."

Ed, unsure, waited. What did no more refer to? The session? The beating? Magnus slumped forward, elbows on knees, hands cupping his forehead. His breaths came jaggedly. Ed thought he might be sobbing quietly, but could not tell. He sat still, watching.

Magnus hardly moved, but his breathing slowed. He lifted his head. He had not been crying; his gaze was a desert, dry and barren. "My mother died two weeks later."

Ed took that in, imagining the grief welling in that desert. "Was her death related to Daryl's hitting her?"

Magnus looked puzzled. "He beat her on my account."

Ed spoke gently. "Did you think you caused her death, Magnus?"

Magnus put his head back in his hands. "A minute, Ed. I need a moment." As he spoke, his telephone rang.

22

Mack groaned, but he carried the phone over to the window. "Anderssen here," he said. Watching his back, Ed could see him straightening, facing into something.

For a moment he listened, then said, "Take her to the ER now. I'll call ahead." He punched numbers into the phone. After a few moments, he looked toward Ed while he spoke into the phone, "Connect me with Doc Keeley. This is Magnus Anderssen." Quickly, he added, his voice softening, "I'm sorry. Please. It's an emergency."

Ed said, softly, "What?"

Magnus shook his head, held up his index finger. In a minute, he mouthed.

After a few moments, Magnus said, "Yes, I'm he. I'd like to speak with John Keeley." He listened. "Okay, the daughter of one of my men is very sick and she's on her way to your ER." He listened. "No, I don't know that. Can you connect me with John?"

When Keeley answered, Magnus repeated the information. "Look, John. Do what needs done for her. Send me the bill." He listened. "Yeah, whatever it costs. And John, the family is, ah, undocumented."

He held the phone a bit away from his ear for a moment, then said, "So tell Ben Stewart to arrest me. But take care of the kid, okay?" After a moment, he smiled. "You're a good man, Keeley." He ended the call.

Putting the phone back in its cradle, he looked sheepishly at Ed. "So. You never heard that."

"Heard you helping somebody out?"

Magnus blushed. "Yeah, that. And that I hire the undocumented."

"Hell, we all know that."

23

Magnus took his seat, looking brighter. "Poor woman's beside herself with worry. It's her only child." He shook his head. "Those folks have no end of suffering. Glad I can help."

"You're a good man, Mack."

His friend looked grateful. "I try. Not so good a man lately."

Ed nodded, glancing at the wall clock: 5:40. Time left to process the story. He waited a moment, then said, "Just before the call came, I'd asked if you think you caused your mother's death."

For a long moment, the rancher looked at the ceiling, breathing heavily. He lowered his eyes to Ed. They were dark, afraid. "I think I've had enough today."

24

On the drive north to Jefferson, Ed's hands trembled on the wheel. Over the years, he'd heard many violent stories—too many—but this story, from one of his oldest friends, weighed heavily in his chest. His eyes misted, so he pulled onto the shoulder and stopped. He sat, breathing slowly, letting grief well up from that deep place where, long ago, he'd discovered he could bury the sorrow that filled him about his patients.

For ten minutes, he watched the snowy ridges of the mountains brightening in the late sun, and, then, feeling settled, called Andi.

"Hi, sweetness," he said. "You coming over tonight? I could use a dose of Dr. Pelton's love medicine."

"Not going to happen. We've got a warrant, so we're heading over to search Jared's room, then we're meeting back at the department. Looks like a long evening."

"Me too. Patients at seven and eight. I should be home by 9:30 or so. How about a glass of wine on the porch? This warm weather's too good to waste."

"Make that ten or ten-thirty. I need to pick up a clean uniform for tomorrow."

He waited a moment, then took the plunge. "Andi, just move in with us. You're there most nights anyway."

"This isn't the time for that." She sounded annoyed. "I'll see you ten-ish."

"I don't mean *move in* tonight. Just talk about it."

"Don't push your luck. If you seriously want to talk about that tonight, I'm sleeping at my place."

"Ouch. Got it. Ten-ish it is, and no talk. See you then."

He sat in the truck, windows open, letting the last ripples of his sadness for Magnus smooth themselves; Andi was right. Neither of them was in a sane enough place to talk about living together. He picked up the phone again, and tapped in Grace's number.

"Northrup? Why are you calling? Can't you text?"

He smiled. She loved teasing him about his old-fashioned telephone habits, as much as he enjoyed correcting her grammar. "My mother taught me when you're inviting a young lady out to dinner, you use the telephone."

"Who are you inviting to dinner?"

"You."

Silence.

"You still there?"

"Northrup! I would, but you should've told me sooner. I already had pizza with my girls."

Ed felt a twinge of disappointment. *Strike two*, he thought. "No problem. We'll do it another time."

"Northrup?"

"What, honey?"

"Can we please talk about a car for me? Like, soon?"

"Andi said you told her to withhold sex until I buy one."

"Oh." She was quiet a moment. "That was kind of a joke. Sorry. But I need a car before summer vacation, Northrup."

"Oh? Why so soon?"

A long silence. "Uh, we can talk about that later."

Ed heard what sounded like embarrassment in her voice, which set off a chain of thoughts familiar to any father of a sixteen-year-old daughter: Andi had told him she'd seen Grace riding, in the center of the bench seat, in Zach Norlander's old F-150. Lately, Grace had been mentioning Zach a lot, in a tone Andi called "smitten." The bench seat in beat-up '86 Ford pickups wasn't large enough for the play of two teenage love-birds, one of whom was a six-two lineman. Thus, a car—specifically, a vehicle with an ample back seat—was needed. And "soon" did not bode well.

Grace had recovered enough to say, "Why so soon? I don't know, I was just thinking about how I hate to keep imposing on you and my girls for rides."

You don't know? Time for that boy-girl refresher chat. He decided that had to wait for face-time. He also decided on a frontal attack about the car. "Honey, are you and Zach Norlander going out together? Is that why you want a car?"

He heard her gasp. "Northrup! No! Him and me, I mean he and me, we're just friends. What does having a car have to do with me and Zach?"

If you don't know now, you'll learn soon enough. "Well, nothing, I guess. But yeah, we can talk about the car."

"When?"

"How about tomorrow, on the way into school? I'll expect you to make your case, okay?"

"Yeah, okay. I'll make my case." She made a small sound that might have been "bye," and ended the call. Ed smiled for a moment, feeling mostly recovered from Magnus's session. He opened his contacts and tapped Lynn Monroe's number. She was staying at the Jefferson House Motel during this crisis week; maybe she'd have a quick bite to eat with him before he met his seven o'clock.

Her phone rang once, then rolled to voicemail. At the beep, he said, "Lynn, it's Ed. I've got an hour before I see evening patients. Interested in a burger at the Angler Bar? If you get this in time, let me know."

He chucked the phone onto the seat beside him, checked his mirrors, and pulled back onto the highway. *Strike three.*

A few miles north, he pulled off again and grabbed the phone.

"Speak," Ben Stewart's growl greeted him.

"I've got an hour. How about meeting me on the corner?"

"Ain't our day."

"And so I repeat, how about meeting on the corner now?"

Ben grunted. Ed expected strike four, but Ben said, "You're on. Ten minutes."

He tossed the phone onto the passenger seat again, and pulled onto the highway. The phone buzzed. He answered, wondering if Grace had reconsidered. Or Andi.

"Doctor Northrup, this is Donna Ratner. I am Jared Hansen's lawyer. We would like to retain you to examine him."

Startled, Ed said, "Can you give me moment, Ms. Ratner? I'm on the road and I have to pull over." He found a wider spot on the shoulder and stopped. "Ms. Ratner? Thanks for the call. Look, I don't do a lot of forensic work. I think Jared would be better served with an expert. How about Jack Pullman in Bozeman?"

"I'm quite familiar with Mr. Pullman. Unfortunately, the Hansens are not wealthy, and his fees make even us lawyers blush, not to mention the travel time he'd charge them. Additionally, the Hansens requested that I contact you." She hesitated. "I discouraged them from using someone who is not, how shall I put this, a specialist in court work."

"I completely agree, Ms. Ratner. So you're calling me why?"

"The Hansens are not wealthy, and they insisted on you. So the first thing I need to know is, have you any court experience?"

Ed felt the old, familiar shame. Court experience, yes. Good court experience, no. He said, "I do, but it's not extensive." He didn't mention that it was as a defendant.

"May I ask what your fee would be to accept this assignment?"

"Before we go any further, Ms. Ratner—"

"Please, Donna."

"Donna. You need to know that I'm in a relationship with the lead investigating officer."

He listened to the silence, imagining her calculations. Finally, she said, "That complicates things."

"I imagine if it comes to a trial, the prosecutor will impugn my objectivity."

Another silence stretched out. "I have to contemplate the implications of that. You're right, it puts my client at a disadvantage. But we've worked with other more complicated situations before. Maybe..." She didn't finish.

"I think you should use Jack Pullman."

"I'll take that under advisement. But in case my partners and I can figure out a way that you'd not be a liability—sorry, not you, the complication— what would your fee be?"

"Same as my regular fee: seventy-five an hour, plus expenses."

"Come on, Doctor. Be realistic. Here in Missoula they get three-hundred an hour."

He frowned. "Here in Jefferson, Donna, I get seventy-five. You mentioned the Hansens not being wealthy. I can't see charging them more just because it's forensic." His voice carried an edge.

"My apologies, Doctor—"

"Accepted, and please, call me Ed."

"Ed. I have no business questioning your business practices. Seventy-five an hour plus expenses will be the ticket."

"But there's still my relationship with Deputy Pelton."

"Yes, there is that. I'll consult with my partners, then the Hansens, and I'll get back to you. Let me ask, though. If I decide to go ahead with you, will you accept the job?"

Ed looked out the windshield at the rugged height of Hunter's Peak. He and Magnus had scouted elk there last August, preparing for the autumn hunt, during which they'd both been skunked: Magnus had harvested no meat, Ed no photos. Now his friend was caught in some maelstrom Ed had no idea how to calm, and the valley was reeling from the revelation of Jared's weapons cache. Ed suspected mental illness, but that wouldn't calm people's fears. Jared would suffer, no matter the outcome. Could he play a part to help the boy? The kid needed someone, and he was going to need that someone more than ever when legalities heated up.

"Yeah, Donna, I will."

25

Nearly every Wednesday, Ed and Ben sat together at the corner of the Angler Bar, across Division Street, opposite the building that housed Ed's office and the sheriff's department. They got together to talk about anything and everything and nothing in particular. All year, four days a week, Ben met on the corner with men living in the valley; he felt that meeting with the women might be misconstrued. Between elections, Ben listened to the concerns and heard the issues brewing in the valley, so he could arrange whatever help the department could offer. When the election came around, Ben didn't need to campaign: Everyone believed he knew their problems and would help to whatever extent he could. He hadn't faced an opponent in twenty-four years. Wednesdays, though, belonged to Ed, and they met on the corner for business; their Wednesday meeting refreshed their long friendship, now twenty-nine years old.

Ed had been surprised that Ben had agreed to meet on a Tuesday. *No citizens available today?* Then it occurred to him—Ben might not want to field questions about the Jared Hansen rumors swirling around the valley. Yesterday's press statement hadn't quelled the innuendo.

Ed arrived first. Ted Coldry, the owner-bartender of the Angler, waved. "How nice to see you on a Tuesday, Edward. Your usual?"

"Yep." He yawned. "Excuse me!"

"Your exertions with Andrea keeping you awake at night?" Ted asked, looking sideways at Ed, as he poured the ale and spun a coaster onto the polished bar in front of him.

Ed chuckled. "Uh-uh. I spent all day at the high school, calming kids down about the Jared Hansen thing." He rubbed his eyes. "I can't make sense of it myself. Anyway, in an hour I have to see my own patients. Makes a long day."

"And you've been going out to the Anderhold the last couple of afternoons, I hear."

Ed flinched. His seeing Magnus should be private, but the valley's communications networks put Verizon to shame. *How did Ted know?* The bartender answered his unspoken question. "Luisa called and said you and Mack were working on a project for Magnus's Labor Day fireworks. Any advance notice for a poor bar owner?"

Ed smiled. Magnus couldn't have fashioned a better cover story, or picked a better person to spread it around. Ted talked to everyone. "We'll want your beer tent, of course."

Ted and his partner, Lane Martin, had bought the decrepit Angler, a dead-on-its-feet beer-and-burger joint, in 1998, and renovated it into a city-class restaurant, blond wood and red brick. The old bar itself had been refinished, keeping the dark, smoky atmosphere, the varnished bar and back-bar, and the soot-stained fireplace. The valley folks loved the place, both the upscale restaurant and the old-time bar. Then, last year, after Ted and Lane had opened their Monastery Valley Brewing Company next door to the restaurant, Magnus's annual fireworks show had decided it needed a beer tent.

Ben Stewart pushed roughly through the swinging doors separating the restaurant from the bar. Just behind him, someone Ed didn't recognize pushed in. Ben fell onto his regular stool, his wide haunches overflowing it. "Bring me a beer, Ted, or I might shoot up your bar." Ed saw him glare at the stranger. "And I ain't givin' no interviews, Jack."

Ed nodded. *Ah. Reporter.* Under his breath, he said, "Suddenly you're popular."

Ben glared at him, then swiveled on his stool and said to the reporter, "Give me a break, Jack. I know you got a job to do, but I do too. We'll have that presser tomorrow mornin' and you'll get whatever we know then. Give it a rest tonight, okay?"

The reporter, burly, with a thin, whitening beard and a shock of wild brown and gray hair, said, "Come on, Ben. Everybody's saying it's a kid and he's piling up weapons for a mass shooting. Can you at least confirm that?"

"How long you known me?"

Jack looked surprised. "I don't know. Twenty years?"

"You ever know me to bullshit you guys?"

Jack smiled. "Once or twice."

Ben chuckled. "Yeah, well, *this* ain't bullshit: I ain't doin' no confirmin' or denyin' till tomorrow at nine. Let's give 'er a rest and let me visit with my pals, here."

Jack pocketed his pen and stuck his notepad in his bag. "Can't fault a guy for trying. Okay, Ben. Tomorrow at nine." He looked at Ed and Ted. "Gentlemen," he said, and gave a small salute, then left.

"A rough day, Benjamin?" asked Ted, as he poured Ben's beer. "Town's buzzing about the boy."

"Got that right." Ben turned to Ed. "How you doin', pal? You handlin' the counselin' chores at the high school?"

"I am, with Lynn Monroe. She agreed to stay here all week. I'll be seeing my own patients after we talk."

Ben nodded sympathetically. "Not to mention driving out to Mack's place every day."

"How the hell do you know that?"

"Luisa called. You're workin' on the fireworks together. I'd join you boys, but I'm up to my kisser with this damn situation."

"Yeah," Ed ventured. He changed the subject, careful of Magnus's confidentiality. "What're you guys learning about the boy?"

"Damn little. Nobody's got a bad word to say. Pure as the driven snow, except for the damn weaponry and talkin' about killin' his friends. We're stuck. Andi's searchin' his house as we speak. Got us a meetin' at eight-thirty to see what they find."

"Yeah, she told me."

"Well, God help us if she and Ordrew don't turn up some good bugs under the rocks."

"Working them overtime?"

Ben ran his fingers through his curly, graying hair. "Yeah. My budget's over the cliff, with the flood and now this. We have us a wildfire or some other damn nonsense this summer, I'll be borrowin' money from you and Ted here. What do you think?"

"About your budget?"

"No, joker. About the boy."

He hesitated. If Donna Ratner decided to hire him, talking with Ben—

and Andi—would be off limits. "I really shouldn't say. I haven't examined him."

"That ain't helpful." He picked up and sipped the beer Ted had coastered in front of him. "He looks to me like one of your cases of disorderly thinking."

"The term's *thinking disorder*." Ed paused to think about what he should say. "Could be paranoid psychosis, but I couldn't say without examining him. You should have Jack Pullman in Bozeman take a look. He's excellent."

Ben looked hard at him, and centered his beer glass carefully on the coaster. Ed knew he'd touched a nerve.

"Why should I have Jack Pullman take a look? I got me a shrink right in my building."

Ed felt a twinge of guilt for concealing Jared's lawyer's offer, but he said nothing for the moment.

Ben said, "Ted?"

"Benjamin?" Ted came over, wiping a glass with a towel.

"You run a business."

Ted glanced around his bar. "So it would seem, Socrates."

"When your budget gets tight, what do you do?"

"What sanity dictates, Benjamin: cut costs, and God help us, raise prices."

"So, hypothetically, if I got me nothin' but dust in my till and I need a psychologist, do I hire me a top-dollar shrink from Bozeman, or do I get me a Freud from the neighborhood?"

"Well, hypothetically, a wise manager would shop locally and land a bargain."

Ben grunted and turned his head toward Ed. "You trackin' the gist, here?"

Ed felt himself tense, felt his face flush. "You're not exactly subtle."

"So what sort of deal can you give me?"

"To examine Jared?" Ed tried to delay the inevitable. Ben was going to be furious.

"No, to sell me a Ford. You suddenly develop Alzheimer's for this conversation?"

"Just making sure." He swallowed. "No deal, I'm afraid." This wasn't going to be pretty. "I just got off the phone with Jared's attorney. She wants me to examine him." He paused. "For the defense side," he added, making sure Ben got it.

Ben swung ninety-degrees to look hard at him. "And you said what?" he started, then stopped, his face registering puzzlement, or maybe hurt. "I ain't sure I expected nothin' like this." He turned back, staring at the back bar. "You goin' up against us?"

"I'm not going against you, Ben. This boy's in big trouble and his folks want somebody local. I'm it. And I want to help him if I can."

"Small comfort." Ben shook his head. "Ain't easy not to feel it's a personal slap."

"Damn it, Ben, you know better than that. You're one of my oldest friends." Ed's irritation was growing. "Look. I know it's awkward, but it's not personal."

Ben grunted. "You work the other side of the street, I ain't allowed to even pick your brain. That's hard."

"It's going to be even harder with Andi."

Ben sprayed a mouthful of beer across the bar. "Keep the details of your love life outa this conversation, bud."

Good sign, Ed thought.

Ted, leaning over his crossword puzzle at his end of the bar, obviously eavesdropping, straightened. "A question, gentlemen?"

"Sure," Ben said, wiping the splattered bar with a tiny paper napkin. "Could use a bigger washcloth, first."

Ted brought over a bar towel and wiped the bar. "Edward, are you allowed to have a conflict of interest on a case?"

Ed swallowed his beer, suddenly nervous. "No, of course not."

"How does your having a relationship with the lead investigator on this case fit with your being on the defense side?" He looked expectantly at Ed, then at Ben.

Ben turned on his stool. "Yeah. How's that work?"

Ed stretched, uncomfortable. "Been thinking about that. Told the lawyer too. Could be a problem. I'd have to check my ethics code."

Ben spluttered again, and Ted quickly mopped up the second spray. "Your ethics code? That the same ethics code you keep quotin' whenever I ask you a shrink-type question about a suspect?"

"The same." He hesitated. "I'm not clear how conflict of interest applies to this situation, though."

"Well, I ain't no fan of you working against us. Seems, well, unfriendly."

73

As they sat in silence for a few moments, Ed felt a growing discomfort with his decision to sign on with Ratner.

Ben turned to him again. "Suppose your ethics code says it's a conflict of interest. You willing to work for me? Or the prosecutor, technically?"

"If it's a conflict for the defense, it'd be a conflict on your side too."

"What say we gut that fish when we catch it? If you do it, what's your fee?"

Ed chuckled. "I'd do it *pro bono*. Service to the department. Maybe that'd show there's no personal gain in it. No conflict." As he said it, he knew it was wrong. The conflict wouldn't be about money, but about his relationship with Andi.

Ben was moving on. "Huh. Free, eh? Nothin' for me to pay you?"

"Yeah." Ed thought about why he'd offered this. Friendship? Or maybe he *had* a conflict—a desire to please Andi? He shrugged. *I'll gut that fish when I catch it.* He glanced at Ben. The sheriff looked to be over his hurt feelings. Ed said, "You could buy me a beer to show your gratitude." He held up his empty glass.

As Ted poured a fresh one, Ben said, "You sure you can afford evaluatin' the kid free of charge?"

"Sure."

Ben looked smug. "Then buy your own beer."

26

When Andi and Ordrew arrived at the Hansens', Marie said, "I have to call my husband. I want him here while you search." Her eyes were red, her face haggard and pinched. "Is Jared all right?"

Andi flushed. She'd looked in on the boy before they went to the unit. Although he was awake, he hadn't responded to her. Following the lawyer's advice, probably. Or sunk in paranoia. She said, "He didn't want to talk when I last saw him. At morning report, they said he had a rough night."

Marie Hansen's eyes misted. "You have no idea what this is like, Deputy."

Andi touched her arm gently. "I imagine it's hell, Marie. And call me Andi, okay?"

Marie dabbed her eyes. "I just talked with Phil. He'll be home in twenty minutes." They sat in the living room to wait. Marie said, "I should ask if you'd like coffee or a soft drink."

Ordrew shook his head. "Not necessary, ma'am. We know how very difficult this must be for you."

Marie stiffened. "No, Deputy, you don't."

He nodded. "Well, that's so, isn't it?" He glanced at Andi, who nodded. On his best game, she thought. They all sat quietly for a time.

"Mrs. Hansen," said Ordrew. "We're sorry for the inconvenience of all this. I just wanted to alert you that one of the things we've been told to look for is evidence of..."

Marie interrupted. "Drugs and alcohol." She looked disgusted this time, not sad. "You won't find it, Deputy." She started to say something else, but the front door opened.

Phil Hansen came through, looking furious. "What's this search for?"

Andi and Ordrew stood up. Andi said, "Thanks for coming home, Phil. We've been advised that some of the things Jared's been saying may represent a mental illness, but that usually those kinds of problems don't just pop up. When they do, and from everyone we've talked to, including yourselves, it seems to have happened very suddenly and very recently. We've been advised that either drugs or alcohol may be the cause. So, we'd like to search Jared's room, with that in mind. And other parts of the house where he might have hidden alcohol or drugs."

Ordrew took the warrant out of his pocket, held it up. "We have a warrant, sir."

Phil snatched it, read it, handed it to Marie. She gave it to Ordrew, unread.

Andi searched Phil Hansen's face, which had not softened. Indeed, his eyes were red, hard, and very angry.

Marie shook her head. "You can search, but you won't find anything, at least not alcohol." She looked at Andi. "It's a little embarrassing to say, but Jared still kisses me goodnight every night." She glanced at Ordrew.

He said, "That's very sweet, Mrs. Hansen. But we're not —"

She cut him off. "Every *single* night, Deputy, and I have never smelled alcohol on his breath. And he never gets slurry in his language or forgetful or irritable. He doesn't hide things from us. I don't know what other signs of drug use we'd see, but those are the ones we've always been told to watch for."

Andi said, "Told to watch for? May I ask by whom?"

"Our church has parenting classes for members with teenage children. They tell us what to look for."

"Thank you, ma'am," Ordrew said, his voice soothing. "We got it. But we haven't found a single thing that explains those guns or the secrecy, or the threat to kill his classmates either. So we need to dig deeper. I'm sorry. We understand how painful this is for you."

Phil Hansen shook his head. "Do what you have to, but don't condescend to us. You have *no* idea how painful this is for us." He turned away, then turned back. "Please, put his things back where you found them. When Jared comes home, it'll be hard enough for him without seeing how his privacy has been violated."

Andi nodded and stood. "Thanks, both of you. We'll start in his bedroom."

Three hours later, they had nothing. The bedroom and the rooms in the basement and attic were as clean as a baby's nursery. There wasn't even a *Playboy* rolled up in a boot.

27

The deputies' chatter buzzed around the conference table until, promptly at *8:30*, Ben Stewart came in and dropped into his usual chair at the head of the table.

"What've we got?" he said, cutting off the talk. All the deputies turned to Andi.

She felt a weight on her chest. "Nothing. Jared's room was clean, except for another jar of those seeds we sent up to DCI. Brad says it's a normal seventeen-year-old boy's room." She glanced at her partner, and forced a smile. "I wouldn't know. Never was in a seventeen-year-old boy's room."

Tentative chuckles around the table.

Ben drummed his fingers on the conference table. He hadn't chuckled. "What about the rest of the house?"

"The Hansens showed us all the hiding places they knew of. Nothing there, either."

Ordrew grunted. "All the hiding places they *said* they know of."

Ben looked hard at him. "You got reason to think they're concealin' somethin'?"

Ordrew shrugged. "We've got murder threats, nine rifles, and a goddamn pressure cooker. *Somebody's* hiding something. And the parents admit the kid's been real moody lately."

"What's *lately*?"

Andi said, "Six, seven weeks. And they didn't say real moody, just *moody*. And they keep insisting it's nerves about college next year."

Chip Coleman raised his hand. "What about his past? Anything?"

Ordrew looked disgusted. "The parents *claim* he wasn't bullied or abused. Of course, they wouldn't admit that—it'd blow back on them."

Andi looked hard at him. "It's not just the parents; everybody we've talked to so far likes him. You guys hear anything different?"

All the deputies shook their heads. Andi said, "Ed Northrup thinks we should be looking for signs of mental illness. I'm no psychiatrist, but he does seem paranoid. But other than that, there's nothing we've found to substantiate it."

Ordrew scowled. "Except for wanting to kill his friends."

Andi ignored the contempt in his voice and scanned the table. "What've you guys got?"

Heads shook. Pete said, "I covered the teachers we didn't get to yesterday. None of them could think of anything negative. Oh, he sucks at calculus." Ben's glare short-circuited the chuckles.

Chip Coleman said, "The neighbors all say more or less the same. Old Miz Kenneally said Jared mows her lawn twice a month, for nothing. Seems he shovels her sidewalk in the winter."

Andi said, "Like I say, we have nothing beyond his crazy talk during the interview."

Ordrew's annoyance was visible. "You call it 'crazy talk,' I call it serious threats. You saying we need something beyond that?"

"Loretta Tweedy says he's been staying in that storage unit for a couple of hours four or five afternoons a week for the last few weeks. That's really the only difference from his usual routines—generally, he hangs out after school with friends, but we're told he's been doing less of that."

Ben asked, "Loretta says 'the last few weeks.' How many weeks she talkin' about?"

"She mentioned the big thaw in February. I don't know how long ago that was."

Pete said, "That'd be early or middle February. My kids were pissed we couldn't ride the snowmobile."

Andi nodded. "Then Loretta's saying roughly six or seven weeks."

"What's he been doin' in the unit all that time?"

Andi shrugged. "Reading, I suppose."

Chip said, "Yanking his wiener, would be my guess." Everybody laughed, and Ben glared again.

Ordrew said, "We didn't find any light source for reading, did we?"

Andi nodded. "An electric lantern." She looked at Ordrew. "You have anything else?"

"Just what my gut tells me," he said. "This kid's bad, people. First, he collects all that weaponry, then he tells us he wants to kill his classmates. And a guy doesn't hang out in a goddamn storage unit with guns unless he's planning something. In my book, we got all the evidence we need. And in my book, it adds up to big trouble. Something terroristic, if you think about the anti-government aspect. And as for mental illness, almost everybody agrees terrorists must be mentally ill, by definition, and that's not our business."

Pete shook his head. "I've known Jared for ten years, Brad. I've coached all his teams since he was seven. He's a good kid. The weapons collection and the threat buffalo me, but I can't see *terrorist*. We didn't find any notebooks or journals or diaries, either. No written plans anywhere."

Ordrew frowned. He scanned the deputies. "For Christ's sake, people! I realize we've got a small town, but that doesn't mean we can't have the same shit as Los Angeles or Chicago or Boston."

Ben intervened. "Well, we ain't Los Angeles, so let's put on our thinkin' caps and dig a little deeper. What about this paranoid mental illness business? I ain't hearin' nothin' supports that besides the one comment."

Nobody spoke. Finally, Andi said, "Well, there's the moodiness."

Ben leaned back into his chair. "Crap on toast, *moody*. I get *moody* when my electric toothbrush don't run. Moody don't add up to killin' the senior class, for Christ's sake. Somebody get me one damn piece of evidence I can build a criminal charge on."

Again, the table was silent. Ordrew barked into the silence. "Jesus Christ! The fucking kid collected weapons and threatened his classmates with them, then told us the government's out to kill him. What am I missing here?"

Ben rubbed his eyes. "Weapons ain't against the law here in Montana, and we don't issue permits for long guns, so that ain't no help," Ben said, visibly frustrated. "What did the parents say about their guns disappearin'?"

Andi said, "Until we told them, they didn't know. Seems that Phil doesn't hunt, and he inherited them from Jared's grandpa, who taught Jared to hunt. They've been locked up in his gun cabinet for years."

"So the boy took the guns to his storage room without them knowin'?"

"Looks that way."

Ben looked pained. "Makes a guy sympathetic to Brad's thoughts, don't it? They maybe don't know as much about their son as they say. But his grandpa taught him to hunt. That helps."

Ordrew said, "Can we get back to the point? This isn't about hunting, damn it. This is about amassing weapons to use against his friends." He stopped, shaking his head. "No, it's even clearer than that: He's talking about killing people because he's afraid the government is after him. In my book, that's a terroristic threat."

Ben half-smiled, although he didn't really look amused. "Well, Brad, at least your book ain't cluttered with ideas." The deputies chuckled, while Ordrew's face darkened further.

Andi felt obliged to say, "Brad's got a point: We have the threat."

Pete spoke up. "And there's the issue of mental illness."

Ordrew waved that off. "He's gaming us on that. It'll be his defense. Anyway, that's for the county attorney and the boy's lawyer to fight out."

Ben rubbed his eyes. "Well, we either charge him, or we let him go." He stretched. "Maybe you're right, his threat's the ticket. I gotta talk to Irv Jackson about that, but I suspect he ain't much interested in filin' any charge on the nothin' we got. So unless you all get your asses out there and find something stronger, I'm probably gonna have to let this boy walk."

Ordrew barked, "Fuck that, Ben. Just fuck it. Only chicken-shits and liberal dupes let a terrorist go."

Ben jumped up fast, crashing his chair over backward. "My office, Ordrew. Now." To the others, who had gone stone-still, he barked, "We're done here."

28

Ben waited while Ordrew entered his office, then slammed the door. "That's a step too far, Ordrew. You can toss around your opinions all you want, but you insult your colleagues again, you're suspended. You clear about that?"

Ordrew folded his arms across his chest.

"I want an answer."

"You're making a mistake here, Sheriff. This kid's going to kill somebody."

"You think I ain't aware of the chances? Before you say any more, are we clear about showin' respect to your co-workers?"

After a moment, Ordrew nodded. "Clear. I'll watch my step. But we can't let him go."

"What evidence we got to justify holdin' him?"

"Making a terroristic threat. It's on the damn tape. No-brainer." Disgust tinged Ordrew's voice.

Ben looked at him. "Maybe. That's between me and the county attorney. My own view, that's a bullshit political charge, not a legal one."

"That's crap, Sheriff. It's the law."

Ben squinted at him. "You want a pissin' contest about the law? Okay. We need three elements to charge makin' a terror threat. We got the threat. That's one." He held up one finger. "We got specificity, his classmates. That's two." The second finger lifted. "But number three's *reasonability*, evidence the suspect had reasonable means and opportunity to carry out the threat. Nine single-shot rifles ain't persuadin' me about reasonability. And I sure as hell don't take what he said to be terroristic. The kid ain't political. I think he's either crazy or he's been doin' too many video games."

Ordrew shook his head. "Screw reasonability. Let the lawyers argue that one. And you can't be serious, Ben. Terrorism isn't a 'bullshit charge.'"

"Sure it is. Since them Twin Towers came down, there's been politicians screamin' 'terrorism' to justify any damn hair they got up their ass. We got us damn-near a police state, and I for one don't like it." He grunted. "Times have changed, but that don't make this kid no terrorist."

Ordrew grimaced. "You're wrong, Sheriff. He may be a lone wolf, but he says he has to kill before the government kills him: That's political. Charge this asshole under the Patriot Act or whatever act you come up with. But charge him, damn it, before he kills somebody."

Ben rubbed his eyes, giving himself a moment to rein in his annoyance. "Give it a rest, Brad. What I do with the boy is one thing, and Jackson and I'll make that decision. You 'n me are havin' this little conversation for another reason. If you ever call out me and my deputies like you just did, you're suspended with pay. This here's a warning. Do it again, it's without pay, and if you're dumb enough to repeat, you can pack your bags. You clear on that?"

Again, Ordrew said nothing.

"Answer me, Brad. I ain't playin' a game here."

Ordrew smirked. "I already told you I'm clear: When I see stupidity, I'm to keep my mouth shut."

Ben glared at him. "I'm developing a real dislike for you, Bradley. You better walk the line."

Ordrew shrugged. "You want to know what I wish, Sheriff?"

"Yeah. I'm plain dyin' to know."

"I wish that kid had taken a shot at us when we opened that unit door."

"You do?" Ben was genuinely surprised.

"Yeah. 'Cause then I'd have blown him away without a second fucking thought."

29

As Ed had predicted, talking about Jared's defense attorney was harder with Andi, and that didn't refer to Little Eddie. Furious, she sat in the dim light of the porch lamps, staring out at the night.

"You're working for the defense?" she said, not turning to look at him. "You expect me to be good with that?"

"I'd like it if you were, but I don't suppose I should expect it. And it's not for sure yet."

"You 'don't suppose'? Jesus, Ed. This means we can't talk about the case anymore, you realize that?"

"I do."

"This sucks. Not only do you take yourself out of the game, you jump back in against me."

"Damn it, Andi, I'm doing this for *Jared*, not against *you*!" He eased up. There was no reason for Andi to like his decision. Or Ben either, though the sheriff had come around.

"Works out that way, though, doesn't it?" she said, her voice still angry. "You could help Jared from *our* side, if you'd have just talked to us." She folded her arms and turned her body away on the porch swing.

Ed waited to see if she'd turn back, but after listening to the silence for a couple of minutes, he stood up and walked down the steps into the yard and then out into the long, sloping field that led down to the highway, the Monastery River, and Jefferson. *Give her some time.* Thirty yards or so into the field, he turned and looked back. Andi still sat, arms folded, looking south, backlit by the porch lights. Had he made the wrong decision? Maybe he should rescind his agreement to take the job. He turned and walked a little farther into the darkness, hands in his pockets. New-thawed mud and early grass smelled green all around him; he heard the rustling of night animals. No, working for the prosecution would make it tough for Jared to open up to him. *If he's truly paranoid.*

He stood still, watching the stars. Andi's anger—and probably the hurt just below it—made all the sense in the world. Overhead, a satellite moved silently down the southern sky. He jerked his head up: Something had flashed above him. A meteor streaked south, flaring out. A flash, then extinction. He turned back toward the house, walking slowly, dreading what came next. The porch swing was empty.

Inside, Andi was making up the couch. She straightened when he came in. "Grace is asleep. I'm too tired to drive home now, so I'm sleeping on the couch. We can try to continue this discussion tomorrow."

He started to speak, but she turned away.

"Not now, Ed. I'm done talking for tonight."

WEDNESDAY, DAY THREE

30

Ed gave up on sleep. The bedside clock showed a red *4:45*. He'd slept fitfully, an hour here, a half hour there, upset by Andi's anger and worrying the ethical dilemmas from every angle he could think of. He got quietly out of bed, hoping not to waken Andi, but he smelled coffee brewing in the kitchen. She was already dressed for work; seeing her in uniform and wearing her firearm in his peaceful cabin unnerved him; they'd never bothered him before this morning. She looked as haggard as he felt.

"I made coffee," she said, pointing to the kitchen area. "I'm going home before my shift. Need to clean up."

Her voice, more distant, colder than he'd ever heard it, troubled him. He poured himself some coffee. "Thanks for making this." He leaned against the counter and looked at her. "Let's talk, Andi. I hardly slept all night."

She said nothing for a moment, then, "I didn't either, but I don't see what there is to talk about. It's your decision."

"I need to talk about it. I'm not so clear."

"What's not clear? If you take this case, we're on opposite sides. I can't be sleeping with the defense psychologist—your lawyer will make mincemeat of my testimony, not to mention our lawyer crucifying you. We'll have to stay apart for the duration of the pre-trial and trial—completely apart. And that could be a long time, Ed."

He shook his head. "As far as that goes, if I'm on your side, sleeping with you is still a problem. Donna Ratner'll claim I'm biased in your favor. Still, while I lay awake, I realized a couple of things during the night. For one thing, I think my ethical code is on your side."

"A first. What the hell does that mean?"

"It's kind of complicated." He yawned. "Especially after a lousy night."

"I can handle complicated, damn it. Explain it."

Her tone annoyed him. He took a long breath. "If I work for the defense, our forced separation could reduce my objectivity. I could be torn between loving you and wanting to help Jared."

"You could be torn? Thanks a lot."

"Give me a break. Okay, I *would* be torn. And if I lack objectivity, that harms Jared, and taking a case in which I lack objectivity would be unethical."

She dropped the folded blankets on the couch. "So don't take the case." She went to the coat rack and lifted her jacket and belt. "I'm going. Let me know what you decide. If you take the case, I'll send Callie over to pick up my things."

Ed's chest tightened. "Wait. There's another thing."

Her hand was on the door handle. "What?"

Why was she giving up on their relationship without fighting? "I don't want us being separated." He took a step toward her, but she warned him back with her eyes. He stopped, peering at her, trying to detect any softening.

None.

She said, "If you feel that way, don't take the case." As if it were only his decision.

"No matter which side I work for, the other side will argue I'm not objective because we're lovers. So how do I help the boy?"

"That's yours to figure out. Let me know."

"Damn it, stop being such a hard-ass!" he snapped. "This isn't just my decision—it affects you too."

Her lips formed a line. She folded her arms, leaned back against the door. After a moment, she said, "It *is* your decision, and it sounds to me like you made it without talking to me first. So, what's there for me to say?"

"You could say how you want this to turn out."

"I've said it: Don't take the case."

"That's the logical conclusion, isn't it?" He felt something firm up inside. "But I'm torn. If Jared's paranoid, I can't imagine him opening up to me if I work for you guys." Some of the annoyance crept into his voice. "What's my duty to *him*, damn it?"

"You don't have any duty to him, unless you take the case."

"So I should let him down so I can keep you? That's not a decision."

"Sounds like a decision to me."

Even as his anger mounted, Ed realized what was happening: Andi was a cop, not a psychologist. Except maybe where hostages are involved, cops don't talk about tough situations, they contain them. Control is their therapy. She'd told Ed about her marriage, back in Chicago. Two months in, she'd caught her husband in bed with another woman, and a month later, she'd divorced him. He relaxed a bit. Confronted with something tough, Andi didn't work through the thing, she steeled herself, built a wall. Containment. He said, "This thing ate me alive last night. I don't want us to be apart."

Her jaw clenched. "Then don't take the damn case. If you work for either side, and we stay together, Ben'll take me off the investigation, which puts Jared in Brad Ordrew's hands. I won't allow that."

"Sounds like I'm not the only one making unilateral decisions."

She opened the door. "Maybe." For a brief moment, her eyes softened, before he saw her stiffen. "Call me when you know which way it'll go." She stepped part-way out, her hand resting, almost pausing, on the handle.

"Andi." Something about her setting the terms of this galled him. Then he thought, if he chose to let her control him, wasn't *he* the one in control? He took another long breath. *Psychobabble. But true psychobabble.* He made up his mind.

She waited, looking back at him. "Well?"

He looked at her hand on the door, realized it signaled her desire. "I'll turn the case down. Won't work either side. Being apart from you isn't acceptable."

Abruptly, Andi was weeping, flowing back into the room, rushing to his arms. "Oh, Christ, I didn't want you to let me leave," she murmured into his chest.

They were where he wanted them to be, only Ed didn't like how they'd gotten there.

31

Grace came into the kitchen a few minutes after six. Ed and Andi, calm now, sat across from one another at the table, coffee steaming in their mugs, quiet in a way that reminded Ed of the stillness after sex. How deeply Andi had moved into his life. Into his heart. It had surprised him, some time ago, to realize that he'd never let anyone so close before. He watched her face as she gazed at the lightening dawn through the kitchen window. Had she really meant her tears twenty minutes earlier?

Grace banged out a bowl, poured her cereal and milk. "Any fruit, Northrup?" Her voice was thick with sleep.

"Mexican bananas," he said.

Grace put the bowl on the table, began slicing a banana onto the oat flakes.

Andi said, "Grace, I've got a question about Jared. Has he seemed different lately, like the last six or seven weeks?"

"Diff'r't?" Chewed bananas blurred the word.

"Angry? Moody? Not like himself?"

Grace chewed thoughtfully, then swallowed. "Me and him haven't had much to do with each other lately. It's spring, and he's a senior. I don't know." She swallowed. "I haven't noticed any difference."

Ed glanced at Andi, and when she didn't say anything, he said, "Grace, it's 'he and I.'"

"What's he and I?"

"Grammar. Your sentence should be, 'He and I haven't...'"

"That's what I said." Halfway between amused and annoyed, Ed shook his head. Grace glanced at Andi, and both women began giggling. His daughter said, "God, Northrup, you're so easy to tease."

"Glad to give my ladies a laugh in the morning." He got up and refilled his coffee cup. To Andi, he said, "Want some?"

"No thanks. I'm out of here. Got a case to solve."

Ed sat down and looked at the clock. To Grace, he said, "We leave in a half hour, kiddo."

Grace swallowed her mouthful. "Northrup, I've prepared my case." She looked embarrassed.

"Great."

Andi, nearly out the door, came back, looking curious. She leaned against the counter, arms folded.

Grace said, "Well, here goes." She flicked a look at Andi, then set her shoulders. Ed could see this was tough for her.

"First thing is, I'm a good driver."

"You are. You're as good as any sixteen-year-old who's had her license for four months."

Andi looked at him quizzically; he gave a slight shrug.

Grace said, "Well, I'm not going to get any better if I only drive your

86

truck with you sitting in it."

"Sure you are."

"Northrup!" She shook her head. "God!" She poured herself a cup of coffee and started to leave the kitchen. "I'm taking a shower. Then you can drive your baby girl to school."

Ed said, "When we're on the road, you can make the rest of your case."

"Whatever." When they heard the bathroom door slam, Andi said, "You're being a bit patronizing, aren't you?"

"Patronizing? Protective, maybe, but I don't see patronizing. Come on, let's not start another fight."

She ignored that. "Protective? From what?"

"Risk. Danger. Sixteen-year-old drivers have a terrible accident rate."

"So wrap her in cotton so she never gets hurt. Besides, she'll still be sixteen in September."

"Andi, what is this? You know what sorts of things happen with kids on the road."

"Sure I do. But most kids around here get an old beater when they get their license. You're the only parent I know who drives his daughter everywhere."

"Hey! I let her drive."

"You know what she wants, and it's not to drive with her dad in the seat beside her."

Ed said nothing, annoyed again. He stood up and looked at his watch. *Argument number three and then the day at school and patients all evening. Jesus.*

Andi said, "And if you're really so worried about sixteen-year-old drivers, you sure don't show it."

"Meaning?"

"You let her ride with Jen and Dana and her classmates all the time. They're all sixteen."

Ed felt the air go out. She was right. "All right, maybe I'm over-protective, but you're a cop, you know the odds. If she were yours, would you buy her a car?"

Andi flinched. "She's not mine."

"Yeah, but would you?"

"Hell, Ed. I don't know. Maybe, maybe not."

"Then why are you siding with her?"

Andi looked reflective, and didn't answer for a moment. "I supposed it's because my dad bought me a rusty old VW right after I turned sixteen. He was a cop and he knew the risks, too." He saw her eyes. They were looking into the past. "He let me grow up." She came back. "I guess I want you to do the same for Grace."

He refilled his coffee, calming himself. Andi's eyes had told him something. Something he liked. "All right. Maybe I should re-think this."

Andi softened. "You're different from most guys. You listen."

After a pause, Ed wiggled his eyebrows. "How about a little reward while Grace's in the shower?" He nodded in the direction of the bedroom.

"I take it back. You're just like most other guys."

32

As he pulled onto the highway, Grace said, "All right, I'm sorry, Northrup." Her voice had none of the edge he'd expected. "I should tell you why I need the car."

"I'm sorry, too, honey. Andi pointed out I'm being kind of a jerk about this."

Grace looked at him. "She did?"

Ed nodded.

"I called you a Nancy Reagan to Jen."

" 'Just Say No' Nancy Reagan?" He chuckled. "So what's this 'real reason'?"

He glanced over at her. She looked nervous; he turned back to the road.

"Me and Ardyss were talking and Ardyss asked me to drive Meals-on-Wheels for her this summer, and I said I would. Her car's like a hundred years old, so I need a safer one."

Ed's throat thickened; he had to wait a moment before he could speak. "Grace, that's really generous of you. Why didn't you tell me?" He looked at her again.

She shrugged. "I don't know. I didn't want to seem like a do-gooder."

"What's wrong with doing good?"

"Look at Jared."

"I don't understand that. Look at what about Jared?"

"He was always doing good stuff for people, and now everybody thinks he's a phony."

Ed drove, thinking about that. "Do you think he is?"

"No!" The fierceness of her answer surprised him, but not the answer itself. After a few minutes, Grace said, "So what do you think about the car?"

"How about we make a deal?"

She looked sideways at him. "What kind of deal?"

"You work on your grammar harder and we'll get the car."

"What's wrong with my...oh. 'Me and Ardyss,' right? I should say, 'Ardyss and me.'"

"Ardyss and I."

"Ardyss and you?"

"No, you said, "Ardyss and I were talking...""

Grace opened her mouth to object, then closed it. "Yeah, okay. I'll work on it."

"Great. I'll start looking for cars. Stay tuned."

As they pulled into the high school lot, Grace touched his shoulder. "Thanks, Northrup. You're not a Nancy Reagan."

33

Fifteen minutes before the students started arriving, Ed sat in Lynn Monroe's office, sipping another cup of coffee. Although she looked as tired as he felt, her hazel eyes twinkled. Yesterday, Ed had occasionally heard her talking with a parent or a kid; her steadiness and compassion, and the practicality of her advice, had impressed him.

"Mind if I ask you a question?" he said. Andi's idea that he patronized Grace troubled him. The girl had come into his life only two years ago, when her mother abandoned her in his office, so he'd been focused on learning to love her, not on letting her go. Not yet. He almost chuckled at the irony. When parents complained about their teenager's self-centeredness, he'd always told them, "Adolescence is nature's way of preparing you to say goodbye." *Psychologist, heal thyself.*

"Sure," Lynn said. "Fire away."

"It's about my daughter, Grace. She wants a car—well, turns out she needs a car so she can drive Meals-on-Wheels this summer. I've been resisting but I think it's time I get her one. Any thoughts about kids her age and cars?"

Erin's eyebrows lifted a trace. "I've only met Grace a few times."

Ed felt a chill, and looked at her sharply.

She said, "No, not in counseling. I meet with the class officers and the student council once a month; we talk about the conflict resolution skills needed for committee work. Grace strikes me as quite level-headed."

He nodded. "She is. She's had a lot of independence as a kid, so she learned early to take care of herself."

She looked at him, still smiling. "I don't want to step on your toes, but a lot of juniors seem to drive their own vehicles around here."

Before he could respond, the hall bell rang, and he checked his watch. "Damn. Here come the huddled masses." He smiled. "Thanks for your thoughts."

"My pleasure," she said. "In fact, my partner in Missoula has a car for sale. A '96 Volvo. Solid as a tank. I could call her. I'll bet she'd drive it over for you to look at."

He took a deep breath, feeling almost excited. "Why not? If she's willing. Or I could drive there."

"Okay. I'll let you know."

Ed heard kids outside the door. He sobered.

Lynn looked at the clock. "Show time. We're in the middle of a community nervous breakdown," she said.

"Got that right," Ed said. As he stood, the cup slipped in his hand and coffee sloshed on his shirt. "Damn."

Lynn chuckled.

"Not funny! You can't get coffee stains out. So much for this shirt."

"No, no," she said. "I wasn't laughing at you. The thought popped into my head that if I hear one more dad worrying that what Jared's done might threaten his Second Amendment rights, I'll pull a pistol out of my bra and shoot him between the eyes."

"Wow. Talk about concealed carry!"

She laughed. "Black humor. And if I hear one more mom call these high school kids 'my babies,' I'll turn the pistol on myself."

34

"I want to look at the storage unit again," Andi said to Ordrew after the press conference. The reporters had been angry at the lack of information. Many had driven over from Missoula or Bozeman, leaving well before dawn. Ben had told them about Jared's arrest and the weaponry, but he offered very little else during the questions, repeating his mantra: When they had some information, the media would be the first to know. Nobody had left the conference satisfied.

Ordrew looked at her. "The unit? Why? We cleaned it out."

"Standing up there behind Ben and only saying 'the investigation is continuing' just galled me. Maybe we missed something." She shook her head. "Nothing's adding up."

"The goddamn unit's empty."

"Look, you don't have to come. What are you going to do?"

"I think I'll take another shot at the boy. Push hard."

She shook her head. "No. His lawyer's instructions are clear, so anything you might get without her there won't be admissible."

He frowned. "Fuck that. Let me front him in his cell. Nobody needs to know. Any fallout's on me."

Lousy idea, she thought, but time was running out and they were at a dead-end. She had a thought. "Let's do the unit again. If there's nothing there, we'll figure something else."

Ordrew shrugged. "You're in charge, but that unit's clean as a choirboy's pecker. If we don't shake something loose, I'm visiting his cell, lawyer or no lawyer. You don't have to know about it."

She hesitated. What if they let Jared walk and somebody died? Andi narrowed her eyes, then nodded. "You're on." She forced a smile. She'd have to come up with something better if the unit didn't pan out.

Andi stood still in the middle of the small space, trying to see it from some new angle. "Might be something hidden in the walls or the floor."

Ordrew grunted. "Let's see." They worked their way around the unit, tapping the walls for loose boards or different, hollow sounds. Finding none, they worked over the floor. Tight. Solid.

"Is it worth having the crime lab come in and tear this place apart?"

Ordrew looked at the walls. "I didn't get any feel for a hidden space. And the kid left all his shit out in plain sight."

Andi nodded. They looked up at the ceiling. Ordrew said, "I'll get a ladder." While he was gone, Andi continued tapping the floor again, hoping they'd missed something the first time. She thought about the ceiling. *If we can't reach it without a ladder, how could Jared?* No ladder had been listed when Pete inventoried the evidence from the unit.

They had no more luck with the ceiling. The plywood ran up to the ridgeline, and their tapping suggested no hollow spots.

"Our warrant's good for twenty-four hours. Let's go back to the Hansens' and tear his bedroom apart again, and if we don't find anything, the rest of the damn house." He paused. "And if that craps out, I'm talking to him. Hard."

Andi didn't want that, but she was starting to feel desperate. She said, "Okay, but no rough stuff."

Ordrew's lip curled, but he said nothing.

35

In the squad, driving back to the department from the Hansens' house, where they'd found nothing new, Ordrew said, "We're striking out. Let's go back and push the friends harder. A *lot* harder. They'll know about drinking or drugs. After that, we hit the kid. Or I do." He plainly didn't believe Andi was up to being hard.

She recoiled. Coming down heavily on the friends made some sense: They probably knew more than they'd let on during the first round of questions. The idea of Ordrew interrogating Grace, though, made Andi shiver. Still, they had only a couple of shifts left to dredge something up. She looked at the dashboard clock. "Twelve-forty-five," she said. "There are twenty-eight seniors without Jared. That's fourteen each. We'll start there." Maybe they'd learn something from the seniors and could leave Grace out of it.

At *3:35*, Andi climbed back into the squad and waited for Ordrew to emerge from the school. Her argument with Ed, last night's lousy sleep, and the day's dead ends left her tense, frustrated. Her mind raced about their next move.

A few minutes later, he came out of the school, scowling. He climbed into the passenger seat and slammed his door. "Squat. Absolute. Fucking. Squat. Two kids say the little shit got wasted on Beam-and-Cokes sophomore year. One damn time! Nobody's seen him take a fucking drink since. Not even at keggers down at the river."

Andi shook her head. "That's being drunk once more than I heard about. I'm starting to think this guy's too good to be true—which means maybe he *is* too good to be true. Who's the last high school senior *you* knew who *never* drinks?"

"Huh. Pisses me off. I make this kid to be bad, but bad guys leave traces, and we got no traces. Nada. He's a fucking ghost. Young Methodist League, my ass!"

"Well, we've got an hour before shift change." She hesitated. "I'm staying on this. I want to talk to Jared again." She looked at Ordrew. "Without you."

He glared at her, then looked straight ahead, out the windshield. "What about the lawyer's gag? You shut me down on that."

"Not the same thing. You wanted to confront him hard. I don't."

"Sweet-talk him."

"Well, not exactly." *What exactly?*

Ordrew smirked. "Won't work. The kid's playing us, Andi. You won't get shit from him."

"You got anything better?"

He thought for a moment. "Other than me grilling him?" He made a little nod. "You said you talked to your boyfriend's daughter. I think I ought to talk to her, too. Lean on her a little." He said it cautiously, watching her from the side. "You know, adult authority."

Andi stiffened. She didn't want him to be hard on Grace, but she had to trade something to keep him away from Jared. A confrontation with the boy would give the lawyer all the ammunition she needed to dismiss the case. She took a deep breath. "I guess you should. But if you hurt her, Brad, you won't have just her father to contend with."

He didn't smile.

36

Ed pulled into the yard of the Anderhold at a few minutes before five. He climbed out of his pickup and walked slowly across the gravel yard and up the steps onto the big porch. He wondered what his friend would reveal today.

At his knock, Magnus pulled the great oaken door open, and Ed must have looked surprised.

"Luisa's preparing dinner. You'll join us after our talk." Magnus's eyes searched Ed's.

Ed thought Magnus half-expected rejection, as if yesterday's story of Daryl's violence would somehow push Ed away. *Delicate moment.* He said, carefully, "Well, let's see about that, Mack. I generally avoid socializing with the folks I'm helping."

Magnus's broad brow furrowed. "Maybe these talks aren't such a good idea."

Thought so.

The rancher turned abruptly and led the way toward the small office at the back of the Addition. When Ed followed him in, Magnus closed the door.

Even before he sat down, Ed said, "I want to tell you, Mack, that your story yesterday broke my heart, and I think these talks are a very good idea. You can't carry that kind of poison inside forever, and I'm honored you shared it with me." He sat down.

Magnus nodded his white head. He looked calmer. He sat. "I was afraid you'd decide I was weak."

Ed shook his head. "Just the opposite, Mack. I've been thinking since yesterday about your kindness to people. Abused kids often grow up closed in on themselves, but you didn't. I appreciate you even more."

Tears came to Magnus's eyes, but he said nothing. Minutes passed. Ed reflected on the hours of his life he'd sat silently like this, leaving open space into which a patient, like a wary animal, might venture. Like hunting elk.

Finally, Magnus shifted. "Ask a question. I'm stuck here."

He nodded. "Let's talk some more about why you think you caused your mother's death."

The big man seemed to gather into his gaze a strength born of decades wrestling with adversity, from his violent father to the Montana weather to the economics of cattle. The voice coming out of this gaze was granite-ribbed as the mountains. "You think I killed my mother." Magnus did not inflect it as a question, but Ed knew his reply could go badly wrong. In Magnus's eyes, Ed detected as much fear as challenge.

He considered his answer a moment, then said, "No. I suspect that's what you think."

Magnus stood abruptly, strode to the gun closet, unlocked it, and lifted out an old rifle. Sitting again, he gazed at the rifle for a long, soundless moment. Behind him, the door of the gun closet drifted silently closed. Finally, he said, in a voice darkened with emotion, "Yes. You're right."

Ed waited, very still, his heart pounding. "Magnus, is your rifle loaded?"

Magnus smiled grimly. "Not yet. This is my great-great-grandfather's deer rifle, *Kött Hitta*. Swedish for *Meat Bringer*."

"I thought that exploded and killed your brother?"

"No, that was Günter's elk rifle. *Kött Hitta* hasn't been fired since Anders passed." He looked out the window. Beyond the glass, sunlight and shadows dappled the eastern mountains. "Daryl kicked her because of *me*. That killed her." He shouldered the rifle, sighting through the window at something outside. "So, yes, I killed her as much as if I'd used this rifle. I know it in my belly. You can't tell me different."

"I wouldn't try. You were there, I wasn't."

Magnus swiveled his massive head to squint at Ed, the rifle still aimed out the window, unwavering. "So I killed her?"

Ed swallowed. The rifle distracted him; the pounding of his heart hadn't slowed. "I didn't say that. I said you saw it. You know what the truth is, but—" He gestured at the rifle. "Mind putting that away while we talk?"

Magnus lowered the rifle, resting the stock on his thigh, the barrel aiming just above Ed's head. "I see: No drinking *and* no gunplay during our talks, that it?"

"Yeah. This isn't cowboy time."

"You sure as hell got that right," Magnus said, standing and returning the rifle to the gun closet and turning the key in the door. At the cabinet, his back turned, he said, "Anders' rifle can't fire. It's been rusted for a century." He returned to his chair, sat. "You said *but*."

"But?"

"You said I know the truth, *but*. *But* what?"

"*But* I can't see any connection between what you did or said and your dad hitting your mother."

The big man jerked forward. Ed couldn't read the look on his face. Fear? Anger? "Don't call that man my *dad*." His whisper was fierce. "He sired me, but he was no *dad*."

"Sorry." Ed waited a moment until Magnus looked more composed. "What about what I said, though? What connects what you said and Daryl hitting his wife?"

"He was killing mad at me..." But then he fell silent, looking confused.

Although he knew this was hard for Magnus, Ed decided to push. "Suppose two of your cowboys get drunk, start a fight. You try to break them up, but one gets in a kick that kills the other. Your fault?"

"Not the same thing." Magnus's shoulders were high, his hands gripped on the arms of his chair. Tense.

"No?" Ed kept on. "You're telling me that you suddenly started drinking yourself unconscious over your son's leaving college because Daryl hit your

95

mother and you think you killed her? I don't get it."

Magnus visibly relaxed. A smile almost flickered across his thin lips. "You're not buying it."

"Nope. Don't forget, I've known you going on thirty years, and I've always known your ideas to hang together. Not this time." Before he continued, he watched Magnus's eyes, expecting to see anger, but although the rancher narrowed them, Ed saw only relief. "You're right. I don't buy it."

"That my father abused me?"

"No, *that* I buy. Hell, Daryl beating up Magnus is old news. Everybody knows it. Blaming *yourself* for your mother's death, though? That doesn't compute. If it did, why wait thirty years for it to bother you so much you start drinking?"

Magnus rested his cheek on his right hand, his elbow dimpling the soft leather arm of his chair, his long fingers buried in his thick hair. "You think I'm hiding something." Again, it did not come out as a question. Ed saw mixed sorrow and fear in the rancher's eyes.

"Or hiding *from* something," Ed ventured, then sat back. He'd made his point, so it was time to be still and see what it might yield.

Magnus closed his eyes and, almost imperceptibly, began rocking back and forth in the big chair, his head still resting on his hand. "I am," he said softly, his eyes still closed. His breathing came heavily, and Ed saw the big veins in his forehead throbbing.

The big man rocked quietly another moment before continuing. "When I was eighteen, the spring before I graduated from high school, she'd been dead three years. Living with Daryl was hell. He was angry all the time." His breathing was labored now, his body stiff.

Ed said, "Hold on a minute, Mack. Let me help you relax." He proceeded to teach Magnus how to breathe calmly, to focus his attention on soothing himself. They practiced using cue words to trigger relaxation. After practicing for a few minutes, the big man was calm again. Ed thought, *Good student.* "Go ahead, Mack. You were telling me about that summer with Daryl. If you get upset, use your words to relax."

Magnus nodded. "That felt good." He looked gratefully at Ed. "Thanks." He looked out the window at the rounded mountains. "Daryl. Sometimes he'd start a fight with one of the men or kick a heifer almost to death. Mostly, he left me alone, but everybody knew he hated me. When he was drunk, which was most nights, he'd sit alone in the living room and talk to himself. I'd hear him muttering about how I was to blame for Mom's death or Calvin's. Every bad thing in his life he blamed on me. I kept my bedroom door locked."

He fell silent.

Ed wondered. More violence? More abuse? It would explain the growing darkness in his friend's eyes. He thought about Elizabeth Murphy, back in Minnesota, hanging herself behind her own locked door, terrified of her mother's wrath. He felt his heart sink. *Please, not again.*

Magnus gathered himself and began again. "One Sunday at Mass—you remember that I went to the Catholics when I was fourteen?"

Ed nodded. "To spite your father."

"Yeah. Anyway, at Mass, I thought to myself, *Why not join the monastery?* Get the hell out of the valley. Daryl wasn't teaching me about running the ranch, so what would it matter?" He shuddered. "Well, it mattered. The acceptance letter came in June and he opened it. He beat me so bad I couldn't get out of bed for days. I probably had broken ribs, but he wouldn't take me to the hospital. Sometime during that summer, though, he gave up."

"Gave up beating you?"

"Everything. He stopped looking at me, yelling about me. I was dead to him." He paused and looked expectantly at Ed, his eyes clouded with emotion.

"He was suffering."

Magnus nodded.

"Were you pleased he was suffering?"

"Wouldn't you be?"

It caught Ed off guard. "Maybe. I suppose so."

Magnus looked out the window for a moment, as if he could read something in the pale sky or the afternoon mountains. Still gazing out, he said, "No, I told myself I was pleased, but I wasn't. I kept hoping he would come up to my room one night and we'd talk, that he'd forgive me. He'd ask me to stay and run the ranch with him. Take Calvin's place." His eyes dampened. He coughed and rubbed them vigorously with his fingers. For a moment, he waited. "Anyway, that first year in the monastery was the happiest year of my life. There were three of us rookies—they called us postulants—and I loved everything. It was heaven." He smiled grimly. "I guess anything would have been, after living in hell." He stopped.

After a few moments, Ed asked, "What happened?"

"They accepted me as a novice after that postulant year. Things changed then. It got rough."

Magnus stopped and abruptly stood and strode to the window and stared out. After a silent moment, Ed said, "How did it get rough?"

"It just did, damn it." It came out rude and hard, and Magnus quickly swung around, looking sadly at Ed. "I'm sorry. No call to take it out on you." He turned back to the window.

Ed thought, *Hiding from what he has to say.*

"It got rough, and I couldn't take it, so I crawled home that following August. Two damn years, then I collapsed like a weak calf."

Ed heard the self-loathing in that, but said only, "That must have been hard." Shame was an emotion he'd never detected in Magnus. Somehow, through the years of their friendship, the rancher had buried this so deeply that Ed doubted anyone in the valley knew it. He wondered if even Luisa suspected this.

Magnus turned back, stared above Ed's head, avoiding his eyes. "I failed. I was everything Daryl said I was. Weak, a coward. He sent me to live in the bunkhouse with the hands. He never once asked me about what happened, but he'd make damn sure to laugh about it in front of the men." Magnus shifted his voice into a sneer. "*Don't push him too hard, boys—never know what he'll run away from next!* Most of the men were kind to me. They told me to ignore him, that he didn't mean it, but..."

Ed heard anger beneath the harmonics of Magnus's shame-washed voice, a bass note resonating below the words of failure. That was the question. Which engine—shame or rage—drove Magnus's drinking?

Magnus's eyes locked on Ed's, defeated. "That explain things to you?"

"I guess so. You came home in disgrace and—"

Magnus finished it. "And when my own boy fails college, it all comes back to me and I can't stand the thought that he's like me. End of story." Again, he looked toward the window.

Ed thought, Not end of story. Junior hadn't failed anything—Magnus was perhaps projecting his own story onto his son's, but Junior's taking time off from college to contemplate his future was no species of failure. Also, how the heavenly monastery life had turned rough wasn't yet in the plot. That will come. He couldn't avoid the obvious question, either: Had Mack been abused in the monastery? While Magnus stared out the window, Ed felt his own sadness begin to swell. Something bad was coming.

Magnus rubbed his hands briskly together, as if an unpleasant job had been finished. "So, we're done here. Time for dinner."

Ed smiled but shook his head. "No, Mack, I don't think we're done. How about I take a rain check on dinner? Just till these conversations are done."

Magnus flinched visibly. "Ah." He got himself under control.

Ed thought, *Feeling rejected after that painful session.*

"Well," Magnus said. "I'm done."

"For today."

"Yes, for today."

Ed relaxed. "Good. You're working hard, Mack. This'll work out. See you tomorrow. Same time."

Magnus did not answer as he opened the door and led him into the hall. As they passed the kitchen, Luisa came out, smiling. Magnus said, unable to wash the disappointment out of his voice, "Ed can't stay for your dinner, Luisa." His voice sounded dismayed, and very far away.

Ed felt a chill.

37

After Ed left, Magnus, disgruntled, lit a fire in the dining room. He sat in the big chair at the head of the long oak table, absently rubbing the finger-smoothed carving in the dark oak. His great-grandfather Günter had scratched a big "G" into the oak table during his eighth birthday dinner, with the new penknife he'd just gotten. Over the years, Anderssen fingers had rubbed it smooth. Magnus watched the flickering fire, listening to the sounds of Luisa cooking in the kitchen. He resisted the urge to pour himself another Scotch. He'd had one in his study before coming down to the dining room. Telling the story of his failure at St. Brendan's left him unsettled, fretful. Could he bear much more? Ed seemed to think there was something left to face. He stood and paced around the table. The thought there might be something more frightened him. He no longer felt safe, even here, at the family table.

Luisa came in from the kitchen, a platter of thin-sliced steak, onions, and beans in one hand, a salad bowl in the other. Earlier, she'd laid a bowl of steaming pinto beans on the table. She called out, "*Hijo! Comida!* Dinner!"

Magnus sat down as footsteps pounded down the staircase. His son burst into the dining room, fell into a chair, and looked at the platter of steak. "Mind if I just grab some beans and salad, Mamá? I'm cutting down on the animal protein."

Magnus looked at him. "We raise beef, Junior, not lettuce."

Junior laughed as he ladled a pile of beans atop the salad on his plate. "Beef's just a roundabout way of eating veggies, Dad. I'm cutting out the middle-man. Or middle cow."

Magnus chuckled; Junior always found a way to amuse him. "Suit yourself. Beef is something *else* you quit at college?" he teased, but seeing the quick hurt in his son's eyes, he felt a pang. "I'm sorry, son," he said. "No call to bring that up."

"You're still upset about my decision."

Magnus felt heat flushing his face. His erratic behavior, his drinking, the sessions with Ed—all of it had to be as plain to his son as it was to Luisa, and the boy probably blamed himself. Magnus nodded. "It'll pass."

"Dad, we should talk about it. I still plan to go back, when I figure out what I want to do. I'd like us to talk." Junior's eyes pleaded. "Your advice would mean a lot to me."

Am I misjudging my son? Magnus thought. *As Daryl misjudged me?* He said, "You're right. We need to talk. After dinner maybe?" Perhaps talking to his son would delay, or even prevent, his late-night descent into the cloud of alcohol.

Junior had wolfed down the beans and salad and was already standing. "Can't tonight. Some of the seniors are meeting about supporting Jared Hansen. They asked me to come."

Magnus felt the too-familiar claw of anxiety in his chest. He took in a few long breaths and recited in his mind the relaxing words Ed had taught him. When he felt collected, he said, "Not sure you ought to be doing that, son. The boy did threaten to kill people, if I heard right." Had he heard correctly, or had he, in his Scotch-drenched fear, twisted something? He felt a stab of, what? Anger? No, harsher than that, a black sliver of rage.

He gripped the edge of the old table, then ran his fingers again over Günter's scratch. He'd rubbed that long deep scratch since he was a boy; the ancient gesture brought some calm. But only some. Both Junior and Luisa were watching him, intent. Luisa's eyes narrowed.

"You all right, Dad?"

Magnus nodded, then shook his head. "No, I'm not. Something...bothers me. I'm working it out with Ed." He took a deep breath. "I'd prefer us not getting involved with Jared's problems."

"You always get involved in people's problems," Junior said. "You've taught me—"

Magnus, confused by a sudden flood of affection for his son—where had the anxiety gone?—lifted his hand to interrupt, but found his throat too thick for speech.

After a moment's wait, Junior went on. "Dad, I've known Jared since I was his 'Second-grade Buddy,' the year he started kindergarten. It can't be true, what they're saying about him." He looked hard at his father. "Would you abandon your friends if they were accused of something you knew they couldn't have done?"

Magnus felt a war in himself: pride in his son, and yet...He deflated. "No, of course not. But none of my friends have threatened to kill me." It felt weak, like an excuse. Magnus hated excuses.

Junior shrugged. "Well, maybe our generations are a little different." He stood and left the room. In a few minutes, Luisa and Magnus heard his pickup crunch down the driveway.

Magnus sat staring at his plate.

Luisa pushed the platter closer to Magnus's plate. "Eat, *mí esposo*. You are losing weight." When he did not look up, she added, "Mack, I am afraid."

He looked at his wife, tears close to his eyes. He looked down, cut a small piece of meat. "I am eating. I'm fine," he said, softly. That he was frightening Luisa tore at his heart.

"You are dark, Magnus. Talk to me, *mí amor*."

He felt the heat in his face again, but he cut a bite of now-cold steak and chewed in silence.

"It is unlike you not to talk to me, *mí esposo*."

His head snapped up. "Luisa! Leave me alone, damn it!" About to burst, he remembered his mother standing at her sideboard, her back to them, just before his father had stricken her down. Shaken, Magnus silenced himself and carefully laid his fork beside his plate. His hand shook.

Where is this violence coming from? He forced himself calm. "Forgive me, Luisa. I've no cause to bark at you."

She touched his arm gently. "You are suffering, esposo. I will help when you are ready."

Although he trembled inside, he put on his most careful smile and nodded. "It's a rough patch for me, but Ed has helped. I'm good now." He hoped his voice did not betray him. He cut another slice of beef to reassure her.

Luisa was not meek in the face of his passions; Magnus understood that. If she backed off, he knew it was not from fear. Still, he felt shamed by his sudden burst of anger at her. He glanced at her. She sipped her coffee and quietly watched him eat. *Waiting for me.* He chewed quietly, tasting nothing. *When will I be ready to tell it?* A flare of anxiety closed his throat and he coughed. He wiped his lips; his next words surprised him.

"Let's go down to *Árboles Blancos.* Tomorrow. We could use a change of scenery, and down there, we could talk about it."

Luisa leaned back, frowning. "Tomorrow? *Esposo,* I need time to prepare such a trip!" *Árboles Blancos,* their ranch in Sonora, was their February refuge from the brutal Montana winter. Going down late in April, just when the Double-A was coming to springtime life with the new calves and preparation of the fields, was something they'd never done. Her tone said it was something they could not do.

"I've decided," Magnus said, his emotion flaring again, anger threaded with shame. He slapped the oaken table. "I need to get out of here." He heard the feeling in his voice, added, "For a rest."

Luisa shook her head. "*No es posible,* Mack. Too much is unprepared. We have no airline reservations." She reached over to collect Magnus's dish and silverware. He gripped her wrist.

"I said I have *decided,* Luisa. Tomorrow. Perhaps the next day." He dropped her wrist, but not her eyes. She lowered them to her wrist, then raised them back to his. "Although you have *decided,* it cannot be. There is too much to do before we go." She rubbed her wrist, but did not release his eyes.

Magnus looked away and he forced his body to relax, using Ed's words and rubbing his great-grandfather's scratch. He watched Luisa gather the dishes and carry them to the kitchen; he heard their sound, being laid in the sink, hot water splashing on them. She came back to the dining room and refilled their cups.

"Thank you, Luisa. I'm sorry. I'm not myself." He stood and picked up his cup. "I'll take this to the study," he said. "I have work to do." He pitched his voice to a calm he did not fully feel.

Luisa nodded.

She is not fooled, he thought.

She returned to the kitchen and he heard more water splash into the sink. Magnus climbed the stairs to his study and his bottle of Scotch.

38

After dinner, Grace and a group of juniors were working in the gym, prepping for the prom. She was teasing Jen Fortin about the lop-sided paper flowers Jen had cut at the last meeting when her cell phone buzzed. It was Andi.

"Hey, Grace, we need to talk to you some more about Jared Hansen. Can you come over to the department and meet with Deputy Ordrew?"

She felt a flutter of worry. The news had wild-fired through school that Andi and the new deputy had interviewed the seniors that afternoon; the word was, Ordrew had been a hard-ass. She said, "Why?"

"We're still trying to learn whatever we can about Jared. We decided that he might pick up something that I missed when you and I talked."

Grace wanted to delay it. "Well, I guess. But I have a prom meeting now, Andi. Maybe later."

Andi hesitated, then said, "No. Now's better. Sorry to push, but we're down to the wire and anything you can help us with is important."

Fifteen minutes later, Callie pointed Grace back toward the deputies' squad room. "Don't you worry, Gracie. It's just talk," she said kindly.

Grace wasn't relieved to hear it. When she stood in the squad room door, Andi stood up and introduced her to Ordrew, and Grace felt guarded as she shook his hand.

Grace turned to Andi and said, "So when I'm done, can I get a ride home?"

Ordrew answered. "Sure. I'll take you. I've never seen your place."

Grace felt her heart speed up; looked a question to Andi, who nodded.

As Ordrew pointed down the hallway toward the interrogation room, Andi said, "Okay, then. I've got my own work to do. See you at home, honey." When Grace caught Andi's stern glance at Ordrew, her heart jumped again. *He's going to be tough.* She hunched her shoulders. *I can be tough, too.*

He surprised her. Opening the conference room door, he said, "Can I get you a Coke or something?" His voice was friendly.

"That'd be good," she said, carefully. While she waited for him, she sat quietly and pretended to feel unconcerned.

When he returned, he put a Coke on the table in front of her. As he took his seat, he pulled a little pad and a pen out of his shirt pocket. His opening was easy. "I understand from Andi that you're good friends with Jared."

Grace opened the can, took a sip. "We're friends, but I guess not so much *good* friends. What I mean is, he's a senior and I'm just a junior. He helped me when I came here. He's a good..." She paused, unsure of the right word. "A good guy."

"That's what we're hearing from everybody. So we're a little confused, to tell you the truth." His voice shifted to a softer tone. "Maybe you'll help us out?"

Grace looked at him for a moment, put a little off balance by his tone. "Okay. If I can." She held the Coke still in both hands, but didn't drink. She'd felt awkward drinking in front of him.

"Jared's said some pretty scary things, you know. Your dad told us to look for drugs or alcohol." He looked at Grace as if she might know about this.

She shook her head. "You won't find any. Jared doesn't drink. Some kids say he got drunk once in sophomore year, but I've never seen him drinking."

Ordrew's eyes narrowed slightly, although his voice remained friendly. "That doesn't mean he doesn't drink, just that you haven't seen it."

"Well, sure. But there've been quite a few times he could've been drinking, when I was there to see him, and he wasn't."

"So you've been present at drinking parties." His smile tightened.

Grace felt her face warm. "I thought we were talking about Jared."

"So far, we are." She heard threat in his voice. Or maybe she imagined it. "But if *you're* doing something illegal, I guess that's not about Jared, is it?"

Not imagining it. She asked, "How is being at a party illegal?" Her voice sounded wiggly.

"Underage drinking is illegal." He snapped it out. No more smile.

Grace put the Coke on the table, wiped her hands on her jeans, and thought about what to say. "Yeah, it is." Then her anger stirred. "And if you find out I've been drinking at these so-called drinking parties, you go right ahead and do something about it. Till then, let's get back to Jared."

Ordrew leaned forward, closing the space between them. "Look, sweetie, it won't be hard to find out exactly what you do at these parties, so quit playing around. I want the truth about Jared's drinking. Or drugs."

Grace pulled away, fully angry now. "Don't call me *sweetie*, Deputy. I'm a young woman and you need to show respect." She pushed her chair back farther. "I told you the truth about alcohol—I've never seen Jared drink. And I don't know anything about drugs."

Ordrew's jaw muscles clenched. "All right, Grace." His words were arrows. "Listen up. Jared's planning to commit mass murder, and everybody's lying about him. Don't get caught on the wrong side."

Mass murder! Andi never said that. "What? I mean, why would he say that? I can't believe Jared would..." She stopped. Was there something she'd missed about Jared? Her conversation with Andi: What *had* she said? That he had nine rifles, some ammunition, a pressure cooker. Had there been anything about mass murder? Grace couldn't remember. Would Andi hide that? Grace didn't notice her arms folding across her chest.

Ordrew noticed. His voice made her jump. "You're telling yourself Jared's a great guy, because you want to believe it—but he's not. He wants to shoot his classmates. A lot of people could die because you kids are hiding what you know."

Jesus, was this true? What if she'd forgotten something? Northrup had talked about how people can forget scary stuff. Could she be doing that? She knew she needed to say something. But what?

Ordrew's tone softened. "Tell me about the first time you met Jared." His voice sounded almost friendly, confusing her for a moment, because it didn't match the anger in his eyes. She decided to stay with what his eyes said. The topic change jarred, too, along with the mismatch between his softer voice and his pissed-off eyes. She tried to parse out her confusion, but couldn't.

"The first time I met him? I guess it was when my mom—" Her eyes misted, which made her mad. She roughly brushed them with her hand, and as she did, her confusion lifted. She knew what she knew. "When my mom left me here." She hesitated. "No, *abandoned* me here. They said I had to go to school while they looked for her, so I went, and right away, Jared introduced himself. He was a sophomore and I was a freshman, so I was, you know, impressed. Nobody talks to freshmen. He was real nice. And real mature." She thought back. "The only other boy not in my year who was nice to me was Junior Anderssen. They both took me under their wings."

"Magnus Anderssen's boy? The big rancher?"

"Yeah. You should talk to Junior too. He knows Jared better than anybody. They're best buds, although Junior's two years older." She added, "He's taking a break from college."

He made a note on his little pad. "I'll do that. So was there anything you noticed about Jared then, freshman year? Anything that made you uncomfortable?"

"Yeah," she said, and noticed his eyes brightening. She smiled inside. "I didn't like his talking about becoming a Marine. I'm against war as a solution to international problems."

She watched his face shift into a sneer, but he kept his voice even; obviously, her views did not interest him. "Why did Jared want to join the Marines?"

"He wanted to introduce Buddhism to them. Also, he says he loves our country and thinks he should give back."

"But that's bullshit, isn't it?" His tone darkened again. "Patriots don't think the government's out to kill them."

Grace bristled. "Did he say that? Well, on TV a lot of people call themselves patriots and hate the government. I believe Jared."

"Nobody cares what you *believe*, Grace. What matters is that Jared's going to murder your friends. Good Marines, or Buddhists, don't kill innocent people."

Grace froze: That sounded right. Was Ordrew lying? Do cops lie? She couldn't imagine Andi lying, but Andi hadn't said anything about mass murder, had she? Grace wavered for a long moment.

No! She knew Jared. He wasn't a murderer. What had Ardyss said? Trust your heart. "Look," she said, intense now. "Jared's a serious guy. Real serious. He takes Buddhism seriously. He even meditates. You're overlooking that."

Ordrew looked dismissive. "Meditates? Jesus." He shook his head. "Look, if I'm wrong, nobody dies. But if you're wrong, people could die. That'll be on you, Grace."

A chill shot through her. She didn't want to back down, but...She squared her shoulders. "I don't know what else to say. To me, Jared's always been a good guy, and I can't believe what you say is true."

"Oh, give it a goddamn rest! I'm—" He stopped himself, drew in a long breath. "I'm sorry." His voice took on the gentle tone he'd started with. "It's just that nobody's this perfect."

"I never said he's perfect. He complains about homework and chores. He told me he gets tired of being nice sometimes."

"When did he say that?"

"I don't know exactly. But he doesn't stop doing the right thing just because he's tired of it."

She saw his eyes light. "Tell me about that."

"Uh, so, a while ago, he told me he wished he wasn't class president, because everybody expects him to solve their problems."

"So he's angry at his classmates."

Grace snapped, "Don't put words in my mouth. I said he was tired, I didn't say he was angry. Train your brain to listen."

Ordrew looked hard at her; she could tell he was struggling to stay calm. "Oh, come on, Grace. If you were tired of people expecting you to do things for them, wouldn't you eventually get angry?"

"Maybe. But not everybody's like that. I expect Northrup to buy me a car and I keep nagging him, but he doesn't get angry about it. I never saw Jared get angry. Just tired."

"*Tired*, right," Ordrew said. Grace felt contempt come off him like heat off a sun-baked rock. "Nothing worse than *tired*, for God's sake?"

"No, just tired."

"Huh," he grunted. "Looks like I pursue this drinking-party business." He looked intently at her, as if this would shake loose some revelation.

All of a sudden, Grace was tired of *him*. "Deputy Ordrew, if you come up with anything about me drinking, I'm sure you'll be in touch."

He started to say something, but she stood up. "Can we be done here?"

39

As Ordrew showed Grace into the interview room and closed the door, Andi had lingered, tempted to watch through the one-way. She promptly dismissed the thought. She didn't trust him much, but he hadn't given her reason to think he was incompetent, just a jerk. At some point, she'd have to learn to trust her partner. *No time like the present.* She walked down the hall and let herself in the cellblock.

Jared lay on his bunk under a faded gray blanket, arms rigid at his sides.

He looked asleep. Or dead. He didn't move when she clicked shut the cellblock door and walked toward his cell, letting her heels sound against the concrete floor. His closed eyelids rippled, though; he was awake.

"Hi, Jared. Got a minute?"

He opened his eyes and turned his head toward her, then sat up. "Time's about all I've got, I guess."

Andi noticed his shy small smile, which clashed with his sad eyes. *That's new*, she thought. "May I come in and talk with you?"

"*You* can talk, but my lawyer told me not to say anything unless she's here."

Andi smiled. "Yep, you can stop me. Just say you won't talk to me without your lawyer and I'll shut up. Or you can decide for yourself." She was treading on risky ground. She had to get something.

He shrugged. "We can talk."

"May I come inside?"

He nodded. She opened his cell door, watching carefully, but he didn't bolt or move, except to swing his feet slowly to the floor.

"Mind if I sit?" she asked, pointing to the end of the cot.

He shook his head without looking at her.

"How you doing?"

He shrugged, looking to her like a regular seventeen-year-old, alone in a terrifying place, trying to hide it. She hesitated, then asked, "You feel safe here?"

He shook his head. "I doubt anybody feels safe here."

"You still feel I want to kill you?"

His eyes widened and he glanced sharply at her. "I said that?"

"You did. And sounded like you meant it."

"Really?"

She smiled. "Apparently not so much today, eh?"

He shook his head. "No, I'm just scared. I don't really remember much about what happened and how I got here. I guess I did something awful?"

Andi saw tears fill his eyes. "You don't remember what you're here for?"

"Not too much. I guess my storage unit. The guns? Did I..." His voice caught. "Did I hurt somebody?"

Andi shook her head. "No, you didn't. But you threatened to kill the senior class."

He shuddered. "My God." He blinked. "Sorry. I try not to swear."

Andi suddenly remembered Ed's occasional conversations about multiple personalities. Could Jared have some kind of other self, murderous and paranoid? The nape of her neck prickled.

Jared took a deep, shuddering breath. "I can't believe I would say that." He looked around his cell and the cellblock. "But I guess I wouldn't be here if I hadn't."

Andi thought, *Nothing paranoid about that.* This wasn't helpful; she was getting more confused, not less. *What the hell's going on here?*

"Jared, you know how, when a person is having ideas or doing things that don't make any sense compared with who they usually are—"

"You mean, when a person acts out of character?"

She chuckled. "Exactly—you put it better than I did. So when that happens, sometimes drugs or alcohol are behind it. We've been asking around, and everybody tells us you don't do either one. If you do, honestly, it would be helpful for us to know. Drinking or taking drugs are a lot less serious than threatening to kill people." She saw the fear in his eyes, and touched his arm softly. She could feel his flinch. "What can you tell me?"

"Maybe I should wait till my lawyer..." His voice trailed off uncertainly.

Andi nodded. *Damn.* She started to stand. "That's definitely your right, Jared."

"No, please stay." He looked flushed.

She felt a momentary excitement. Might this be the breakthrough?

"I don't know if this matters, but I don't drink. Or use drugs." His blush deepened, spreading across his jaw. "Well, I...back in sophomore year, I got drunk at a party. When I felt better, I hated myself for doing that. I promised I'd never drink again, and I haven't. Drugs either."

She felt herself deflate. Just what they already knew. So what the hell is going on? And why is he so different today? Andi patted his knee. "Plenty of sophomores get drunk, but not many quit. Good for you." She considered what to ask next. "What do you think might have caused you to think we want to kill you? Or to threaten your friends?"

He shivered. "I don't really remember that, or not too clearly anyway. Kind of. I remember being really afraid when I was in the storage unit."

"Afraid of what?"

He spread both hands, palms up, a gesture of confusion. "I don't know. Just scared. And mad. Really mad." The tears in his eyes gathered again. "I don't know much more," he said, brushing his eyes with a finger.

"Has anybody threatened you or bothered you? Attacked you?"

He shook his head again. "Uh-uh. Our class gets along really well. We're pretty much all friends."

"How about somebody else?"

"Threatening me? No, nobody."

"So you remember being afraid and angry, but not much else?"

He looked adrift. "Yeah, I guess."

"Do you remember when the fear started? Or the anger?"

"Uh-uh. No." His eyes widened suddenly.

"Are you feeling afraid right now?"

"Yeah. Real afraid." Again his eyes swept the cell block. "I hate it in here. But no, not afraid like I was."

"Good. We want you to feel safe in here." Andi was surprised at the depth of her feeling for Jared. All of a sudden, he struck her as no more than a sad, vulnerable, very lost boy. She gently touched his arm. "We'll take good care of you."

At her touch, he flinched again. "How long do I have to stay here?"

She pulled her hand back quickly. "Well, we have to investigate. The combination of those guns and your threat to kill your friends is something we can't be too careful about."

His head jerked straight, face stiffened with fear. "Deputy, please. Don't let me hurt anybody." Tears welled in his eyes, but they did not fall. He looked down at the floor.

40

On the ride home, Brad Ordrew continued to question Grace about things with no link to Jared, which annoyed her. When he asked her if she was dating anybody, she said, "Could we just drive, please? None of these questions are any of your business."

"Hey, I'm just trying to be a friend."

She looked at him with narrowed eyes. "I have friends already, thanks."

His eyes narrowed, but he said, "You're a very nice-looking young woman."

She thought, *Eeeuw.* She didn't respond.

After a long pause, he said, "I didn't mean anything by that."

Again. *Eeeuw.*

She thought he looked angry, but he said nothing for the rest of the trip.

As they turned onto the long drive that curved up to the cabin, he said, "You remember what I said about drinking parties?"

Grace looked at him. "Uh-huh. And do you remember what I answered?"

He glanced over at her. "No. What?"

"You don't remember? What kind of interviewer are you? I said, go ahead and investigate. You'll come up as empty as you're doing with Jared."

Ordrew looked annoyed again, which pleased her. When he pulled up to the front steps, she opened the door and got out. "Thanks for the ride," she said, and started to push the door closed.

"How about showing me around?" Ordrew said, gesturing toward the cabin.

She looked back. "No, I can't. Northrup tells me not to let anybody in I don't know and trust."

"Hey," he said, frowning. "I'm a deputy, just like Andi. You know me."

She looked hard at him. "Yeah, well, I *don't* know you, and I don't trust you." She slammed the door. To herself, she muttered, "And bullshit, you're 'just like Andi.'"

She stood in the doorway, keeping her eye on him. Ordrew waited, both hands clasping the wheel, peering intently around the yard and up at the cabin. When they locked eyes, Grace went inside and closed the front door, but peered through the door's window, watching, her hand resting on the deadbolt. After a few minutes, he backed the squad car around and moved slowly down the driveway toward the highway.

She squinted and wondered if she should tell Northrup.

41

A few minutes past ten that evening, Ed climbed the steps to the porch, bone-tired and stiff, the way his father had walked when he got old. He stopped a moment to gaze out at the valley, at the town lights shimmering in the warm air, at the hazy stars clustering overhead. *Beautiful*, he thought. *No more work today.*

As he closed the front door and tossed his jacket on the couch, Grace came out of the bathroom, wrapped in a large towel, a smaller one turbaned around her hair. "Northrup, Magnus Anderssen called. He said to call him back, no matter how late."

As if he'd reached a campground with no vacant spaces, Ed deflated. He ran his hand through his hair. "Did he say what it's about?"

"Uh-uh. Just to call." She went halfway into her room, then turned back. "And Andi called—she had to work late. Somebody called in sick. She'll come over about eleven."

Instead of eating, Ed had seen patients all evening, after spending the day with upset students at the school. Hungry, he debated grabbing some food before calling Magnus. *No. Get it over with.* He dialed the Double-A.

Magnus answered. "Ed, thanks for calling back. Look. I'm canceling our visits. You've done a superb job, and I'm fine. I haven't had a drink since our first visit, and I'm sure everything will work out. So thanks, and let's get back to being friends again, shall we?"

Ed frowned: After today's revelation about Mgnus's failure at the monastery, he could understand Magnus's wanting to avoid going further, but his intuition said this was not the time to stop. "You've been doing well, Mack, but I think we need a few more."

"No, I'm doing just fine. No drinking, no problems. You were right—getting it off my chest was just the ticket. Look, if I get shaky again, I'll give you a call, and thanks for all your help. I'll send you a check. Well, good, then. Take it easy." He hung up, leaving no space to edge a word in.

Ed cradled the phone, then rubbed his face, annoyed with himself for not insisting. *The man is scared of something.*

While he made himself a peanut butter sandwich, he beat himself up for not having pushed harder. When he finished the sandwich, he dialed Magnus again. After ringing and ringing, the call rolled over to voicemail. He left his message, but he guessed that Magnus wouldn't be calling back tonight.

42

As he was hanging up, Andi came through the door. Her eyes were as dull and tired as his felt. She sagged against his chest. "Caught a double shift," she murmured. "Half the damn department's got the flu." For a moment, she rested against him, then straightened. "I have to talk with you about Jared. It's very weird."

"Weird? Come sit down. What's weird?"

They sat on the couch. Andi said, "I talked to him this afternoon. He wasn't paranoid at all, and he hardly remembers the things he said Monday. He looked upset when I told him he'd threatened to kill his classmates."

As tired as he was, Ed tensed. "Upset? Like angry?"

"Uh-uh. Tears. A shocked look. He begged me not to let him harm anyone."

"Huh." He thought about it, intrigued. "No paranoid thinking?"

She shook her head. "What do you think about him maybe being one of those multiple personalities?"

Ed frowned. "Before that, I'd wonder if he's playing you." He considered her question. "Multiplicity? It's unlikely, I'd say. Those folks—by the way, it's called dissociative identity disorder nowadays—they've usually been abused multiple ways, multiple times, by multiple people. Starting when they're kids, usually little kids. Any evidence of that with Jared?"

"None, but the parents would cover that up, wouldn't they?"

Ed rubbed his face. "Yeah. You interviewed them—what do you think?"

She shook her head again. "They weren't covering anything up, and everybody says the same damn thing. No sign of abuse." She shook her head. "So, this disassociation thing, it's not likely?"

"The kind of family that creates dissociative disorders is secretive. No friends, no visitors. No outsiders get in. I don't see the Hansens like that at all."

Andi looked at him. "You know them?"

Ed nodded. "Not well, but Phil Hansen and his crew helped me with some remodeling a couple of years ago. Before you came to the valley. Nice guy. He invited me to his house to go over the plans; I didn't pick up any bad vibes. While I was there, it was a revolving door, neighbor kids in and out all afternoon. Not like an abusive home at all. "

Just then, Grace came out of her room, dressed in baggy sweatpants and one of Ed's t-shirts, the one with the four Beatles marching across Abbey Road. "You guys talking about Jared?"

Ed nodded. "Come join us. I have a question for you."

"For me?"

"Yeah. About Jared. Have you ever noticed him getting very angry, then later being very different, and not remembering being angry? Or anything else like that?"

She nodded. "Well, he gets angry sometimes, but not real angry, and I don't think he forgets it."

"Give me an example."

She thought about it. "Remember when Kenny Daggett was accused of cheating and Ms. Sergeant suspended him for a week? Jared was mad. He said Kenny hadn't cheated—he sits behind him."

"How did he show he was angry?"

"I guess a normal way, for him. He swore a couple times, then he apologized to us. Afterward, he said, 'I can prove Kenny didn't cheat.' He did too. He figured out what had happened and went to the principal's office and told Ms. Sergeant about it, and she let Kenny come back, and she had an assembly and apologized to Kenny in front of everybody. Me and lots of kids were crying."

Ed ignored Grace's grammar and arched his eyebrows at Andi. "That sound like the kind of anger you saw Monday?"

"Uh-uh. Not even the same planet." To Grace, she said, "Have you ever seen him threatening anyone, or talking as if anyone was threatening him?"

"No. I keep telling everybody, Jared's not like that."

Andi shook her head. "*Damn.* I need something that *explains* something."

Grace yawned. "I can explain it."

Ed and Andi, simultaneously, said, "What?"

"Temporary insanity." She stood up. "Gotta sleep." She smirked at Ed, then said to Andi, "My *chauffeur* leaves early in the morning."

When Grace's bedroom door slammed, Andi whispered, "The car campaign heats up."

Ed closed his eyes, muddled between Andi's case and about Magnus's sudden—and probably unreal—cure. After a moment, he said, "Lynn Monroe thinks I should buy Grace the car."

"That's three against one, cowboy." She rubbed his neck for a moment. "You still think you'll turn down Jared's case?"

Ed felt himself tighten. *No more arguing*, he thought. He didn't answer.

"Earth to Ed."

"Sorry." He thought about Magnus, wondered what was going on.

"Jared's case? You turned it down?"

"Uh, yeah. This afternoon."

"What'd the lawyer say?"

He felt annoyed, decided he was just tired, and gave a long, frustrated sigh. "Look, can we talk about this later?"

Andi looked momentarily hurt, then nodded. "Yeah. We've both had a hard day."

Ed frowned. "And nothing makes a damn bit of sense."

THURSDAY, DAY FOUR

43

Luisa Anderssen drifted up from sleep into a hazy awareness that Magnus's side of the bed was cold. She came instantly awake. Was he drunk again, passed out in his study as on those other terrible nights? She grabbed her robe, glancing at the clock's red *5:11*, and hurried down to his den. It was empty, so she ran to the small study at the back of the Addition. Empty. She slapped on the porch lights. Nothing outside. She ran upstairs to Junior's room and roused him. "*Hijo*, go out to the garage. Tell me if your father's truck is gone." Befogged, the boy sat up.

"What's wrong, Mamá? Where's Dad?"

"I do not know. Go look for his truck. I will call him." As Junior pulled on his sweats, she went back to the big kitchen and snapped on the lights. She dialed Magnus's cell phone number. The rings were an agony. His voice answered. Luisa cried out, "*¡Esposo!* Where are you?" But his voice continued over hers: "… leave a message and I'll return the call when I can." She banged her hand on the counter with frustration.

"His truck's gone, Mamá. What's going on?"

"Did he speak to you? Did he say anything about …" She stopped. About what?

Junior, recently turned a man, wore the bewilderment of a boy. Trying to decipher what his mother needed from him, he snagged on the edge of her fear. Should he comfort her, or be afraid?

"Mamá? What's happening?"

She heard the quaver in his voice and steadied herself. She touched the boy's shoulder. "I am sorry, *hijo*. I became startled when I could not find him. I am certain he has gone to deal with a problem on the ranch."

"Was there a call?" His voice was steadier.

"Perhaps one we did not hear. I am sure it is something on the ranch. Go back to bed."

116

Instead, he went to the stove. "No. I'll start some coffee. You call Dobie and find out what's up." Dobie was the head foreman on the Double-A. Luisa, one of the strongest women in a valley of strong women, relaxed for a moment into her son's charge. She repeated to herself that it was something on the ranch, though Magnus's troubles made her fear something worse. She dialed the head foreman's house, and let the phone ring until it clicked over to the voicemail. She left a message. Then, knowing that Dobie would have wakened to the ringing, dialed again. He would answer now.

44

Ed awoke to the phone's insistent ringing. He craned his neck to the alarm clock: *5:38. What the hell?* He looked at the caller ID: *Anderssen.*

Andi groaned beside him. "God, don't let it be for me."

He thought, *Mack's had a rough night.* He whispered to Andi, "Go back to sleep. It's mine."

He went outside the bedroom. "Morning, Mack."

"Ed? It is Luisa."

"Luisa?" His heart sank: Something was wrong, her voice told him. Very wrong.

"Ed, Magnus has disappeared. I have called everyone—our foreman Dobie, the bunkhouses, the mine, the sawmill. Do you know where he might be?"

Ed groaned, and instantly regretted it.

"What do you know?" Her voice rose. In the background, Ed heard Magnus Junior's voice: *Mamá? What?*

"No, no, nothing like that, Luisa. I have no idea. He cancelled his appointments with me last evening. He said he was doing fine. Perhaps he needed to go to the capital, or to Missoula? On an errand?"

"He would have told me. He does not answer his cell phone. This is unlike him. It frightens me."

Ed wondered what she knew. And what he'd missed. "What frightens you, Luisa?"

Luisa said, "Is he all right? Will he...harm himself?"

"He seemed to be doing much better." The words tasted bitter, hollow in his mouth; he'd missed suicide before, when Elizabeth Murphy had hanged herself. *God, not again.* "Has he seemed happier than normal lately, or acting like he's tying up loose ends?"

"*No comprendo,* ah, this phrase, 'loose ends.'"

"I'm sorry. Putting his affairs in order."

He heard a muffled sound on the line. After a moment, she spoke with difficulty. "Ed," she managed, "is my husband going to kill himself?"

He flinched. "I saw no recent...obvious sign of it, Luisa." *Except he told me,* he thought. "That's why I asked if you had noticed something I haven't."

"About these loose ends? No, I have noticed nothing like that. We had a small argument last night, but..." She gasped. "*¡Dios mio!*"

"What is it, Luisa?"

"I will call you back." She hung up.

Ed put down the phone, hoping against hope that Mack was running. People who are running are alive.

45

Buzzing with worry, Ed left for his morning run a half hour early. He pushed himself, running hard. When he returned, he stood panting on the porch, watching the first sunlight brush the western snowpack with morning rose. Behind him, Grace opened the door and stepped out onto the porch, her arms folded against the chill.

Ed turned. "You're up early."

"I heard you talking on the phone before you ran. Has something happened to Jared?" Tears were gathered at the corners of her eyes.

Still breathing hard, Ed tossed his running gear on the porch swing and reached toward her, pulled her to him. "Want coffee?" His shower could wait.

She pushed him away. "Come on, Northrup. I need to know what's wrong with my friend."

"The call wasn't about Jared, Grace. Let's go inside and get some coffee. We can talk about Jared." He needed a moment to think. He didn't intend to reveal information he really ought to keep private, but what information did he actually have? He poured two mugs, and set them on the kitchen table. "First of all, it's all guesswork at this point. I haven't examined Jared, so I only know what Andi's told me. And I need you to keep anything I say to yourself. Understand?"

Her hands gripped the mug. She nodded. "Me and my girls were talking about him. We just don't think he could do what everybody says he said he wanted to do."

Ed started to correct her grammar, then held back. Grace usually spoke bluntly, so her avoiding the words "shoot the seniors" meant she was scared. He said, "I don't think that's what's going on. There's no real sign of it."

"But something's wrong, isn't it? Me and my girls—"

Second offense. He couldn't resist. "Your girls and you."

"Yeah, I said that. Don't do that active listening stuff, okay? This isn't one of those teachable moments."

"Whoa, honey. It's not active listening, it's grammar. Say 'my girls and I,' not 'me and my girls.'"

Her eyes flared. "Oh man, Northrup. I'm talking life and death here, and you're worried about grammar?"

Ed bristled. "Weren't you thinking you want to be a lawyer or an FBI agent after college? If you want a good college for that, you've got to use good grammar, not 'me and my girls.' 'My girls and I.' Otherwise, you can forget law school or the FBI academy." His pique faded before his lecture did; he immediately regretted what he'd said.

"Fine." He could see her gather herself. "Back to Jared. Me and my girls, sorry, my girls and me—"

He felt his mouth open, but he said nothing, just looked at her.

"Give me a break, Northrup! *My girls and I* talked about Jared and we think there's no way he'd do a school shooting. Unless he was one of those multiple personalities, and we don't think he is."

"Me neither," he said.

"'You neither' what?"

"I don't hear anything that suggests he's got multiple personality."

Grace softened. "So what's wrong with him?"

"I don't know, Grace. It could be half a dozen things. All I know for sure, he's in big trouble." *Like Magnus*, he thought. Unsure of his next words, Ed bought time, pouring himself another cup of coffee. His hand shook, coffee splashed on the counter. Grace noticed, her eyes frightened.

"We'll figure it out, honey."

She pushed close to him, and let him put his arms around her. "I'm scared, Northrup." She paused. "Everybody's scared around here."

He tightened his embrace. "We'll figure it out, pal."

She pulled back, looked up at him, her face questioning. "Pal? That's a new one." She turned away. "I gotta get ready for school."

Ed sipped his coffee and returned to the table. Sat. Mused. Watched the long dawn shadows stretch across the down-sloping fields. Pal. Was Grace a pal? Magnus wasn't just a patient; he was a long-time pal. *If I missed something...*

He shook himself. *Stop this.* Mack was most likely somewhere out on his ranch, helping with a late calf's birth. Or a sick horse.

Or somewhere in the foothills, dead.

46

On his way in to town and the high school, Ed got a call.

"Ed? John Keeley here. Say, we've admitted Art Masters. He says you're seeing him. Can you stop by?"

Ed's heart sank. First Magnus, now Art. "Is he...?" He didn't say the word.

"Dying? Not today. But he's in and out, and it won't be long now. Asked for you."

Ed glanced at the dashboard clock. "Sure. I'll swing by on my way to the school."

"You're counseling kids about the Hansen thing? They pretty jittery?"

"Yep. Nobody's feeling safe here these days. What room's Art in?"

"Room 121."

"Okay. I'll be there in fifteen minutes.

Art lay, diminished, in the big bed, eyes closed. On Monday, in the office, he hadn't seemed as withered as now, framed by the white sheets. Ed marveled at the damage the cancer had done in only three days. Art's face was gaunt, its skin yellow and taut, the eyelids gray. Ed knocked softly on the doorframe. Art opened his eyes, smiled weakly. "Grab a chair, Ed. Had me an insight last night."

Ed smiled back. "Tell me about it."

"You know how people are surprised I'm not angry about the cancer?"

"Sure do. I believe I'm one of them."

"Yep. Well, I figured out why I'm not."

Ed waited.

"When I was a kid, maybe sixteen, seventeen, I got me my first job. I cowboyed with an old gent everybody called Buddy. Don't recall his Christian name. Anyway, one morning a cow spooked, took off running. I tore off after her, but she got herself lost way down in some brush by the river. I rode all over hell, getting all pissed off 'cuz I couldn't find that damn cow. Old Buddy, he just rode up a hill and sat his horse, smokin' a cigarette, calm as can be. I got pissed at him too. After an hour or so crashin' around in the woods like a crazy man, I rode up the hill to Buddy and started yelling at him. He just smiled and said, 'Look around, son. From here we can see this whole stretch of country. Just sit your horse, keep your eyes open, and watch. We see movement, we got us our cow.'" Art chuckled, then started to cough, painfully. After a moment, he composed himself. "That ol' Buddy, he laughed at me. 'Works like a charm so long as you're up here and not riding around like a damn fool in the brush.'"

Art lapsed into a quiet place, his eyes dimming for a moment before he stirred himself and looked back to Ed. "So Buddy and me, we sit maybe fifteen more minutes, then we see the cow moving off east. No use in getting angry. Taught me, just sit my horse and watch for what moves."

Ed imagined the scene. "So you're watching your cancer?"

Art nodded. "The whole damn thing." His eyes dimmed again. His breathing stretched out, and in a moment, Ed thought he was sleeping. But as Ed stood quietly and turned to go, Art's old voice crackled. "You're worried about things, Ed. I can tell it."

Ed hesitated. He didn't share much about himself with patients, even those he'd known for years. Believed it'd interfere with whatever they were working out. But Art..."You're right, Art. Lots of trouble in the valley just now. I can't figure it out."

Art took a long breath, adjusting to pain. "You're talking about Mack Anderssen and that boy with the rifles?"

Ed nodded, torn about exposing them, but understanding that everyone knew about the two of them.

Art coughed again. "Just sit your horse and watch. Don't get out ahead of things."

Doc Keeley came in. "Hey, Art. Sleep all right?"

Art nodded. "How about you let me go home and die, John?"

Keeley hesitated, glanced at Ed. "We can control your pain a lot easier here, Art."

The frail shoulders shrugged. "Pain ain't all it's cracked up to be. Learned a long time ago, don't give it the time of day. I'll do better at home."

"Well, let's give it a couple days, shall we? We can revisit this tomorrow or Saturday. That work?"

"Sounds like how my mom said *no*." He chuckled, then coughed. A spot of red bloomed on his lip. "Well, how about getting me a room where I can see the mountains?"

47

Toward the end of their shift, Ben called Andi and Brad Ordrew into his office. "Close the door," he said, signing papers. After a moment, he looked up. "What we got?"

Andi said, "Nothing. We've canvassed all the classmates, a bunch of other kids, the neighbors, the members of his church. He's Jared the Just, everybody's perfect friend. Model citizen."

Ordrew said, "Who wants to kill his friends because he cares so much about them."

Andi ignored that. "I talked with him again yesterday. He doesn't really—"

Ben, looking surprised, interrupted. "Lawyer present?"

"Uh-uh. He gave the okay. Anyway, we just chatted. He doesn't remember much about Monday, and he says he doesn't want to hurt anybody."

Ordrew frowned. "Which is exactly what I'd say if I was sitting in that cell."

Andi shrugged, then ignored him. "We talked with the parents again, this time separately. Brad got something interesting."

Ben turned to him. "What?"

"Only one thing's off-message." Ordrew opened his notebook and glanced at it. "Turns out the kid's been a vegetarian for a year or so, since he took that course on Buddhism." He looked up from the notes, scorn in his eyes. "Anyway, he's also into organic food, which is hard to find here in the valley, so he's been going to Missoula frequently. The father says that over the past six weeks or so, Jared hasn't gone to Missoula even once, and he's been..." He looked at his notes. "And I quote, 'kind of irritable at home.'" He put away the notebook.

Ben's face clouded over. "That's it? Irritable? What the hell's that mean?"

"I asked him to tell me more, and he said the kid's been 'testy,' like when they'd ask a question he'd look annoyed and not answer. He said the kid's got—" Again he glanced at his notes. "—and I quote, 'too many irons in the fire, or maybe it's the pressures of college coming up.'"

Ben said, "Hell, a teenager lookin' annoyed and not talkin' to his folks ain't breakin' news. Any of the friends mention this testy business?"

Andi said, "One of his buddies said he'd noticed Jared's seemed quiet lately, and one girl said she thought he was mad at her, which everybody says would be unusual. But nobody else observed anything."

"What about mom?"

Ordrew shook his head. "Dead end. Cried like a faucet, but told the same story."

"Crap on toast." Ben went to his desk and picked up a paper. "Talked with Irv Jackson. Like I thought, he ain't keen on the terroristic threat charge, based on the nothin' we've got. He's a little more open to chargin' the boy with suspicion of makin' terrorist threats, which is a non-stick charge, but then we can release him on bail and Irv'll get a court order for a psychological examination." He looked at Andi. "Which your boyfriend can't do."

"Why not?"

"He's signed on with the defense."

Andi's heart hammered. "What? He told me..." She shut up, in turmoil. Why had Ed lied? She remembered his evasiveness last night, his refusal to talk about the attorney's reaction. *He lied to me!* Her reaction boiled up like a thunderhead in July. This was wrong. Ben was studying her, but Ordrew was smiling. She pushed air out through her nose. *Get on top of this, now*, she ordered herself.

Ordrew said, "Trouble in paradise?" He snickered.

She wanted to smash his smile off his face. But yeah, trouble. She back-burnered her anger and focused.

Ordrew was mid-sentence. "...due respect, Sheriff, letting him go is fucked." His voice stayed level. "The bastard's a danger to those high school kids, and no shrink'll stop him from doing what he *told* us he's going to do. You let him go, and I guarantee we'll have a tragedy on our hands."

Despite her half-angry, half-sick feeling, Andi said, "Ben, Jared was different yesterday. Not angry, not paranoid. He hardly remembered the things he said on Monday. He sounded regretful, sad."

Ordrew laughed, but without humor. "Let me see. On Monday, the kid tells us he wants to kill people because they might discover he's a bad guy. Then after two days in the can, a miracle: He's Mr. Rogers. Give me a break. He's gaming us."

Ben said, "Maybe so. But Irv says, and I agree, Dickie Flure ain't likely to go for a high bail on a kid for one statement, specially a kid like Jared Hansen. So, either way, he walks. And we're right up against the time-limit for holdin' juveniles."

"Charge him as an adult. Making terroristic threats is a felony, for God's sake." Ordrew's voice snapped.

Ben shook his head. "Can be a felony, but it can also be a misdemeanor. For a misdemeanor, seventeen is juvenile, and Irv ain't sure we can prove the actual intent of the threat. When he made it, Irv says the kid wasn't intendin' to scare his classmates, which we'd need to prove for the felony."

"What're you saying, Sheriff?" Ordrew snarled.

"He was just answerin' your questions. Ain't no way to prove he actually *intended* doin' it. Whole thing's murky as hell. He ain't lost his civil rights, you know."

Ordrew started to object again, but Ben waved him silent. "The *suspicion* charge will buy us time to find a shrink to examine him, and we might find somethin'. Me and Irv listened to the interview tape. Our opinion, you both got a point: Either he's got a mental problem or he's playin' games, hidin' behind the crazy talk. But Pete tells me this boy ain't the devious type, and I ain't heard nothin' so far to tell me he's playin' a game, so my money's on mental illness. So here's how we're doin' this: We charge him with suspicion of makin' a terrorist threat, the parents make bail, and he walks, and Irv gets himself a court order for a psych eval. I want you two to keep diggin'—get me somethin' more than the squat we got so we can go to trial, if we get there."

Ordrew, though he looked disgusted, didn't immediately respond. After a moment during which Ben said nothing, he stood up. "Well, Sheriff, I'd say the crap he spewed in that interview is more than squat, but you're the boss." He headed toward the door, then turned back. "But it's on you when this blows up and people die."

When they reached the squad room, Andi said to him, "What the hell did that last crack mean?"

"Ben might just find himself facing some opposition when the next election rolls around. People will remember who made this decision."

Her anger rose fast and hot, but she said, "I'm going to forget you said such a stupid thing."

"The stupid thing's letting Jared Hansen go."

Andi glared, but said nothing. She had an argument with Ed Northrup to finish.

As she left the department to go across to Ed's office, Jack Kollier, the reporter from the *Missourian*, was waiting in the hall. "Deputy Pelton, is he being released?"

Andi took a deep breath. She wanted to tell him to fuck off, but waited till she was calmer. "You're persistent." She forced a smile. "I really can't say anything."

"Is that because you've been told not to, or because you folks don't *have* anything?"

Andi heard the trap. "Department rules. Information to the public comes from the sheriff, not from me." She smiled; she knew Jack was the only reporter still staying at the Jefferson House; the rest had gone home. "You must have a family over in Missoula. Why hang around here?"

At the word "family," Jack's face had changed. "No, no family. News is my family nowadays."

"I'm sorry to hear that."

His eyes closed briefly, almost as if his eyelids were warding something off. His eyes opened again. Andi saw she'd missed their sadness before. She wondered what his story was. "What happened to your family?"

He looked away. "Same thing that happens to lots of people. She left, took the kids. I see them twice a month." He gave a thin half-smile. "So how about it? What have you got?"

She almost gave him something, which is to say, she almost told him about the nothing that they had. But she remembered the rules, and her upcoming fight with Ed, and shook her head.

48

When she entered Ed's waiting room, his office door was ajar, so she went right in. "You told me you wouldn't sign on with the defense. Why the hell'd you lie to me?"

He hard the fury in her quivering voice, saw the raw look in her eyes. He kept his voice easy, though he didn't feel it. *This case is ripping us apart.* "I didn't lie to you."

"Ben just told me you signed with the defense, but you—"

"Oh." He took a relieved breath. "I forgot to fill Ben in. I called Donna Ratner yesterday. I'm not taking the case on either side."

He watched her visible effort to calm down. After a moment, she said, "Truth?"

"Andi, I don't lie to you." He waited.

Finally, she nodded. "I know you don't. So." She was quiet another moment. "I guess I owe you an apology."

"Naw, you don't. I'm the one who needs to apologize. To Ben."

49

That afternoon, after District Attorney Irving Jackson had presented his charges in district court and Judge Dickie Flure had set bail at fifty thousand dollars, Andi waited with Jared in the conference room while his parents posted a bond. He sat hunched over, elbows on his knees, staring at the floor. Andi noticed the scars on the backs of his hands again, white and puckered. Burns? She hadn't asked about them before. Could they point to something about his mental state?

"How you doing, Jared?"

After a moment, he said, "I'm real low. I've never felt so sad."

She wanted to reach over and touch his arm, but remembered how he'd flinched when she'd done that before. "You feel like telling me?"

He looked up at her, almost gratefully. "It's about what you told me, the things I said to you and the other deputy. It's all kind of like a dream. No, not a dream, just hazy."

"So you still feel like you did yesterday?"

He looked down again. For a moment, Andi thought he wasn't going to answer. Perhaps he hadn't heard. After a moment, he said, "Yeah. I think on Monday I maybe meant those things I said, but, really, I'm not sure." He paused. "I suppose I must've meant them."

She hated to remind him, but had to. "Remember, whatever you say can be used against you in court."

He nodded, still looking at the floor. "It's like I don't care, you know?

Use it. The things I said seem all fucked, now." He looked up sharply. "I'm sorry. I shouldn't swear." He lowered his head again. "All I want is to get home and eat well again. The food here's—" He paused. "It's not so good." Even this complaint sounded apologetic.

Andi remembered the father's comment about Jared eating vegetarian. "What do you eat? At home, I mean."

"Organics," he said, looking shy. "Good stuff: vegetables, nuts, grains. Grass-finished beef when I can afford it. My seeds. Healthy food." He smiled, but his eyes were sad. "My mom worries I don't like her cooking."

His shift in mood puzzled her, the way Monday's aggressive hostility seemed to have burned down to this sober, somber sadness. A ploy? If he was gaming her, why contradict himself by acting so sad, so confused, and so clearly *not* paranoid? To confuse the picture even further? His downcast look and palpable sadness argued against it. Besides, if it were a play designed for a defense, why admit that he may have meant the crazy talk on Monday?

"There's something I forgot to ask you earlier," she said. "Why'd you rent the storage unit in the first place?"

He slumped. "I'd rather not say, if you don't mind."

"You're free to do that. But it might help us understand."

He just shook his head.

"Jared, do you—" But the door opened and Phil and Marie Hansen came in. Marie rushed to Jared, eyes welling, and pulled him into her arms. At first he held back, stiff, but then he melted, sagging against her, his head on her shoulder, his eyes filling.

The tears running down his cheeks distracted Andi. She sensed there was something important about the storage unit. His tears got in her way of seeing it.

50

Delta flight 8021 banked steeply into a long swooping curve high above the Sierra Madre Occidental, making its final turn toward Hermosillo. Magnus Anderssen looked down, watching the forested mountains flattening westward into desert plains. The spring rains must have come late or lasted long. Wide swaths of reds and yellows still patched the red-brown desert floor. The plane leveled and he gazed over the wing to the low hills rolling west across the Sonoran plain, beyond the sprawl of Hermosillo, out to the distant blue-black shimmer of the Sea of Cortez. Red jewels paved a gleaming sun-road on the rippling water. The three legs of his flight—Missoula to Salt Lake, Salt Lake to Phoenix, Phoenix to Hermosillo—had been uneventful, but it'd been a long, tiring trip. He'd left the Double-A at 2:30 in the morning. He stifled a yawn.

The attendant came through collecting trash, and the captain announced their descent into Hermosillo. Magnus closed his eyes and dozed. A bouncing touchdown rattled him awake.

The customs agents were polite. When Magnus came through the international arrivals door, a powerful man lifted a hand, sun-darkened like his face, in greeting. Calm red lips smiled beneath a bushy, black mustache, and his salt-and-pepper hair was pressed flat from the big Stetson he held respectfully in his other hand.

"Ernesto!" said Magnus, stiffening. How had his foreman known he was coming?

"*Señor* Anderssen. *¡Bienvenido!*"

"*Gracias, 'Nesto, mí amigo. Cómo estás?*" As he shook Ernesto's hand, Magnus recalled the start of their long friendship, during Magnus's first visit, in 1992, to *Árboles Blancos*, Luisa's father's ranch. Ernesto had been a *caballero* then, assigned to show *el norteamericano* around the ranch.

They'd been riding up an arroyo, under a gray-green arch of mesquite and scrubby eucalyptus trees shading the dry creek bed. Suddenly, Magnus's mare shied at a snake gliding underfoot. He managed to keep his seat.

"Whoa, there," he said softly, rubbing her neck. She stood panting, her withers quivering. Ignoring his own beating heart, Magnus gentled her patiently, talking softly, and after the animal was calm, Ernesto said, "You are *muy serio* with her, *señor*."

Magnus heard the compliment and pondered the word. "Why do you say *serious*, Ernesto?"

"Many men would beat her for startling them. You comprehend that a horse can bear snakes even more poorly than we do."

The following year, after Luisa left *Árboles Blancos* to marry Magnus, her father had promoted Ernesto to head *caballero*, and later, to chief foreman. After the old man died in 2003, they learned he had willed Ernesto a tenth share of the ranch, and Luisa gave him an additional twenty percent to stay on and run the spread in her absence. Magnus, who'd never stopped grieving his older brother, Calvin, valued Ernesto as the brother of his adult age.

Now, standing awkwardly in the airport, Magnus felt confused, and then embarrassed. Luisa must have figured out where he'd gone and called Ernesto, but what had she told him? Had she mentioned his drinking or his trouble?

A short, stocky man walked up slightly behind Ernesto. His wide brown face, broad nose, and hooded eyes made him Indian. Magnus questioned Ernesto with his eyes.

"Señor Anderssen," said his friend, "allow me to present el Jefe de Policía de Hermosillo, Atl Yaotl." He pronounced the short man's name "Aht Yah-oat." Magnus knew that few Aztecs lived in Sonora, but the name sounded Aztecan.

The men shook hands, Magnus warily. The chief's eyes examining him were soft, but penetrating. Magnus covered his growing embarrassment, and asked, "*¿Porque este honor, Señor el Jefe?*" To what do I owe this honor?

The policeman answered in beautiful English, his baritone rich and fluid. "Please call me Al, as my friends do, *Señor* Anderssen. Your lady, *Señora* Castellano Reyes de Anderssen, requested that I accompany *Señor* Escobár—" He nodded gracefully up at Ernesto. "—in meeting your plane. Your friend, Sheriff Stewart, joined her in this request, which I am honored to fulfill." He nodded in what could only be a bow.

Magnus flushed. *Luisa must've called Ben.* It was a dance, so smoothly had the police chief fenced the issue. "You're here to see how crazy I am," Magnus answered, more harshly than he'd intended. The embarrassment mounted. *Jefe* Yaotl smiled. "You do not appear crazy to me, Señor. Weary, perhaps, from your long flight, and therefore understandably annoyed to be greeted by the police."

"Ben Stewart asked you to be here," Magnus said, flatly.

Yoatl nodded. "As I mentioned, *Señor*. Both Sheriff Stewart and your spouse."

Magnus felt his face tighten. Ernesto, looking very uncomfortable, extended his hand. "Amigo, allow me to take your bag to the truck." He extended the handle and rolled the bag slowly through the big doors of the airport. The chief stepped closer to Magnus and warmly touched the taller man's forearm, a strangely intimate gesture that left Magnus momentarily shaken. He could come to like this small man.

The chief smiled. "*Señor*, you are a man of the world." He pronounced it as a compliment. "I am certain that you realize that your wife has informed me—privately, and I assure you, only me—of her worries for you. I do not care to have any additional information. Hermosillo knows you, and we welcome you. *Árboles Blancos* is a proud member of our community and you will not be bothered. Every *caballero* needs a place of peace at times, and *especialmente* when troubled. We will not disturb you more."

Despite his embarrassment, Magnus was oddly touched by the small man's courtliness and understanding. *If it's real,* he thought. Aloud, he said, "I appreciate your frankness, *Jefe*. Al. May I ask what you will tell my wife?"

"Of course. I will say that you arrived safely, that you seemed to be quite, ah, *regulár*." He used the Spanish word, with its connotation of sobriety. So Luisa had told him about the drinking. "And I will say that your eyes were very sad."

The policeman bowed and turned as Ernesto came back though the large door. Magnus watched the chief walk away. Ernesto said, "Only one bag, *amigo*?"

"Luisa will bring the rest of my things later," he replied, still watching the chief's back. "I need to cancel the rental car, `Nesto. Then, let's go home."

They drove in silence the forty miles up the Nogales highway toward the turn to *Árboles Blancos*. Magnus's sense of humiliation swelled as he wondered who else in the valley was talking about his disappearance. Perhaps Ernesto sensed his friend's discomfort; in any case, he said nothing. Ordinarily, this ride was a pleasure for both men, talking of the ranch and Sonoran politics and their lives since the last visit, but there was no such pleasure today, even though the late April sun was hot and the dry air was filled with the fleeting fragrance of the fading spring flowers. The highway meandered up a long desert valley of mesquite and ironwood stands, graced by swaths of flowers that would be dry and brown in a week. The flanks of the hills to the west were pale yellow-green with *palo verde* trees. Even the old gray eucalyptus trees in the arroyos looked fresh. Magnus registered none of it. He was agonizing over what to tell Ernesto.

He asked one question: "Did Luisa call you too, `Nesto?"

"*Sí, amigo.* That is how I knew to meet you."

Magnus said no more, although he was desperate to ask Ernesto what Luisa had said.

At the store-girdled junction where they turned off the Nogales highway to head northwest toward the ranch, he asked Ernesto to pull in at the *licorería*. He went in and came out quickly, carrying three large bottles of Johnny Walker Red, the best Scotch the store carried. Ernesto looked at him askance. He looked away.

"*Amigo,* I do not remember you drinking."

"Well, it seems I've started." The embarrassment rose, almost unbearable now. Magnus looked out the window at the desert hills, then opened the first bottle and took a long swallow, avoiding his friend's glance.

51

Andi sat on the porch, uncomfortable despite the soft darkness and the warm evening air. Last night's argument with Ed bothered her. Worse, how she'd handled her anger felt like a failure, a slip into something old and deep. She'd thought she was over that, the angry withdrawing when she was losing control of something she cared about. Two years ago, after she'd been shot and Ed had started pressuring her to stay in the valley with him and Grace, she'd reacted by pulling angrily away, even though she'd really wanted to stay. Since then, though, she'd learned to trust Ed's love and had hoped she was done with that fearful place again. She owed Ed an apology. Hell, she owed herself one.

The rugged ridges of the Monastery Range were black against the fading sky. Early stars thickened above them. She watched headlights turn into the drive and sweep up the long curve from the highway. In a moment, Ed's pickup pulled into the yard. She smiled at his wave as he got out of the truck. As he climbed stiffly to the porch, she stood, and kissed him when he reached her.

"Now that's the best thing that's happened to me all day," he said, and they kissed again. "Let me get a glass of wine and we can talk."

As he started into the cabin, she put her arms around from behind him and slipped her hand into his pants pocket and began rubbing him. "Talk?" She felt his stirring beneath the clothing. He pushed against her hand, and his left hand reached behind, to her groin. She shivered, and kept rubbing.

"I guess all is forgiven, eh? Let's go inside."

Through his clothes, she took his erection in her hand, and pressed herself against his hand at the same time. But she whispered into his back,

"Later. I want you good and ready. Grace is on her way home, so let's get her settled first."

"Quit rubbing Little Eddie, then."

"I like feeling him get hard."

With his other hand, he tugged her hand from his pocket. "You keep that up and there won't be any later."

She laughed and backed up. "Right. Get yourself that glass of wine."

When he returned, he sat down with a small groan and said, "Lots of women angry with me these days. Donna Ratner, Grace, a couple of woman patients I couldn't see." He glanced at her. "You."

"I'm sorry about that. Momentary insanity. Don't feel bad."

He let out a long breath. "I'm too beat to feel bad."

"Okay, good. I still want to apologize, though. I was harsh yesterday."

"When you get scared, that's how you handle it—control. But I asked for it."

She took that in. "You're analyzing me."

He lifted his glass in a mock toast. "Bingo."

She shrugged. "Anyway, I'm sorry."

"Me too."

"Okay. That's finished, then."

"So, put your hand back in my pocket."

"When your daughter goes to bed."

He laughed. "Worth a try." He sipped his wine. "What's new with the investigation?"

"We released Jared on bail today. Charged him with suspicion of making terrorist threats. Judge Flure ordered him to be evaluated. Ben'll be calling you in the morning to set it up."

Ed was quiet, frowning.

"Something wrong with that?"

"Well, sure. If I sign with you guys, same problem—you and I are a conflict of interest. I can't take the case for you either." He stood up and looked toward the town lights below, stretched in a line along the dark river. "But that's not what I was frowning about."

She looked at him. "What was it?"

"The mood in the valley, it's tense as hell. Releasing Jared isn't going to

132

sit well with a lot of folks."

"Tell me about it. Brad's angry about it. He's predicting bloodshed."

"By Jared? Or against Jared?"

"Well, he means by Jared, but the other's a possibility too." She let out a long breath. The turn in the conversation had sapped her romantic mood. "We really don't have anything besides his statements to go on, and who knows..." After a moment, she finished. "Who knows any damn thing about this case?"

"You don't sound confident." Ed sat down again beside her.

She pondered the rush of sympathy for Jared that had surprised her in the conference room. "There's something about him I don't get. His paranoid talk made my hair stand on end, but he's got another side to him, a kind of gentleness. I get the feeling he's a sweet kid, just like everybody says. Brad's convinced he's gaming, setting up a defense, but I don't buy it. He wasn't paranoid at all, yesterday or today, just sad, regretful. I felt sorry for him."

"Maybe Brad's right. Could be he's crazy like a fox."

"Sure, it's a possibility. Wouldn't be the first perp who played crazy."

"But?"

"I don't think so. For one thing, he admitted he meant what he said when he was paranoid."

Ed looked at her. "Really? That's unusual. Still, can't ignore the chance he's setting up an insanity plea."

She let that play against her experience of the boy. She shook her head. "Still don't think so. He's very mixed up."

"Well, looks like it's my job to un-mix him."

Andi stiffened. "You said you wouldn't take this case for either side. Don't—"

Ed reached a finger, touched her lips gently. "Shh. I talked to Phil and Marie; they agreed to let him see me as a regular patient. That will allow you and me to stay together and help Jared."

"What about testimony? You'll be subpoenaed by somebody. Probably everybody'll want a piece of you."

"Just as a fact witness, not an expert."

More headlights came up the drive, and Jen Fortin's car pulled into the yard. Andi smiled. "Beater," she said to Ed.

He nodded. "Noted."

Grace jumped out. "Later, girl," she yelled through the window. Jen waved, turned the car around, and drove out. Grace carried her backpack up the steps and dropped it in front of them. "The radio just said you let Jared go."

"Not exactly," Andi said. "He's been charged with a crime and he's out on bail."

"The kids are gonna be freaked."

"Are you?"

Grace shook her head quickly. "No. Jared wouldn't hurt anyone."

"How can you be sure?" Ed asked.

"Easy. He's always helping somebody. Remember that fire we had last February?"

Andi looked at Ed; they both nodded. Andi thought of Jared's scarred hands, tried to remember the details. She said, "In the chem lab, wasn't it?"

"Yeah. The teacher yelled at everybody to get out and she tried grabbing the fire extinguisher but it was too close beside the fire. She jumped back and tripped and I guess she hit her head. Anyway, she wasn't moving. We were all screaming, but Jared ran back into the smoke and grabbed the fire extinguisher and put out the fire, then he carried Ms. Andrews out."

And burned his hands, Andi thought.

Grace stopped, still shaking her head. "Jared wouldn't hurt anybody," she repeated, then yawned. "Man, I'm really tired. I'm going to bed. Good night."

He and Andi, sitting side by side on the porch swing, listened as her bedroom door closed, then opened, then the bathroom door closed, then opened, and then her bedroom door closed again.

Ed whispered, "Is it later yet?"

Andi chuckled and slipped her hand back inside his pants pocket.

FRIDAY, DAY FIVE

52

As Ed drove into town the next morning, he wondered about the previous night. After Grace had gone to sleep, they'd played in bed until almost midnight. Had they used sex to push away the worry they both were feeling? He knew he had. Whatever, morning had come too early. First Tuesday night's argument, followed by not much sleep, then last night and, once more, not much sleep. Still, sex was a damn good reason for missing his beauty sleep. He chuckled.

Turning into the high school parking lot, smiling, Ed spoke to the windshield. "Is our sex good because we're in love, or are we in love because the sex is good?" He pulled into a parking space. When the windshield didn't answer, he shrugged and said, "Must be a question for a philosopher's truck."

His good humor faded when he saw the cars already lining up to park in the high school lot. Parents, protectively walking their kids into the school. Men with angry faces, arms folded, stood at every door. Word of Jared's release must've burned through the valley.

Ed approached the nearest one. "Morning, Jim. What brings you here?"

"Hey, Ed. A bunch of us dads are manning the doors in case that maniac kid shows up." He patted the bulge under his jacket.

Ed tensed. "Carrying on school grounds isn't legal, man. Let me call the sheriff to handle the guard duty."

Jim shrugged. "We're not letting that creep harm our kids. Tell Ben Stewart, he wants us gone, he should get his ass—and his men—over here first."

This could turn bad, Ed thought. What if Jared came to school? He stepped away and lifted his cell phone, dialing the Hansens.

"Phil? Hi, it's Ed. Look, keep Jared home today. There are some angry parents here at school."

"We weren't going to let him go anyway. The court order forbids it. Thanks for the heads-up, though." Ed heard him telling someone, either Jared or Marie. Then Phil said, "Jesus. What the hell's next?"

"Don't know. These guys look serious. I've gotta give Ben Stewart a call, but I'll let you know if anything starts going south."

He ended the call, his tension mounting as he saw more men arriving. Armed, no doubt.

Inside the small conference room, before starting his meetings with upset students, he called Ben. "We have a problem." He explained about the men guarding the doors.

"Crap on toast. That's a time bomb. The boy's not there, is he?"

"No. I called Phil Hansen. They're keeping him home."

"I'll be over in five minutes."

Hanging up, Ed remembered Magnus. Luisa had called late yesterday, after she'd figured out he was en route to their Mexican ranch.

At least Mack's safe, he thought.

53

After eating a silent breakfast, Magnus rode with Ernesto out from the corral. Spread across the foothills of the Sierra Madre, the ranch overlooked the Sonoran desert to the west. Magnus had awakened hungover and stiff, and the soft air and the fragrance of the *palo verde* trees revived him. He stretched in the saddle. *This ranch will heal me*, he told himself. *Or else*.

Ernesto, riding beside him, noticed. "You are well this morning, amigo?

Magnus shook his head. "Not so well, `Nesto. But riding helps. I'll feel better."

Ernesto turned in his saddle. "May I ask a question?"

Magnus looked over at his old friend. "About the drinking."

"*Si*. It is unlike you." He looked ahead at the trail going up among the pale green trees. "I do not mean to intrude."

"That's all right. You have a right. I'm going through a rough patch. Something is troubling me and I drink to sleep." He gave a rueful laugh. "Although it didn't work last night."

"You have dreams?"

"*Si, `Nesto*. Bad ones. But I fail to remember them." Magnus half-smiled. He'd noticed before how, talking with Ernesto, he slipped unconsciously into the more formal grammar that he loved in Luisa.

Ernesto remained quiet, and the two rode side by side. After a few minutes, they left the *palo verde* grove and rose up into the mesquite. "I will be all right, don't worry," Magnus said.

Ernesto looked over and smiled. "Perhaps I will worry less, *amigo*." They both chuckled, and continued up the trail in silence.

As they rode into the yard of the upper bunkhouse, high in the mesquite-timbered bench-lands where they summered the cattle, eleven *vaqueros* gathered around his horse, quiet, but smiling. Magnus was a good boss. Despite not having seen these men in months, he remembered most of their names and greeted them one by one. He noticed one he didn't recognize hanging back behind the others, his head bowed. He quietly asked Ernesto who it was.

"Paco Olivéz. A few days ago, he let a calf fall into an arroyo. He has been acting—how do you say—guilty?

"Why? Did he do something wrong with the calf?"

Ernesto shook his head, and reached forward and stroked his horse's neck. Surrounded by men, the animal was shifting on its legs, restless. Quietly, so the men wouldn't hear, Ernesto said, "No, a storm came fast off the Sierra. The calves were all running around, and he couldn't keep them together."

"Who could? Was he alone?"

"*Sí.*"

"How is his work?"

"He is young, Mack, but conscientious and skillful. I trust him. He is just feeling culpable."

Magnus nudged his red horse, Rojo, forward. The other hands opened a path for him. He dismounted and approached the young cowboy. "You are called Paco?"

"*Si, señor.*" He looked quickly up at Magnus, then at the ground.

Magnus switched to Spanish. "I understand you know what happened with one of my calves."

"*Si, señor.*"

"*Señor* Escobar tells me you did nothing wrong."

"*Señor*, your calf died. I did not prevent it."

Magnus put his hand on the young man's shoulder. "I know it. So I must ask you to repay me."

The young man, really still a boy, looked up from the ground. "How, *señor?*"

"I will ask *señor* Escobar to take it from your wages, every month one-sixtieth of the calf's cost for five years." He heard Ernesto's quiet chuckle behind him. The boy looked at Magnus, a calculating look on his face. After a moment, he said, "*Señor,* for a calf in Hermosillo, one-sixtieth is only thirty-four pesos."

Magnus nodded, thinking, *The boy is smart.* "Your pay is how much each month?"

"Twenty-five hundred pesos, *señor.*"

Magnus nodded again. "For five years, then, you will make thirty-four pesos a month less. That is what you will do." He started to mount Rojo, then turned back to Paco and said, "Of course, with good work, you will get the usual raises."

Behind him, Ernesto said, in English, "But *señor* Anderssen, what if Paco does not work for you for five years?" Magnus could hear amusement in his voice. Fortunately, none of the *vaqueros* spoke English well enough to pick up the nuance.

The boy looked hard at him. Magnus shrugged. "If he leaves *Árboles Blancos* before he pays, I will suspend his debt. Until he finds another job."

The men around them went still. Magnus wondered what their reactions were. Resentment? Respect? He hoped it was respect, but feared it was resentment.

When he and Ernesto rode away, Ernesto said, "You were wise to give him a task to repay you; it will remove his guilt. And your generosity will shame him into staying all five years." Ernesto's chuckles bubbled in his throat, a soft liquid sound.

"How do you think the other men took it, 'Nesto?"

"Some will resent your generosity, but most will decide you are God. Just, but merciful." Magnus laughed.

He rode awhile, feeling the grip of anxiety growing in his chest. "Sometimes being God is a burden, *mi amigo.*"

Ernesto looked at him from the side. "You will make money. The boy doesn't know how little a new calf is worth."

Magnus nodded. "Nor does he know how often calves die." After a moment, he said, "But he will learn."

They rode in silence a mile or so into the timber. When they came to a ford across a wide creek rushing down from the Sierra, Magnus said, "I want to ride up farther, 'Nesto. I know you have work to do. I'll go alone. We can have dinner together when I return."

Ernesto nodded. "Take care, my friend. Let the mountain heal what troubles you."

54

A half hour after calling Ben, as Ed was listening to a girl explaining, while she glanced at her cell phone, how terrified she felt, the sheriff stuck his head in the door. "A minute?"

The girl stopped talking. Ed said to her, "Do you mind? This'll be quick." The girl nodded, unflustered, and lifted her screen closer to her eyes. He stepped into the hall and asked, "What's going on?"

Ben walked a short way from the door. "Sent the posse home. Pete's on the front entrance, Xavier's on the back, and Monica locked the side doors. Thank God it's Friday. Hope to hell this blows over by Monday."

"Is that safe, locking the doors? What if there's a fire?"

Ben squinted at him. "School doors lock on the outside, not the inside. You smell smoke, just stroll right out into God's sweet air, bucko."

Embarrassed, Ed said, "Thanks, Ben." He turned to go back inside.

"Hold your horses," the sheriff said. "I need you to evaluate Jared Hansen. You still willing to do 'er free?"

Ed felt uncomfortable. "Look, I changed my mind, Ben. I can't work for either side."

The sheriff looked at him from under gathered brows. "Crap on toast, here we go again. Why the hell not?"

"No matter which side I work for, my testimony will be compromised by my relationship with Andi, and I'm not willing to give that up."

"Damn it, Ed. It ain't forever."

"I have a better idea. I'm going to work with him privately, as his therapist. I can find out what's wrong with him and I can still testify as a fact witness, but I'm not on either side, and I can keep my opinions to myself. You can pick my brain all you want—within confidential limits, naturally."

"Or unnaturally." Ben's tone was sour. "No way you'll help me out? Judge Flure ordered this evaluation at county expense."

"Hire Jack Pullman in Bozeman. He's good, and it's kosher if he consults with me on the facts of the case."

"What's *he* gonna cost me? Hell, him and you talkin' could rack up a fortune, and that's money the county ain't got."

"I'll work with Jared *pro bono*—including consulting with Jack."

Ben was quiet. After a moment, he said, "Real sorry to hear this, Ed. Gotta say it. Was countin' on you."

"You can still count on me to help Jared and you guys too, if I can."

"Uh-huh. That *if* sounds a hell of a lot bigger than the *can*." Ben grunted. "Leastways, you'll help the kid." But he didn't sound pleased. Ed watched his head shaking as he walked away.

Ed went back inside and sat across from the student, feeling uneasy. He waited while she finished texting. *If I can help him, indeed.*

55

Magnus rode alone up through the birch forest blanketing the lower shoulders of the Sierra Madre. Rojo climbed the twisting trail easily. As they gained altitude on the mesquite-shaded switchbacks, Magnus rested his eyes on the craggy, pine-softened peaks above him. Snow swathed the higher reaches, reminding him of the Monasteries at home, and a loneliness settled on him. He remembered walking with Father Jerome up the trail to the Coliseum. In his affections, the gray granite cirque had become attached to fond memories of Jerome. A quiver of anxiety broke through the loneliness. He rode on, using the calming words and breathing Ed had taught him. Alongside the trail, the arroyo ran full with snowmelt. He stopped to allow Rojo to drink, and took a long swallow from his water bottle. His morning hangover was gone, but the thirst remained.

Rojo climbed. In an hour, they reached the second, higher ridge, passing into the big firs. His loneliness had faded, leaving an ache he could not name. Rojo walked into a grove of white birches among the firs, through which the arroyo riffled over rounded cobblestones. In a month, it would be dry, its stones hot in the sun, but now the rush of water and the grove's shade refreshed them both. Magnus rode up here whenever he was at *Árboles Blancos*. A granite rise lifted above the trees; atop it, he could look down to the valley and the hacienda two thousand feet below. He dismounted. Rojo ambled over and gingerly placed his forefeet in the cold water, leaning down to drink.

Magnus climbed the granite outcrop and gazed down. Far below, he saw the hacienda, four-square, the red tiles of its roof glowing in the sun. The courtyard, surrounded by the arches of the interior walkway, was visible only as a shadowed square. He could picture the bougainvillea clinging to the arches, in rich, red spring bloom. Their beauty was a consolation. In the center of the courtyard, he could faintly make out the fountain, a tiny dark circle. The fountain bubbled all year, no matter how dry the season. The square courtyard reminded him of the monastery cloister. He felt a wash of sorrow. It would be so hard to say goodbye to this place. Then, a burst of terror struck, a shock exploding in his chest.

His eyes went dark and he was falling, unaware of the pain when he struck the granite rock and slid roughly down against the trees. He rolled, then lay motionless, stopped sharply by a tall birch.

56

As Ed was leaving the high school at the end of the day, Lynn Monroe waved at him down the hall. He walked toward her.

"My friend—her name's Rachel Anders—can't bring the car this weekend, but she's got the day off next Thursday and could drive it over then. She can stay overnight with me and, if you like the car, she can go back with me on Friday after school. That work for you?"

"Let me check." He pulled out his appointment book. "Oh, man, I'm booked all day. I'm playing catch-up, re-scheduling the patients I canceled this week. I don't want to put anybody off a second time."

"Makes sense. How about your lunch break?"

He winced. He'd penciled Jared's name in on his lunch breaks, so he'd have some time for the boy. He knew he needed to work as fast as he could. He shook his head. "Can you keep a secret?"

"Can Mona Lisa smile enigmatically?"

He chuckled. "I'm seeing Jared. As a patient."

Her eyebrows arched. "Wow. You're gutsy. He's not real popular at the moment; that'll rub off on you."

"Could be, but he needs somebody in his corner. For him, nothing good's coming out of this thing."

"Boy, that's the truth." She was quiet a moment. "Do you want to look at the car Wednesday evening? Rachel's coming over after work."

"What time?"

"She'll get here around ten."

"Not a chance. By then, I'll have fallen into the arms of Morpheus." He chuckled, then scratched Jared's name off his Thursday lunch hour. "Let's do it at noon Thursday."

SATURDAY, DAY SIX

57

When Ed started climbing out of bed, Andi rolled toward him, put her hand on his back. "How about an eye-opener?" she murmured.

"Sorry, gotta prep for Jared." When he'd called Phil Hansen and offered his services, Phil had jumped on it, but said he had to ask Jared.

"Of course. Just let me know."

A half hour later, Phil had called back. "He's scared, but he'll see you." He paused. "We made him an offer he couldn't refuse."

"Oh? What was it?"

"Either he sees you or we stop paying for his organic food."

Ed laughed. "Let's start tomorrow morning. How's ten?"

They'd made the appointment. Now, as he drove into town, Ed caught himself tapping his thumbs hard on the steering wheel, a sure sign of nerves. He wrinkled his nose and thought about it. How many new patients had he seen in thirty years? A few hundred, maybe a thousand? "So why the anxiety?" he asked aloud, then got it: How many of those new patients were seventeen, threatening mass murder, and facing a long stretch in prison?

At the office, he watered his plants and tidied the waiting room. Then he made coffee, straightened the books in the bookcase, even considered dusting, which made him laugh.

He opened his email. The first address was unfamiliar—*Los_Árboles@hotmail.com*—but the subject line was not: *Luisa insists I speak with you.* Magnus. Ed started to read.

> *Ed,*
>
> *I am writing at Luisa's insistence, although it is becoming clear to me that something is indeed very wrong with me. What it is, you will have to figure out, because I cannot.*
>
> *I suppose you know that I left the valley two days ago. Luisa is hurt and*

angry, with reason: I acted selfishly. I lied to you. I lied to her. At the time, I thought being alone here in the desert and riding in the hills would straighten me out. It is beautiful here at this time of year, but I feel removed from beauty. No sooner had I arrived but I resumed drinking. Luisa called yesterday evening, after I had had an experience up in the hills, which I need to tell you about. I was already drunk.

We argued. I told her I would stop drinking, but after what happened, I could not. When I told her what had happened up in the hills, which, I admit, terrifies me, she demanded that I write you.

Ed paused at that, thinking, *Magnus does not frighten easily.*

I have told you that every night, fear wakes me, but I have not told you how. Perhaps you will comprehend it, but I do not. It feels like a claw seizes me out of sleep and crushes me till I cannot breathe. I sense a presence that I am sure will destroy me, but I see nothing. The silence frightens me so completely I cannot think or even move. As I write this, my throat tightens, and I can hardly breathe. Your calming words help, but I cannot feel safe here. I told Luisa that only if I drink enough can I sleep through the night, but she cannot bear my drinking. Some time ago, she told me the reason, a horrible thing done by her uncle Agosto when she was a girl. It broke my heart to learn it. The fact that I cannot stop drinking even though it pains her so is almost more than I can bear. This is the first thing that made me agree to talk to you.

Ed could only imagine what anguish Magnus must feel at causing Luisa's pain.

Here is the experience I referred to. Yesterday I was riding in the hills above the hacienda. I had hoped the ride would help me. Up high, where we summer the cattle, there are groves of birch and cottonwood drained by arroyos down from the Sierra Madre. I stopped in one of these to water Rojo, my horse, and, I suppose, to calm myself. I had decided that, if I could not break through this terror, I would kill myself rather than inflict more pain on Luisa. Such a decision is irrational, and yet it seems right to me.

I am telling you this detail so that someone will know that if I do end my life, it is out of love for Luisa.

Ed felt a shiver of dread. He walked to the waiting room and poured himself a cup of coffee. Jared would be arriving soon, and Ed knew he should be in as positive a frame of mind as possible; reading more of Magnus's message might rule that out, but he felt compelled. He looked at the clock: *9:42* a.m. He took a long breath and resumed reading.

From where I stood among the birches, I could look down the slope of the hills and see the hacienda. It is built around a courtyard, like St. Brendan's monastery up on the mountain. Even in the dry season, a fountain bubbles in the courtyard, and the bougainvilleas bloom. I was thinking of how I will miss that courtyard if I kill myself, when the second thing occurred.

I must have lost consciousness. I fell down, which I know only because I was on the ground when I awoke, and bruised. I must have slid down six or seven feet. As if in a dream, it seemed to me that I was hiding, or maybe cowering is a better word, in a dark corner of an arcade, which felt familiar although I did not recognize it. This arcade framed a dark courtyard and it was heavy with snow. I was shivering, but I don't know whether from cold or from fear. The only thing I knew was that I needed to hide. I heard words. No, that is not right, it is more like I felt the words: "Stay away from the infirmary." There was no voice, the words seemed to shake me, like a buzzing in my chest, and I had no idea what they meant; I still do not. All I could see were shadows of the arches above me and beyond them a blacker darkness. Even now, as I write this, I need to stop and breathe.

Then came the last thing. Without any warning, a terrible pain gripped my gut, like a cramp, but much sharper, a tearing stab. I was too frightened to cry out, but I believe I moaned.

While this pain gripped my mid-section, something touched me and I almost screamed, but it was warm and soft. Rojo had come over—this is why I think I must have moaned—and was nuzzling me. I was lying on my side against a birch tree. Rojo nuzzled me again, then lifted his head, but continued watching me. I sat up and pulled the flask from my pocket and drank, and gradually came back to myself. The experience lasted only a few minutes—I could see the sun had not moved very far above the trees.

Please Ed, help me.

Mack

Jared hadn't arrived. Ed considered the email. Hallucination, unexplained sensations, the gut pain, an enveloping terror blotting out rational thought. The phrase, *and beyond them, a blacker darkness* intrigued him. He dampened his worry, and hit *Reply*.

He typed.

Mack. Put your rifle away. I will call you later this morning.

Just as he hit "Send," he heard a knock on his office door.

58

When Ed answered the door, expecting the Hansens, Lynn Monroe surprised him.

"Hey, Lynn. What's up?"

"I'm heading back to Missoula for the weekend, but I wanted to apologize for not calling back on Tuesday. I should have done it yesterday when we talked about the car."

"Not a problem. I figured you were either busy or tired."

Ed thought she looked embarrassed. *Curious*, he thought.

She shook her head. "Oh, god, this is so stupid. Anyway, when you invited me to dinner, I thought you were going to make a pass, and I didn't want that to interfere with our professional relationship. Next day, when I asked Monica about you, she told me about your relationship with Andi, and I felt terrible. I just avoided the whole thing. I'm so sorry I misjudged you."

Ed chuckled. "Hell, I'm flattered you'd think an old guy like me was going to make a pass."

She laughed, looking relieved. "Well, that's good. I didn't want—" She stopped.

Outside the window, they both saw the Hansens getting out of their SUV, Jared last.

"Good luck," she said, and touched his arm as she left.

59

When the Hansens came in the door, Ed felt their tension like an electric current. Ed shook hands with the three, noting how stiff their hands felt. Jared kept his eyes down. Phil Hansen said, "So how does this go?"

Ed explained that he and Jared would talk for an hour or so, and said, "I need to warn you that I won't be telling you what we talk about."

Phil stiffened. Marie glanced at him, and said, "Of course, Ed. We know that Jared needs to know that whatever he has to say won't be coming back to us." She put a calming hand on her husband's arm. Phil said nothing. Ed offered them coffee and the parents took seats in the waiting room. Phil was watching Jared, but Marie, acting relaxed, which Ed doubted she felt, picked up one of his two-year-old magazines; Ed winced. *Got to renew those subscriptions.* He ushered Jared into his office. Jared said nothing, and still averted his eyes.

"Mind if I start out with a couple of questions?"

"I'm only answering the ones I want to."

"Fair enough," Ed said. "Want to tell me what you think this interview is about?"

Jared waited a moment, looking cautious. "The police think I'm either insane or faking it, and you're supposed to find out which."

"Nope. I'm offering to help you figure out what's going on, and to help you fix it if we can. I'm not working for either your lawyer or the sheriff. Just for you."

"Sure."

Ed waited, hearing a hint of paranoia in that word. Or perhaps a healthy skepticism.

"What if I don't trust you?"

"You shouldn't trust me, not yet. And I have to decide if I trust you. Trust runs both ways in therapy." Ed watched surprise work its way across Jared's face.

"I *shouldn't* trust you?"

"Not at all. You're in huge trouble. The cops say you made explicit threats to kill your friends, and claimed that the government is out to kill you. If you think that, why *would* you trust me? You need time to find out if I tell you the truth. Don't trust me before you're sure."

Jared's mouth opened, then closed. His hands gripped the chair. Hard. "Everybody knows you and the deputy are sleeping together. You're on her side."

Ed nodded. "We do a lot more together than sleep." The boy's eyes widened a little, which Ed decided was a good sign. "We're in love, but I don't tell her about what my patients say. It's the same deal with your parents—they won't hear a word from me about what we talk about, and Andi won't either."

He took that in. "What about Grace? She's your daughter, right?"

147

"Same thing." He waited a moment. "So don't trust me until you decide it's safe."

"So what should I do in the meantime?"

Another good sign, that 'meantime.' Ed smiled. "Do what you're doing. Challenge me, and think about my answers. If you don't believe something, test it. Find a way to make me show my true colors."

"How do I do that?"

Ed smiled. "How do I know? I don't know what your true colors are. Yet."

Jared paled. "And then?"

"And then, if you decide to trust me, we work on how to help."

Jared's arms crossed and his eyes narrowed. "If you decide you can trust me."

Delicate moment, Ed thought. He nodded. "Yep."

"No. What if they find out my *true colors,* Doctor, then they kill me?"

They. Not *'you.'* Ed breathed quietly a moment. "Do you believe that might happen?"

Jared looked away. "I don't know. It just came out."

"So at the moment you're feeling that way? That they might kill you?"

He looked back at Ed. "I don't think so."

"When you said, 'Then they kill you,' *they* is who, exactly?"

Now Jared looked uncomfortable. "I don't know. Maybe the government? Like I said, it just came out."

"The government's a big thing," Ed said, softening his voice. He was disappointed to hear the paranoia, but for the moment, he felt more curious than concerned. "So it just came out. Does that happen to you a lot?"

The folded arms loosened. Jared shook his head. "Uh-uh. Just this time." He looked down a moment, then back at Ed. "You're not going to argue with me?"

"About?"

"Them wanting to kill me."

"No."

"So you agree with me?"

"I don't know about the government wanting to kill you, though I doubt it. I know Deputy Pelton doesn't want to kill you. Or Principal Sergeant or Ms. Monroe. Or me, or my daughter Grace and her friends."

Jared jumped up, startling Ed, who started to get up to stop him from leaving, but sat back when he saw the boy was walking to the window. He relaxed. Jared looked out for a time, then turned back. He looked confused. "The other deputy hates me." He sat down again.

"What makes you say that?"

"He got angry right away. Said there'd be shit landing on me. He called me 'asshole.'"

Inwardly, Ed seethed, but kept his face neutral. "Yeah? I can see why you think he hates you." He paused. "Think he hates you enough to kill you?"

Jared's face contorted, his lips locked in a grimace, his forehead creased. "I sound paranoid. Don't you think I know that?"

"I didn't, but thanks for the honesty." Ed considered what he'd just learned. True paranoids don't exhibit that kind of tortured insight, or confess to it. And gamers, trying to play the crazy card, aren't distressed by their manipulations. After a moment, he said, "Are you okay talking about your conversation with Deputy Pelton last Monday?"

Jared's face paled. "She told you about things I said?"

He nodded. "She's not required to keep your confidentiality like I am."

He considered this. "What I say can be used against me."

"Yep."

"What about what I say to you? Can that be used in court?"

"Yes and no. Do you know what a 'fact witness' is?"

Jared shook his head.

"It means I can be called to testify about facts—did you come to see me, did you talk about the guns, did you threaten anybody while we talked, that sort of thing. They already know about what you said to the deputies from the sheriff's reports, so I won't be adding anything new if they call me."

"That's it?"

"They can also ask my professional opinion about what's going on with you, although your lawyer will object like hell to that and anyway, I won't tell them."

Jared looked at him. "I'm young, Doctor, but I know that a court order can make you tell them what they want to know."

"Yes, but I can refuse. You're my patient, if you agree to be, and there's the psychologist-patient privilege."

Jared relaxed. "I read about that after my dad told me I was going to see you." He waited a moment. "If you refuse a court order, you could be in contempt of court."

"I could. But you have my word, I won't reveal anything you tell me they don't know already." Ed reconsidered. "Wait, that's not entirely true. If you tell me you're about to harm someone else, I'm required to alert the sheriff and the intended victim."

Jared said nothing.

Ed said, "So my advice is, don't tell me." He smiled, hoping Jared would take it as a joke.

The boy's face stayed sober and distant. "You want to talk about what I said to Deputy Pelton?"

Ed nodded.

"I can hardly remember it. But, yeah, okay."

Ed relaxed as Jared's arms fully uncrossed, his hands resting in his lap.

"Deputy Pelton filled me in on the conversation, so I'll jog your memory. She said you believed you should kill your classmates to fight back against the government, because you believe that it wants to kill you. Do you remember any of that?"

Jared nodded. When he spoke, it came out almost too softly too hear. "I remember saying something about the government killing me, and I had to fight back. I know it's paranoid. I believed it when I said it, I think, but not now." He swallowed and looked down. "And I know, that sounds insincere, after what I just said."

When Jared looked up, Ed saw tears gathering in his eyes. He felt a surge of relief. They were past the trust issue, faster than Ed could have hoped.

He waited while Jared composed himself. "Don't worry, Jared. Just tell me the truth and we'll figure this out. So, are any of those parts true today?"

"Parts?"

"The part about the government or the part about having to kill your friends or the part about compassion for your friends because they'd discover how evil you are?"

Jared looked puzzled. "Oh. I said all that?" His smile was shy. "I guess I was pretty confusing."

Ed smiled too. "I'm an old fart. I can be a little slow."

"Well, I don't know about some of it, but I guess the government part and the killing my friends part are true. I mean, they were true on Monday." He looked down. "Not today."

Was Jared concocting his defense? True on Monday, not true today.

"Which parts are true today?"

"I don't feel like I have to kill my friends. I know I've scared a lot of them—my dad told me about the fathers at the school—and I feel bad about that. So I guess that part."

Ed nodded. "Okay. Deputy Pelton—can I call her Andi?"

Jared nodded.

"She says you told her you're evil because you want to kill your classmates, but you have to kill them out of compassion."

At that, Jared squinted, and Ed thought he detected a shift in the boy's mood. His reddening cheeks suggested arousal. Anxiety? Embarrassment? "I said that?" He was still for a moment. "I don't remember that one. It sounds sort of, I don't know, illogical."

"How so?"

Jared's eyes narrowed. After a moment, his arms again folded slowly across his chest.

Damn, Ed thought. *Losing him.* For a moment, he waited, thinking about why Jared could acknowledge his circular thinking, but couldn't or wouldn't answer Ed's question about it. Jared didn't speak, so Ed said, casually, "I suspect something in my question offended you."

At first, Jared stared at him, his eyes hard. After a moment, he said, "It didn't offend me. It was a trap."

Ed nodded. "Like I wanted to force you to speak against yourself?"

His eyes barely softened. Jared spoke very slowly. "If I deny it was illogical, you'd think I'm playing games with you. If I talk about why it's illogical, I'm admitting there's something wrong with me."

"I see." Good insight, quick intelligence, the ability to see consequences. Not commonly seen in delusional paranoids. Nor in someone building an insanity defense. Ed said, "Well, you said you didn't remember saying that in the first place, so let's drop it and focus on the compassion part. Would you be willing to explain that to me?"

Again, the boy squinted. *Trying to see if I'm setting another trap*, Ed thought. Jared said, "Maybe. What about it?"

"You're active in the Methodist youth group. You learn compassion there?"

He shook his head. "No, I told Deputy Pelton, it's Buddhist. I think I might be a Buddhist. Compassion is important in Buddhism."

"So you might be a Buddhist."

Jared looked hard at Ed, calculating something in his mind. "Does it matter?"

Ed shrugged. "Maybe, maybe not. Do you meditate?"

"Why?" The voice was edged, sharp.

Warding me off. "I'm curious. Interested."

Jared frowned. "Answer me, please. *Why?*"

"I practiced Buddhism for a few years. Meditated, no booze, ate vegetarian. Then all of a sudden, poof." He snapped his fingers. "I just stopped."

"What happened?"

"Got seduced by a ribeye steak and a bottle of pinot noir."

Jared almost laughed, checked himself. "Okay, yeah, I meditate, some days. I try to eat vegetarian and organic. I like the Buddha's teachings."

"About compassion."

"Yeah."

"So I'm confused about how killing people to prevent their suffering is compassionate."

"Deputy Pelton asked that too."

"What did you tell her?"

"That no one will understand."

Ed had a hunch. "Jared? Do *you* understand?"

It was as if a curtain dropped between them. Jared's arms locked hard across his chest again and he leaned back, closing down. "No more questions." But when Ed didn't move, he added, "Today."

60

When Ed called her, Andi asked, "How'd your session with Jared go?"

"Hello to you too." He considered what to say. "I see what you mean about not being able to pin anything down."

"Any first impressions?"

Here comes the crunch. "You know I can't discuss anything he said."

No response. *Can't be good*, he thought.

"So you called why?"

"Say hello to my girl, be a responsible relationship partner. Things like that." He kept it light.

"Well, then, duty done."

Her tone made him think of thin ice. "Hey, Andi. Give me a break. You know I can't—"

"—Talk about your case. Or my case. Which I have to get busy on at the moment."

The call ended. He laid his phone on the desk, suddenly annoyed, but it buzzed. Andi.

"Sorry about that. Just feeling the pressure and hoping you'd find something to help out."

Ed didn't answer right away, torn between annoyance and understanding, a miniature version of Jared's conflict between rage and compassion. He said, "Yeah, I know. Look, I'm thinking I'll give Merwin a call."

"Yeah. Do that. And if he tells you anything I'm allowed to hear, let me know."

She hung up again. The second ending didn't feel much better than the first.

61

"Charlie Merwin here."

Ed smiled. He enjoyed the sound of Merwin's voice, which reminded him of a gravelly old comedian who was just about to laugh at his own joke. "Merwin! It's Northrup. How've you been, old man?"

"Ed, you rascal! I'm exactly your age, dear. What the hell is manifesting your ignorance this time?" He laughed.

"I've got another nut that's hard to crack." He always started these calls to Merwin with the old grad student joke.

"As always. Well, my brain's yours for the picking, such as it is."

Ed chuckled. "Merwin, you're the smartest, funniest, and most cynical friend I've got."

Merwin laughed. "That's a vanishingly small comparison pool."

"Okay, look, I've got a stumper, and I need your help."

"A Montana stumper? Will wonders never cease? Well, you can run it past me, but don't expect me to keep up." His laugh filled the phone. In grad school, Merwin had been short and skinny, but in the thirty years since, he'd gained 120 pounds and no inches; he'd turned into a pink beach ball. His rotund and rosy looks were as infectious as his good humor—people chuckled when they saw him—and he enjoyed laughing at himself as much as those people enjoyed looking at him.

"Seriously. I've got a problem."

"You always call with a problem. Why don't you ever call just to schmooze?"

"Because you don't like to schmooze and because you do like to help me solve problems. Makes you feel smarter than me."

"True, true, and related. I *am* smarter than thou, my son." Merwin chuckled. "Okay, so what's the stumper this time?"

He told Merwin about Jared, detailing carefully the contradictions and the confusions. Merwin, as always, listened quietly from start to finish before asking any questions. Charlie Merwin was one of the best clinical listeners Ed knew.

"You've considered schizophrenia? Age of onset is right."

"Yeah, but he's got no risk factors for that. And the paranoia is intermittent, which is wrong."

"No infections during pregnancy? No autoimmune diseases during childhood?"

"Nope. No family history either, back three generations the parents know of. I asked them yesterday about all that. He's clean as a whistle. I don't like the suddenness of the onset either."

"Okay. His friends and his parents say he's been quieter and maybe more irritable than usual, for how long?"

"Six, maybe seven weeks. No longer."

"And he rented this storage unit when?"

"Seven weeks ago."

Merwin was quiet. Ed read his mind. "I wondered too: coincidence, or connection?"

"Your sheriff, what's his name? What does he say?" A few summers ago, Merwin had vacationed in Jefferson. He and Ben Stewart, as different as a beach ball and a boulder, had taken an immediate liking to one another. Ben, six-two, 260 muscular pounds, rough-voiced and commanding; Merwin, five-six, round and ruddy, refined as an oyster's pearl. Merwin called Ben's sayings "picturesque." He was asking about one now.

"The sheriff's name? Ben. What's he say about what?"

"Coincidences." Merwin answered his own question. "He says, 'Coincidences ain't.' Love that man's way with words." Merwin laughed.

"Anyway, back to your case. Don't chalk it up to coincidence unless more evidence arises. Treat the two as connected."

"So he becomes irritable and rents the unit at the same time, for the same reason."

"Indeed, my friend. The question is, what's the reason? Let's go through the contradictions again."

They did, laboriously.

"I'm curious about your hunch. You think maybe the boy—what's his name?"

"Jared."

"Jared. So you're thinking Jared is delusional, paranoid, but has simultaneous, or at least retrospective, insight into it, and also may be puzzled about why he believes his delusion. Did I understand that correctly?"

"Yeah, exactly. When I asked him if he understood himself, he shut down the interview."

"Aha! We have ourselves a clue."

Ed chuckled; Merwin loved drama. "And what does our clue mean, oh sage?"

"Damned if I know." His laugh echoed in the phone. "For some reason, he acknowledges his confusion, but refuses to talk about it. What might that presage?"

"If I knew that—"

"You wouldn't have called. Sadly, I'm as flummoxed as you. Why would a...young man...?" Merwin went silent.

Ed waited.

"Don't leave me to labor alone," Merwin said.

"Okay. Two things come to mind. He's trying to control things, or he's afraid of what he'd say."

"Do you find the lad to be controlling?"

"I don't see it."

"So."

"So by elimination, he's afraid of what he'd say." Ed remembered what Jared had said during the interview. "When we talked, he said something quasi-paranoid, then said it just came out."

"He could be afraid he's not in control of his thinking. Or of what he'd learn by talking. I'd wager on one or the other, boyo. I presume you've scheduled another interview?"

"Yeah, tomorrow morning."

"Ah. And how did Jared react when you proposed it?"

The light went on. "Oh! He agreed immediately. No hesitation. As if he wants me to find out what frightens him."

"You know what he's frightened of already."

Ed hesitated. Merwin usually brought him to this point, the moment where something became obvious to Merwin, but remained shrouded from Ed's view. "Help me out, Charlie."

"Think."

"He's frightened...no, terrified...of..." Of course. "Of his delusions. He's afraid they mean he really is a killer."

"No shit, Sherlock." Both men waited. Finally Merwin asked, "Was there anything else the lovely Andrea told you about her second interview?"

Ah. "She said something about health foods."

"Health foods?"

"Apparently he eats a lot of organics. I think she said he told her he just wanted to get home so he could eat healthy again. He complained about the jail food, but she said he sounded apologetic about complaining."

"Unlike someone who actually believes the government wants to kill him."

"Exactly. Totally confusing."

"Not at all. Take a look at his organic foods. Jared could be poisoning himself. We had a case here in Minneapolis a year or so ago, some fly-by-night Internet organic food supplier with no toxicity controls. Spread ergotism across a dozen zip codes. Let me think."

Ed waited, thinking about the organic food connection.

Merwin asked, "How many days did he spend in jail?"

"He was brought in Monday morning, and released in the late afternoon Thursday."

"Something more than seventy-two hours. Perhaps long enough for whatever he was eating at home to leave his system, so his thinking cleared somewhat. I'm speculating, of course."

"I considered physical causes, but I was thinking brain tumor or an injury. I couldn't see how either one would account for delusions flaring up, then returning to normal."

"Perhaps you're right. No, correction. Probably you're right. With a brain lesion, the fluctuating psychosis has quite low probability."

"So, what foods have you got in mind?"

"That, my friend, is your homework. I have no clue, but I'd start with ergotism."

"Ergotism?"

"Think the Salem Witch Trials."

Merwin was laughing as they hung up. Ed was not.

62

Ergotism? Ed Googled the word. As he read the article, his frown deepened. A disease caused by consuming grain products infected with the fungus ergot, symptoms included hallucinations, but also convulsions, and over time, gangrene. Some people apparently believed that the witches of Salem had hallucinations and seizures from eating ergot-infected rye bread.

Convulsions? Nobody had mentioned Jared having convulsions. Ed leaned back and rubbed his forehead, thinking. Was it likely that Jared ate infected bread at home but his parents didn't? For that matter, everyone in Jefferson bought their bread at Art's Fine Foods, so if there'd been an infected bread delivery six or seven weeks ago, wouldn't there have been more cases?

Ed thought for a moment about Art's advice to sit his horse and watch what develops. "Well, Art," he said, reaching for his phone. "Not this time." He dialed the hospital.

Doc wasn't there. The receptionist said he was probably at home. Ed dialed there.

"Hi, Ed. Calling about Art?"

"Something else just now. How is he, though?"

"Hanging on. But it won't be long."

"Figured that, when you kept him there." Ed took a moment. "Anyway, I have a question. Have you seen any cases of ergotism here in the valley in the last, oh, three months?"

"Ergotism? No, none. Why?"

"I'm trying to figure out what's going on with Jared Hansen."

"Ah. You're thinking of the hallucinations. Is he having convulsions?"

"That's what bothers me. No sign of them."

"Looks like you're back to the drawing board."

"Looks like it." As he ended the call, Ed thought, *Scratch ergotism. Damn.*

He glanced at his watch. *11:30.*

He had a date for lunch with Andi at the Angler. On the Saturdays she wasn't on duty, they'd make a long afternoon of it, often ending up in bed. Or, last summer, lying naked in the soft warm grass by the river. Given how frustrated she was about the case, though, that didn't look likely. Ed turned back to his computer, checking the weather anyway. Afternoon temp: 73 degrees, full sun. He smiled. *A fellow can always hope.*

Then he remembered Magnus's email, and his promise to call the rancher this morning. *Damn.* He dialed Andi.

She answered with a long, breathy sound, her voice sounded sultry. "You about ready for lunch and some, ah, afternoon delight?" She made a soft come-hither sound into the phone.

He smiled into the phone. "Guess you're feeling better."

She chuckled. "You could say that. Shame to waste a warm afternoon."

Ed felt his erection stir. *Hell, sexually I'm not a day over 35.* "I'm up for it." He matched her smoky voice. "Literally."

"Glad I still have an effect."

"Oh, girl." He paused. "But I have to call Magnus first. I have no idea how long that'll take."

"Magnus? What for?"

He hesitated. *Damn confidentiality.* "He's down in Mexico on some business; I told him I'd call today before lunch." *Mostly true.*

"Well, it can't take all afternoon. I'll wait for you at the Angler." Her heavy breathing filled the phone a moment. "Or we could just skip the meal and..." A pause. "Gather by the river." She let her voice trail off, then hung up.

Ed enjoyed the momentary arousal, but thinking about Magnus settled him right down. He called Luisa Anderssen.

"Luisa, Ed here. Can you give me Mack's number at your ranch in Mexico? I promised I'd call him."

"What is wrong?" Alarm tinged her voice. "Has something happened? Has he told you about falling?"

So she knows that much. "Yeah, he sent an email." He hesitated about what to say. "I just want to stay in touch with him while he's down there. We'll work it out when he's back here in the valley."

"Ah," she said. "That is good of you. They gave us a new number, which I do not yet remember. Let me find it."

While she was away, Ed considered how much he cared for her, and could only imagine the anguish she was feeling at this insidious change in her husband.

Luisa returned to the phone and gave him the number. "Please, Ed. You will tell me if something has grown worse?"

Again he hesitated, his responsibility to keep Magnus's privacy weighing on him, but then, frustrated with holding back from this friend of twenty-five years, said, "Of course I will, Luisa."

"Thank you, Ed. Please help *mi hombre.*"

63

"What's wrong with me?" Magnus said immediately after picking up the phone. Static crackled on the line.

"Whoa, Mack. I need information first. Is this a good time to talk?"

Magnus said, "The email had all the information I can give. Can't you tell me what you think it is, or what it *might* be?" His impatience was palpable.

"Can't do that without more answers, Mack."

Magnus was silent. "You're right, Ed. I'm sorry. Do your job and I'll be patient. You'll tell me after the questions?"

"If I can."

"All right. Forgive my impatience. I'm not handling this well."

"No apology necessary, Mack. You have reasons to be upset." He paused to frame the first question. "When you found yourself huddling in that cold courtyard, was it so vivid that it felt like it was actually happening? At that moment?"

"I didn't make that clear?"

"Yes, you did, but I need to be sure: Was it like it was actually happening *right then*, or like you *remembered* it happening at some earlier time?" For no reason, the static on the line reminded him of Andi's sultry breath. He jumped up and began pacing, scrambling to keep his focus.

Magnus's voice sounded raw. "It was actually happening. Or felt like it was."

"Describe the pain that you felt in your gut."

Magnus repeated what he'd written in the email.

"But where exactly? When you say 'in your gut,' where precisely do you mean?"

"Cramps. In the bowel."

"Upper or lower bowel?

At first, there was no answer. Then, hesitant, "Lower."

"*Where* lower?"

"Please." This came softly.

"I'm sorry. But..." He didn't want to say what he suspected, in case he was wrong.

Magnus said, so softly Ed barely heard, "In the anus."

Ed nodded. *As I feared.* He gave Magnus a moment, heard a ragged breath. "Thank you, Magnus." He waited another moment. "Have you had any digestive problems in Mexico? Did you drink the water?"

Magnus snapped, "*Árboles Blancos'* water is pure, Doctor."

Doctor? Ed caught the anger embedded in that title. "Sorry. So, no digestive problems, then?" He took the silence as assent. "Okay, has this happened before yesterday?"

"Which? The terror at night or seeing the arches or the pain? The fear has been happening for weeks—it's why I drink. What I saw and felt on the hill, only once."

"Just a few more questions, then, Magnus, bear with me. Still having nightmares?"

"Yes, every night I don't drink, but I don't remember them. I think they wake me up, and that's when I feel the claw on my chest."

"But you remember nothing at all about the nightmares? If you think about it?"

Again, a pause. "I don't think about it, and when I say nothing, I mean nothing."

Ed felt Magnus's frustration flaring. "All right, Mack. Do you have headaches?"

"No. Never." The voice came clipped.

"Are there times when you just feel numb?"

"No. When I'm not afraid, I feel only a deep sadness. For part of the time, riding Rojo, or sitting last evening on the porch talking with Ernesto, I felt happy. Or at least less desperate."

"Ernesto?" Perhaps a clue?

"He owns one-third of the ranch and runs it for us. He's an old friend."

Ed thought he heard some emotion in Magnus's voice. He waited, but only silence followed. Finally, he said, "Mack, with your permission, I am going to say some words. I want you to tell me exactly what you experience when I do, all right? This might be quite painful for you. May I say the words?"

"Wait. Tell me why."

"Because I suspect it will give me a clue to what is happening, but it could set off that fear or that pain again, or maybe both. If it does, it will only be temporary and I'll help you with it."

"And if nothing happens?"

"Failed experiment."

"Very well. Say the words."

Ed hesitated, then said, "Stay away from the infirmary." Ed strained, listening. Ragged breathing mingled with the static on the line. After a moment, he said, "Magnus?"

Gasping sounds came back, then a faint "Here."

"Tell me what's happening to you."

"I can't...breathe. It's...back. Help me!" He was almost whimpering. Ed felt a stab of sorrow, his friend so afflicted.

He kept his voice calm, assuring. "Breathe like we practiced, Mack. Slow, easy. Use your calming words. Breathe into the phone so I can hear you." Ed listened carefully to the sound of Magnus's breaths, which after a moment began easing, stretching out. After the episode passed, Magnus's voice cracked, "What...was that?"

"Was it like the night terror, the claw?"

"Yes. I couldn't catch my breath. What is it?"

"Was your heart pounding?"

"Damn it, what the hell *is* it?"

"Take it easy, Mack. I can only give a hunch, but it sounded like a panic attack to me. And the fact that you responded well to what we do for panic attacks—"

Magnus interrupted. "So what caused it?"

"Could be a number of things, but I think you were starting into a flashback, and that the panic attacks are associated with that. A flashback is—"

"I know damn well what a flashback is. What caused it?"

"That I don't know," Ed paused, unsure whether to ask this; he'd prefer being face-to-face. He asked anyway. "Maybe *you* know?"

Magnus breathed into the receiver, but did not reply.

Ed waited.

Magnus asked, "Can you help me?"

Ed hesitated. He knew the added suffering his help was likely to cause his friend. "Yes, Mack, I can, but you'll feel worse before you're better. When can you come home?"

Another long pause. "But I'll feel better?"

Ed hated to promise. Too many variables. But he said, "I'll do everything I can." He heard a rustling sound, pages being turned.

Magnus said, "I'll fly back tomorrow. Tomorrow's Sunday, right?"

"Yeah. We can meet on Monday, then." He flipped through his own appointment book. "Noon is my only free hour." At the word "noon," the picture of Andi and himself on their blanket by the river invaded his mind. He shook his head, refocused on Magnus. He considered how to say the next thing. "Mack?"

"What?"

"Put away the rifle."

"Why?"

"I can't help you if you're dead."

64

Andi was waiting at the Angler, chatting with Ted Coldry at the bar. She winked at Ed as he approached them. "Hey, good lookin'," she said.

Ed said, "Whatcha got cookin'?"

Ted smiled beneath arched eyebrows. "Perhaps a pre-prandial drink, before breaking into song and dance?"

Ed couldn't remember what the word *pre-prandial* meant. Something about foreplay? Had Andi told Ted about their afternoon delight? She couldn't have. "What's 'pre-prandial'?"

Ted said, "Latin scholars inform us it means *before lunch*."

"Ah." Ed looked at the glass of wine resting in front of Andi. "Sure, Ted. Anything new on pour?"

Ted said, "Yes, as a matter of fact. Bitterroot Brewery's summer ale just arrived. Care for one?"

"Perfect. It almost feels like summer outside, although it's still winter in here."

Ted nodded. "Furnace went out last night. Lane's downstairs working on it."

Ed smiled, thinking of the soft river grasses and the springtime air waiting for Andi and him this afternoon. He started humming "*Down by the Old Mill Stream.*"

Ted set the beer in front of him and winked. When he went back to his end of the bar, Ed grinned and whispered to Andi, "A loaf of bread, a glass of beer, a bite of thou."

She laughed. "Not quite Omar Khayyám."

"A loose rendering."

"But I like its, ah, thrust."

" 'Thrust,' is it?"

Ted rubbed a wine glass with his white towel. "You two look enraptured."

"We're taking the afternoon off, Ted," said Andi.

Ted looked beatific. "Ah! One wonders what, besides the afternoon, will be taken off. In any case, to enhance the festivities, may I recommend the mussels Scampi?"

While they waited, Ed filled her in about his conversation with Merwin, or at least what he could share without breaching Jared's privacy. He mentioned the poisoned food hypothesis.

She said, "Is that possible? A poison?"

Ed shrugged. "Sure, but the question is, which one? I considered one kind, but it didn't pan out. There are thousands. The one advantage to the poison theory is that it could explain the changes you observed in him between the first day and his release."

"How so?"

"Well, hypothetically, if he ingested something that caused the paranoia, he presumably didn't have access to it while he was in custody. After two days, it could have been eliminated or at least metabolized enough to end the delusions."

"He peed it out, eh?"

"Hypothetically." He waited a moment. "There's a flaw in Merwin's theory, though."

"What's that?"

"The food in your jail is a poison in its own right."

She punched his shoulder.

He chuckled. "Or maybe the jail poison's an antidote to our real poison—like using chlorine to kill bacteria in water supplies."

"Well, it gives us a direction to look. We'll expand the tox report from DCI to look for any poisons they can find."

"Do that. So you already did a urine test?"

"Of course we—" but she started to giggle. "Urine. Pee. Penis. Puts me in mind of our upcoming festivities, as Ted calls them. I say we grab our mussels and a bottle of wine and mosey down to the river."

Ed was starting to say something about Mosey in the bulrushes when his cell phone buzzed. He glanced at the screen. "It's Grace." As he listened, he grimaced. "When was this?" he asked. After a moment's listening, he said, "I'm on my way."

At the same moment, Andi's phone rang. She listened, said, "On it!" As she jumped up, she said, "I've got to get over to the school. Somebody just called in—"

Ed interrupted. "Grace is there. Jared just came into the school and is ranting about everyone hating him." He stood and took Andi's arm. "He's my patient. I'm going."

She pulled free. "This is a police issue, Ed. The court order prohibits him from going to the school for anything."

Just then, Ted came out of the kitchen with their mussels. "Whoa! Your mussels! Are you minks that hot?"

Andi barked, "Trouble at the school. Jared's there."

Ed pointed at the mussels. "Refrigerator?"

"I could, but I wouldn't sell you cold mussels; the butter clumps. I'll make another order when you're ready." Ted looked at them. "Be careful over there."

On the way out, Andi repeated, "This is my job, Ed."

He jumped into the passenger side of her Suburban. "He's my job, too."

Andi shrugged and backed out onto Division Street and turned toward the high school at the edge of town. After a hundred yards, a siren sounded in the distance, and Andi's phone rang. She said to Ed, "Take it for me."

He hit *Speaker*, then *Talk*.

Callie's voice said, "Dispatch here. Backup's on the way, you can hear the sirens. Our caller didn't know if the boy was armed, so they're coming armed and vested."

Andi glanced at Ed. "Got it," she said. To Ed, she said, "Hang up." For a moment, she watched the road, then, as they approached the school, looked at him. "We may have a shooting about to go down. You stay in the car."

He shook his head. "Grace is inside." His phone buzzed again. He snatched it and hit the *Talk* button." Grace? You okay?" He listened, then relayed to Andi, "Jared ran when he heard the sirens. The kids don't know where he went."

Andi said, "Is he armed?"

"Grace, was he armed?" He listened, then said to Andi, "No sign of a weapon."

"How'd he leave? Car? Bike? On foot?"

Ed repeated the question on the phone, then said to her, "Driving." To Grace, he asked, "What kind of car?" To Andi, he said, "Green Dodge Ram pickup. Older model, pretty beat up."

Andi handed him her phone. "Call Callie—dial 137." He did, put it on *Speaker*, held it near Andi. She relayed the information to Callie. "Reroute everybody. He's not at the high school now. Send cars north and south to watch the highway, and the rest start patrolling town and the surrounding roads. He's driving an older green Dodge Ram, pretty beat up. Consider him armed." She looked over at Ed. "And dangerous." As she finished speaking, she spun the wheel and her tires squealed into the high school parking lot.

"Let's go see what happened. The guys'll find Jared." They ran into the school and down the hall to the cafeteria.

SUNDAY, DAY SEVEN

65

The deputies did not find Jared, not that afternoon nor that evening, nor had he surfaced by Sunday morning. A little before seven, the sun just lighting the mountains, Ben Stewart finished talking on the phone and for a moment, before hanging up, stared at the receiver. Andi and Ordrew waited on the far side of Ben's desk, yawning. They'd been prowling the back roads of the county all night. Ben, ignoring his overtime budget, had kept all but two deputies on duty overnight, searching. Now he slammed the phone roughly in its cradle.

"The Hansens are frantic. They ain't thinkin' any too clear, but they can't figure out where he might have gone. Crap on toast! I got my own hunches, but what do you think?"

Ordrew said, "Like I said, this was gonna happen if we let him go."

Ben raised his hand and waved him off. "Don't break your arm pattin' yourself on the back. Answer my question."

Andi said, "I'm thinking Missoula. He could hide around here, but he can't get food and water without drawing attention."

Ordrew grunted. "Farther than Missoula. Some place where he can rent another unit and start over."

"With what?" Ben grunted. "According to his dad, the boy didn't take no money, no clothes, nothin'."

"That means squat," Ordrew said. "He hid nine rifles and 200 rounds, for Christ's sake, and nobody would've found *them* if the old lady hadn't got suspicious. The kid's a planner. He could have money, clothes, even more weapons stashed anywhere."

Andi nodded. "Possible. He goes to Missoula to buy organic foods." She jotted a note. "Brad, when we're done here, call Missoula County and ask them to canvass all the rental units and organic food stores in the Missoula area. Get his DMV info and fax it to them." She handed him the note. "I'll

166

call Marie Hansen and find out what food Jared buys in Missoula."

"Have somebody else do it. I want to keep looking for the little shit."

Ben said, "The canvass's yours, Brad. You're needin' to win some points around here."

Ordrew grabbed the note and stuffed it in his shirt pocket.

Andi said, "The kids in the cafeteria said he sounded agitated. What he said to them sounds like what we heard in the first interview, pure paranoia. Ed said he was acting 'disorganized,' which I guess is a bad sign. When he heard the sirens, he took off. Monica Sergeant saw him run past her office and she confirmed he looked both terrified and angry at the same time. Ed said that's disorganized."

She waited a moment, but neither Ben nor Ordrew spoke. Her partner was visibly angry. "Brad's right, Ben," she said. "Jared's a planner." She waited another moment. "But I don't think *this* was planned."

"Explain that," Ben said.

"Ed's got a theory that Jared is somehow getting some poison in his body, maybe from his diet at home. It causes the paranoid thinking. While he's in custody, he doesn't get the poison, and the level in his system drops, so he calms down. When he's at home, he gets another dose somehow, so he's paranoid again."

"Are you serious?" Ordrew said, visibly angry. "Poison? You people'll try any damn idea to avoid the obvious, won't you?"

Andi bridled. "What's so obvious, Brad?"

"This kid's a killer and now he's in the wind."

Ben said, his voice very low, "We got us two kinds of mistakes on this job, and like you say, Brad, one is avoidin' the obvious. The other one is jumpin' to conclusions without no evidence. My question for you is, if he's a killer, why'd he only yell at those kids? Why didn't he shoot?"

Momentarily, Ordrew looked surprised, then said, "We've got his weapons."

Andi said, "Ben's got a point. He could find a weapon if he wanted to."

The sheriff said, "No use arguin' what-ifs and maybes." He looked at Ordrew. "If the *evidence* rules out poison or mental illness or whatever the hell, and we're left with your killer theory, we'll be all over it. Either way, we gotta find the kid. Until we got us something to go on, I want you to open your mind." He rubbed his jaw, considering something. "No, I ain't just wantin' it. I'm makin' it an order. You got that, Bradley?"

Ordrew glared a moment, then quickly closed it off. "Sure, Sheriff. Open it is."

Andi met Ben's eyes briefly. "Okay, then," the sheriff said. "Get your butts out there and find me that kid."

66

Jack Kollier was hanging out at Callie's reception desk. When Andi and Ordrew came out of Ben's office, Callie gestured Andi over, and said, "What say you arrest this character for disturbing my peace?"

Jack laughed, but Andi thought she saw something in his eyes. Loneliness? "Just asking questions, Callie. It's my job."

Callie grumped. "Well, your job's keeping me from doing mine."

Andi smiled at the reporter. "Like I said, Jack, you're persistent."

"This case is big. First, we have terrorism in Monastery Valley. That's news. And now the terrorist's disappeared."

Andi felt a chill. She narrowed her eyes. "Who says we've got terrorism?" *Ordrew?*

"I have to protect my source, Andi. But it's a good source."

Ordrew.

She struggled to think of something to say. "We'll find the boy. But who told you this is terrorism?"

He shook his head. His eyes did look sad. "I won't, Deputy. I can't."

Andi smiled. "Good for you, Jack. Doing your job." His sadness brought out the protector in her. And reminded her of Jared.

67

Ed was beat. They hadn't found Jared all night. While Andi and the deputies were searching, Ed had waited up, checking in periodically by cell phone. A little after six, he crawled into bed, exhausted, but worried about everyone, Andi out on the night roads, Jared lost somewhere, Magnus in a crisis. Who could sleep?

With a groan, he surrendered and got out of the sleepless bed at seven-thirty.

After showering and having a cup of coffee, Ed cleaned house. Vacuumed the carpet. Dusted the fireplace mantle and the tables in the living room. Did the dishes. Cleaned the toilet and sink and shower, wiped the bathroom floor. None of his clanking disturbed Grace, who slept till noon. At lunchtime, as he spooned tuna fish salad onto a slice of wheat bread, she opened her bedroom door, a bear emerging from her den in springtime. "Thanks for the quiet morning, Northrup," she growled, and stomped grumpily into the bathroom for her usual 45-minute Sunday shower. He leaned against the counter and stared out the window at the mountains, and took a bite of his sandwich. *Worrying about your girlfriend and having a teenage daughter were fun. Real fun.*

His cell phone buzzed. Thinking it was Andi, he hit *Talk*.

"I have to see you this afternoon," Magnus Anderssen said, his voice sandpapery.

Ed thought he sounded angry. *No, not angry, desperate.*

"I just landed in Missoula—I can't wait till tomorrow. I'll be back to the valley in three hours." A pause. "Ed, I'm sorry to demand. Can we please meet? At the Anderhold?" The question softened it.

Ed held the phone away from his mouth and rubbed his neck. The endless night had drained him, and he had hoped to salvage some afternoon time with Andi. "God, I'm sorry, Mack. I have a lot going on this afternoon. We've got that appointment for noon tomorrow; let's do it then."

Magnus's voice wavered. "I can't wait, Ed. I won't make it through another night." Ed heard a cough, or perhaps a sob, half-smothered. "Luisa had to stay on the phone with me all night long to keep me...alive." He whispered the last word.

Alarmed, Ed said, "Okay, but I can't make three-thirty. I'll come out to the Anderhold at, let's see..." He looked at his watch. "How's five o'clock?" Maybe he could still manage a little time with Andi, if she ever came home from work.

"Can you make it four?"

Ed winced. *Was he being selfish? Maybe. Well, yes.* "Five o'clock," he said. "I'll be there. Wait for me."

After ending the call and finishing his half-sandwich, Ed poured a rare after-lunch cup of coffee, thinking of Ted's word. *Pre-prandial.* What he had was post-prandial guilt at putting Magnus off. He shifted to thoughts of the afternoon. *If I'm going to be selfish, might as well go all out.* If Andi got home soon enough, maybe they'd squeeze the riverbank in.

No way, he thought, giving it up. *She's been up all night.*

He took his coffee out to the front porch. The silky spring sky was a streaky blue, with ribbons of thin, white cloud stretching over the mountains. The buds on the hardwoods and the tips of the pines glowed, a pale chartreuse coloring the sloping valley below his ridge. He wondered when the surprise storms of April would strike.

Hell, there'd already been the flood. Come to think of it, weren't Magnus and Jared Hansen surprise storms? Whatever Jared's problem—a toxin, some mental process, or God knows what else—the boy was in trouble, trouble that could tear the valley apart, and Ed had no working theory that tipped in any helpful direction. Instead of an afternoon with Andi, he should get back on his computer and search for paranoia-stimulating toxins. He took a last look at the soft, inviting sky, and stood up, resigned to work instead of play. Inside, he heard Grace's bedroom door creak open. *Gotta oil that hinge.*

A thought: Maybe he could get Grace to do the research for him.

Grace came onto the porch. Ed started to ask her if she was free for the afternoon, but her troubled look stopped him. A long Sunday sleep and luxurious shower always left Grace sunny. "Northrup," she said, her voice low, anxious. "I gotta talk to you, but you have to, like, promise only me and you will know about what I tell you."

"Only you and me."

"Yeah, that's what I said."

"No, I was correcting your grammar. 'You and I' is correct, 'me and you' isn't."

"Forget that, Northrup. I've got something huge to tell you and you gotta keep it between us."

A hollow space opened in his chest. "Sounds serious."

"Totally. Really, nobody else hears about it. *Promise* me." She looked frightened. "Please?"

"Tell me what it's about first."

She shook her head. "Promise. *Please.*"

"Okay," he said. "I promise."

She took out her cell phone. "I got this text," she said, tapping the screen and then handing the phone to him.

He read.

grace, help. police looking for me. they'll kill me. need talk to your dad, but he'll hand me over unless you help. get him to promise not take me to police? pls? need his help. PLS!

He took a long breath to calm himself. *A rough day just got rougher.* He handed the phone back to Grace. "When did that come?"

"While I was in the shower."

"Do you know where he is?"

She shook her head. "What you read is all I know. You've gotta help him, Northrup."

He nodded. "Yep, I do," he said. He thought of his appointment with Magnus at five, frowned.

Grace said, "What?"

"What what?"

"You made a face."

He forced himself to relax. "Just worried. I have to see Magnus later this afternoon." He looked at his watch. "In four hours."

"You won't turn Jared in?"

Ed looked at the greening trees on the slope down toward town, then up to the blue-white springtime sky. The afternoon had just stretched too thin. "Well, I can't promise that completely, Grace. Jared's ill, and it could be important to protect him from getting worse. Do you understand that?"

"Kind of. But me and him, I mean, him and I are friends, and if you turn him in, he'll hate me."

Ed instinctively started to correct her grammar, but bit his tongue. Instead, he said, "Look, Jared's sickness already makes him hate you and the other kids, at least some of the time. It's a good sign that he wants help, but if he doesn't get the protection he needs, it could flare up and somebody could get hurt. Badly hurt."

Her eyes had widened as he spoke. "You're talking about those guns?"

He nodded, although the guns were in custody now. "So if I can't give him what he needs, and I need to bring Andi or Ben Stewart in to keep him safe, I'll have to do it, Grace."

She nodded slowly. "Yeah. I guess." She looked at him. "What should I tell him?"

"Tell him I'll meet him in my office in a half hour." He considered something. "And tell him I won't turn him in when we meet." That much was true, as far as it went.

She tapped it into the phone. They sat silently until her phone beeped three times. She grabbed it, read the text. "He says, 'Not office. Sheriff's office too close. Meet me…'" She handed him the phone. He read.

"…meet me at river. lovers lane. nobody there til night."

Ed nodded and gave her the phone. "Tell him yes. Thirty minutes."

She tapped the phone. A few moments later, they heard the beeps. She scanned it. "He'll be there. He says come alone." She looked at Ed. "Maybe I should come with you?"

For a moment, Ed hesitated, remembering the psychotic rage. Would Jared be safe? He shook his head. "No, he says alone. Tell him okay. Alone. Say I trust him."

"Do you, Northrup?"

He thought about it. "Yeah, I do. Enough to start this, anyway." He knew Andi would be furious that he wasn't looping her in.

Nothing about this felt right.

68

Lovers' Lane was a narrow strip of gravel that passed for a parking lot alongside the Monastery River, shaded from the afternoon sun by a grove of tall cottonwoods and larches. Five or six vehicles could park, noses toward the river, leaving enough respectful space between them that the sounds and the rocking of the other cars wouldn't be too distracting. From the parking area, well-worn paths threaded into the trees, leading to grassy patches along the riverbank. On cool spring evenings, the grass flourished and grew tall, but when the weather warmed enough, it lay flat, pressed down by nightly blankets and the rolling weight of young bodies. In the summer, unless it was pouring rain or cold, the deputies visited the lane during the evenings, until ten o'clock at night. Before ten, everyone stayed in their cars. After ten, the grassy areas took their pummeling.

The lane was empty. Ed eased his pickup up to the trees and glanced at his watch: a few minutes before one-thirty. He climbed out of the truck and leaned against the tailgate, listening to the river rushing spring-high over rocks. The snowmelt, fed by the hard snows of winter and then the rain-gorged flood, still swelled the river, which rolled high and violent but was holding within its banks. The soft gauze of new growth on the cottonwoods and larches cast a filmy shade, but diamonds of glinting sunlight sparkled off the river water still spreading ten yards beyond the farther, lower bank. This near the water, the afternoon air smelled wet and fertile, and the dark blue sky, the morning's ribbons of cloud now melted off, poured like liquid through the yellow-green canopy. Ed wondered what condition the boy would be in. If he arrived at all.

Gravel crunched behind him. Ed turned. Jared stood at the far edge of the parking area, resting a rifle in the crook of his arm. "I'm not going to shoot, Doctor. But I need to protect myself."

How had the boy gotten another rifle? Alarmed, Ed forced himself to speak calmly. "I understand that, Jared. Is the safety on?"

"Yes, sir."

Ed relaxed. "Sir" meant, if not respect, at least a degree of rationality. "Where do you want to talk, Jared?"

The boy looked around. "Right here. Where I can see everything."

Ed nodded. "Fine. How about if we sit on the tailgate?"

Jared shook his head. "I'll stand here."

Ed nodded, lowered the gate, and settled himself on it. "So, how can I help, Jared?"

"Something's wrong. Yesterday, I hated everybody" He paused. "No, I didn't hate them, I was terrified of them." He stopped. "No, I think I was afraid of myself. I wanted to kill again. I went to the school to do something—I don't really remember what. I didn't remember it wasn't a school day. Then I heard a siren and got scared and I ran. I've been hiding all night and all day. Can you help me?"

"I want to, but I need to talk to you a lot more."

"If I go back, they'll arrest me again."

Ed nodded. "Yeah, they will. So, let's talk about what we can do. You were scared of yourself, but you scared the kids at school yesterday."

"I did?"

Ed was struck by the innocence in those words. "You didn't know you scared them?"

"No. I was trying to warn them about me."

"So why did you run away when you heard the siren?"

"Because the siren meant the government was coming for me. That made me want to kill them. It was awful." Even across the gravel expanse, Ed could see his clear brown eyes filling with tears. *This is no act*, he thought.

"But you don't feel that way now?" He glanced at the rifle.

Jared shook his head slowly. "No, sir. I feel...confused, I guess. And I'm scared, but I don't want to hurt anybody."

"What do you think makes the difference, Jared? I mean, between one day wanting to kill people, and another day feeling like this?"

Jared stared a moment at the rifle cradled on his arm; his shoulders, so squared against danger a moment ago, slumped. "I don't know." Ed heard the gravel-rasp of sorrow in the boy's voice.

"What have you been doing since yesterday?"

"Hiding. I drove toward Missoula, but I realized I didn't have any money or clothes, so I hid in an abandoned barn just north of Mr. Sobstak's ranch. I'm pretty hungry."

"You haven't eaten anything since yesterday noon?" A toxin in Jared's diet that metabolized out when he didn't eat?

He shook his head. "No, sir." He carefully let the rifle down, resting the stock on the gravel. He looked down at it. His fingers curled softly around the blue steel barrel.

"Can you tell me about your diet, please? You told Deputy Pelton you eat a lot of organics?"

A shadow crossed Jared's face. "Why?"

"What if something you're eating causes these episodes?"

Jared suddenly squatted, watched Ed intensely, and lifted his rifle. "You're going to make me stop eating healthy food?" He didn't point the weapon at Ed, but rested it across his thighs, pointing into the woods. Ed was reminded of hunters, waiting.

Any sudden move, and Jared could shoot him before he moved five feet. He knew the boy had hunted with his grandfather for years. He wouldn't miss. Ed slowed his breathing and held up his hands and said, "No, man. I'm just thinking out loud. Some of the organic foods might not have been checked for their effect on people. If we could make a list of all the things you eat, we might find a culprit in one of the foods. Doesn't that make sense?"

"I only eat good things." Although challenging, the voice sounded unsure.

"Okay, Jared. It's just a possibility. Nobody—" He stopped. *Keep it here, just between us.* "I'm not interested in changing your diet." *Absurd, talking diet with an armed paranoid.*

Jared stood, backed a short distance away, again rested the stock on the gravel. He held the barrel gently in his fingers. "You can help me find out? If something is poisoning me?"

"I...can." Ed heard the thinly veiled doubt in his voice, and Jared's face grew hard. Perhaps he'd heard Ed's hesitation? The boy looked past Ed's pickup, toward the river.

Ed heard the sound of the water, thinking that the next few moments could be decisive. Jared might bolt, or he might let Ed help him. "No," he said. "I can help you."

But Jared lifted the rifle and pointed it at Ed, holding him in place, then started angling toward the water.

Ed turned carefully, watched him move toward the cottonwoods, backing up slowly, still holding the rifle on Ed. Suddenly, Jared swung around, walked more quickly toward the trees, then into them. Under the umbrella of the cottowoods, he dropped the rifle, then began to run across the grassy bank.

Ed jumped off the tailgate and chased after him. Jared dashed toward the river. Pushing himself, Ed grabbed Jared's shirt and they tumbled together onto the crumbling bank, then rolled into the swirling, angry water. Ed grabbed the boy's belt with one hand and a dogwood bush with the other. Jared slipped under the roiling waves, struggled, couldn't get a foothold, arms and feet flailing in the flood. One hand struck, weakly, at Ed's grip on his belt, but as the snowmelt flooding over Jared's head gagged him, he slumped again beneath the surface. Ed felt his hold slipping in the frigid water. He shuddered, gathered himself, grunted, dragged the boy limp and heavy back up onto the muddy grass.

After a few moments sputtering, gagging, catching breaths, Jared gasped, "Why did you stop me?" His voice broke.

Ed, breathing hard, spoke between gasps. "I promised Grace...I'd help you."

69

Jared was shivering, dripping water on the seat and floor of Ed's pickup. Ed was shivering too; the pickup's heater, dialed up all the way, couldn't pull the chill out of their wet clothes. As he cranked up the fan, Ed felt the urgency. The dashboard clock read *2:05*, only two hours before he had to leave for the Anderhold, and he had no plan for what to do with the boy. He pitched his voice as kindly as he could. "Jared?"

Dazed, the boy turned slowly toward him, then stopped part of the way, as if he forgot Ed had spoken. After a moment, he said, "What?"

"Where's your truck?"

Jared turned away, staring straight out the windshield. "Why?"

"We can't get it just now. Is it exposed?"

"We can get it. I'll drive behind you." His voice was flat, empty.

No way, Ed thought, but he hesitated. Almost anything could wreck Jared's tenuous cooperation. "We'll get it later, but I'm worried somebody might find it if it's in the open."

The boy was silent.

What's he thinking? "Jared?"

He turned his head toward Ed. "Sir?" His eyes looked vacant.

"Your truck? Can anyone see it?"

Jared stared through the windshield. When he answered, Ed barely could hear him. "It's hidden. In the woods near the lane."

Ed nodded. "Good. We'll come back for it." He put his hand in front of the heater vent. It was warming.

Where to go? Not the department. If he took the boy in now, Jared would never trust him. Was his cabin safe? Jared could bolt, or maybe the paranoia would recur and Grace might be in danger. Not to mention the fact that Andi would find him there. Ed ran his fingers through his hair. *Jesus*. It didn't sound like a prayer.

Ed drove slowly, tracing out the risks. What about the gun? He'd picked it up when they'd walked up from the river and unloaded it before putting it behind his seat. Did he dare hide Jared? How long would be enough to figure out what was causing the psychosis? And how much would Magnus, approaching his crisis, need him? Art was near death too: he might be called in for that. Ed gripped the steering wheel fiercely.

Jared looked at Ed's hands on the wheel. "What's wrong?"

Ed flexed his hands. "Nothing. It's all right."

"You said we have to trust each other, but you're not being honest."

Ed bristled. "Your little run into the river put a real chill on my trust."

Jared turned away. Ed searched for words to apologize, but Jared spoke first. "I'm sorry. You're right." He folded his arms. "I won't kill myself. I'll let you help me."

Ed pulled out of Lovers Lane and onto the highway. He drove for a few minutes, then said, "You were right, Jared. I'm worrying about what to do."

Jared looked at him. "With me?"

"Yeah. I want to keep you at my cabin, so we can talk and I can figure out how to help you. But that plan's got some problems."

"You're afraid I'll run."

Ed nodded. "That's one. And Deputy Pelton stays at my cabin most nights. I have to talk her into helping me."

Jared shuddered. He was silent for a mile. Then, "Don't let her take me back to jail, Doctor."

"Yeah. Exactly." After another moment, he said, "Maybe she won't be there when we get back. And Jared?"

"Sir?"

"Call me Ed."

They drove another five minutes, then turned up his drive. Andi was there.

Ed parked in the yard, beside her black-and-tan sheriff's department SUV. Grace and Andi sat on the steps, in the sun. Andi was squinting at his passenger, her face dark. Ed collected himself. This was going to be damn tricky.

70

When he spotted Andi's black-and-tan squad parked in the yard and Andi in her uniform, sitting on the steps, Jared stiffened. Ed put his hand softly on his shoulder, which was quivering. "Easy, man. This'll work out." He rummaged behind the seat and pulled out a blanket. "Wrap up in this while I talk to Deputy Pelton. Just wait here."

"You said you'd help me!" Jared started to open his door.

Ed tightened his grip on the shoulder and pulled him back. "Yes, and I meant it. Just wait here in the truck. If you run, she'll be on you in a minute and she'll take you in. Let me talk to her."

Ed looked hard at him, hoping the glare would underscore the warning. Jared held the stare, almost angrily, then dropped his eyes, nodded. "Okay."

Ed lifted the boy's rifle from the rack behind the seats. "By the way, where'd you get this?"

After the silence stretched and Jared was obviously not going to tell him, Ed decided to back off.

As he got out, Jared said, quietly, "You can leave the rifle here."

Startled, Ed looked back at him. "If you were me, would you leave it?"

Jared's eyebrows lifted, dropped. Then he smiled weakly. "I suppose not."

"Okay, then. Anyway, I've got the round." He patted the shirt pocket where he'd put it. "Just wait. This'll work out."

Andi was standing at the edge of the porch. As he climbed the steps, she whispered, "What the hell's going on? Grace told me—" She looked at his wet, muddy clothes, then down at the rifle. "That his?"

Ed nodded, starting to shiver again in the spring breeze after leaving the heat of the pickup cabin. "He wouldn't say where he got it."

Her lips were tight. "Give it to me."

He passed it to her, and fished the round from his shirt pocket. She marched them down to the squad car and locked them in the trunk. When she returned, he said, "I want him to stay here for a couple of days."

Andi looked at him as if he had grown a new nose. "You're kidding."

He shook his head. "He asked for my help, and I'm giving it. I only have ninety minutes before I have to go keep another patient alive, so I need your help. We can debate it later."

"My help? For *what*, goddamn it! The whole department's searching for this kid and you have a secret meeting with him and don't call me? What if he'd killed you, for God's sake?" She shook her head. "Jesus, Ed. Put him in my vehicle. I'm taking him—"

He interrupted her. "He's terrified, Andi, and he's suicidal. If we take him in, we'll lose him. He'll clam up tighter than a Master Lock and we'll never learn what's going on. But he trusts me for now, and if you'll give me two days alone with him, I think I can figure this out."

"*Two days?* Are you crazy? That breaks every rule in the book. I can't just let him go."

"Not *let him go*, damn it! He'll be here the whole time, or with me. Or you." He softened his tone. "If you'll help." He took a breath. "Yeah. Break a rule. Please."

Andi stalked to the end of the porch and stared out toward the trees, arms folded tight. Grace was watching the exchange from her chair, her eyes wide, darting between Ed and Andi arguing, then glancing toward Jared, sitting stiffly in the truck.

Ed said, "Grace, could you make a couple sandwiches for Jared? There's tuna fish in the refrigerator. He hasn't eaten since yesterday. Oh, and find him a pair of my jeans and a shirt and socks."

Grace said, "Maybe I should go sit with him?"

Andi whirled. "No way! We don't know what he'll do."

Ed said to Grace, "Please, just make the sandwiches and get some clothes ready, okay?"

Saying nothing, Grace went into the house and let the screen door slam.

Andi turned her back on Ed, facing toward the woods. "Ed, I love you, and there're a lot of things I'd do for you, but you can't ask me to violate my oath."

Ed moved close and put his hand on her shoulder, turning her back to face him. "Can I ask you to help me for two days?"

"Help you how?"

"Let him stay here, let me try to figure out what's making him sick. Forty-eight hours. Then you can take him in."

"Damn it, no, you can't ask that."

"Please." He felt time pressing. "I've got to go soon, Andi, and we need a plan."

"What? You need to leave? *Now?*"

He nodded. "Afraid so. Another patient's suicidal." He went to the edge of the porch and leaned on the railing. His fight with Jared at the river caught up to him. His shivering worsened, not just from cold this time: It was fear. This could go so wrong, so fast. He looked out across the valley, down the sloping fields toward the greening line of trees along the river in town. He forced himself to breathe slowly, willed the fear to drain. Finally, more in control, he turned back to Andi. "I love you too, and I hate putting you in this position, but I can't see any other choice. Think about it. If we lock Jared up, what have we gained? He'll never—"

Andi cut him off. "What we've gained is a potentially dangerous kid under control."

He nodded. "Okay, right. But look. If you take him in, he'll never trust anybody again. If keeping him here works out, we'll find out what's causing his delusions and maybe a way to save him—and save the county a lot of money."

"Oh, screw that, Ed. We're talking about my integrity here, not Ben's budget."

"Sorry. But I'm not asking you to violate your integrity; I just need you to help me protect this boy for forty-eight hours."

She turned away again, gazing out over the valley. "I don't see the upside for me or the department—or Jared. I'd be violating my oath and lying to my partner and my boss, and what good will come of it?"

"You'd be giving the kid and me the time to maybe sort this mess out."

She narrowed her eyes. "You honestly think you can do that?"

"Honestly? Maybe. Probably. Nothing's for certain."

She shook her head. After a long pause, she said, "If I say yes, you give me everything you learn from him."

He felt his throat tighten. "You know I can't talk about what he tells me."

She threw her hands up. "Jesus Christ, Ed! You're asking me to violate my oath while you shut me out with your damn *confidentiality*?" She moved close to him and put a hard finger on his chest. "Enforcing the law is *my* ethics. You can't have yours without giving me mine."

He stepped back. She was right. He had to break his own rules here. "Okay, anything I learn that's germane to your case, I'll give you. Just you. But look, Andi. This is *all about* law enforcement. Do you want to *solve* this case, or do we just hand Jared over to Brad Ordrew?" Ed regretted saying it, but he felt desperate.

For a moment, Andi just stared at him. "Fuck you, Ed. That's low. You know me better than that." She shook her head. "At least, I thought you did."

He steeled himself. "You're right, I do. Now that Jared ran away, though, won't Brad's theory gain traction?"

She shrugged, looking out again to the pines. "Probably. But your remark sucks."

"Maybe, but figuring out what causes his delusions is the key. Will you give me two days with him? And stay with him when I can't?"

She turned her face further away. Ed held his breath. Then, without facing him, she whispered, "All right, two days, no more." Then she faced him. "But you blindsided me, Ed, and I won't forget that."

He cringed. Andi had never said something like that to him. *Well, I never did something like this to her before.* He tried a small smile. "Well, I didn't know you'd be sitting on the porch."

"After your two days are up, I won't be sitting on your porch for a while."

71

Walking toward Jared in the pickup, Ed wondered what his advocacy had just cost him with Andi. How long would that "for a while" be? He felt the same sick tightness in his chest he'd felt when Mara, his wife, had announced she was divorcing him. Since he and Andi had been together, they hadn't had more than minor collisions, and those were when they both were too tired from work. He'd believed, or persuaded himself, that their being older had saved them from the petty ego dramas of youth. Now, pressured by his ambush, she'd compromised her professional standards for him, and already Jared's case had caused two serious arguments. Would their relationship withstand the demands he, pleading Jared's case, was putting on them? As he climbed into the truck, he thought, *And will it even be worth it?*

"What'd she say?" Jared asked.

"We've got two days. She won't take you in till then."

Jared shuddered. "Then?"

Out of nowhere, he thought of Art Masters. "A friend of mine told me just to sit my horse till the cow shows up. That cow shows up in forty-eight hours."

The barest smile touched Jared's mouth. "My grandpa used to say, 'We'll butcher that deer when we've shot it.'"

Ed smiled. "Right. You and I have two days to figure out what's causing these changes in you. Then we'll deal with whatever comes next."

"I'm not going back to jail. I can't." Under the blanket, he started shivering again. Ed glanced at the porch; Andi stood stiffly at the steps, arms folded, watching them.

He turned to Jared. "You need dry clothes. And food. You hungry still?"

For a moment, the boy said nothing. Then, "Starved."

"Come on. Grace is making sandwiches."

At the porch, Ed said, "Jared, this is Deputy Pelton."

Jared nodded. "We've met." He paused, then said, "Hi, Deputy. I'm sorry I'm causing you so much trouble."

Andi looked surprised. "You're going to help Doctor Northrup figure things out?"

He nodded. "I'm going to try." His voice was small, unsure.

"Two days is all you've got. Better try damn hard." She stepped aside.

In the kitchen, looking nervous, Grace waited with a couple of tuna fish sandwiches and a glass of milk. Ed tensed again. How would Jared be around Grace? Was she in any danger? He watched them carefully from the door.

Grace pushed the plate across the island toward him, and said, shyly, "Hey, Jared. The lettuce is organic."

His face lightened. "Thanks, Grace. That means a lot to me." Then he bit into the first sandwich. Grace started talking about school, as if nothing had happened.

Jared followed her conversation, chewing hard, nodding, working fast through the food.

Ed waited a moment, relieved, then went back to the porch. "Thanks, Andi."

She didn't respond.

He said, "Look, I've got a patient who's on the verge of suicide. Can you stay a couple hours while I go do what I can?"

"Jesus, Ed, you're asking a lot. I'm still on duty."

He almost snapped, but instead waited, trying to look patient. Probably failing.

She frowned and reached for her phone. "Go. I'll call Ben and tell him I'm taking a couple hours to rest. Everybody's bushed after searching all night." She looked pained. "For a kid you're hiding in your damn kitchen."

He leaned forward to kiss her.

She stepped back, shaking her head.

72

Magnus sat slumped in his small study. Patchy whisker stubble splotched across his jaw, as if he'd started to shave and given up partway through. His hair was ragged and uncombed. The gun case door hung open. *Kött Hitta* lay across his lap.

Ed reached across and lifted the rifle away. Magnus watched him, his eyes slack with fatigue. Ed checked the bolt: rusted hard shut. He replaced the weapon in the gun case and closed the door.

"I take your point, Mack," he said. "You can't take any more."

"It doesn't stop. I keep seeing those arches, and feeling the pain in my backside. My...*anus*."

He snapped the word, but Ed felt the desperation behind it, and waited.

"Even drunk as I can get, the words don't stop."

"You're hearing them now? While we're talking?"

"All the time. I can't do this, Ed. You've got to stop it." Ed had never seen such pleading in a man's eyes, especially not in this man's.

Ed started to ask what the words were, but changed his mind. They were probably the same as before. *Stay away from the infirmary.* "Mack, let's just talk for a bit. Then we'll—"

"God, no, no talk! Just *do* something. *Anything.*" Magnus looked beaten. "Please, Ed."

Ed heard the raw fear lacing the words. He nodded. "How long since you slept?"

"Days. A week. Since before I went to *Árboles Blancos.* I don't know."

"Let me take you to see Doc Keeley in the ER. He can give you something so you can sleep. At the moment, you need that more than anything."

Expecting a fight, Ed was surprised that Magnus merely waved his hand. "Whatever you say."

Ed asked, "Have you remembered or heard anything else? More words, different images?"

Magnus leaned forward, lifting his hands to his face. Ed saw tears welling in his eyes. "Just *help* me."

"Right." He reached over and took Magnus's hand in his and pulled him to his feet. "I'll drive you to the hospital. Luisa can follow with your things."

Magnus's expression swiftly changed, from defeat to horror. He snatched his hand violently back. "*Hospital?* That's an *infirmary.* No, I'll kill him first!"

Confused, Ed spoke as softly as he could, forcing Magnus to listen. "Mack, calm down. Who will you kill?"

As abruptly as it had come, the storm passed, and Magnus fell back into his chair. He put his hands to his ears. "Just stop the words."

Everything could wait until Mack had slept. "Let's get Luisa and go up to the..." He paused. "To see Doc." Would this trigger another outburst? But Magnus only nodded, his eyes closed, his face twisted up against the words he must have been hearing. Ed felt a wave of compassion. Mack had never seemed so broken. Compassion for his friend warmed his eyes. But behind that lurked something different. Futility. After Magnus slept, what would they do? *Am I merely buying time?*

He opened the office door and led Magnus down the hall, his hand gentle on the big man's elbow. *Of course I'm buying time*, he thought. *Sleep's what Mack needs now.*

Sleep would help.

If it doesn't, God help us both.

73

At the hospital, after Ed explained what he wanted, Doc Keeley said, "I need more to go on than that, Ed. What's your diagnosis?" They stood outside the ER cubicle where Magnus lay on a gurney, eyes frightened, darting.

"Can you live with 'unspecified sleep disorder'?"

Doc crinkled his nose. "You're playing this close to the vest."

"Uh-huh. Just till Mack gets a good sleep. I don't factually know what's going on, though I have my suspicions."

"Which you're keeping mum about."

Ed nodded. "Until I know more. And Mack needs sleep before we can dig any further."

Doc nodded. "Okay. I'll admit him and get him sedated. After he's been asleep a few hours, we'll let him go on his own and see if he's able to sleep. That work for you?"

Ed smiled. "Perfect, John. Thanks."

Keeley shook his head. "Very unusual, but I'll trust you. Be grateful we're a small-town hospital."

"Don't I know it?" Ed yawned. "I could use some sleep myself."

Doc looked at him. "Long days, eh? They find the Hansen boy yet?"

Ed swallowed. Unwilling to lie baldly to Doc, he threaded the needle. "The deputies can't find him."

"Bad luck. By the way, you probably want to stop in and see Art today."

Ed felt his shoulders slump. "How soon?"

"Soon."

"*How* soon, damn it!"

Doc touched his arm. "Easy, man."

Ed felt himself slump. "God, I'm sorry, John. You're right. I'm running four directions at once, on about two hours sleep."

Keeley patted his shoulder, and for a moment, Ed felt the man's warmth; tears filled his eyes.

Doc looked at him a moment, then said, "My best guess, Art'll die tomorrow or the next day. I'll be surprised if he lasts much longer than that. He'll probably slip into a coma before the end."

Ed took a long breath, glanced at the clock on the wall. He'd almost used up the two hours he'd promised Andi. She'd be furious. "Thanks for the heads-up, John. I'll stop in right now."

"We moved his room. He can see the mountains now."

74

In his new room, facing the mountains, Art slept. New tubes snaked into his veins. Oxygen seeped slowly from the white tube below his nose. Ed looked out to check the view. At the southern end of the long valley, he saw the Coliseum's dark granite amphitheater framed by the soft green blanket of pine and fir, snow glistening in the afternoon sun. Quiet beeps broke the silence every couple of minutes. Ed peered across the bed at the heart monitor. It read *125*.

Art's whispery voice startled him. "Nice view, isn't it? I'll miss the valley."

"You're awake. How're you feeling?"

A feeble shrug. "How's it feel to die? Not so bad, I'd say. Mostly, tired." A small smile tugged at the corners of the old man's mouth. "Guess I'd say I'm ready, far as that goes."

Ed watched a wave of pain cross Art's face, followed by calm. "What about that thing that needs sorting out?"

"Ah, that." He closed his eyes for a moment. "What's going on with the boy?"

Ed hesitated, said, "The sheriff can't find him."

The silence felt uncomfortable; Ed hated his half-truth, and could tell Art was uneasy too. Could he know where Jared was? No. Whatever Art needed to talk about was what made him hesitate. Ed waited a moment, then said, "So, what needs sorting out?"

Art's lips thinned in a weak smile. "You're right, time's come." He stopped, short of breath.

When he recovered, he nodded. "Here we go. It's a guilt I've carried since I was a pup."

Ed pulled up a chair. "Tell me about it."

Art said, "I never thanked my old man for a thing he did." He paused, coughed. "A big thing." He licked away a drop of blood on his lips. "I was a kid. It was '68. Vietnam, bad times. The old man and I, well, he was Nixon, I was Bobby Kennedy. Hell, we fought about every damn thing, not just the damn war. I said I wouldn't go, so he called me a pussy and kicked me out of the house. When I got drafted, I refused to go in. I said I was a CO." He coughed, hard, took time settling down. "My ma told me he went ape-shit."

"CO?" Being a young teen during the Vietnam war, Ed hadn't absorbed much of its lingo.

"Means conscientious objector," Art smiled. "Forget you're just a youngster." He chuckled, which made him cough again. When he could speak, he said, "Draft board called me in to explain myself. So I'm halfway through my little speech, and it's obvious they think I'm talking bullshit—not one of 'em would look me in the eye, just scribbled on their notepads, looked at each other. Right about then, there's a knock on the door. It's the old man, dressed in his Army uniform from World War Two, battle ribbons, the whole schmear. He comes in, never looks at me, salutes the flag, and asks permission to say something." Again, he coughed, hard, rasping, bloody. The cough went on and on.

Ed leaned forward. "Should I call the nurse, Art?"

Art shook his head. In a moment, the coughing slowed. Another few moments, he lay still, collecting himself. Then he said, "The chairman says, 'And who the hell are you?' My old man, he gets all red in the face, but he says, 'I'm this young man's father. I want you to know I don't agree with a damn thing he says, but I fought the Japs so he'd be free to say it, and even though he's wrong as a nun in a whorehouse, I'm tellin' you he's goddamn sincere when he says it.'"

Art's rheumy eyes were moist. "Never talked to him about it. Never thanked him. About a year later, he had a stroke, real bad one." He rummaged on the bedside table, pulled out a Kleenex and blew his nose. Ed saw red on the tissue. Art panted a few moments before going on. "Never thanked him before his stroke shut out the lights."

"Your father sounds like a good man."

"In his way." He coughed, winced. "In his way."

"I doubt he'd have done what he did if he wasn't secretly proud of you."

Art gazed out at the mountains. "Think so?" The worried look in his eyes softened. "Why, that'd be a fine thing to think." He took a long, shuddering breath. "A damn fine thing." After a moment, Art's own lights went out. Ed sat forward, then sat back, counting the shallow breaths, watching the rapid pulse in Art's neck.

Then the watery eyes opened, dim, but clear for the moment. "Well, guess I'll get to tell him thanks soon enough." He looked up. "My gratitude, Ed. Secretly proud of me, you think?" He closed his eyes. "I think she's sorted out now." He patted Ed's hand. "Go out there and find that boy. He's in need of your help, I'd say."

75

With each mile toward his cabin, Ed's tension grew, competing with his fatigue. Andi wasn't really on board with this; he hoped nothing had gone wrong while he was away.

Andi was reading the paper in the living room, her face carefully neutral. Ed saw she wore her weapon belt; she'd never done that inside his house before. Grace, doing homework at the table, looked up when he came in. "He's sleeping in your bed," she said. "I got him dry clothes of yours to wear, and put his in the laundry room. Oh, and I gave him one of those toothbrushes you keep for company we never have any of."

Ed smiled, although the sight of Andi's weapon had unsettled him. A precaution, he knew, but still. "How'd he seem to you?" he asked Grace.

"He's not like himself, Northrup. I think he's sick. He just keeps looking away."

"He's probably ashamed of himself in front of you, Grace."

"Why? Me and my girls, we know he's not serious about what he said."

"Your girls and you. He doesn't know that. He's too confused."

Andi broke in. "I'm starting to feel a little like Brad," she said. "Aren't we taking this compassion thing a little further than we should, under the circumstances?"

Grace said, "You gotta let Northrup help him, Andi."

"I'm asking your dad, not you." Ed had never heard Andi speak coldly to Grace; to Ed, it signaled more than anger.

"Just two days."

"And what do I tell Ben—and everybody else?"

"Nothing. You don't know he's here."

She slapped the newspaper down. "Oh, violate my oath and lie to my colleagues."

"Goddamn it, Andi! You know better than I do that locking Jared up now won't accomplish a damn thing!"

Andi stood up, her eyes narrowing. "Problem is, I *don't* know that. Locking him up would make this whole situation a hell of a lot safer than it is right now."

Grace jumped in, loud, "Stop it!" Then looking quickly in toward Ed's bedroom, she lowered her voice. "You guys! Something's wrong with Jared, and that's the only thing that matters here. Me and him talked while he ate, and he said he's scared he'll die in jail." She looked at Andi. "You gotta help Northrup help him, Andi. Please."

Andi frowned. "Some things I can do to help, and some I can't."

Grace's interruption had given Ed a moment to regroup. He said to Andi, "Okay. Let me call Ben. I'll tell him I've got Jared and try to persuade him to let me have the time. I won't tell him you're here or know anything about it. I won't lie, I just won't say. If he agrees, you're off the hook."

Andi shook her head. "No, I'm not. Ben knows I sleep over most nights. He'll know I know."

Ed stretched his shoulders. "I'm not thinking this through, am I?" He yawned. "Any ideas?"

Andi was silent for a moment. "I think you tell him the full story. Tell him I said I'd only go along with this if he okays it."

He nodded. "Better." He went inside for the phone. He noticed a light on in his bedroom.

When he stepped back out on the porch, Andi said, "And if he says no?"

"Then I'll take Jared someplace safe. I'll make sure nobody finds us for two days."

Andi grimaced. "For God's sake, Ed, *bend* a little. If Ben says no, and if you hide the boy anyway, we'll have to arrest you for obstructing justice."

Grace growled. "You two! If me and my girls were as stubborn as you two, we wouldn't stay friends."

Ed was too tired to argue any more. "It's 'my girls and I.'"

"That's what I said."

Andi looked at Ed and, surprising him, chuckled. "We're half-way to divorce court and you're obsessing over grammar!" She shook her head.

Grace gasped. "You two are married?"

Andi shook her head. "Just an expression."

Ed relaxed. "You're right, both of you. I'm being stubborn. If Ben doesn't go along, I'll step aside. You can take him in." He paused. "But Jared'll never trust me if that happens."

Andi said, "That may not be your call, big guy."

Behind them, from the doorway, came Jared's voice. "You're going to arrest me, aren't you?"

76

"No, Jared. I'm calling Sheriff Stewart to get his okay for this plan. Otherwise, it can't work. I need you to take it easy while I call, okay?"

Jared's eyes darted from Ed to Andi, then to Grace, then back. Fast. His jaw was clenching.

Ed put his hand on the boy's shoulder. "Calm down, Jared. I'm going to do everything I can to make this work. If Sheriff Stewart agrees, you'll be safe. Without his help, the plan breaks down."

Jared glared. "How do I calm down? You want to kill me." His glare suddenly softened, tears following the anger. "I'm sorry, Doctor. I'm just totally scared. I know you don't want to kill me." He looked at Grace. "Nobody does. I know that."

Andi said, "I'm not trying to hurt you, Jared. I'm thinking we all have to trust each other one more round."

Jared took in a long breath. "Okay. Yeah. Okay." He looked at Grace. "Will you wait with me on the porch?"

Ed watched them carefully. Jared looked shaky as he and Grace went out. Andi positioned herself where she could see them, sitting on the top step. Her hand hung quietly beside the grip of her handgun.

Ed dialed Ben's number. When he picked up, Ed gave him the story fast and made his pitch for the two-day deal.

Ben exploded when he heard about the two days. "Christ in a sidecar! You been hit on the head? Bring that boy in! Pronto."

Ed took a deep breath. "Wait, Ben. Let me talk, will you?"

"Talk till your teeth fall out, but bring him in while you're jabberin'."

"This is a courtesy call, Ben. I didn't need to let you in on this. You clear on that?"

"Clear as mud. It ain't changin' a damn thing."

"Okay, but look. We'll be with Jared every minute—he won't be out of our sight. He's not paranoid now, and that fits my poison theory. Whatever the poison is and wherever he gets it, he won't get it while he's with me. And two days will give me time to get to the cause."

"Explain this poison theory."

He's listening. Ed explained the theory.

"For somebody who don't know what the poison is, you're awful damn sure he won't get some at your place."

"Granted." Just then, Jared and Grace came inside. *Damn.* He thought a moment. "Ben, I need a minute here. Can I put you on hold?"

Ben growled. "Ain't polite, but under the circumstances...do it."

He hit the *Hold* icon and said to Jared and Grace. "Guys," he said, "I need privacy for this call. I don't mean to be impolite, but I'm going to take it in my truck, okay?"

Jared looked immediately suspicious. "Are you——?"

"Damn it, Jared, no!" He held up his phone. "I'm on with Sheriff Stewart. We're figuring out how to keep you out of jail, but I need privacy."

Jared's eyes went wide at Ed's angry tone.

Seeing the boy's fear, he ratcheted himself down. "I'm sorry I barked at you, Jared. Just give me a couple minutes, okay?"

Andi stood up. "What's Ben saying?"

"Nothing yet. We're still talking." As he stepped down to the gravel, he heard her mutter, "Fuck this."

A moment later, he was sitting in the pickup and Grace and Jared were sitting on the porch steps again, watching him. Andi carried a tray of Cokes out, and she glared at him too. *Great. Everybody's pissed off.*

He took Ben off hold.

77

Ben said, "Speak."

"Okay, Ben. We both know this kid's not a killer."

"That ain't somethin' I know."

"Fine. I need time to evaluate him. Give me two days."

"Bud, you can have a month. But he sleeps in the jail. He violated a court order."

"Because he got into whatever poison he's eating. Now he's thirty-some hours without it, and he's normal again." Well, not quite normal, but close enough. "Ben, the kid's scared to death of jail, and he's starting to trust me. If we bring him in, I'll never get close to him."

"Not sure that's my concern, Ed. I got laws to enforce, and closin' my eyes to a violation of a court order ain't gonna happen."

"I'm not asking you to close your eyes, Ben. I'm asking for two days. If I can't crack this by then, I'll bring him in."

"You the same shrink that's always talkin' your rules about confidentiality and professional ethics?"

"Guilty as charged. But this isn't the same thing."

"My big butt it ain't. I got rules to follow too. You're interferin' with me enforcin' the law."

"Not true, Ben. I'm *helping* you enforce it. Think about it: Right now, your only evidence is his single statement that he wanted to kill people. And you don't know whether he's serious, crazy, or gaming us. Am I right?"

For a moment, Ben didn't answer. Then he said, "For the sake of argument."

"And we've got to find out what caused that single statement if you're going to have a case. I've got a theory that could make sense of everything, but I need a couple of days."

"Your poison theory?"

"Yeah. Jared's the only one can tell me what I need to know, and I need him to trust me enough to do it. If I'm right, you'll have your explanation, and that helps law enforcement."

"You say."

"I say."

Ed waited. For more than a minute, he listened to the crackle of occasional static on the line. After that minute, he said, "Ben? You still there?"

Ben's voice growled. "Hold your horses, I'm thinkin'." In a moment, he said, "A while back, you said somethin' like, 'we'll keep him in our sight.' Who's we, bud? We talkin' your girlfriend? Who last time I looked was also my deputy?"

Now comes the hard part. "We are. She was here when I brought Jared home."

"And?"

"And she wanted to arrest him on the spot, but agreed to wait if I called you."

There was another tense silence. While he listened intently to nothing, his back stiff, Ed checked the porch. All three watched him, looking no happier. Jared's eyes were jumping again; he looked spooked. Andi's lips were tight. Grace's face was red. Angry.

"Tell her to bring the boy in."

Ed sagged against the seat back. *Damn.* "Ben. Listen. I can figure this thing out but I'll lose him if we put him in jail. Nobody but the three of us needs to know."

"Somebody always finds out." Ben was quiet a moment. "What if your poison theory's wrong and he goes crazy, somebody gets hurt? Killed. Picture *that* on the damn TV news."

Ed felt chilled. It was hardly a sure thing. Keeping Jared from whatever was poisoning him—if anything was—might have nothing to do with his illness. *Maybe I'm barking up the wrong tree.* He started to speak, but Ben started sooner.

"Ed, tell me straight: How sure are you about sortin' the kid out in a couple days?"

Ed let out a long breath. *Maybe, maybe.* Ridiculously, he crossed his fingers. "I can't guarantee anything, but—"

Ben interrupted again. "I ain't lookin' for guarantees, bud. What I'm needin' is that boy safe and sound, not a threat to the community. You gotta give me somethin' for that."

"I realize what I'm asking, Ben."

The sheriff didn't answer. Ed took a breath and said, "But if we can get a cause for his delusions, you'll know how to prosecute your case."

Ben's breathing was deep and loud. "I gotta think this over. I'll call you back in a half hour. Just keep a halter on that boy till I do."

"Ben, wait, I—"

Ben hung up.

Is Ben sending a deputy to arrest Jared? Ed took a long, trembling breath, decided to drop the thought. *Sometimes you have to trust your friends.*

He walked slowly to the porch. The three, sitting on the top step, looked at him. "Half an hour," he said. "We'll have it arranged then." He made it sound like a done deal, but inside, he was quaking. No telling what Jared would do if Ben's verdict went against him. Nobody moved, so he couldn't climb the steps. He sat on the lowest step, his back to them. *It'll be a damn long half hour.*

The phone rang in seven minutes. "You have forty-eight hours," Ben growled. "Me and you never had this conversation, and anybody says we did, I expect you to lie through your ass. We clear?"

Ed was almost staggered with relief. "Very clear, Ben. Not a word."

"Forty-eight hours." A pause. "That's *6:48* Tuesday evenin'. Have the boy here, and bring the evidence for your damn theory." Ed started to thank him, but Ben rushed on. "And I'm callin' his folks. They deserve to know we have him and he's safe. At least we better hope to God he is."

Ben hung up. The three others were studying him expectantly. "We've got forty-eight hours," he said. Grace squealed and swung to Jared, giving him a hug. Andi frowned when he caught her eye, and looked away.

Jared did not return Grace's embrace. He looked lost. Lost and very afraid.

MONDAY, DAY EIGHT

78

Monday morning dawned clear and still warm, although a stiffening breeze had rattled the windows a few times during the night. Ed got up first. During the miserable night on the couch—so Jared could sleep in his bed—he'd awakened to every noise, anxious that Jared might run. Andi had slept with Grace. Ed decided not to take his morning run.

Andi got up a little after six. Ed was reading about ergotism on his laptop. He said, quietly, "Coffee's ready."

After pouring herself a to-go cup, Andi pulled her duty belt off the clothes hook, checked the weapon, and slung it over her shoulder. "Heading home for a new uniform; my clothes are in your closet and I don't want to wake Jared. If you need me, call. I'll make some excuse and come out as fast as I can."

Ed hesitated. "I need to take Grace to school. Can you hang around till I get back?"

Andi shook her head. "Grace can take a sick day. It's probably better she doesn't talk to her friends too much." She snickered. "Wouldn't be a problem if you'd bought her a car."

True enough. He stood up. "You still angry?"

She took a moment. "Yeah. Maybe not as much. This is a tough deal, Ed."

He nodded. "I'm sorry I put you in this position."

She looked at him. "I'd gotten to like how easy things were between us."

"Were?"

"Yeah. This eats a lot of trust, big guy. And I don't come by trust easily."

"I'm sorry. Again. I'm not going to let you down."

"Well, we're in it up to our asses. Let's make 'er work."

"I'll do my best."

"We probably need better than that."

194

He chuckled.

"You see humor here?" Her face registered annoyance.

He nodded. "You remind me of my fourth-grade teacher, Sister Alberta. 'Good, better, best, never let it rest, till your good is better, and your better, best.'"

A hint of a smile touched Andi's lips. "That's something you Catholics are good at."

"What?"

"Making it hard on a person."

79

Not long after Andi left, Jared came out of Ed's bedroom wearing Ed's old robe. Ed stood up, studying him. He didn't seem agitated, just sleepy. "Can I use your bathroom, Doctor?"

"Sure, Jared. No need to ask. And it's Ed, remember?"

A few minutes later, Jared came out. He looked embarrassed. "I'm sorry for these clothes." He looked down at himself.

The boy'd found his clothes from yesterday in the laundry hamper—no one had remembered to wash them—and put them on, dirt, wrinkles, damp spots, and all. Ed said, "You don't need to wear those till we wash them. Wear my clothes from last night."

Jared looked embarrassed. "I didn't want to impose."

"No imposition. Let's get you something clean and we'll wash yours."

After they found another pair of jeans and a shirt and underwear—Ed was six feet, Jared about five ten, so the fit wasn't bad—Ed tossed Jared's clothes into the washing machine and went into the kitchen. "Coffee?"

The boy recoiled. "I don't do caffeine. It's toxic."

Hmm. "What *do* you do for breakfast?"

Jared looked into the kitchen area. "Fruit, usually." There were bananas and oranges in a bowl. Ed nodded. "Help yourself."

After he ate, Jared went back into the bedroom. He came out five minutes later. "I made your bed. Sorry you couldn't sleep in it."

"No problem." Just then, Grace came out of her room, rubbing her eyes. "Geez, you people talk loud."

"Good morning to you too," Ed said. Grace saw Jared and gave a start. "Oh! I forgot..."

Jared backed up a little. Ed said, "Grace, how about we call today a sick day?"

"Really, Northrup? You never..."

"Today I do."

"Okay. Then I'm sleeping in." She went back in her room and closed the door.

Ed smiled and said to Jared, "She'll sleep till noon. How about a walk?"

Jared nodded. "Yes, sir."

After they'd walked a while in silence, Jared said, "So what do we do?"

Ed didn't answer for a moment, looking up to the mountains. He pointed. Yellow patches of early sunlight played up high, across the dark green swath below the peaks. In the distance, an eagle moved slowly across the morning sky. Jared looked, nodded. "Pretty." After a moment, he said, "Have you ever wished you could fly away, Ed?" He'd seen the eagle too.

Ed looked at him, thinking of his own near-suicide up on the Coliseum two years ago, just before Grace came to town. He'd stood on the granite lip, thirteen hundred feet above the glacial lake below the Coliseum, debating whether to step off. He'd seen a hawk soaring below him that day, and unexpectedly, today's eagle's graceful passage across the sky filled him with gratitude. "I have, Jared. I almost killed myself once. It was before Grace came. I was pretty depressed. I think she saved my life."

The boy's eyes widened for a second, then he nodded. "I never thought I'd understand that, but I do now."

"Down at the river?"

Jared nodded. "My thoughts scare me. Or, I should say today they scare me. When they take over, they're so real. It's like the only way to stop them is to kill somebody."

"Any ideas about what causes them?"

He shook his head. "It's, you know, like I just *know* that killing will solve something. Today that makes no sense at all, but when I wanted to drown, it did."

"So you don't know *anything* about how the thoughts come?" He thought of the poison theory. Time to get into that.

Jared shook his head. "Not really. Sometimes, though, maybe I know."

"Sometimes you know? So, what do you know?"

Jared looked at him sharply, almost angrily. He turned away and looked up at the mountains.

Ed said, "I'm sorry, man. I'm just trying to understand."

Jared turned back, his eyes sad now. "I know you are," he said, quietly. "I guess I'm still tense. No, suspicious."

Ed caught the returning arc of the eagle out of the corner of his eye. Neither of them spoke for a while. After they had walked a couple hundred yards, Ed said, "So when you shift from thinking about killing your friends to thinking normally, like today, are you aware of how it happens?"

"What do you mean?"

"What things might have changed that could cause the change in you? Like food or stress or...well, anything?"

Jared stopped. A hundred yards away, a doe had carefully stepped onto the drive. Behind her, two fawns stopped in the grass beside the gravel. The doe looked back. They gingerly followed her.

When they'd gone into the trees, Jared said, "I'm sorry, but I'm not sure I understand."

"Let me give you an example. Suppose a guy has an allergy, but he doesn't know it. He just notices that sometimes he can't stop sneezing, but other times he's fine. What he doesn't know is he's allergic to his girlfriend's dog, so when he visits her house, he sneezes, but when he's not around the dog, he's fine. Get it?"

Jared nodded. "Like an environmental toxin," he said. In a moment, he said, "You're going to tell me it's my organics."

"I don't know that. It's what I'm looking for, whatever makes you change, either from being in your right mind to being a killer, or back."

"Yeah, I get that." He said nothing for a moment, then said, "Maybe I have a demon."

Is he joking? Ed looked at him, but Jared looked serious. "What makes you think that?"

"I don't know. I never thought it before now." His voice wavered. "I didn't think I believed in demons."

"I don't. There's a natural explanation."

"Like what?" He stopped in the road and turned to face Ed.

Ed stopped too, and faced the boy. "Well, two things come to mind: One possibility, you might have a mental illness that suddenly flares up, then dies down."

"Does that happen?"

"It's not the usual picture, but it can."

"What's the other possibility?"

"Could be that there's some kind of poison in your system. As you say, an environmental toxin of some kind."

Unexpectedly, Jared laughed, a short, tense laugh. He resumed walking. "What about brain tumors?"

Ed looked at him. "Considered that. It'd be really unusual to have a brain tumor if the symptoms come and go like yours do."

"So, which one do you think it is?"

"At the moment, I don't know." Ed hesitated, then pushed on. "I'm thinking we should talk about your diet."

Jared stiffened. "My diet's healthy, Doctor."

"Not saying it isn't, Jared. But we've got to explore everything, right?"

Jared looked west to the rugged sierra of the Monastery Mountains. "Those mountains have always made me feel safe," he said quietly. Ed waited. The deer had vanished into the woods lining the road. The eagle had disappeared.

Jared said, "Doctor Northrup, I mean, Ed, do you think we could go back and get a cup of your coffee? I think I'll need it for this."

80

When they were settled at the kitchen table, Ed said, "Let's start with your diet."

"You get right to the point." Jared sipped the coffee, then looked at the cup. "You know, sometimes these bad things sure taste good."

Ed chuckled. "An unfortunate truth."

"All right," Jared said. "What about my diet?"

"Let's name all the foods you eat." He took the pen from his shirt pocket and set the yellow pad on his lap. "Give me a list."

Ed wrote them as they came. Toward the end of a long string of unsurprising vegetables and grass-finished meats and free-range chicken, Jared said, "Morning glory seeds."

Ed looked up. "Morning glory seeds? Are they like sunflower seeds?"

Jared shook his head. "Not really. They're small and dark. I don't know much about them, except I figure the seeds must be nutritious."

"Are they?"

Jared looked sheepish. "Well, the first time I tried them, I got really sick."

"Sick?"

"Vomiting, nausea. I thought I was going to die. But I went online, and it turns out you have to clean them because the manufacturers coat them with a poison."

Ah. "Why?"

"I don't know, but they do. So I cleaned the seeds and now they don't make me sick."

"How do you clean them?"

Jared blushed. "It's kind of complicated. You soak them in lighter fluid first, till the fluid evaporates. Then you soak them in ethanol till *it* evaporates."

"Lighter fluid and ethanol," Ed said. He jotted a note. "What if they don't evaporate completely?"

Jared shrugged. "The Internet said that if the seeds are completely dry, the liquids have evaporated."

"And your seeds were dry?"

He nodded.

Ed jotted another note: *Lighter fluid/ethanol—cause paranoia? Toxin incompletely cleaned?* Then he asked, "So why go to such lengths to eat these seeds?"

"Morning glory leaves are incredibly nutritious. I figured the seeds would be concentrated, so they'd be that much better."

Ed nodded. "So when did you first eat the seeds and get sick?"

Jared took another sip of coffee. He shivered slightly. "Wow. Strong."

Ed chuckled. "Grace accuses me of making weak coffee."

"No way! I'll be buzzed in a minute." He waited a moment. "What did you ask me?"

"When you first ate the seeds and got sick."

"Yeah. I guess it was the middle of February."

Ed's pen poised in mid-air. "You're sure?"

"Yeah. Actually, I remember, it was Ash Wednesday. We'd gone to evening service and the seeds were dry when we got home, so I tried them."

Ed noted it. *Ash Wednesday. Check date.* "That's about, what, eight weeks ago?"

"I guess so."

"People have said you've been different the last seven or eight weeks.

That you've been more moody. Do you think that—"

Jared looked up sharply. "What people?"

"Your parents. Some of your friends."

"Which friends?" His face had tightened. A flare of paranoia?

"Jared?"

The boy collected himself. "I'm sorry. I guess that sounded like they're talking about me."

"They are. But do you know why they are?"

He shook his head.

"Because they care about you."

Ed watched sadly as tears filled the boy's eyes. After a moment, he said, "Let's take a break. But I have one more question first."

Jared nodded, wiping his eyes.

"When did your thoughts about killing people start?"

The boy looked out the window. At last, he said, very quietly, "About the same time." Ed wondered if there was something else he wanted to say, but when Jared said nothing, he let it go.

81

After a moment, Jared said, "Do you mind if I use your bedroom to meditate a little? I'm pretty tense about all this."

Ed nodded. "Sure, be my guest."

Grace was still sleeping, so Ed dialed Andi, hoping to catch her at home before she went in to work.

She answered, "How's it going?"

"I think I found a possible toxin he's been eating. Look, can you get out here and stick around for a couple of hours? I have to go in to the hospital and see my patient."

After a moment, Andi said, "Mack Anderssen."

Ed felt the familiar apprehension when a patient's identity became known. "How do you know?"

"I don't, but it's a good guess. You don't need to drive out to the Anderhold every afternoon to plan next Labor Day's fireworks."

"Damn. You're not supposed to know."

"And you're not supposed to be harboring a kid who violated a court order. Helping you means I'm playing outside the rules, Ed, so don't talk ethics at me."

He smiled. "Ah. Hoist on my own petard."

"What the hell's that mean?"

"Not sure, actually. Something like stewing in my own juice."

Andi chuckled. "Yeah. Stewing's good."

"Guess I don't win many rounds for a while, eh?"

"Not one, partner," she said, but her voice sounded friendly. "I'll stick close to Jared while you're gone."

Ed said, "Thanks, Andi. You're not angry?"

"Sure I am. But I'm a big girl, and you put shit aside when you have to."

"So you'll maybe be sitting on my porch again after this is over?"

"Not so fast, Romeo. I'm still a quarter angry."

"Got it. So you'll come out?"

"Give me a half hour."

"Maybe you can work on that last quarter while you drive out?"

"And maybe you can get elected pope."

82

At the hospital, Ed paged Doc Keeley. They met at the door to the physicians' lounge, and Doc led him inside. "At last check, Mack was still sleeping. We stopped sedating him at around eleven last night, per plan. Apparently, he slept on his own all night. I don't know if he had nightmares, but the nursing notes say he was never awake when they checked."

"How often did they—"

"Check? Every fifteen minutes."

"That's good. Well, thanks, John. I'll look in on him."

Magnus's door was wide open. Ed knocked softly on the doorframe.

The rancher, awake, though still in bed, called, "Come."

"Mack. How are you feeling?"

"I'm better. Must've slept all night."

"Glad to hear that." Ed yawned. "John tells me you were asleep every time they checked."

"I think I had a couple of hard dreams, but nothing like before. I went right back to sleep. Can I get out of here? I feel like a bull in a pen." He tried a small smile, which seemed like it hurt.

"That's up to Doc, but the plan was if you slept through the night without sedation, he'd release you. He's probably going to want you to take an anti-depressant medication."

Magnus shook his head. "No drugs."

"Why, Mack? It'll help you sleep through the nights. And I don't recall you balking at your personal medication." At the puzzled look, Ed added, "Quantities of scotch."

"Hmm," Magnus muttered, "I see." He changed the subject. "Luisa's on her way in with Junior to pick me up."

"You'll have to wait until John sees you and writes the order."

Magnus frowned. "And when does that happen?"

"I just talked with him in the hall. My guess is he'll see you shortly."

"Ed, I appreciate your getting me the sleep I need, but I'm a little nervous. I'd like out of here before the gossip starts. Can you arrange it?"

Concern about gossip wasn't Magnus's style. His usual confidence was obviously badly eroded. Ed pushed the door closed behind him. "I'll ask the nurse to get John. But whenever you leave, I want you in my office at five this afternoon." He'd figure out how to handle Jared later. One problem at a time.

Magnus groaned. "I can't come back into town today, Ed." His eyes took on the haunted look again.

"Yes, you can." Ed sat down on the bed, surprised at his own calm. "You came back from Mexico suicidal and desperate. You've had a good night's sleep, and it's understandable you want to forget the whole thing." He stifled a yawn. "Excuse me. Anyway, I promised you and Luisa that I'd help you, and I'm going to. So, five o'clock."

Magnus tried to smile. "Ed, we've been friends a long time. You're being helpful, but—"

Ed stopped him with a hand on his arm. "And we'll be friends for a long time to come, Mack. But right now, I'm your psychologist and I call the shots."

Just then, Ed's cell phone buzzed. Magnus nodded. "You're needed, my friend. I'm not the only one. I'll see you at five."

Ed stepped into the hall to take the call.

83

While Ed was at the hospital, Andi stepped out to the yard and called the department on her cell phone. Grace had gotten up, again, and she and Jared were eating a late breakfast. "Callie? Andi here. Is Brad Ordrew in the squad room? No? Okay, I'll call him on his cell."

She hung up and dialed Ordrew's mobile. "Hey," she said. "It's me. What's going on?"

"I'm going out to the Hansen's. It's time to push them harder on where the kid is."

Her stomach tightened. "Brad, they're worried to death. Don't—"

He cut her off. "It's a week since we found his cache, and so far we've got shit, nothing but his crazy talk, a pile of guns, and our suspect in the wind. I'm going to shake every tree I can find till something about this little bastard falls out."

Andi looked toward the cabin, trying to ignore her guilt at hiding him. "I don't want you upsetting them, Brad." She felt her voice rise.

"Upsetting them? Their kid threatens mass murder and violates an express restraining order, and you're worried about *upsetting* them?" He paused, then added, "It's time everybody gets a little more upset than they are, if you ask me."

"Give me a break," she snapped, letting her voice rise. "We put out the statewide APB within a half hour of his disappearance, and *everybody's* been busting their butts looking for him." She felt a twinge at her deception. She hadn't exactly lied, but...

"Well, I'm out here trying to get information, while you tell me to back off so the goddamn parents don't get fucking upset! What kind of female bullshit is that?"

Andi felt her face reddening. Jared had come to the screen door, watching her. She calmed herself and smiled at him. He gave a weak wave and went back inside. "Well," she said to Ordrew. "Wait for me." She wondered how long Ed would be—he'd promised no more than an hour, and he'd been gone, what? She checked her watch. Forty-five minutes. She felt her heart pound. *God, what a mess!* "I'll meet you back at the office in a half hour. I have to finish something up here. We'll go to the Hansens' together."

"No. I'm going now."

She turned slightly away from the screen door and lowered her voice so

Jared couldn't hear. "I'm lead on this investigation, Brad. You'll wait for me. Period." She listened to the silence.

Finally, he said, "Whatever. You're lead. But I'm not playing nice with them this time."

Andi debated confronting him on his tone, but decided that, even with Ben's approval, hiding Jared put her on shaky ground. Her issues with Ordrew could wait. She couldn't escape the nagging sense that the situation could go bad at any moment.

She ended the call and quickly dialed Ed's cell.

"What's up?" he answered. "How's Jared?"

"He seems all right," she said, annoyed because she was losing control— of the investigation, of the whole situation. "When are you coming back out?" Her tone was sharp.

"I'm on my way," he said.

She made an effort to soften it, but her irritation sounded in her voice. "Look, just make it fast."

"What's wrong?"

"This whole damn thing is wrong." She felt a chill. *What if Ordrew's right?* Were they all playing this too soft?

84

On his way out of town, Ed called Merwin.

"Ed, my friend! How's that mystery boy of yours? What's his name again? Jeremy?"

"Jared. Complicated. The fluctuating psychosis continues. When he left jail, he was paranoid again within a day. He scared some kids at school, but then he disappeared. A day later, he was relatively normal and texted me, asking for help. But I'm a little concerned there's some suicidal thinking going on under the surface."

"Texted!" Merwin laughed. "Aren't these youngsters fascinating?" He paused, then got to work. "What makes you think he's suicidal?"

"We met, and after we talked a while, he agreed to let me help him, but then he tried to throw himself in the river."

"You say he 'tried to throw himself in the river'? Literally, I presume."

"Yeah. I tackled him."

"Ah. Was it nostalgia for your football days, or just your Messiah complex?"

"I never played football."

Merwin guffawed. When he settled down, he said, "So he goes home, gets sick, then leaves home, and in a day or two, he's back to normal."

"Uh-huh. And we talked about his diet this morning. Mostly it's the usual health foods, organics, pastured meats, that sort of thing. But he tells me he eats morning glory seeds because they're so nutritious, but that he has to prepare them with a mixture of lighter fluid and ethanol before he can eat them."

Merwin said, "I've heard of that. Apparently, the manufacturers coat the seeds with some toxin."

"Yeah. Jared doesn't know why, just that they do. Lighter fluid and ethanol remove the poison. Anyway, my question is, Can lighter fluid, ethanol, or some combination of both cause paranoid psychosis? They might be the cause we're looking for, but I haven't had time to look them up."

"Or the original poison might be something to look at. I don't know the answer, at least about the lighter fluid, but morning glory seeds are a hallucinogen, a cousin to..." He paused. "Let me think. LSD, if I remember."

Ed felt excited. "So the seeds might be the cause of the paranoia, even without the ethanol or lighter fluid?"

"I don't know enough to answer that, but I know whom to call. You at home?"

Ed smiled at the *whom*. Merwin's care for grammar should rub off on Grace. "No, but I'll be there in ten minutes."

"Good. I'll call you back."

85

Ed turned into the long, up-curving drive to his yard, fretting about the phone call with Andi. *Something's wrong.* She'd sounded upset on the phone, but that didn't make sense if Jared was all right. When he pulled into the yard, she was standing on the steps, jiggling her keys.

"Where's Jared?" he said, getting out of the car.

She looked up, pointed back toward Ed's bedroom. "Sleeping again."

"You sounded upset on the phone."

"I am," she said over her shoulder, moving fast toward her Suburban. "This situation's a powder keg." She climbed in. "I have to go with Ordrew to interview the Hansens again—and pretend I don't know where Jared is."

"Damn."

"Yeah. And don't forget, I'm on swing shift today. I'll be back around eleven-thirty tonight."

Ed's heart sank. "Oh, man."

"What's wrong?"

"I have to see Mag—" He stopped. "Someone, at five, and I don't want to leave Jared here alone." He caught her annoyed look. "I'll think of something. Don't worry about it."

Andi climbed into the vehicle, shaking her head. She slammed the door and started the engine.

Ed watched her turn around. He waved. Andi didn't wave back, just drove down the hill.

Inside, Grace was texting someone.

"Jared's sleeping?" he asked.

"Yeah. Northrup, can I ask you something?" She put the phone in her lap.

"Sure." He wanted to make a note about the morning glory seeds, but Grace looked urgent.

"Me and Jen are texting and she says there's a used car for sale. Can we go see it?"

" 'Jen and I were texting.' "

"Really? Why were you and her texting?"

"No, grammar. Say 'Jen and I were texting.' "

She rolled her eyes. "I know, Northrup. I just like to see you get all grammarly on me. Anyway, can we?"

He shook his head. "Not today. Too much going on and I can't leave Jared alone." That reminded him of the problem coming up this afternoon.

"Maybe tomorrow?"

"Let's get Jared's problem settled and get him someplace safe, then we'll do it."

She nodded. She lowered her voice, glancing at Ed's bedroom door. "Northrup, something's wrong with him."

He tensed. "What?"

"He asked me if I believed in demons. I told him no, but he said, 'I think I have one in me.' That was, like, spooky."

The demon thing. Is he going psychotic again? "Did he say anything else that spooked you? Anything, like, angry?"

Grace shook her head. "Uh-uh. Not angry at all. He sounded kinda, like, shy. You know, like embarrassed."

Ed considered this. He made his decision. "I want to take Jared out to the Anderhold when I see Magnus. Would you mind coming with us so he doesn't have to be alone with Luisa?"

Grace shrugged. "Me and him can play cards. He likes cribbage."

"He and I."

"You don't like cribbage."

"No, your grammar."

Grace smiled. "Gotcha."

Ed smiled, but the good feeling faded quickly. He was skating too far out on the edge of something bad. He felt in his pocket. "Grace, I must've left my cell phone in the car. Back in a flash." It was sitting on the front seat. He called the Anderhold. Luisa answered. Ed explained the change of plans—he would drive out to the ranch for Magnus's appointment—and asked if she'd be comfortable with Jared and Grace coming out with him.

"This is the boy with the guns? The radio said he is still missing."

Ed hesitated. How to ensure that Luisa and Mack never let on Jared was with him? For that matter, that Grace and Jared never let on he was seeing Magnus? He clenched the phone, said, "Well, it's him. I'm doing the psychological evaluation, and I don't want to leave him alone while I see Mack. I'd appreciate it, Luisa, if you didn't tell anyone he's with me."

Luisa was silent for a moment. "Is he, what is the word? *¿Peligroso?*"

"Uh, dangerous? No, I don't think so." Ed hoped he was right.

"*Bueno.*"

"But I'm responsible for him while he's with me, and Mack needs another session."

"Yes, I understand. Certainly, bring the children along. Junior is also here, and he is a friend of Jared's. He does not believe the rumors." She paused. "We will tell no one."

"Thanks, Luisa," he said. "I'm obliged." After ending the call, he went back inside. "It's on. We'll head out to the Anderhold around four this afternoon. MJ's there too."

Grace brightened. "I have a crush on Junior Anderssen."

"Wow. Does Junior know that?"

She shot him a sour look. "No! And don't you tell him!"

86

Just as he'd started toward his bedroom to wake Jared so they could continue their conversation, Ed's cell phone buzzed. He walked outside as he answered.

"Eddie, Merwin here. Two tidbits of news."

"Great. Tell me." He sat down on the porch swing; at the moment, the warm weather was about the only thing to enjoy.

"First, inhaling lighter fluid could make a person somewhat paranoid, but not as delusional as your patient—what's his name, Jason?"

Ed smiled. Merwin was as lousy with names as he was brilliant with most everything else. "Jared."

"Ah, yes, Jared. And that reaction lasts only about ten or fifteen minutes. You'd have to keep inhaling it for hours to make it last, and doing that would severely damage your brain, fry it if you will, if it didn't kill you. And ingesting lighter fluid normally brings on nausea, not serious psychiatric symptoms."

"It was a long shot."

"Very long. Of course, ethanol is known to cause psychosis."

Ed frowned. *Only in quantities.* "A few tablespoons of ethanol, though..."

"Not a chance. You'd need late stage chronic alcoholism. A little dried ethanol on the seeds wouldn't do the trick. You're out of luck in that causation department."

"Damn," Ed muttered. "I was hoping..." He looked through the porch window. Grace was still texting. No sign of Jared. "What about the original poison?"

"Unfortunately, manufacturers use different toxins. Equally unfortunate for your theory, the compounds they select cause nausea, but nothing psychiatric."

"Crap." He took a deep breath. "Wait. You said there were two pieces of news."

"Indeed I did. The morning glory seeds themselves. They're meant only to be planted for flowers. The poison coating is designed to prevent people ingesting them."

"Why would people eat them?" Then it dawned. "Ah. For their hallucinogenic effect."

"Righto. The seeds are a cousin to ergot and lysergic acid."

"LSD. So the seeds could trigger his delusions."

Over the phone, Ed could almost feel Merwin's shrug. "Might, or might not. Lysergic acid amide, LSA, is their active ingredient. It's not tested for in your standard tox screen."

"So I should request it. Do they have a test for it?"

"Indeed, they do, but it's seldom used. Maybe never, actually. Anyway, another hypothesis I'd suggest you consider would be that he's somehow pre-disposed to psychosis and the seeds tip him over the edge. Those are certainly two options to consider." He paused, and Ed heard a rustle of paper. Notes. "Ah, here we are. Ask the boy if he ever got nauseous after he treated the seeds. If not, you can absolutely rule out lighter fluid or ethanol, and you're left with three theories."

"Which are?"

"Think about it."

Ed flinched. He'd been so tense, he'd stopped thinking clearly. He squinted at the mountains, cornering his thoughts. "One: The poison coating causes the paranoia."

"Which is refuted how?"

"Come on, Merwin," he said, cutting short the words. "Can we skip the Socratic method?"

"Which is refuted how?" Merwin repeated.

Ed relaxed; he had no reason to rush Merwin; they weren't due at the Anderhold for a couple hours. Besides, he needed to think this through so that he could present a sound theory to Andi and Ben. "It's refuted by the fact that to avoid liability no manufacturer would use a poison that would cause actual psychosis, only one that causes nausea."

"Indeed. Next theory?"

"The seeds tipped him into a psychosis he's already disposed to."

"For which our evidence is?"

"Insufficient."

"Woefully. I'd be tempted to use the adjective non-existent. And your third theory?"

Ed looked at his pickup, suddenly feeling the absurd urge to drive away, to go someplace quiet and fish. Like Jared's wanting to fly away. He pulled his thoughts back. "Some organic cause of a psychosis that fluctuates. Tumor, injury, something like that."

"Which fluctuates? The psychosis or the organic cause?"

Ed smiled. Grammar matters. "The organic cause, resulting in the psychotic effect."

"Exactly. Which tells us what?"

He thought it through. "A brain injury would be unlikely to fluctuate, right? It's there, or it isn't. Which maybe leaves a tumor."

"Generally true. Nothing in the brain is absolute, so don't rule it out entirely."

Ed thought about it. "The odds of a tumor causing intermittent paranoia and suicidal thinking, though? Probable, likely, unlikely?"

Merwin was quiet a moment. "I'd go with unlikely. But note, not impossible. Let me talk to a neurologist I know. If it's known, he knows it."

"Okay. But I'm thinking the odds bring us back to thinking about an external toxin again." He paused, thinking. "If not the seeds, then another one."

Merwin was silent. Then, "Of course, nothing's certain in the brain, but yes, that's my thinking too, Eddie. I'll talk to this fellow, but you go find your external toxin. And the seeds look like the place to start."

Ed grunted. "Otherwise, there are thousands." He thought about those odds. "Not a pretty thought."

Merwin laughed loudly. "You were hoping for pretty?"

"Screw you, Merwin. I thought you delivered answers." He smiled.

Another guffaw. "Never. I deliver only questions." Another laugh. Then, "But don't overlook the seeds. Start there."

They signed off and Ed sat on the porch swing, gliding back and forth quietly, watching the afternoon sky, blue as an infant's blanket, sun-filled and soft. Across that blue, a long black V of geese curved north. From the distance, he could just make out the sounds of honking, talking to each other. Guiding each other. The porch door opened. Jared stepped out.

Ed watched him carefully. The boy looked sleep-socked, but otherwise his eyes were not angry or terrified. He said, "I'm sorry to disturb you, Ed, but could I please make myself a sandwich before we leave?"

Grace joined them. "Me too, Jared. I'm starving."

210

They all went inside. As they made their sandwiches, Ed asked Jared, "Did you ever get sick again after you washed the seeds?"

The boy looked embarrassed. "No, sir. Only the first time."

Grace looked interested, but neither Ed nor Jared said anything more. Ed thought about Merwin's final words. *Don't overlook the seeds.* He made himself a sandwich and sat in the living room. Grace and Jared sat at the island counter in the kitchen.

While they ate, Ed thought about the seeds, and the kids carried on a quiet conversation. Jared spoke too softly for Ed to overhear his words, and Grace listened carefully, nodding. He saw her flinch at something. Then she flinched again, and reached over and touched Jared's arm. The boy looked away. Ed felt a welling sadness for this poor young man, and for his daughter and what she was learning about the world.

87

Andi sat off to the side, letting Ordrew confront the Hansens, as she'd agreed. She'd worried they might ask how Jared was or somehow give away that she knew where he was, but aside from a small look of gratitude from Marie, they said nothing. Ben must've sworn them to secrecy.

As she watched Ordrew take the lead, an unfamiliar self-doubt distracted her. No, not self-doubt, but guilt at deceiving her partner. From his intensity, she knew he cared about this case. Andi studied Marie Hansen, whose eyes were red, her forehead creased. Andi's heart went out to the other woman; even knowing that Jared was safe hadn't reduced her pain. Suddenly, she felt a blush rising across her face. Wouldn't her dad, who was a cop who always played by the rules, look askance at what they were doing? She shook herself. *Get back to this interview,* she demanded of herself. Maybe Ordrew was right. Maybe pushing the Hansens would break something open. Maybe.

Ordrew began slowly, directing himself to Phil. "I realize we've covered a lot of this already, but sometimes asking the same questions a second or third time surfaces details that might've been missed before. That make sense, sir?"

Phil nodded.

After ten minutes revisiting ground they'd already covered, Marie Hansen's hands were wringing; Phil's lips, pressed tight, were almost white.

Ordrew shot a glance at Andi, then sat up straighter and leaned closer, moving in. "So, let's get serious here."

Phil narrowed his eyes. "There's not a single minute of this we haven't been serious, Deputy."

Ordrew brushed it aside. "I repeat, sir: Let's get serious. So far we've talked to you till we're batty, and you've given us nothing but what a great kid you have, what a great job you've done as parents. Which is bullshit. Your miracle boy amassed an arsenal and two hundred rounds of ammunition. He's got the makings of a bomb. All this happens right under your noses and you pretend to know nothing about it."

Pretend? Andi leaned forward to object, but he glared at her. She sat back; she'd agreed to this. *Okay. Let him dig his own grave.*

Ordrew hammered it. "Your *good boy* told us he intended to kill his classmates. That's twenty-nine murders, Mr. Hansen. *Twenty-nine.* Good kids don't murder twenty-nine people. So drop the goddamn public relations campaign and start telling us what you know."

Phil leapt out of his chair, his face red. "For Christ's sake!" He turned to Andi. "Why are you letting him say such, such...outrageous crap?"

Startled, Andi felt herself blush again. *Didn't see that coming. Off my game,* she thought. She cleared her throat. She couldn't contradict her partner at this point. Not yet. "I'm sorry, Mr. Hansen." She glanced at Marie Hansen, whose face was ashen. "Mrs. Hansen. But there is a lot we don't know about your son, and he's a serious threat to many people. We need your help on this."

"My partner's being too damn nice," Ordrew snarled, standing now, confronting Phil Hansen, moving in close. "We're past needing your *help.* You need to convince us that you're not involved in the whole thing." He glared.

Andi thought, *Jesus, he's daring the father to punch him.*

Hansen did not back away. "One more insinuation like that, Deputy, and I'll report you to Sheriff Stewart." His fists were clenched.

"Report whatever you want, sir, but I'm not insinuating. I'm being as clear as I can be. You're under suspicion of concealing a wanted felon."

Andi frowned. *Bullshit.* Jared wasn't a felon, not yet, and the Hansens weren't under anyone's suspicion—except Ordrew's. He was close to the line. She said nothing, but she felt a vice clamped on her chest: She'd agreed she wouldn't interfere. Not yet. But she zeroed in, ready to stop this if it went much further.

Phil Hansen stood stone still for a beat, his face red, his eyes furious. Then he turned and carefully sat down. He glared at Ordrew for a moment, then at Andi. He spoke quietly. "I don't want to make this worse than it is." For that, Andi admired him immensely. His wife put her hand on his arm, rested it there.

Ordrew sat down, perched on the edge of his seat.

Struggling to calm his voice, Phil said, "We have no idea about what's the matter with Jared. We're not concealing him." He glanced quickly at Andi, then looked at Ordrew. "We've told you everything we can. If you suspect us of hiding something, there's not a damn thing I can do about that."

Ordrew, his own face crimson, barked. "You're lying. You know your son. You know the places where he's likely to go, where he'd feel secure. You're not—"

Andi leaned in, said, "Partner?" She hoped he'd get the message: Back off.

He waved her away. Andi, angered now, almost stood up to end the interview, but she saw Phil grasping the arms of his chair and turning to his wife, whose eyes were welling with tears, but whose mouth was working, trying to form words. Andi stopped.

Marie didn't dab her tears away, allowed them to track her cheeks. "Officer, you're being hateful," she said. "But I understand. You don't want..." She coughed on her tears. "...our son to murder innocent people. I can forgive you for doing your job, but I'm asking you to stop personally attacking my husband."

"Ma'am, I care a hell of a lot less about your feelings than I do about saving the lives of the senior class. So I repeat: Where would your son go? Where would he feel safe?"

Marie said, "The church. We told you he's a committed young man, and spiritually inclined. Didn't you think to look at the church?"

For a moment, Ordrew looked surprised, then recovered. "Of course we did. We're not stupid. Give us something better." He let the rebuke hang.

Andi was incensed. They'd searched the church, of course, but Marie triggered a thought that hadn't occurred to anyone. She said, "Does the church own any other property? A camp, perhaps?"

Ordrew glared at her. "Forget that," he said to the Hansens. "We've checked all that."

Andi realized he was no longer probing for useful information as much as trying to terrorize the couple into some bigger disclosure. She looked at the Hansens, ignoring him. "Any other church property?" She heard Ordrew's angry grunt, but refused to look at him.

Phil said, "Yeah. There's a church camp on Washington Mountain. Over in Carlton County, just across the county line."

"Would Jared feel safe there?"

Marie said, "I suppose he would. He spent many summers there."

"Exactly where is this camp?"

Marie looked at her husband. He said, "It's just past milestone 64 on Highway 36. The sign says, 'Camp Wesley.'"

Andi wrote it on her pad. She started to offer thanks, but Ordrew overrode her.

"Where else?" His tone was ice.

Marie said, "There's no place else, Deputy. Not that we know of, anyway."

"Damn it, you're lying! Do you think for a goddamn minute we believe that a high school senior felt secure only at home and summer camp? I'm going to—"

Andi jumped up and pushed her hand against his chest. "Brad, we're done here." Moving into the space between her partner and the Hansens, she warned him with her eyes, then turned toward the Hansens. The wave of Ordrew's rage broke against her back. "I apologize for my partner's accusations." She felt him start to move around her, shifted to stay in front of him. "We're under a lot of pressure to prevent what could be a horrible tragedy, and sometimes even the police let the pressure get to them. I hope you'll accept my apology, and if you think of anything that might help us— anything, really—please call me." She'd given them her card before, but she extended another across the gulf between them. Phil's hand, taking it, trembled. He glared over Andi's shoulder at Ordrew.

"I'm not done here," Ordrew snarled at her back.

She turned and stepped into his space. "Yes, you are."

He stood taller. Andi took another step toward him and whispered, "Turn and leave, or I'll see to it you never work another shift in this department."

For a flickering moment, Ordrew's hand hovered near his weapon. Then, explosively, he turned and stalked out. The front door slammed.

Andi faced the Hansens. "I'm truly sorry. I won't let him near you again."

As she left the house, the adrenaline trembling began. It wasn't helpful that behind her anger, she felt that stab of guilt for deceiving her partner.

88

As he locked his seatbelt, Ordrew snarled, "Listen to me! I don't give a good goddamn that Ben made you the lead. The next time you pull shit like that I'm going to make sure—"

"Shut up before you say something you'll regret," she said. She ignored her guilt. "Those people gave us something we didn't know and you attacked their honesty after being expressly asked not to. You lied to them about Jared being a felon and them being suspects. You stepped over the line and—"

"Fuck your line! I'm trying to save lives here and all I get from you and this damn department is push-back. Maybe you people *want* a mass murder, get yourself on fucking TV."

Andi went silent, still angry, but caught by something in Ordrew's tone. She just looked at him.

"Well, what?" he demanded.

"What's with the attitude, Brad? It's always you versus us, as if we aren't on the same page."

"We're not. You're small-town, nice-guy types. You wouldn't know the real world if it grabbed you by the tits."

"I wouldn't?"

"Hell, no. In LA, ten-year-olds shoot to kill, damn it. They don't smile at the nice policeman."

Andi looked at him, more curious than furious, straining to hear what was behind his rage. She said, "I'm from the Cook County Sheriff's Department. That's Chicago." His head snapped forward; he stared out the windshield. She kept her voice even. "I got shot. Was about to be promoted to lieu and given the medal of valor." She touched her right earlobe, which was notched.

As he turned toward her, he looked startled. "Cook County? You were shot? What went down?"

"A sex ring bust went bad. I was first in, and when I went through the door, the pimp took his shot. It nicked my ear. That was the second time I'd been shot at, so I resigned and came out here. I like polite citizens, and I'm glad people don't shoot cops, but that doesn't mean I don't know big-city policing." She felt something change in the car and tried to lighten it up, chuckled. "Of course, then I got shot here. Almost killed me." Ordrew's red face didn't lighten, but something had changed in his eyes. She looked at him hard. "And I've known my share of asshole male cops throwing their weight around. It doesn't work for me."

Ordrew seemed ready to strike back, but suddenly sank back in his seat, flattened by something. After a moment, he said, "I didn't know that—the shooting. Or about Chicago." He took a deep breath. "Maybe I owe you an apology."

"Uh-uh. Fuck apologies. What I want is an explanation of your attitude in this case." She looked at him hard.

He looked out the windshield again, his jaw muscles working, saying nothing. Andi watched his right index finger rubbing minute circles on his knee. When he spoke, his voice came out strangled, almost too soft to hear. "There was a kid in my precinct, fifteen, maybe sixteen." He stopped, his voice catching. "Cached some weapons in his parents' basement. One of his friends tipped us. Told us his friend wanted to shoot up the school. Somewhere mid-way through the investigation, it comes out he's autistic or some damn thing, and..." He stopped a moment, then took a deep breath. "Well, long story short, everybody felt sorry for the fucker. Tried him as a juvie, gave him three years' probation and *therapy*." The word sounded like it tasted foul. "Six months after the trial, he opens fire in the high school cafeteria, kills a kid and the teacher."

"Huh." Andi felt it rip through her belly, how she'd feel if that happened on her watch. She got it, his attitude. It'd be hers too.

Brad nodded, looking her way. "It wasn't my case, but it was my precinct." His voice thickened. "If it's your precinct, it's yours."

Andi nodded. She reached across the console and touched his arm. "I get it now."

He looked at her hand, then pulled his arm away. "Okay." He looked at her, a war in his eyes between sorrow and fury. "Show-and-tell time over?"

Andi felt the whiplash of his emotions. And her own. "Are you going to let go your hard-on about Jared?"

Ordrew forced a half smile, and offered a truce. "You interested in my hard-on?"

More whiplash for Andi. "Don't go there, Brad. You know I'm with Ed."

Ordrew winked. "Your choice of words."

"Bad choice then." She lowered her head, looked at him. "Seriously, are you going to let an autistic kid in LA drive your reaction to Jared Hansen?"

He nodded. "Yeah, I am. I couldn't live with myself if this bastard came back and snuffed his friends. Not twice."

He muffled a cough. Andi heard the grief.

89

In the threshold of the Anderhold's big front door, Ed gave Luisa a hug, felt the tension in her body, knew she could feel his. After a long embrace, he stepped back and introduced Grace and then Jared, who kept his head down, although he shook Luisa's hand when she offered it. Magnus Junior came down the hall, calling out, "Hey, man!" to Jared, and they did a ritual handshake that had been the rage when MJ was himself a senior, Jared a sophomore. Ed watched Jared closely; the boy seemed a bit more at ease, but not relaxed. Yet.

Grace moved close to Ed, and kept her voice low. "He's okay, Northrup. They're friends."

Ed nodded. Junior reached out to shake Ed's hand, smiling. "Nice to see you again, Doctor Northrup."

Jared, his voice soft, said, "I call him Ed."

Everyone chuckled, and everyone relaxed.

After the three young people had settled around the table and dealt cards for Texas Hold 'em, and Luisa had gone to the kitchen to make coffee, Ed made his way to Magnus's back office, deep in the Addition.

"Hey, Mack, nice to see you."

"No, Ed, it's not nice to see me," Magnus said. "This whole thing's a pain in the ass—" He stopped, grimaced. "Well," he said, "I guess that says it."

Ed gave a sympathetic smile. "In a manner of speaking, I suppose. Any pain since yesterday?"

"No. It's gone. The sleep seems to have helped." He paused. "Thanks for that, Ed. I can't figure how I'd have ended up without your help."

"Well, I'm glad I could do it. Shall we start?" Ed hoped that today, they could leverage the relaxation techniques Magnus had learned to deal with the symptoms—anal pain and the words in his head—without setting off a flashback or a flood of panic.

Ed repeated the procedure until Magnus was well relaxed, deeply in trance. Ed asked, "Anything new to report?"

Magnus breathed evenly and slowly, his eyes closed. "Nothing," he said. His voice sounded deeply relaxed. "No. Yes, one thing." There was a long pause. "Sometime during the night, I realized the infirmary—" He stopped. Then, "You remember those...words?"

Ed watched Magnus's face, his breathing, his hands for signs of a reaction: none.

Magnus sat perfectly still, waiting.

"Mack? You realized something about the infirmary?"

"You remember the words?"

Ed realized his mistake. So deeply relaxed, Magnus was probably close to being hypnotized, if not fully there, so his thinking would be utterly literal: Having asked Ed a question, he would simply wait for the answer, as long as it took to come. "Yes, I remember the words, Mack. *Stay away from the infirmary.*"

Ed watched Magnus's face: placid, unruffled.

The big head nodded slowly. "That's right." He took a long breath. "The infirmary. At St. Brendan's."

St. Brendan's Monastery perched high up on Mount Adams, in the shadow of the Coliseum. Ed had surmised that the anal pain reflected sexual abuse, and, given the Catholic Church's scandals, St. Brendan's seemed the logical place for that. Ed's sadness was profound. He'd spent time in a seminary as well, and he'd once loved the Church. Suspecting the monks, many of whom had consulted with him about their psychological troubles, hurt. But it made sense. Magnus had joined St. Brendan's and then "failed." So, Magnus's mention of the infirmary was interesting. Where would this lead?

Perhaps to the story of how the heavenly first year had turned "rough"?

Magnus nodded, frowning. In that instant, his tanned face paled, then crumbled in pain. His eyes shot opened. "It's back! The pain! Do something!"

Ed jumped in. "Use your calming words, Mack. *Relax.*" He reminded the

218

rancher of the cues—*safe, calm, breathe*. After a minute or so, Magnus's lips moving silently, repeating the calming words, his face relaxed, its color returning. His eyes drifted closed, and he whispered, "I thought I was done with that." His voice was drenched with disappointment.

"You can control it; you've come a long way. But until we learn what triggers it, you you'll have to manage these flare-ups."

Magnus opened his eyes and looked askance at him. "I suppose." He closed his eyes again, breathing heavily. "But..." His voice faded into silence.

After a moment, Ed asked, "*But* what, Mack?"

Magnus opened his eyes, looking stricken. "When the pain hit me, I remembered something new."

"Can you tell me?"

Magnus slumped in his chair, closing his eyes again. Ed had a sense of the man folding into himself. After a moment, Magnus said, "It happened at the monastery. When I was a novice at St. Brendan's."

Ed waited. This wasn't new.

Magnus turned his head away for a moment, as if looking far away; his eyes remained closed. His body shuddered. "Somebody raped me." Ed could barely hear the words.

He waited, his hunch confirmed, but at what cost to his friend? For a time, Magnus steadied himself, mumbling the calming words—*safe, calm, breathe.*

The rancher frowned. "I remember a black robe on the floor. Not mine." His breathing hurried. Suddenly, his face twisted, and he lurched forward in his chair. "I hate him! I'll kill him!" He jerked upright, his eyes wide, glazed.

Ed said quickly, "Mack! Use the words. *Calm, safe...*" He saw Magnus mouthing them.

Slowly, the big man settled himself again. This time, he looked confused.

"Who do you hate, Mack? Who do you want to kill?"

Magnus shook his head, as if clearing it. "I don't know. I'm hearing the words 'my novice' in my head."

" 'My novice'?" Ed tried to remember if Magnus had named other novices. *If there were any others.* St. Brendan's was a small monastery.

Magnus hunched his shoulders and put his head in his hands, having trouble settling down. Ed said, "Just breathe, Mack, as slow or fast as you want. Your body knows how to relax." He said it again, added the calming words, and repeated them softly again. Gradually, the rancher's face softened and his breathing slowed. Finally, he looked up.

His voice, no longer shaking, sounded implacable. "If I remember who it was, I *will* kill him. I promise you that."

Ed felt the power in that threat, and the truth. "Promise me another thing, then."

The rancher waited.

"Promise me that you will call me before you act on it. Promise you'll talk to me."

"So you can stop me."

Ed nodded. "And so I can help you."

Magnus, moving slowly, seemed to shake himself, stood, and walked slowly to the window. He stared out toward the mountains. "After his stroke," he said slowly, "my father asked me to kill him. When I refused, he called me a coward." Ed watched Magnus's shoulders go square. The big man returned to his chair. "It wasn't cowardice, it was vengeance. I wanted him to suffer. I could easily have killed him." He looked at Ed. "And I will kill this man when I remember him."

"I know you can do that, Mack. Promise me you'll call."

"Why?"

"Because I'm not just your shrink. I'm your friend."

90

Ed chatted a moment with Luisa, reassuring without divulging, then collected Jared and Grace, and they drove down to the log bridge and parked under the apple trees in the Anderssen orchards. Spring buds, hastened by the long warm spell, tinted the orchards a faint, almost ethereal yellow-green. Ed loved the color, but today, he felt a stir of sadness that the color did not move him. Ed turned to Grace and Jared. "I've got a quick phone call to make. You guys mind waiting a little longer?"

Grace said, "We're hungry, Northrup. Make it quick!"

Waiting for Jared's answer, Ed watched him staring out at the acres of softly tinged branches. During apple blossom time, townspeople came out here to picnic under the trees and enjoy their fragrant beauty.

The boy spoke softly. "In two weeks, this'll be a paradise. Blossoms and fragrance. I wonder where I'll be."

Grace touched his arm. Ed noticed Jared didn't flinch. "You'll be all right," she said. "We'll drive out here and enjoy the trees."

Ed smiled at Grace's attempt, though he doubted if that would happen. He said, "I'll be back in a flash."

Walking a short way off, he dialed Abbot Timothy's number at the monastery, and when there was no answer, left a message asking the Abbot to call back.

Twenty miles from town, his cell phone buzzed and Ed pulled over near a stand of yellow willows. He started to climb out of the cab, saying, "Ed."

Grace groaned. "Speed it up, Northrup. Me and Jared are *starving*!"

Jared said, "I've got my license, Doctor. Want me to drive while you talk?"

"Sorry, but I have to talk privately. Just a couple more minutes, please?" Grace groaned again.

Ed rolled his eyes and spoke into the phone. "Thanks for getting back, Timothy. Here's the story. I'm seeing a fellow who once lived at St. Brendan's. He recalls being raped at the monastery back around 1976...Yeah, it *does* suck...He seems to think it was a 'novice,' so it seems likely it's..." He listened. "No, he hasn't given me any names. I wondered if you have records of who the novices were in 1976."

After listening again, he said, "I'd appreciate that. I know how touchy this could be. But it's forty years ago..." He waited. "Yeah. You can just call this number and leave a message. It's my cell phone. And by the way, once you find the names of the novices, you'll know the name of my patient, though you won't know which one it is. I'd appreciate your keeping this confidential?" Satisfied with Timothy's response, Ed ended the call, and climbed back in the pickup.

Grace said, "Northrup, you better hurry. If I don't eat soon, I might die."

Ed thought he heard Jared chuckle lightly. *Good sign.*

91

As he pulled back onto the highway, Ed said, "Jared, let's check out your truck."

The boy looked surprised. "Why?"

"Making sure no one can see it."

"Oh, sure. I kind of forgot about it." Ed heard more than saw him rustling his pockets. "I don't have my keys."

"I've got them. Where is it?"

Grace groaned again. "You talking to me, Northrup? My stomach is growling so loud I can't hear you."

Ed laughed; even Jared smiled. The boy told him where the truck was and they found it in a cottonwood grove a hundred yards south of the Lovers' Lane. From the highway, Ed saw nothing at first, but driving in to the Lovers' Lane, the truck was easily visible. Way too visible.

"Damn," he muttered. Hadn't anyone driven in here?

"What's wrong?" Grace asked.

"I can see the truck. So that means, anybody else could see it and call it in. Everybody knows what kind of truck Jared drove."

Jared's hands balled into fists. "I thought I hid it well enough."

Ed heard the fear in his voice. "Not your fault, Jared. When you parked it, you didn't plan to leave it here." He glanced over; Jared's fists were loosening. "Let's see if we can hide it better." He didn't want to bring it back to his cabin.

But there was nowhere to safely hide the car.

He made a quick estimate of the risks involved, then said, "I think it'd be best if Grace drove your truck back."

Jared grunted. "Why?"

"The truck's too visible here. If we take it up to my place, I think it'll be safer."

"I didn't mean that," Jared said, his voice tense. "Why should Grace drive it?"

Grace looked at Ed, then at Jared.

Ed said, carefully, "I'd rather have you stay with me. Like we agreed."

The boy's face reddened. "You don't trust me. I gave you my word I'd help you, but I guess that's not good enough."

Careful now. Don't push him away. They had only twenty-five or -six hours left, and Ed knew he'd need all the good will Jared could muster. "All right," he said. "You drive your pickup. Grace rides with you."

"That's not trust. That's tying me to you through her." He looked apologetically at Grace. "I'm sorry, Grace. This isn't about you. It's about your dad trusting me."

Grace looked unsure, but her voice came out firm. "He's right, Northrup. You gotta trust him."

Ed squinted up at the cottonwoods, tinged with the chartreuse of early spring. He loved that color. He glanced at his gas gauge: *Three-quarters full.* So, if the boy took off, Ed could easily keep him within sight. Jared's old green pickup was well-worn, probably couldn't do more than sixty. But that wasn't really the point, was it? The kids were right: The issue was trust.

Still, if Jared ran, it would be on him, and Andi and Ben—and Brad Ordrew, for God's sake—would have every reason to be furious. He hesitated, thinking fast.

Ben, Andi, Jared—they're all taking a huge risk based on nothing more than trusting me. Magnus and Luisa, too, letting him bring Jared into their home.

Time to put skin in the game.

"You're right, Jared." He fumbled in his pocket for the keys, then tossed them to the boy. "But make me a promise."

"What?"

"We'll have about ten minutes out on the highway. You'll follow me, I'll lead you the back way to my place, but for those ten minutes, you're exposed. Promise me if the cops see you and pull you over, you'll stop, not run."

"So they can put me back in jail."

"No, so nothing seriously bad happens to you." He hesitated, then added. "They assume you're armed and dangerous. I want you to stop, because if you run, they'll shoot you."

Jared got out, then turned back, his eyes dark. "Okay." He walked to his truck without looking back.

Grace said, "Do you really think they'd shoot him?"

"I'm afraid they could."

Grace watched as Jared's truck backed slowly out of the woods onto the gravel of the Lane. "That's real bad, Northrup."

92

After an anxious ten minutes on the highway and then ten more on the back roads, Ed pulled into the yard ahead of Jared, whose truck slowly edged into the space beside Ed's. Grace popped out and ran over to Jared's truck; Jared got out slowly. Ed's phone buzzed. Grace called back that they were going to put a frozen pizza in the oven. "If we live that long!" She bounced up the steps. Jared walked more slowly behind her, his head low.

Ed took the call sitting in his truck.

"Ed, it's Timothy. I've got your names. In '76, they had three novices up here: Bobby Rancer, a fellow named Loyd Crane, and, you won't believe this, Magnus Anderssen! I had no idea Mack had been with us—I didn't come here till 1986. Bobby Rancer stayed; his monastic name is Father Dunstan. I have no idea what happened to Loyd Crane." He paused. "Anything else I can help with?"

Ed's breath had hit the shallows. "Did you say *Loyd Crane*? How did he spell his first name?"

"L-o-y-d. Just the one L."

Hair raised on the back of Ed's neck. "Timothy, do you remember the shooting two years ago here in the valley? Deputy Andi Pelton got shot when they broke up a tax conspiracy meeting?"

"Sure, why?"

"The guy behind the whole thing was named Loyd Crane. One L." Ed felt himself going very still. There couldn't be a connection, except, as Ben had said, "Coincidences ain't."

The Abbot asked, "Do you think it's the same person?"

"I have no damn idea." He paused. "Sorry."

"No problem. Monks contemplate damnation every day." He chuckled. "Look, keep me posted about this sexual abuse, will you? Especially if I need to call our lawyer."

"Sure, I'll do that." Ed steadied himself. It couldn't be *the* Loyd Crane. He thought about the names. Loyd Crane or Bobby Rancer. Given the evil that Loyd Crane had brought into the valley two years ago, if he had to put money on it, Ed would bet on Crane being the rapist. "Tim, is there anybody up there who knew the novices then?"

"Well, Father Dunstan, of course. Probably the one who knew all three of them best would be Father Jerome, the novice master in 1976. A sweet old man."

"Might I speak with him?"

"Unfortunately, no. He's dying of cancer. The old fellow no longer speaks, and he's seldom conscious. Doc Keeley was up yesterday and said Jerome'll die within the next few days."

Damn. "I'm sorry to hear that." Ed thought about Art Masters.

"Yeah, Jerome's a very important member of our community. We're going to mourn him a long time. Such a sweet man."

93

The kids had baked a couple of pizzas—Jared seemed to have lost, or maybe set aside, his devotion to organic food—and Ed was finishing a piece of the second one when Andi called.

"Look," she said, "I'm running on empty. I'm sleeping at my place tonight. Another night doubling up with Grace the Restless just might do me in."

He couldn't blame her. "Yeah. The couch is mighty unappealing, too." They'd let Jared sleep in Ed's room—because neither wanted to wake up to the sound of the door slamming and Jared fleeing into the night.

"And we have to figure out how to bring Jared in tomorrow evening. You should call Ben and set up a phone meet tomorrow morning, you, Ben, and me. We can set up the arrest scenario. I don't want Brad in on it. He's still real hardass."

"Besides, he'd find out you've been helping me conceal Jared. Not good." He rubbed his eyes. "Okay. I'll call Ben tonight and set it up." He paused. "I'll miss you tonight."

She didn't say anything for a moment. Then, her voice pitched lower, "Handcuff the boy to your bed and come on over. Then handcuff me to my bed."

"Let me count the ways Little Eddie goes for that," Ed said. "And Big Eddie thinks it's impossible."

She chuckled at the other end. "On second thought, I wouldn't get enough sleep either."

TUESDAY, DAY NINE

94

When he and Ben had talked last evening, they'd agreed on a conference call promptly at nine o'clock. Ed decided to make the call from his truck in the yard, so Jared wouldn't overhear. Grace had gotten a ride to school; they'd decided last evening that another "sick" day wasn't necessary, and she'd grumpily called Jen for a ride.

When she left this morning, he'd warned her against saying anything about where Jared was.

"Don't be a helicopter parent, Northrup."

As he climbed into the pickup and dialed the sheriff's department, he wondered what the hell a helicopter parent was.

Ben Stewart's voice growled when he answered Ed's call. "I buzzed Andi. She'll be here in a minute."

Ed heard a string of beeps, then Ben again: "I'm puttin' this speaker thing on." The line went dead. Ed chuckled and called in again.

"I ain't no switchboard operator," Ben grumped. "Lemme give 'er another shot." Another series of beeps alternated with grunts and mutterings. Finally, Ed heard Ben's growl. "Andi, 'bout time. How's this damn speaker thing work?"

A single beep, then Andi's voice: "Ed, that you?"

Before he could answer, Ed heard Ben: "Let's get goin'. Gotta write the screenplay for this evenin's little drama."

Andi said, "How's Jared, Ed?"

"Good. We had a long talk this morning after Grace went to school, and he went back to bed. I think I've found the source of his delusions."

"Which would be what?" Ben asked, chewing something.

Andi said, "Before that, let me fill you two in. I just got the report from DCI. They didn't find anything of interest on Jared's computer. But those seeds, remember the ones we found? They're morning glory seeds. Apparently they're a hallucinogen."

Ed made a private fist pump. "Yeah. Jared eats them."

"Here's what's interesting. Most people who eat them get sick, because manufacturers coat them with poison to make anyone who eats them nauseous, so they don't eat them. But get this: Remember the Zippo lighter fluid and the ethanol we found? It turns out people bathe the seeds in the lighter fluid and then the ethanol. When the liquids evaporate, the seeds are edible. People eat them because they cause hallucinations. They're like a weaker version of LSD." She sounded very pleased.

Ben said something with his mouth full; Ed couldn't make it out.

"Hey, Ben, could you swallow whatever you're eating and say that again?"

Ben was silent a moment, then said, "I said, 'crap on toast.' So, our boy's a druggie on top of a paranoid mass murderer wannabe. Just got worse."

Ed smiled. "I don't think so, Ben. What Andi says is true, and I've been on this already. My consultant and I—"

"Whoa, Pancho! I ain't got money for another consultant."

"He's an old friend, Ben. You remember Merwin, don't you?"

"That bowling-ball-shaped professor from Minnesota? With the big laugh?"

"Yeah, that's him. Anyway, we know that Jared ate the seeds—he did get sick the first time, which shows he didn't understand what he was doing, and probably didn't know they were mind-altering."

He paused. *Jesus L. Christ on a crutch!* To learn how to clean the seeds, Jared must have Googled them—and that would have told him they were hallucinogens. He must have known, but he'd pretended not to. Suddenly Jared's all-American image had cracked. Was he taking drugs? Maybe other than the seeds?

"Earth to Ed."

"Sorry, just thought of something I need to, uh, follow up on. Anyway, Jared thinks the seeds are nutritious. Merwin and I are thinking the seeds might cause the delusions. Could be why his thinking clears up when he can't eat them."

Andi said, "So that explains why the crazy talk comes and goes?"

"Yeah. Have you got the tox screen back yet?"

"Not yet. A few more days."

"Well, I'd like you to ask them to test for lycergic acid amide. It'll tell us if the seeds were causing his psychosis on Monday when you arrested him."

Andi jotted a note. "On it."

Ben grunted. "Still thinkin' it just got worse. Drugs ain't easy for juries to overlook."

Ed shook his head at the phone. "Or it just got better, because it may show he's innocent. He thought the seeds were a health food, and he's known for being a health nut."

Andi said. "That fits what we've seen."

Ben was silent for a moment. "Or he's shinin' us on. It don't make me happy, whatever it means." Then he must have put something else in his mouth, because Ed barely made out what he was saying. "Well, kee' on 'er. Wha's 'a plan...bring Jared in?"

Ed took a stab. "First thing, I don't want to deliver him to Ordrew. Jared trusts Andi now—"

"Sorry, Charlie, Ordrew's got the desk during swing shift. He's the one to book the boy. I switch out assignments and somebody'll get curious."

Ed sighed. "Okay, then let's do it this way: I claim neither of you knew I had Jared. Andi stayed all weekend at her place, not out at the cabin. Tonight, after her shift, she comes out to my place and sees Jared's green pickup in the yard, finds him inside, arrests him, brings him in. I take the rap, and I tell you what I've discovered and how that makes this a medical issue, not a criminal one."

"*Medical or criminal* ain't your decision, pal. Up to a jury." Ben said. "But listen up: The rest works. I expect your expert report on my desk by tomorrow morning, eight sharp."

Ed took a deep breath, glad he wasn't face-to-face with Ben. "I can't do an expert report, Ben. I'm seeing Jared privately, remember? You'll have to subpoena my file." He expected Ben's anger to blister the phone. To pre-empt it, he jumped ahead. "But my notes'll state my impression the cause is the seeds, which will jibe with the DCI's findings." Lame as a congressman's apology. He pushed on. "So it makes your case even stronger."

"My big butt it does, Ed. I ain't pleased how this is turnin' out. I've half a mind to arrest your ass for obstructin' a police investigation."

"Well, if you have to. But I wasn't obstructing. I was helping."

Ben grunted again, but didn't say anything.

Andi changed the focus. "Ed, when you're talking with Jared today, before he comes in, ask him why he rented the storage unit in the first place. I asked, but he didn't want to say. Maybe he'll open up to you."

Ed made a note. "Will do."

She went on, "How should I react to you 'keeping a secret' from me?"

"Act pissed I didn't loop you in."

Andi laughed. "Brad'll love that. He thinks I'm interested in his hard-on."

Ben choked, and something sounding like a mouthful of liquid spattered the speaker phone. Ed frowned. "Interested in his hard-on? What's that mean?"

Andi sounded coy. "Worry about it, big guy."

Ben snorted audibly again. This time with no waterworks.

95

After the call, Ed went inside. His bedroom door was open. He called Jared's name, but heard nothing. His heart jumped into his throat. Running?

On the table was a note:

Going for a walk in the woods behind your cabin. I'm okay. I saw a trail out the back door and I'll just follow it. I left around 9. I'll come back. Jared.

Ed glanced at his watch: *9:16. Oh, man.*

After making sure he still had Jared's truck keys, Ed stopped. Was the note meant to decoy Ed, get him to leave the yard so Jared could hotwire his truck? Did the boy know how to do that?

Better safe than screwed. Ed lifted the green truck's hood and took out the spark plug wires, then dropped the hood. He stashed them in his truck and locked the doors. Then he walked fast down the trail, one he'd walked a hundred times. It occurred to him that if Jared were escaping, he wouldn't have left a note. *Unless it's a distraction.* He picked up his pace, ducking the low branches. Needles and small forest debris crunched beneath his boots, and through the trees he saw towering pillars of cloud rising above the crests of both the eastern and western mountains. Between them, the sky was clear as a child's face.

Ed hurried down the trail. *Please don't let this kid be in the wind again.*

96

Deep in the quiet stand of mid-sized ponderosa pine and grand fir, Ed found Jared sitting on a stump in a wide clearing. Jared stood up when Ed came into the clearing. "I heard you coming." He looked nervous.

Ed put his hand on the boy's shoulder. "How're you doing?"

Jared shrugged. "The usual, scared." He looked up between the trees at the soft blue sky, then drew a long breath. "What happens now?"

Ed nodded. "It's going to turn out all right. I—"

Jared cut him off. "No disrespect, Ed, but I need to prepare myself for what's going to happen next. Just tell me the plan."

"Got it. Andi is going to come out here after work, and she'll take you in."

Jared seemed to shiver. "So I'm going back to jail?"

"Yeah, unfortunately. As soon as your lawyer can, she'll get you out, of course, but it might take a couple of days."

"Can you call her, so she meets me when Andi takes me in?"

Ed sighed. "Can't. If we do that, we tip our hand about you being here all along."

Jared nodded. "Probably doesn't matter. How can she get me out? I ran away the first time. Nobody'll trust me now."

He's looking at facts. Ed found himself admiring the boy's courage. "Yeah, that'll be a problem. But what we've figured out should help us get closer to the end of this mess."

"I'm not so sure there's any end to it." He looked away into the trees for a long moment. "So, what've you figured out?"

"I believe we know what triggered your condition."

"My condition?" Skepticism colored the fear in his voice. "I don't have a condition." But before Ed could answer, he said, "Oh. The paranoid thoughts. Wanting to kill my friends."

Ed nodded. He waited for Jared to ask about the trigger.

Instead, as if he hadn't heard, Jared said, "I don't think I can stand going back into jail." His face was white and his hands fisted and released, over and over. He was restless, but didn't move away. He was breathing hard.

"We'll go over some meditation techniques—they're good for managing anxiety. You did tell me you meditate, right? And I've got books you can read to pass the time. They allow that—as long as I don't hide a hacksaw in them."

Jared didn't smile. "I meditate now and then. Not as much as I should, I guess. How can that help?"

Ed nodded. "What's the worst part of being in jail?"

"Fear."

"Exactly. Meditation knocks fear down."

Doubt crept across his face. "It didn't do that when we practiced it in class."

"Were you afraid then?"

Jared half-smiled. "Good point."

"Want to practice?"

Jared glanced around the grove. "Here?"

"Why not? You can meditate anywhere."

"Even in jail, eh?"

They sat on stumps and Ed reminded Jared about breath-counting, one to ten, over and over until thoughts and fear diminish. Ed watched Jared's body relaxing, impressed with him. *The kid has practiced before.* After ten minutes, he said, "Okay, stop."

Jared opened his eyes.

"How did it go?"

"You're right. A couple of times I started to get scared, and I just looked at it and accepted it, then went back to counting. Like they taught us. It helped." He looked at the forest around them. "But the woods aren't jail."

"Are you free to go anyplace?"

Jared shook his head. "That doesn't make it jail."

"No?"

For a moment, Jared looked annoyed, but then, he smiled bashfully. "I see what you're getting at. It's how I think about it that makes it jail, or woods, or whatever."

"Exactly. Think about Nelson Mandela."

For a moment, Jared said nothing. Then, "Mandela was innocent. I'm not."

"Wrong on two counts. One, Mandela was a terrorist. He wasn't innocent, although be became a good man in prison. And two, you haven't done a damn thing."

Ed felt the pressure of time: He was due at Magnus's in less than an hour. Andi was working and Grace wouldn't be home from school till late. He said, "Look, Jared, I have to go back to see Magnus Anderssen again. I need you to come with me."

Jared shook his head. "I'd rather stay here and practice my breathing. I'm going to need it."

"Ah, man, that's hard." He thought. "You can practice at the

Anderssens'. I can't leave you here alone, Jared."

"You can trust me, Doctor." The voice sounded hard.

Ed grimaced: *Doctor?* Damn. Was he losing him? "This time it's not about trust. We need to talk some more about the seeds, and I'm afraid there won't be time if we wait."

"You're afraid I'll jump in my truck and leave."

"No. I trust that you'll keep your word. Anyway, I've got your keys." He tried a small smile, but Jared didn't return it.

"I don't want to go back to the Anderssens."

"Why? You and Junior are buds."

He looked at the sky again; Ed saw tears form in the corner of his eyes. "I'm ashamed."

Ed nodded. *Poor kid.* "Come with me anyway. You can wait in my truck, and practice meditating."

"You're afraid I'll kill myself if you leave me."

"Would you, if I left you?"

Jared's eyes narrowed, but he shook his head. "No. Grace would find me. I can't promise I won't do it some other time, maybe in jail. But I won't do that to her."

Ed heard the compassion in the boy's voice. Decided to trust it. The problem hadn't changed, though. "No, Jared, you've got to come. Like I say, wait in the truck and practice. But we have to hit the road."

Jared looked at Ed for a long moment, then shrugged, resigned. "All right." They walked the trail back to the cabin, and after getting water and some cold pizza, they climbed into Ed's pickup.

Driving south on the highway, Ed asked, "Do you have any morning glory seeds that you could eat?"

"With me here? No. Why?"

"You should be aware what the morning glory seeds are doing to you."

"Aren't they a health food?"

Ed looked across at him. Why was he playing innocent? "Uh-uh. They're hallucinogens. I believe they make you paranoid. We're pretty sure that's what caused all this." But the crack in Jared's image nagged him.

Jared looked away. "Shit. I didn't know."

"You never looked them up?" He glanced again at the boy.

"Uh-uh." His face had paled.

Ed considered confronting him, but under the circumstances, decided to wait. Instead, he said, "You haven't had any seeds for a couple days, so I think you'll be all right. But you've got to promise me you won't touch them again, when you finally do go home."

"I haven't had any since the first time I was in jail." His eyes went to the sky again. Thinking. "No, maybe that's wrong. I maybe ate some Saturday morning before I went up to the school."

"Ah. That would explain what you did, why you ran. Good. But you'll help your case a lot by not getting paranoid again. I'm going to ask Doc Keeley to prescribe some medication for you to take while you're in jail. Combined with meditation, it should make sure you stay in a calm frame of mind. And keep you from getting paranoid again."

Jared looked frightened. "But if it's the seeds, and I don't eat any, why would I get paranoid again?"

"I don't expect you will—if it's the seeds, and that's still an *if.* We need to talk a bit more this afternoon about that. But if I decide you should take the medication, will you do it?"

The boy looked up again at the pure sky, as if solace were in the blue. He shook his head. "I hate this. How will it end?"

Ed touched his shoulder. "I don't know. But I think you're going to be okay."

Jared frowned and looked at him. "No, Ed. I won't be okay."

97

Brad Ordrew drove back roads, searching for Jared Hansen, stewing. He wasn't on duty till the afternoon, but he was pissed. Pissed about Jared's disappearance, pissed about everybody's apparent unconcern with what was going on. The whole clusterfuck infuriated him; no, to be honest, it terrified him. He kept glancing at his cell phone lying on the dashboard, expecting any moment the call to come: *All units to the high school. Active shooter inside building!*

Shit. He needed action. *Somebody fucking needs to do something!* He turned around and drove back into Jefferson, then drove slowly up and down streets, peering into alleys and behind garages. No green pickup. He really didn't expect to see it; hell, every goddamn inch of the county had been searched. *We ought to be scouring the shit out of Missoula.* The Missoula County sheriff and the city police hadn't turned up any storage units in Jared's name. Yet.

When the houses gave way again to fields and patches of forest, he remembered that Ed and Grace Northrup's cabin was out this way. He picked up speed. Ben had mentioned that Northrup was acting as the kid's psychologist. *Fuck that.* Northrup would know where Jared was.

At the shrink's driveway, he turned in, and drove up the long rising curve toward the cabin and its gravel yard. He conceived a plan: Interrogate Northrup hard, and if he doesn't give anything up, do Grace again, and push her hard. Real hard. Screw Andi.

Cresting the rise into Northrup's yard, he smiled at the thought of screwing Andi. Then he gasped.

In the yard sat a battered green pickup. *The kid's ride*, he thought, his anger flaring. *What the fuck?* There were no other vehicles.

He parked behind the green truck and walked up the porch steps and pounded on the door.

After a long wait and another round of pounding, he debated going in. Without a warrant, there could be trouble. *Shit. The fucking shrink's the one in trouble. There's a fugitive in this house and I'm not letting him go.*

He opened the door and stepped inside.

98

No lock on the door? Ordrew considered taking off his shoes, wanting to leave no evidence of his being in the cabin, but decided against it. *Might have to get out quick.* To his scan around the living room and the open kitchen, nothing presented itself. He listened for sounds, but the house was still. He went into what was obviously Grace's room. Girl stuff everywhere. Stuffed animals. Cosmetics on the top of the dresser. *The Hunger Games*, all three books, on the bedside table. A poster of some woman named Zadie Smith—*What the hell kind of name is that?*—hanging beside another of Rachel Maddow. Ordrew wrinkled his nose. He knew Maddow. *Liberal twit.* But no sign of the boy.

In the other bedroom, he found women's underwear in a basket in the closet, and in one of the dresser drawers, more women's T-shirts, socks, and underwear; the other drawers contained men's things. *Andi stays here.* He lifted a pair of panties and inspected them. Tempting to put them in his pocket. Instead, he laid them back in the drawer.

He checked the bath. Four toothbrushes rested in the rack. Puzzling. *If*

Andi sleeps here, she'd have one. Grace and the shrink. That's three. He peered at them. One brush looked new. Using his handkerchief, he opened the medicine cabinet, then the drawers below the sink. In the bottom drawer, he found two unopened, packaged toothbrushes. *For guests.* So the fourth might have been opened for Jared Hansen. Where's the package? He checked the wastebasket. Bingo.

Fingerprints? Carefully, he wrapped the toothbrush and the package in his handkerchief, then opened one of the new ones and placed it where Jared's had been. He put the two newly opened packages in his pocket. On an impulse, he looked in the clothes dryer. *Ah!* One pair of jeans, a T-shirt, a flannel shirt, underwear. *Could be Northrup's, he thought. Or the kid's.*

He heard a sound outside. *Goddamnit.* He froze, but the sound didn't repeat. Feeling vulnerable, he went out, down the steps, and around the pickup into the grassy field beyond. With his cell phone, he took two photos of the green pickup framed in front of the cabin. He moved around the front and photographed the plates.

He was deciding how to use this. The kid was here, he knew it, and for damn sure, Andi had to know. Maybe he should print the toothbrush, then come back and grab the kid. No, skip the fingerprints, no way you could use them without a warrant. So maybe wait till he shows up and nail him.

Or arrest the shrink. The son-of-a-bitch.

He re-thought fingerprinting the package and the toothbrush; do it. Even if he couldn't use them, at least he'd know for sure the boy was here.

As he climbed back into his squad, thinking about the beat-up green truck, he wondered, *Where the hell is everybody?* Andi's on duty. The girl's at school. From the truck, the kid had to be around. Unless Northrup had him hidden somewhere. No, there were the clothes and the toothbrush.

Or unless the kid killed the girl and Northrup, and stole the shrink's truck.

99

Ed pulled into Magnus Anderssen's yard. He dropped his keys in his pocket and turned to Jared. "You'll be all right out here. The air's warm. I should be an hour, maybe ninety minutes."

Jared nodded. "I'll be okay. I'll practice."

Getting out, Ed patted his pants again, re-checking that he had his keys.

He hoped Jared didn't know how to hotwire a car. *No use in worrying about that now.* At the top of the porch steps, he turned and waved. Jared was watching him. He waved back.

Luisa looked past Ed toward the truck. "He does not want to come inside? I have coffee on."

Ed shook his head. "He's embarrassed. I think he'll be all right out there. The truck is plenty warm."

Magnus came down the stairs from his den and took Ed's arm, directing him to the office at the back of the Addition. Closing the door, he said, "Let's get this done, Ed. Use your hypnosis or whatever, and let's figure out the rest of this crap. I need it over." The man's urgency was palpable.

They sat. "Okay, Mack. Lay out what we already know."

Magnus looked confused. "You know what I know."

"Not to refresh my memory. To refresh *yours.*"

"Oh." Magnus lifted an eyebrow. "Priming the pump?"

Ed nodded.

"Okay. In the infirmary at St. Brendan's. Somebody raped me. In the ass. The words 'my novice.' A black robe on the floor." His face twisted, anxious. "Enough?" He was breathing heavily.

Ed nodded. "Let's get to work." He wanted to flesh out the images so Magnus could penetrate further into the story. "Start with your breathing. Use your cue words and get as relaxed as you can."

A ready student, Magnus quickly closed his eyes and slumped in his chair. After a few moments, he was breathing slowly and deeply and Ed began the induction of hypnosis proper. When Magnus was well into his trance, Ed said, "And so, when you're ready, you can see the next things you're ready to know, and—" He did not have to go on.

Magnus spoke, his eyes closed, his voice deep and slow. "I see it. Johnny and Loyd are with me. We're waiting on somebody."

"Where are you waiting on somebody?"

"In the...in the infirmary." His breathing picked up slightly and his eyelids moved.

Ed said, "Easy, Mack. Use your words. Stay relaxed." Magnus quickly settled, his eyelids still.

There was a long silence. Ed said, "So you were waiting for someone in the infirmary, you and Johnny and Loyd."

Magnus's eyes moved side to side behind his eyelids. "I see him coming in. Father Master." His voice sounded strained.

"You saw Father Master coming in."

"Father Jerome." Rapid, shallow breaths now, shoulders hunching.

Ed pictured Father Jerome, the Abbot's *sweet old man,* dying of cancer. "You saw your novice master, Father Jerome, coming in. How were you feeling as Father Jerome is coming in?" He was careful to use Mack's words, to add nothing of his own.

"Something bad is happening."

Ed repeated it, held his voice neutral.

Magnus's breathing came faster, his fists clenching, unclenching, clenching. Sweat dewed his forehead. "Johnny and Loyd. He's sending them away. Very bad."

Ed started to remind him to relax when Magnus slumped back in the chair, his face pale. His whisper was barely audible. "My God."

Ed waited a moment, then asked, "What, Mack?"

Magnus's eyes opened and he looked directly at Ed, his face, if possible, becoming even whiter. He shook his head.

"You can say it, Mack."

Again, he shook his head.

Ed waited.

After a few moments, Magnus gathered into himself a long, ragged breath. Still whispering, as if trying to keep a secret from escaping, he said, "Jerome drugged me, then raped me." Leaning forward, he looked into Ed's eyes, as if searching for something there. Suddenly, long desperate moans came from deep in his chest, and he sank back into the chair and began sobbing. His face cradled in his hands a long time, his wide chest heaving, Magnus wept.

Minutes passed. Magnus would calm, then be wracked again, blown by gusts of weeping, bursts of pain. Finally, he was still. His eyes, when they opened, were red and heavy-lidded, glazed. He briefly caught Ed's eye, then looked down, whispered: "Now you know."

Ed brushed the tears that had gathered in his eyes. He shook his head gently. "Now *you* know."

Magnus looked out the window, his breaths stuttering with small sobs. "I loved that man. That whole first year, he was the good father I never had." He wept again, quietly; Ed handed him a fistful of tissues. The two men sat silently for a very long time, Magnus's eyes brimming over. During lulls between gusts of grief, he kept his eyes on the floor, or looked out the window. After ten minutes of calm, Ed asked, "Mack, how're you feeling?"

Magnus looked up, eyes lost. "Like a whore."

The shame comes before the rage, Ed thought. He said, "You're not a whore, but after what you went through, shame's natural."

"After being turned into a whore."

"That's how it seems to you?"

"That's how it is."

"We'll argue about that later. For now, just let yourself feel whatever you feel." He thought about Magnus's coming evening—and Jared's. In a flash, it could turn ugly for either of them. Ed shivered, blocking his apprehension. "Stay in touch with me, okay? We'll get through this."

Magnus's eyes filled again. "I loved him. He was my good father, and he made me his whore."

Ed disliked ending on that, but he had to get back to Jared. He made the calculation quickly: Magnus was strong, a man well aware of the cruelties of human nature. The rape—like his father's brutality—had not soured him on people. He'd always borne his responsibilities to his workers and to the valley people graciously, and he treated everyone with fairness and friendship. Except in the recent weeks, he hadn't withdrawn from life or turned sour. He loved Luisa, and Luisa was here, and Ed knew she would call if anything went wrong. It was probably safe to leave. Still, he felt uneasy.

What he'd just witnessed washed over him, not only Mack's enormous sadness, but the unutterable humiliation the man had endured. At least, now they knew the origin of his suffering, and that offered a release from the prison of pain in which Magnus had been trapped. With a catch of sadness, he thought of Jared's returning to jail, and whether he could find a way to end the boy's suffering. The enormity of it swept over him, a rogue wave.

Magnus must have seen it on his face. "You look as bad as I feel, my friend."

Ed could only nod, his throat too full.

The rancher said, "I'd offer to listen, but I'm, ah, spent."

Ed rubbed his eyes. "Yeah, let's pack it in for now. How about meeting again this evening?" He thought, *After Andi takes Jared in.*

Magnus shook his head. "No, I can't take—" He stopped, then looked at Ed. "I said I wanted to get through this, didn't I?"

Ed nodded. Perhaps Magnus was ready to fashion some healing from his tragic knowledge. Moving on it quickly seemed a good idea. "I can drive back out about seven-thirty or eight tonight. That work for you?"

The rancher nodded. As Ed opened the office door, Magnus touched his arm. "Thank you. I think."

100

Four o'clock in the afternoon—deputies' meeting at shift change. Andi sat uncomfortably at the corner of the table, worrying about the upcoming charade with Jared. The meeting's focus on Jared's disappearance didn't help; she tried to come up with things to say, but failed.

Ordrew reported on his drive up Highway 36 to the Methodist camp. "The pastor gave me the master key, but the place is a goddamn ghost town. No sign of the little prick."

Andi felt his eyes on her. Throughout the briefing, he kept glancing at her. *He knows something.* Since their talk yesterday, she'd tried to give him the benefit of the doubt. His side looks worried her, though.

Ordrew was the on-call deputy this evening, which meant he'd be the one to book Jared. As the meeting broke up, she wondered how she could get around that. As they filed out of the conference room, surprising her, Ordrew took her arm.

"Got something for you."

She couldn't decipher his look and resisted him, but he pulled her into the empty interrogation room. Inside, when he dropped her arm, she said, "What the hell's—?"

"Shut up," he said. Pulling out his cell phone, he brought up a photo. "Take a look," he said, handing Andi the phone. Andi went cold. The picture showed Ed's cabin and yard, with Jared's green pickup parked in front. Ordrew reached in and tapped the photo: The time and date stamp came up: Today, *11:13* a.m.

Andi felt her breath catch. "I can—" She stopped herself. Ordrew didn't know she was involved.

His voice was hard. "No, you can't, *partner*. You went off on me for thinking somebody's hiding evidence, and all the time, it's your damn boyfriend! And you had to know it."

Andi let her guilt morph, swiftly, into anger. "Fuck that, Brad. Drop the crap. Nobody's hiding evidence. Ed's *job* is evaluating Jared, and he had to spend time with the boy to figure out what's wrong with him." Even as she said it, she disgusted herself: Ordrew had caught her. She tried to recapture her anger. "If you don't trust me on this, fine, but don't bullshit me about how *you* know how *real* police work. Real cops support their partners."

He shook his head. "*Real* cops don't lie to their partners."

She flinched, her anger evaporating. She sighed. "You're right."

"You let me bully the parents, and all the time you knew where the boy was, didn't you?" He sounded disgusted.

Andi grimaced; all her conflicted feelings about this situation came to a head. "I'm sorry, Brad. I handled it wrong."

Without warning, he smiled. "To quote you, 'Fuck apologies.' This shit happens on the LAPD every day. All of a sudden, I feel like I'm Home Sweet Home." He opened the door of the conference room. "You *do* know big-city policing, don't you? Better yet, now you owe me big time. And I think I'll let your boyfriend pay."

101

When Ed said goodbye to Luisa at the Anderhold door and stepped out on the porch, his truck was empty. *Damn. He's gone.*

When he went around the truck, though, he found Jared sitting at the edge of the terrace overlooking the valley. The truck behind him had blocked Ed's view. He relaxed.

"How are you doing, man?"

Jared slowly looked up at him. "I've been practicing. I'm calm. I think I can do this." He smiled. "Thanks for reminding me about meditation, Ed."

"You're welcome. Look, I still have a few more questions. You up to a conversation on our way home?"

"Yeah. When do I go to jail?"

Ed looked at his watch: *3:55.* "Three hours. We'll talk, then I'll make some supper, and Andi will come out and officially arrest you."

At the word "arrest," Jared flinched, his eyes frightened, but he narrowed his eyes and breathed slowly for a minute or two. He opened his eyes. Ed was impressed with his talent. "Okay, I'm ready."

Ed backed the truck around and started down the two-mile driveway to the highway. "I'm still thinking about the morning glory seeds. Tell me more about how you ate them."

Jared looked confused. "Uh, I put them in my mouth and—"

Ed laughed. "Sorry, lousy question. Let's start with the time of day when you ate them."

"Oh. I used to eat a handful or two every afternoon after school. When I rented the unit, I took a bottle of the seeds there, so I'd go there and eat them." He stopped. "Oh, you probably know that."

"No, I knew there were seeds there, but not that you ate them. So it was, like, every afternoon after school?"

"Well, except weekends. I ate at home then."

Ed struggled to formulate the next question. It had nagged at him since learning about the seeds. "Jared, how did you learn about washing the seeds?"

Jared hesitated. "On the Internet, I guess."

Ed considered how to ask this. "When I told you the seeds were hallucinogenic, you seemed surprised. Didn't you read that when you looked them up?"

Jared stared ahead, his face reddening. After a long moment, he looked at Ed. "I'm sorry. I did know, but I was afraid you'd think I was a druggie."

Ed had to suppress his smile. Being thought a druggie seemed small compared to being thought a terrorist. Maybe not to a seventeen-year-old. "No harm, no foul. But don't hold back any more, okay?"

"Yeah."

"Here's a question. Can you tell the difference between the paranoid thinking and your normal thinking?"

Jared nodded. "I think I can. Pretty much, anyway."

"Okay, so tell me, when you'd go to the unit, before eating seeds, was your thinking normal or paranoid?"

"I never thought about that." He looked off into the distance. Ed wondered if there was something the boy wasn't saying.

Jared said, "In school, sometimes I felt a little down, maybe, but no crazy thoughts. Now that you ask me, after I ate the seeds, I'd start thinking people wanted to hurt me, and I'd read those books about mass shootings and by the time I went home, I'd be angry. And real afraid." He looked straight at Ed. "I pretended nothing was wrong during dinner and homework, then I'd go to bed and just shake, I was so afraid. I even got afraid my parents would kill me in my sleep. I'd lock my bedroom door." His voice caught.

Ed glanced over at him, and patted him on the knee. "Hang in there, Jared. Just a few more questions." He glanced over; Jared nodded. "Can you tell me about those library books, the ones about mass shootings? Why would you read them?"

"At first, school shootings made me sick to my stomach, and I wanted to understand them." He waited a moment, rubbed his eyes. "Later, I read them because...I wanted...to do it too." His voice broke. Ed looked at him; he had tears in his eyes.

For a moment, Jared stared out the windshield; then he turned and looked at Ed. "I've been holding something else back. When they were releasing me, Deputy Pelton asked me why I rented the storage unit. I was ashamed to tell her."

Ed waited.

"Remember how I locked my bedroom door because I was scared my dad or mom would shoot me?"

"Uh-huh."

"I got so scared, I rented the unit so I could hide our rifles there. When I'd get paranoid, I'd sneak down to the unit and sit with them." He paused, looking sheepish. "I'd kind of hug one of the guns. It made me feel safer."

"Got it. So, the morning they arrested you, had you felt afraid and paranoid all night? Is that why you went to the unit before school?"

He shook his head. "By morning, I just felt sad again. And tired because I didn't sleep real good."

"Hmm. But you weren't paranoid in the morning?"

Jared looked up for a moment. "Actually, I think I was. I went to the unit just to feel safe before school, and when I got in there, I ate a couple handfuls of the seeds. Then I had this horrible nightmare or something. But afterward, when I left the shed, I was still tired, but not paranoid."

Ed tried to piece that together. His morning-glory-seeds theory might have just come unraveled. "Well, when Andi interviewed you later Monday, you were paranoid and angry. But you say you were over the paranoia by the time you left the shed, so why do you think you were paranoid when you talked with her?"

Jared didn't answer. Ed waited a moment, then asked, "Something wrong with the question?"

"Uh-uh, I'm thinking." He rubbed his eyes, then said, "Wait. Maybe I ate some more seeds before I stepped outside. I guess I don't really remember."

Maybe didn't help a lot. "So you might have eaten some before leaving?"

"Yeah, maybe." After a moment, he nodded. "I don't really remember. I'm sorry, Ed."

Ed's confidence ebbed. The seeds—it was a lot of theory to hang on a maybe.

102

Andi arrived at a little before six-thirty and found Jared and Ed waiting on the porch. She smiled at Jared, who looked calm enough, though his eyes were wide. To Ed, she said, "Talk to you a sec?"

"Hello to you too," Ed said, glancing at Jared. The boy nodded. Ed followed Andi inside.

She said, "Ordrew knows Jared's been here. I don't know how he found out, but he's got a picture of Jared's truck." She pointed to the yard.

"You're kidding." As it flared, his initial anxiety quickly changed into anger. "Screw him. I don't care. Everybody's going to know soon enough."

Andi looked out to the porch. "He said something about me owing him a big one, and that he'd make you pay."

"What's that mean?"

"No idea." She looked out to the porch again. Jared was staring at the early evening sky. "How is he?"

"Nervous, but he's ready. Still got some loose ends to clear up about the morning glory seeds, but I'm almost certain they're causing his paranoia." He still hadn't remembered what Jared had said in the woods.

"Oh, that reminds me. DCI doesn't have a test for, what was it, LSD?"

"LSA. Damn."

"They can purchase one. Are you sure enough about your theory for me to tell them to do it?"

He scratched his head. "Pretty sure. What do you think?"

"I better. Without proof it was in his system when we first arrested him, the theory is speculation." She looked outside again, then down at her watch. "It's time. I have to take him in."

As she spoke, Ed saw Jen Fortin's car coming up the drive from the road. "Jared," he hollered, "come inside. Don't let her see you here."

Jared jerked, as if startled, then came inside. Ed said, "It's just Jen Fortin bringing Grace home, but it's best that nobody knows you're here, at least till word gets out."

Jared looked apologetic. "I think it's too late, Ed."

"Why?"

He pointed at his truck. "Everybody knows my pickup."

"Oh. Sure. Well, no harm done, I guess."

Jared shrugged. "Makes me feel like I'm a criminal." Then he shook his head, showing a small smile. "I guess I am, huh?"

Grace burst in the door. "We were putting up more decorations for prom. Me and Jen—" She saw Jared's look and sobered quickly. "Is it time?"

Jared nodded, forcing another wan smile. Ed was reminded of dimmed sunlight through thin clouds.

Grace tossed her books on the porch swing and threw her arms around Jared. "I'm so sorry you have to do this, Jared." Her eyes glistened.

"I'll be all right, Grace." He patted her gently on the back.

Ed felt an ache in his chest, seeing his daughter so distressed for Jared, and the young man so considerate at a time like this.

Jared gently unlocked Grace's arms. "Thanks, Grace." He looked at her a moment. "You make good sandwiches." Grace wiped her eyes.

Andi cleared her throat. "Sorry, everybody, but we've got to get this show on the road."

Andi led them off the porch and opened the back door of the squad. She had a pair of zip tie handcuffs ready, but when Jared saw them, his face reddened. "Do you need those?" he asked.

Andi said, "I'm afraid so, Jared." She gently slipped them on, and helped him into the car. She shot Ed a look he couldn't decipher. She mouthed, Wish us luck.

Ed nodded, then leaned into Jared's window. "You'll make it. And I'll be right behind you." He straightened, then leaned down again. "One more thing. Do your meditation."

Jared managed a smile. "Handcuffs don't exactly help the full lotus position, Ed."

103

Across the evening sky above the sheriff's department building, horsetail cirrus clouds were swirls of gray linen. *Storm coming tomorrow,* Ed thought. He hoped it would be a gentle rain, soft and penetrating, a soaking to relieve the fields that had been too dry since the floods. He felt no confidence. He'd driven in behind the squad car, ignoring his tension about Jared, and in the background, Magnus. *No end of their suffering in sight,* he thought.

Parking in his slot, he noticed the reporter, Jack Kollier, leaning against his car near the door. As Andi helped the slumped-shouldered Jared from the back seat, Ed saw the boy's cuffed hands, and felt a wash of sadness for him.

Kollier jumped out of his car and hurried over toward Jared, calling, "Jared! Jared! Tell me where you've been."

Ed jumped out of his truck and got between the boy and the reporter. "Cool it, Jack. They'll be giving us all the information soon enough."

Kollier tried pushing around him, but Ed grabbed his arm. "The kid's my patient, Jack. I'm not letting you upset him."

The reporter hesitated just long enough for Andi to hustle Jared through the door and into the department. Jack snorted. "Thanks a lot, Ed. You lost me a scoop."

They went inside. Ed went through the door to the offices; Kollier had to wait in reception. Jared and Andi were walking down the hall toward the conference room. Ed joined them.

Jared said, almost too softly to hear, "Who was that guy, Ed?"

"A reporter. Don't sweat it, man."

Jared's eyes widened. "Reporter? Am I..." He looked away, then whispered, "I suppose they all want to know."

"Yeah, Jared. Use your breathing and stay calm. I'll be in often to see you, and I'm sure your attorney will work hard to get you out in a day or two." He hoped hard work were all it would take.

Callie Martin came in, followed by Jared's mother, who rushed to his side, but seeing the handcuffs, pulled up short. She looked at Andi. "Can I hug him?" Tears filled her eyes.

Andi said, "Sure," and removed the cuffs.

Callie said, "The booking deputy will be here in a minute," she said. Ed sensed her ambivalence. Was Jared a terrified local boy to be consoled, or was he a killer? He wondered how she was answering that question.

Ed said to her, "Who's booking tonight?" For Jared's sake, he hoped there'd been a last-minute change.

Callie turned a little away from Jared, rolled her eyes slightly. "Brad Ordrew's on the desk."

Ed muttered, "Damn."

Jared said, "He's the one who played bad cop."

Andi said, "I'll be right beside you, Jared. Every step."

Callie patted Jared's arm. "Andi won't let anything bad happen."

Ed thought, *She decided how to answer the question.* Marie Hansen, although she looked miserable, managed a small smile. "Thank you, Callie."

To Andi, he said, "I'll go have a word with Brad." Andi nodded. To Jared, he said, "Wait for me."

Jared tried a smile, though it failed to brighten his face. "Like I could do anything else?"

104

Ed went into the deputies' room just as Ordrew was getting up from his desk. He extended his hand to shake, but the deputy ignored it. Ed thought, *We'll deal with him later. Help the boy.* He smiled, said, "I hear you're booking Jared." He tried to keep his voice friendly.

"I am." He waved the booking folder.

"He's pretty terrified, Brad. Go easy on him, okay?"

Ordrew's eyes flared. " 'Go easy'? Jesus Christ!" He shook his head. "Makes a guy wonder what the hell you people want to happen around here."

Ed bit back his anger. "What you may think of me is no cause for abusing him, Brad. He's in your custody now." He calmed himself with a long breath. "Just take it easy on him."

"Or what, *Doctor*? You folks like thinking things can be easy, don't you? The kid wants to kill people, but 'take it *easy* on him.' Don't scare the poor child. God, you and your girlfriend make me puke." He started to push past Ed toward the corridor, then stopped. "There are procedures for reasons, and they don't include the easy way."

He stepped back to his desk, grabbed a paper, and stuck it out to Ed: a photocopy of the picture of Jared's truck in Ed's yard. "After I book the kid and lock him up, I'm giving the county attorney a copy of this. It's evidence you obstructed justice. Do *that* the *easy way*."

Ordrew pushed past Ed, but bumped into Ben, who'd just come into the doorway. He didn't apologize, but walked fast out into the corridor toward the interrogation room where Jared waited.

Ben, turning to look at Ordrew's back, said, "What's eatin' him?"

Ed, shaken, stared at the picture.

He handed the photo to Ben. "I don't know how he got this, but it's a picture of Jared's truck in my yard."

"Crap on toast." Ben rubbed his chin, studying the photo. "Well, we got the boy safe and sound now, so let Brad bust a gut. It ain't gonna amount to nothin'."

"He said something about the county attorney and obstructing justice."

Ben's face darkened. "Well, pardon my French, he goddamn well better charge me and Andi while he's at it. And if I know Irv Jackson, he ain't touchin' this in a month of Sundays."

He handed the photocopy back to Ed and started toward the door, but turned back to Ed. "That picture ain't nothing but a calf's fart, but still and all, you'd better lawyer up. Call Jerry Francis."

Ed found nothing to say. He thought he should feel anxious, but instead, he only felt irritated. *I don't need this.* He glanced at the wall clock: *6:58.* He needed to get on the road to the Anderhold and Magnus. He nodded to Ben.

The sheriff clapped him on the shoulder. "Ain't nothin' comin' of this, Ed."

"Thanks, Ben. I have a patient to see."

Ben's eyebrows lifted. "Down the valley, by any chance?"

Ed, too drained by the scene with Ordrew and his worry for Jared to wonder how Ben knew about Magnus, merely nodded.

Ben clapped him on the back. "No rest for the wicked, eh?"

As he walked through reception, Ed stopped at Callie's desk. Marie Hansen was signing a paper. He took a breath and let it out slowly, letting his tension drain away. "I think I know what causes his delusions, Marie, and if I'm right, this all can turn out okay."

She shook her head. "I'll certainly pray for that, Ed. But right now, it doesn't feel like anything good will come of this."

He nodded. "Yeah, right now it's real shaky." He watched her sadly as she turned and went out the door.

To Callie, he said, "Andi still here?"

"In with Ordrew and the boy," Callie said, nodding toward the back offices.

Ed leaned on Callie's counter. They'd been friends for twenty years; before she met her husband, they'd almost had an affair, but had decided on friendship. "You're looking whupped, Ed."

"Too many troubles floating around. Seems like nobody's safe here."

"Got that right," she said. "You take care of yourself, hear?"

"Will do. How's your Bill?"

"Saucy as ever. Taking me to Missoula for the weekend. Hot to trot." She winked.

He laughed. "Good for you two. Can I have your pen?"

"Ed Northrup, you could have my virginity," she laughed. "If Bill hadn't got there first." She handed him a pen and a notepad.

He jotted a note. *Andi, remind Jared to meditate.* As he wrote, it hit him: Ordrew's threat suddenly seemed ominous. Ben had said it was a calf's fart, but what if he was wrong? Would it mean prison? What would Grace do without him? He handed the note and the pen to Callie. "Can you see Andi gets this?"

Callie took it, nodded. She looked at him. "You all right? Got real pale there for a minute."

He nodded. "Stress."

She nodded. "Gets us all, sooner or later." She stowed the note on her desk. "I'll see she gets this soon as she's done running herd on Mister Los Angeles in there."

"Thanks, Callie." As he went out to his truck, he thought, *Better call Jerry. After I see Mack.*

105

Ed's first twenty miles south toward the Anderssen ranch went by in a blur, his mind consumed with worry about Ordrew's threat. He tried repeating what Ben had said, but his anxiety trumped it. "A calf's fart" paled beside "Grace in foster care."

To pull himself out of his funk, he called his daughter.

"Hi, honey. Look, I..." he paused, unsure if this was a good idea.

"What?" she asked.

"Well, I wanted you to know Jared's okay. I'm likely out for a while. You okay alone?"

Grace laughed. "Northrup, you're out late every night. Of course I'm okay. Besides, if there's an intruder, I've got your weapons."

He frowned. "I don't have any weapons."

"Your fly rods and cameras. I'll cast a dry fly in his eye, then snap a picture." She giggled.

Ed heard more laughter than Grace's. "Who's there?"

"Dana came over. Her and me, we're doing homework."

He smiled, ignored the grammar. "Good."

Grace's voice lowered, no longer laughing. "Northrup, I've got to admit something."

"What's that?"

"I'm kind of glad you didn't buy me a car yet. Having Dana here tonight really helps."

"What does not having a car have to do with Dana coming over?"

"Because if I had a car, I'd have driven to her house, and tonight, I need to be home in my jammies."

"You're bummed about Jared?"

"Yep. But Dana makes me laugh. Otherwise, I feel like shit on a shoe."

"Yuck."

"But I'll feel better tomorrow, so I'll still need a car, okay?"

He laughed. "You're on." As he ended the call, he thought, *It worked.* He felt better.

Not for long, though. Halfway to the Anderhold, he fallen back into confused apprehension. How was he going to help Magnus?

The next few sessions should tell the story. His mind felt clogged: too much going on, too many unsolved problems. He looked up toward the evening sky. Horsetail cirrus glowed golden against the gray. In the west, the last pink of sunset backlit the mountains. Above them, cloud-mountains lined up, ridge upon ridge, their tops luminous, their bottoms water-heavy gray. Rain coming. He whispered, *What should I do?*

He breathed quietly, attempting to relax. *Face it,* he told himself. *Mack could murder the monk.* "Unless I can stall him until the old guy dies," he said to the night. His voice sounded hollow. Merwin always said, "Start with facts. Build from there."

Okay, then. Fact: Therapy had helped Magnus uncover the truth.

Fact: When Magnus realized he'd been raped, he'd promised to kill the rapist.

Fact: He didn't seem at that point yet—after all, he'd agreed to call Ed.

Fact: Rage would follow the shame; it could lead to murder.

Ed frowned. *This is going nowhere.*

He'd never known his friend to be violent or vengeful. Of course, being raped can cause strange knots in a person's spirit. But if that had happened in Magnus, it'd been well hidden, buried deep, all these years.

Fact: The problem wasn't the murder, it was that knot, and it needed to be loosened. *That's how to save him. The question is, how?*

106

Ed had barely seated himself when Magnus said, "I'm going to kill him, Ed."

Ed said, "You moved from sadness to anger pretty fast."

Magnus frowned. "I'm damn serious about this, Ed. Don't make light of it."

"I'm serious too. We can work on your anger, but killing Father Jerome will wreck your life. You don't deserve to die in prison. And Luisa and Junior don't deserve that either."

Magnus glared. "Don't use my family against me."

"I'm not. I'm using them *for* you."

"Bullshit, Ed. That priest has to suffer. I want him afraid for his life like I was."

Ed shook his head. "He won't be. He's dying of cancer, any day now. He isn't even lucid."

Magnus's eyes hardened. "Say that again."

"He's dying of cancer. He may be dead as we speak."

Magnus's breathing slowed and Ed saw his fingers and knuckles whiten, gripping the arms of his chair.

"Mack? Tell me what you're thinking." He'd never seen such fierceness in his friend; it reminded him of the charged air before the lightning strike.

Magnus relaxed his grip on the chair and stood. "I'll have my justice." He moved toward the door.

Ed stood and barred his way. "There are many kinds of justice, Mack." He kept his voice calm, but he did not feel calm.

"I'll have my justice, even if he's dying." Magnus looked at the door in front of which Ed stood. "If I want to leave, you aren't strong enough to stop me." Although both men were six feet tall, Magnus outweighed Ed by twenty pounds, and his rancher's arms and shoulders were broad and strong. Besides, Ed would never use force against a patient. Or a friend.

He could kill me, Ed thought. "You're right, Mack, but let's talk, not fight."

Magnus looked hard at him another moment, then turned and sat. "A man needs more than talk. He needs justice too." He folded his arms. "But I'm calmer. Say your piece."

"You don't want to kill him, you want him to suffer like you did."

A squint, then a nod. "Agreed. So?"

Ed's face warmed suddenly, and his thoughts came clearer. "I don't think killing him would satisfy you. It isn't what you want. You want him to be afraid."

"I want more than that. I want him terrified, and I want him to know I am killing him."

Magnus wasn't giving up the idea of murder. Ed steadied his hands on his lap. "I'd tell you to do it, if you had time. But you don't. So let's talk about how you might have made the old pedophile suffer, and keep talking till you've become satisfied with that imagery. But don't ruin your life and your family just for the momentary satisfaction of blowing his cancerous brains out."

Magnus gripped the edge of the table and leaned forward. "You want me to *imagine* justice? Are you toying with me? I won't stomach you..." His flaring rage almost choked his voice.

Ed shook his head. "I'm not toying with you. I'm giving you your only real option." He rubbed his eyes, then his face. "If Jerome weren't dying, maybe you could do something to punish him. But he's dying, maybe he's already died. I called the Abbot and he said it would be any day, any minute." He felt his anger rise, and decided not to stifle himself this time. He struck his fist on the arm of the chair. "Damn it, Mack, when revenge is impossible, imagining it is what you're left with. You've got every right to your fury, and to seek justice if you could, but if the monk had no right to rape, then you have no right to kill."

Magnus bowed his head, and his shoulders, which had been so square with rage a moment before, sagged. "That takes the taut out of my bowstring." He stared at Ed for a moment. "And it gives me no comfort."

Ed felt suddenly drained. All this suffering. When does it end? "You're right," he said, as calmly as he could. "But what real alternative is there? The rest of your life either in prison or torn apart by bitterness? Take your vengeance in your mind and be done with it." Ed felt...what? Empty. It didn't persuade Magnus. It didn't even persuade him. "After you've run the images out to their end and you're done, we'll heal the other wounds."

Magnus stood. "I need to think this through." This time, Ed didn't stop him moving toward the door. Magnus opened it. Ed stood, still in turmoil. Had he made headway?

As they walked out, Magnus took Ed's arm roughly. "I still will kill him, Ed. You want to save me, save me from that."

Ed, stricken, looked in his friend's eyes, red with pain. "I will, Mack, if you give me the chance. Come in tomorrow?"

Magnus did not answer immediately. After a moment, he nodded. "Tomorrow."

Ed said, "Between now and then, if you think you're going to act, call me." Down deep, below the crater of sorrow he felt, Ed believed his friend did not want to kill. Or rather, hoped.

107

On the porch, Grace and Andi were waiting when Ed got home. Thunder rumbled over the mountains. Rain coming; the air damp, still warm. Things couldn't be more rotten than they'd been for the last couple of days, but he was glad to see Andi. Her warm body in his bed might ease the heavy ache in his chest.

Grace jumped down and met him as he climbed out of his pickup. "Northrup! Dana just left, but she must've taken my term paper by mistake. I need to use your truck to go get it."

Ed looked at his watch. "It's pretty late. Get it from her in the morning."

"I can't wait. It's due in English class, first hour, and it's not finished yet."

He caught his breath. He'd had a flash of Grace in an accident on a dark road. He almost laughed at himself. *Man, you're worrying about everything.* On the long drive north from the Anderssen ranch, his mood had pin-balled, from concern for Magnus to worry about Jared to anxiety about Ordrew's threat and what it might mean for Grace. Now he'd worry about her out in the night.

Grace cleared her throat. "Earth to Northrup? I have to finish that paper tonight. Please?"

Sit your horse, Ed, he thought. He tossed her the keys. "Okay, sure. But drive defensively. There'll be drunks out."

Andi had observed the exchange from the porch, arms folded. He looked up at her. He walked up the steps and leaned to kiss her. She pulled slightly back, just enough for it to be a message. She said, "You know, worrying about her driving her *own* car doesn't make a lot of sense when you loan her yours."

Ed sat down next to her. "You mad?" He gestured toward her folded arms.

She shook her head. "Uh-uh, just a little chilly."

Ed, restless with worry, stood again and went to the edge of the porch, looking out at the few visible stars. The clouds had thickened over half the sky. "Rain soon," he said. Lightning flickered over Hunters' Peak.

Andi said, "How's Mack?"

More than anything, Ed wanted to tell her about Magnus's threat, but he knew Andi would feel the need to intervene after a creditable threat of murder. He shrugged. "Not good. He's on the brink of either a breakthrough or a breakdown." He smiled. "First poetic thing I've said all day."

"*That* was poetic? You have had a shitty day, big guy."

He heard sympathy in her tone, warmed to it. "Got that right. How's a glass of wine sound?"

"Right on target. And bring me a jacket, would you?"

When Ed got back with her jacket and wine, he could sense that clouds had blotted out the stars. Coming in fast. *Hope Grace gets back before the rain.* He said, "Could be the last night on the porch for a while." He sat beside her again, and leaned his shoulder lightly against hers. She didn't move away. *Good sign.* Ed pulled her jacket over her shoulders.

"A truly fucked-up day," Andi said, after a few minutes.

"Agreed." Ed scraped together some empathy. "Want to talk about it?"

She shook her head. "No." After a moment, she added, "You're wrecked too."

"I've been better. How's Jared?"

"I checked on him before I left work. Gave him your note. He was kind of curled into a shell, and didn't look up at me. But he did take the note."

"Any sign of the paranoia?"

She shrugged. "He didn't say anything, so I don't know. His eyes looked scared, but not angry."

"Did Brad rough him up during the booking?"

"Nope. He kept it low-key. I think he's aiming for bigger game. Namely us. Or me, through you."

"Think he'll go through with charging me?"

"Ben says if he does, he's going to announce he okayed Jared staying with you for the weekend."

Emotion filled him, sunshine after a very gray day. He wiped his hand across his eyes. "Wow. That's huge."

Andi just nodded. "It is. But he still says you should lawyer up, right away."

"Damn. I meant to call Jerry Francis on the way back from Mack's...uh, my session." He shook his head. "In the morning. How serious do you think Brad is?"

"It'll be a clusterfuck. Ben'll have to call in the state police to investigate, since he and I are tainted, and that'll take some time. But the sooner you get a lawyer, the better you're covered, when and if."

"Damn." He sipped the pinot. "You said *tainted.* Have I blown your investigation?" *And pulled Andi and Ben into the ditch with me?*

Again, she shrugged. "Could be. I can't see it, though. If Ben owns it, there'll be trouble for him, maybe an election challenge next year, but I doubt it'll amount to more than a PR hassle. Like Ben said, a calf's fart. For you, I don't see much bad."

"But even so, it'll be a rough patch for a while."

"Got that right."

"So I better start thinking about protecting Grace. I'll call Jerry in the morning." For a moment, he stared out into the darkness. Another dart of lightning danced over Hunters' Peak.

WEDNESDAY, DAY TEN

108

When he saw the clock, Ed stifled a groan: *5:53*. Beside him, Andi breathed softly, still asleep. Ed's night had been fretful, his sleep fitful, even after their love-making had subsided into a warm stillness, like a gentle breeze after a storm. Andi had fallen immediately asleep. Grace came home around midnight. Around three in the morning, Ed had heard the weather change—gusts bumping the house, the log walls creaking as the temperature fell. He couldn't banish worry, about Magnus, about Jared. Andi's leg lay over his, her warm breath brushing his shoulder. He couldn't still his mind.

Gingerly, he extricated his leg from beneath Andi's and climbed out of bed. He dressed, silently closing the bedroom door. Outside the kitchen window, the eastern sky was still gray, although suffused with a pale light. Rainwater streaked the kitchen window. Grabbing a scrap of paper, he wrote Grace a note—*Grab a ride with Andi, okay? Had to go in early*—and pinned it to her backpack. He poured coffee into a travel mug and drove into town. The temperature had fallen twenty-five degrees, and sleet slanted against his windshield, making blotches of icy water.

When he pushed open the sheriff's department door, the night receptionist greeted him. "Ed! Nice to see somebody comin' in with no trouble in his pocket."

"Hey, Shirl. Let's hope not, eh? Can I look in on Jared Hansen?"

Shirl screwed up her face. "Well, you can look at him, but you won't be talkin' to him. I checked him at five-thirty and again at six, and he ain't makin' a peep. Looks madder 'n hell."

Damn. "Did he sleep?"

"Not that I ever saw, and I checked him every half hour."

"Swell. Okay, just let me in and I'll see what's up."

Jared was sitting at the end of the cot, elbows on his knees, chin resting on his fists, staring at the wall. Even in the dim light of the cellblock, Ed could see his eyes were red, rimmed with darkness. The other cells were unoccupied.

"Jared?" Ed said, as quietly as he could and still be heard.

When he heard his name, Jared looked at Ed, his eyes cold, angry.

"I knew you'd betray me."

Ed's heart sank. *Paranoid again?* "You think I betrayed you?"

Jared waved at the bars. "You put me here. I shouldn't have trusted you." He looked away. "It's just a matter of time."

"Time? For what?"

"Till they come."

"They?" Ed asked, although he figured he knew.

"The government. To kill me. And you brought me here so they can do it."

Paranoid again. "Jared." The boy didn't look up. Ed said his name louder. "Jared, look at me."

Slowly Jared turned his face and his hard, hate-filled eyes locked with Ed's. The hairs on Ed's neck tingled. "Jared, have you been eating morning glory seeds?"

Without warning, the boy let out a tense, bitter sound, like a black laugh, drained of humor. His eyes glittered with rage, but his lips twisted into a grim smile. "Right. And a grass-finished steak and two organic potatoes and a nice kale salad and a big glass of hemp milk." He looked away. "Don't ask stupid questions, Doctor. And don't belittle my lifestyle."

"I'm sorry, Jared. But we thought the seeds were triggering the delusions, and you're delusional again." Disappointment bit like a frightened dog. "No one's going to harm you."

"Ah, really. It's such a relief to know I'm delusional." He straightened, snapped his head toward Ed. "And what's the diagnosis when I'm dead, *Doctor?*"

Ed had nothing to say to that. Dismay choked him. He steeled himself. *Got to figure this out.* Out of nowhere, he remembered what Jared had said in the woods that had been nagging him. When Ed had asked if he'd eaten any seeds after being in jail, he'd said, first, no. But then he'd added, "I maybe ate some Saturday morning before I went up to the school." *Maybe can mean maybe. Or maybe not.* Ed thought about that. *Damn.*

"I have to leave for a while, but I'll be back to see you later today."

Jared turned away. "If I'm alive."

256

109

In the minute it took him to walk across the hall and unlock his office, Ed had dismissed the sense of futility that had seized him after seeing Jared; booting his computer, he gathered himself to work out the resurrected mystery. *Not the seeds after all, damn it.* A paranoid illness? *Then why's it so damn intermittent?*

Without knowing what caused Jared's paranoia, what could be done to end it? Back to square one. He picked up the phone.

The hospital operator patched Ed through to Doc Keeley, who was in the ER. "Morning, John."

"Hi, Ed. What's got you keeping doctor's hours?"

"Jared Hansen. He's back in jail, and he's paranoid again. I suppose it's the stress of being there, but he's delusional. Until I can figure out what's wrong, I'd like to see if we can shut down his anxiety enough to short-circuit the psychosis."

"You're talking anti-psychotics?"

"Yeah. Something to even him out while I try to solve this damn puzzle."

Keeley took a moment. "We can try, but what's he paranoid about?"

"The government's going to kill him."

"Ouch. So it's likely he'll think the medication is poison, right? Part of the plot?"

"Yeah, probably. Catch-22. What about an injectable?" *Bad idea*, he thought, as soon as he'd said it.

Keeley saw it too. "We'd have to get a court order, then restrain him. More confirmation of the delusion, right?"

Ed frowned. "And psychologically it could override any good medication effect."

Doc chuckled. "Well, you could just leave the pills in a little cup outside his cell, beside a glass of water, and ask him real nice to take them when he feels like it. Appeal to the better angels of his nature."

Ed thought about that. "Actually, that might not be a bad idea. His delusional periods have been unpredictably intermittent, so he might get lucid for a while and take them. Could you order something?"

"Sure, I'll call it in right away. But wait, did you say his delusions are *intermittent?*"

"Yeah. Why?"

"Well, you're the shrink, but is a paranoid psychosis usually intermittent?"

"Not really, unless there's some intervention, like meds—which is why I'm stumped."

Keeley was quiet for several breaths. "I'm no neurologist, and this is probably a wild hair, but have you considered a small brain lesion, one that slightly affects some area associated with the delusions?"

Ed held his breath for a moment. "I've never heard of that, but why not? It's worth a shot." *A tumor? A brain injury? Is that any better an answer?* "Thanks," he said. "Call in the prescription—I'll pick it up right away."

Ed called Ben.

"Hi, Ben, I just talked to Doc and I want to try to get Jared to take an anti-anxiety medication. That okay with you?"

"Whoa, I just got in. The boy sick?"

"Yeah, paranoid again."

"Thought your seeds theory covered that?"

Ed shook his head. "I thought so too, but I guess not."

"Hell, don't help your answer to Brad's obstruction charge, does it?"

Ed, reminded, started stuttering an answer, but Ben interrupted. "Forget that for now. We'll hang that rustler when we catch him. About this medication business, I can't let the boy have it in his cell. Overdose chances, and all."

"I know. We can control that."

"Damn right we control it. You give the instructions to Pete, and he'll see the boy gets the pills."

Ed hung up and walked the five minutes down Division Street to Art's Fine Foods and Pharmacy. *Gotta see Art today*, he thought. The prescription was waiting at the pharmacy counter. Back at the department, he found Pete in the deputies' room and told him the plan. Pete let him into the cellblock.

Jared was sleeping. *Good sign or bad?* Ed thought about it for a moment, but couldn't decide what it meant, although he decided it probably was good. He left the first dose of pills in a small plastic cup, beside a cup of water, placing them on the floor just inside the cell door with a note: *These will help you feel better. They won't harm you. I want to help. Ed.*

He backed quietly out of the cell block, closed the door softly, and said to Pete, "Two pills every four hours, but only if he takes the previous dose.

Don't talk to him or put any pressure on him, okay? Just leave them on the floor inside his cell door like I did."

"Whatever you say, Ed. With Jared, you're the boss." He gave a little cough.

"You all right, Pete?"

He shook his head, eyes sad. "Nope. I've known that boy since he was seven. Whoever that kid in there is, he breaks my heart."

110

After two sessions with patients he'd cancelled last week, Ed picked up a voice message from Andi. "Ed, we've got trouble. Ordrew gave the county attorney his photos and what he claims is Jared's toothbrush from your cabin. Call Ben right away."

Ed's heart hammered. He deleted the message, then sat down and closed his eyes. Magnus—his next patient—wasn't due for an hour, so after taking five minutes to quiet himself, he walked back across the hall to the sheriff's office. Ben was leaning on the reception desk, chatting with Callie. "In my office," he growled when Ed came in.

Ben pushed the door shut harder than usual. "You get Andi's message?"

Ed nodded. "Took me a few minutes to calm down."

"I ain't calm yet and I ain't tryin' to be. I ain't been this pissed at an employee in thirty years on this job."

"How serious do you think this is going to be?"

"You call Jerry Francis yet?"

"Uh-uh. I've been running around trying to figure out how to help Jared—he's psychotic again this morning."

"Tell me somethin' I don't know. You just called about the pills, remember?"

"Oh, right. Forgot that. Anyway, I'll call Jerry. But what's the story?"

"Well, Irv calls to tell me Ordrew's asking him to investigate you for possible obstruction of justice. He's got that damn photo and a toothbrush he says he found in your bathroom. Took prints off it. They're the boy's."

"What the hell was he doing in my bathroom? I never—"

Ben raised his hand. "And he didn't have no warrant. He's claimin' the boy's pickup in the yard gave him probable cause to enter."

"Did it?"

"Irv thinks Ordrew could win that one, but it ain't relevant at the moment. The judge'll decide, that is, if Irv decides to charge you."

Ed took a long breath. "Will this cause trouble for you and Andi?"

"Ordrew ain't mentioned us so far. Irv says the charge's probably bullshit, but he ain't got no choice but to investigate. He's askin' the state police to do the deed."

"Why?" Andi had predicted this.

"Among other things, since you're sleepin' with Andi, Irv don't want nobody sayin' our own investigation might be 'tainted.' Ain't that a nice word?"

"Not one I like. What'll come of it?"

"You ask me, nothin'. Irv'll play the game and follow the rules and you should too. Trooper already called and said she'd be down here Saturday morning. Ten o'clock work for you?"

"Wow. That quick?"

"Like I told you, bud. Don't fret yourself too much. If it looks to go south, I'll fess up to okayin' you keepin' him at your place. But when all's said and done, my money says Irv ain't filin' no charges against you. I know the man too well."

Ed stood to go. As he opened the door, Ben said to his back, "But run your butt over to Jerry's pronto. Play your part."

He turned back. "My part?"

"This is a goddamn dance, and you gotta do the right steps."

III

Eleven a.m.

Magnus Anderssen stood in Ed's waiting room, gazing out the window, arms at his side, his fists clenching and unclenching. Ed said, "Morning, my friend." Magnus turned. Ed smiled and gestured inside. "C'mon in."

As Magnus pushed past Ed into the office, heat blasted off the big man's body. Ed felt a tremor of anxiety; would what he had to offer be enough?

Magnus didn't even wait to sit. "My blood's real high, Ed. Real high. I need to kill the monk." He spoke, pacing.

"Have a seat, Mack. We'll talk."

Magnus instead kept pacing, the gusts of his words swinging between murderous rage and suicidal despair, fueled by shame and self-loathing. On and on, for ten minutes, then twenty, Magnus roared. Finally, he sat hard in the empty chair, but continued. The word *whore* peppered his ravings: Having made Magnus a whore, Jerome should suffer, or having become one, Magnus should die. The heat of his passion seared the air. Ed waited, keeping himself focused, tuned to Magnus's theme of death in two variations. Ed watched, as one watches wildfire on the night mountains, fascinated, cautious. As Magnus's tirade swept along, Ed began to hear what he had been listening for.

After almost thirty minutes, Magnus collapsed back in his chair, exhausted. "Say something," he said, breathing hard. If nothing else, the gale seemed to have drained him of the murderous conviction.

Ed gathered himself, took a breath. "You loved Father Jerome very much."

Magnus was momentarily startled, his eyes wide, and then he leapt up again, swung around toward the door—and just as fast fell back into the chair, lowered his bullish head, slumped forward, and wept.

When he could speak, the big man began, speaking in a whisper. "You say I loved him. Leaving my father's house freed me from hell. Up at the monastery, I could breathe. No one criticized me, no one hit me, no one despised me. For the first time in years, I didn't have to lock my door at night. Father Jerome took me under his wing; he seemed to like me, although I couldn't figure out why. He took me on long walks in the woods. On recreation days outside the walls, we'd climb the Coliseum. He listened to my ideas. I'd never really *talked* to a man before." He wiped his eyes. "Or been listened to."

Ed nodded, but said nothing.

"I began to think he loved me." A catch in his voice, then a cough. "I began to love him." He put his face in his hands.

Ed waited.

He lifted his head. "There were three of us novices, me, Bobby Rancer, and Loyd Crane. I think Bobby's still up there. He was a good soul. Loyd, though..." He stopped speaking, his face darkening; he looked at the floor. "Well, you know Loyd."

Ed clenched inside. "Andi's shooting?"

Magnus looked up, nodding. "Loyd was a snake. He smuggled in marijuana and tried to get Bobby and me to smoke. He always had a fifth of Southern Comfort in his room and tried to get me interested in porn his dad brought on Family Day. He seemed real cozy with Father Jerome, though, and I couldn't figure that out. I couldn't figure out why he'd entered the monastery either, until one day Father Jerome told me."

Ed waited.

"Crane'd been accused of statutory rape two years earlier. His family was wealthy, and their lawyer claimed Loyd was planning to be a monk and the girl was lying to get at the family money. The judge found him guilty but suspended the sentence, pending his actually entering a monastery and staying at least two years. So, he was doing his time up there, not very monastically. One Family Day, his 'sister' visited and they disappeared for the whole afternoon. Later, he bragged to Bobby and me his 'sister' had been a hooker from Missoula his father had sent up for him."

"Huh." *Once a sleaze, always a sleaze.*

Magnus shifted restlessly in his chair. "How could Father Jerome let him stay? I couldn't figure it. I *loved* Jerome. I thought he loved me." In his eyes, confusion contested with anger. "Now we know how stupid that was."

"And you're angry about it."

"I don't know, Ed. I can't figure it. Why'd he rape me?"

Ed waited a moment, then asked, "Your thoughts?"

Magnus's shoulders rounded. "Father Jerome's pet idea was, we should trust our brothers and confide in them. He called it 'making community.' I wanted to do whatever Jerome said, so one evening after supper, I was talking with Loyd in the monastery library. I told Loyd about Daryl hating me and how Father Jerome was like a real father to me."

Magnus shook his head, his lips curled in disgust. "Loyd was all smiles. He said, 'You wish you were his boy,' very friendly, and I thought he really understood. I said I loved Jerome, and Loyd said, 'I can help you out.' I asked him what he meant, and he said something like, 'I can set it up with Jerome for him and you to have some private time.' I said I already had time with him—our walks and my novice conferences. Loyd smiled a funny smile and said, 'No, not conferences. Time for you to be his boy.'"

Magnus looked up at the ceiling, and rubbed his eyes. "I had no idea what he meant." He paused a long time, one hand shadowing his eyes, head low, elbow resting on the chair.

Ed considered what to say. "Maybe you're angry as much with Loyd as with Father Jerome?"

Magnus sat up, shaking his head roughly. "No! I knew Loyd was a shit, and he didn't rape me. Jerome acted like he loved me, and when I trusted him, he made me his whore."

"His whore? You said that before, and I didn't agree with you then. Or now." He had one more thing to say about this whore business, but held it for the moment.

Magnus snapped, "I said it and it's true. I'm his whore. I told you how he did it. I won't talk about that again. But you see it now, don't you? He made me his boy-whore."

"As you say," Ed said. "But tell me, what did you get paid?"

"What?" Magnus leaned sharply toward Ed, his nostrils flaring. The anger had returned, flushing confusion away.

"Whores get paid. What did *you* get paid?"

Magnus backed a little, seemed to think about it. "Ah." For a moment, he looked away. "I told myself I got Jerome's love. Call that payment, if you want." He shuddered. "What Daryl had always told me was true: I was worthless—I stayed in hell for a year, to get a little love." His face was twisting, his eyes tormented.

Ed cringed at the self-contempt in his friend's voice. "I don't think that's payment. A whore insists on getting something needed—money, gifts, status, something like that. All you got was more pain. That's not what a whore does."

Magnus shook his head fiercely. "No!" he roared—too loudly, Ed thought.

Magnus said it again, fiercely. "I'm a *whore!*"

The moment felt right for the other thing. "You're holding on to that for a reason."

"Bullshit!" Magnus jumped up; Ed flinched, but stayed still in his chair. Magnus stood rigidly at the window. "You're damn right, there's a reason. Because it's true." His anger was mounting.

Ed shook his head. "That's not the reason. There's another."

The rancher turned and demanded, his voice hard, barely in control. Ed had never seen such rage in his friend. "Name your damn reason."

"Jerome's betrayal hurt you worse than the rape did." Ed checked Magnus's eyes—they were veiled, wary, like an animal, screened by a thicket, watching the hunter who hadn't seen him yet. He went on, "Calling yourself a whore gives you control of your pain. You tell yourself that the priest didn't betray you at all, he knew what you were—a whore—and so you *deserved* it.

So maybe, you tell yourself, if you're a whore, Jerome really could love you. Some men love their whores."

Magnus stepped violently toward Ed, his arm raised to strike, then suddenly froze in place. His arm dropped. When he finally spoke, it was a single syllable, "No." It sounded like a lament.

Ed held very still.

Finally, the big man sank into the chair. "You're right, damn it," he murmured. "The betrayal is worse. It's easier to blame myself than to admit he never loved me."

Ed nodded. Magnus was a courageous man.

"I needed him to love me." Magnus's voice was drifting, unmoored. "When I realized Jerome wouldn't stop and I couldn't bear it any longer, I quit and crawled home to the Anderhold. The only thing that kept me from killing myself was believing that Jerome really *had* loved me. After a few months on the Double-A, with Daryl laughing at me, I guess I'd forgotten it." He groaned softly. "Is that possible?" After a pause, he said, "Oh. You told me about that."

Ed nodded. "Traumatic amnesia. It worked until Junior came home from college, like you did from the monastery. That triggered the nightmares, then the other symptoms."

Magnus nodded.

Ed watched Magnus carefully; he seemed to be past the rage and, maybe, the shame; his eyes, lowered to the floor, looked pensive. He decided to push it one more time. "And if you face the fact that you're not a whore, you also have to accept the fact that he didn't love you."

Magnus nodded, his eyes narrowing.

Ed continued. "You said that if you'd faced that when you came down to the ranch, you would have killed yourself. You were what, 20 years old? Now you're 62. What do you think now?"

"About what?"

"Suicide."

Magnus shrugged. "Either the monk dies, or I die."

Ed felt the wind go out of him. The catharsis should have resolved that violent fantasy. Should he risk a confrontation? He settled on, "What do you really want, Magnus?"

"Justice. He dies or I die."

He managed, "That's not justice."

"I want him to suffer like I suffered; call it what you like." He shook his head in disgust. "We've already talked about this."

"So what's the right suffering for him? Anal pain? Losing a father?"

Magnus suddenly looked clotted, plugged up, as if he could not move through something in his mind. Then he stammered, "I want...I want him to feel abandoned, alone, utterly. No hope of redemption."

"As you felt."

Magnus nodded.

"How would you do it?"

Magnus glared at him. "I should confess my intentions? So you can call Ben?"

"No." Ed ran his fingers through his hair, trying to think how to say this. "If you talk about your plan, you won't have to actually do it." It sounded trivial, the wishful thinking of a grad student.

The rancher looked at him for a long moment. "I haven't thought it out." He stood again in front of the window, looking at the mountains. Ed waited.

Magnus turned. "I'll take him up the Coliseum, to the very edge, where we used to walk. I'll tell him why I hate him and I'll tie him so he can't save himself or even kill himself. I'll leave him there on the edge, to die alone in the snow, or perhaps be killed by the wolves. He'll be abandoned by someone he thought loved him."

Ed sat, silent, stunned at the pure, primeval justice of it, its elegant symmetrical irrationality. He struggled for words.

"That would...be murder," was all he could say. He felt a spasm of despair, helpless against the power of Mack's implacable resolve. He closed his eyes.

Magnus's firm voice broke in. "Yes, it will be murder."

Ed opened his eyes. "Please, Mack," he said. "See me this afternoon. Don't do anything. Let me try to help you find another way."

"You've helped me clarify my thoughts, Ed. There's nothing else to say."

"Mack, I have to try. I couldn't live with it if you die or end up in prison."

"Fine, then. Try as hard as you like. I can wait."

Ed wondered if he needed to call Ben, but the cowardice of that repulsed him. This was for him to wrestle out with Magnus. And the longer these talks took, the better chance Jerome would be dead before Magnus took action. Feeling an impotence he hadn't known since his internship, he took

265

refuge in his appointment book. "Come back at five."

Magnus shrugged and stood up. "Five it is, then." For a long moment, he looked down at Ed, who found himself too sad to stand. "I believe you grasp my feeling."

Ed nodded. "Actually, I do. Which makes it harder to talk you out of it."

Magnus gave a hard laugh. "Then we're both crazy."

112

After Magnus left, Ed felt the residue of failure congesting his chest. He'd guided Magnus into a dead end. And Jared—a tumor? What if it wasn't? What if he'd failed to help the boy as he'd promised? Or the obstruction charge? Would Ben and Andi be tainted by his impetuous decision to hide Jared?

For a while, he sat motionless, his energy gone, searching each step in both cases. What had he missed?

After twenty minutes, though, he shook himself. *Enough searching the kitty litter. Work to do.* He looked at his book again—only two patients, at two and at four. When he called them to cancel the sessions, apologizing more than they required, they both told him not to worry. That gave him brief consolation—nothing's as bad as it seems.

He called Andi, who was off duty, but she didn't answer. He left a message, then walked across the street to the Angler Bar. Ted stood behind the bar, drying glasses. "Edward! A welcome face I seldom see at noon."

Ed settled on a stool. "I'm free till five. Lots to think about. Mind pouring me a beer?"

"Now, wouldn't *that* be a curiosity: A bar owner who minds pouring a beer?" He turned toward the handles. "Shall I assume you'll have the usual? Or since the hour is unusual, might the beer be?"

"On second thought, I need a clear head. How about a Virgin Mary?"

Ted's eyebrows sent a message. "A first, Edward. Am I wrong to think your heart is overfull?"

"Either heart or brain, Ted. Or maybe both."

Ted made the drink and coastered it in front of Ed. "So, speak."

"Death and destruction. Which I can't talk about."

Ted leaned against the back-bar and folded his arms. "Of course you can talk. We're in the same profession."

Ed chuckled. "I suppose. What's to say? I'm stumped, and I'm sad." He repeated, "And I can't talk about it."

"Why sad?"

Ed smiled. He knew that Ted, bartender, knew the pathways of confidentiality as well as Ed did, but he held back. "I've got two clients who, far as I can see, are in real trouble and I'm damned if I can figure out how to help."

"Well, aren't we being arcane? You're talking about our friend Mack Anderssen and young Jared Hansen, I presume." He calmly dried another glass. "So why are we so pessimistic?"

"How do you know who they are?"

Ted lifted one shoulder. "I doubt that there are fifty people in the valley who don't know you're taking care of the boy and seeing Mack Anderssen for something."

Ed shook his head, perfectly aware that Ted was right. "There's no confidentiality around here, is there?"

"Which you know perfectly well, Edward. So, stop posing and dish. Why are we so pessimistic?"

"That's what I can't discuss, Ted."

"What *can* you talk about?"

Ed took a swallow of the tomato juice, grimaced. "All right. Bring me a Bitterroot Single Hop."

Ted smiled and turned to pour the beer. "I wondered whether tomato juice and Worcestershire sauce would satisfy." When he returned with the ale, he said, "So, I repeat. What *can* you talk about?"

Ed looked at the beer. "I want so much to help them that I'm losing my perspective." He paused. "This stays between us?"

Ted nodded solemnly. "Edward, speak your heart. It will accompany me to my grave."

Ed took a long breath. "I hid Jared Hansen over the weekend, so I could figure out what's going on with him."

This time, Ted's eyebrows almost bounced.

Ed nodded. "Yeah, professional death-wish. Anyway, now Brad Ordrew's accusing me of obstructing justice, which maybe I did. I don't know. But it might've been a stupid thing."

"Did you figure out what's going on with Jared?"

"Yeah, I thought so. But now it looks like I was wrong, so maybe I've fucked up and on top of that won't help Jared at all."

Ted shook his head. "For which you cannot forgive yourself. And about our friend Magnus?"

Ed shook his head. "I really shouldn't talk about him, Ted."

"Edward, don't be naïve. Most of the valley knows he's seeing you, and half of them have detailed theories about why. And I've heard half of *those*."

Ed took another sip of his beer. "That may be, Ted, but knowing I'm seeing him isn't knowing what about. I can't go into that."

Ted shrugged. "A day of firsts! A bartender his customer won't confide in." He dried another glass. "Want a sandwich?"

"No, what I want is to make my patients safe." He hesitated. "Well, yeah, a sandwich would be good. Make it a Reuben."

Ted smiled. "I love that about you, Edward. Devoted to your profession, but always ready to tend to your stomach." Ed flinched. A couple of years ago, before Andi got shot, Ed weighed thirty pounds more; Ted still teased him about it. He placed the latest dried glass in the rack. "My beloved Lane has a saying about saviors." Lane Martin was Ted's partner—together they'd remodeled the Angler and earned the warmth of most of the valley's people, regardless of being the town's only gay couple.

"What's his saying?"

" 'You can't save somebody unless you fucked them up.' Graphic, but oh, so true."

As if dominoes were falling, click, click, click, it came to him: What he was going to do. Startled at the clarity, he found his voice. "Thanks, Ted. You just gave me an idea. Or Lane did. Can I have that sandwich to go?"

"Oh, Lord, your sandwich." Ted slapped his forehead. "I forgot the order." He called the kitchen, and when he hung up, he said, "Now that is a curiosity, a restaurateur who forgets to order his customer's food."

113

"You can't fix somebody unless you fucked them up." *I haven't fucked anybody up in this*, he thought. Still, he had to save his clients, so Lane's saying wasn't so helpful after all. He'd been sure, leaving Ted's, that Lane's quip solved his problem, but now, maybe not. *Funny how crossing a street can muddle everything.* Munching on his Reuben—he'd left the half-finished beer on Ted's bar—Ed called Doc Keeley, who agreed to order an MRI of Jared's brain. Ed said, "If the Hansens don't give permission for the MRI, we'll need a court order, so write the order for St. Pat's in Missoula specifically, okay?"

"Will do. Who should I send it to?"

"A copy to me and one to Ben." No, wrong. "Wait. Andi's the lead. Send it to her. She'll want to be involved."

Just before hanging up, Ed remembered. "Say, how's Art today?" Doc's answer surprised him.

"Pretty alert all day. I'm thinking he's close to the end. Sometimes they wake up just before they go."

Ed thanked him and decided to get over to the hospital as soon as he could.

He called Andi's cell phone again. She still didn't answer, but he left another message, then called the station. When Callie answered, she told him Andi was home. "She's off today. Some boyfriend, not knowing your squeeze's schedule."

Ed grunted. He'd left Grace needing a ride to school this morning; she'd probably woken Andi up. Thoughtless. He shook his head. *I'm too wrapped up in these cases.* He decided to drive over to Andi's place, hoping she'd be home.

She was. "Thanks for no warning about Grace needing a ride, bucko. She woke me up from a good sound sleep." Despite that, she leaned up and kissed him. "How was your meeting with Mack?"

He sighed. "Rough. I'm not sure I'm going to solve this one." He rubbed his eyes.

"You're maybe in too close."

He nodded. "Yeah, might be. And Jared's paranoid again this morning." He told her about the brain tumor theory and that Doc was writing an order for an MRI.

She grabbed her jacket. "That'll require the parents' agreement, since at the moment we're treating him as a juvenile." She looked at him, and dropped the jacket on a chair, put her arms around him. "You look like a horse dragged you a mile. Was I too rough on you last night?"

He pulled her closer. "Never happen. Your body's good medicine. It's these two cases. Oh, and Art's dying, and Ordrew's obstruction of justice bullshit." He pulled away. "There's not a damn thing I can figure to do about any of it."

Suddenly, he remembered Art's advice and chuckled.

Andi looked a question at him. "What's funny?"

He shook his head. "Something Art said. Told me to sit my horse till I see something move."

"Which means what exactly?"

"Damned if I know."

"Then what *are* you going to do?"

Doc Keeley had said Art might die today. "Go talk to Art before he dies."

114

Art was awake when Ed knocked softly on his door. "I'm not gone yet. Come on in." His voice was weak, but Ed heard and went in.

Art was gazing through the big window toward the mountains. When he turned his head slowly toward Ed, his face lit in a smile. "I saw my dad last night."

"A dream?"

Thin, bony shoulders shrugged. "Who knows, real or dream. I saw him. He said a thing."

"Yeah? What'd he say?"

Art struggled, to weak to hoist himself more upright on his pillow; Ed stepped over and helped him. After a burst of coughing that exhausted him, Art whispered, "Thanks, Ed." He took some ragged breaths. "You remember what I never thanked him for?"

"He told your draft board you were honest."

Art nodded weakly, coughed again, rasping, and his eyes widened; the coughs quieted into gasps, then ragged breaths; he lay back exhausted. After a moment, he looked up at Ed.

"You want to rest? I can come back."

Art shook his head. "Saw my dad." Caught his breath. "Let me...tell it."

"Take your time."

Art nodded. "Not much left of that," he said, smiling thinly. "My old man. He said, 'You're welcome, son.'" He beamed, then, and closed his eyes slowly, like window shades pulled down. Without warning, he slipped away as quietly as a rowboat drifting slowly from the dock in the fading light of a summer evening.

Ed waited, and after a few moments, decided Art had fallen asleep. Or? Suddenly anxious, he stood, looked at the monitor; the heart was still beating. He looked closely at the old man. Art's eyes opened. "Still here." Gave a weak smile.

Ed stood beside the bed, and for a moment let his fingers rest on the old man's hand. After a few silent moments, Art spoke, too softly for Ed to hear. He leaned in. "I'm sorry, Art. I didn't hear."

Art gathered himself. "I said, 'Thanks for getting me sorted out about my old man.'"

Ed smiled. "Glad I could do it, my friend." He started to leave.

Art reached out his hand, took Ed's arm. "Ed?"

He turned back. "I'm here, Art."

"Thanks for these talks."

Ed felt his throat thicken. "You're welcome, man. I'm just sorry—"

Art stopped him with a hand. "Nothing to be sorry for. You're not...my savior." He fell silent for a long moment. Then, Art's hand lifted slowly from the bed. His eyes remained closed. Almost inaudibly, he whispered, "Ed?"

"Yeah, Art."

The wrinkled hand reached out. Ed took it.

"Ed. You're nobody's...savior. Nobody's saved...or safe...here." Art's eyes slowly unfocused. Closed. His mouth opened peacefully, and his breaths lengthened into a smooth, soft flow, then stopped.

How do you watch a man die who has just given you the key? Ed breathed softly and held Art's hand, letting the tears flow down his cheeks.

On his way out, he stopped at the nurse's station, told her Art was gone. Walking toward the parking lot, his thoughts swirled, eddies in a snowmelt river. *I'm nobody's savior.*

115

Pete unlocked the cellblock door and Ed slipped in. The pills lay untouched in the cup outside Jared's cell, but the water glass had tipped, and a pool of water surrounded the cup. The note was gone. Jared lay on the cot, arms behind his head, an icon of the prisoner's boredom.

"Hey, Jared. How's it going?"

Jared turned his head toward Ed. "Shitty. Meditating helps when I'm not crazy." He sat up. "I'm just thinking."

"About what?"

"Why I get those thoughts. Why I get crazy."

Ed was pleased. This didn't sound paranoid. "Any answers?"

"Well, it isn't the seeds. Do you have a new answer?"

Rational, tackling his problem head on. "You're not thinking we're going to hurt you?"

Jared shook his head. "Uh-uh. After I woke up, I felt, I don't know, calmer. Maybe it's the meditation."

"Did you meditate during the night?"

Jared shook his head again. "No. I was paranoid and angry most of the night." He nodded at the spilled water. "I saw your note—it pissed me off." He looked sheepish. "Whenever they checked on me, I'd just get madder. Then around four, I think, I fell asleep, and when I woke up, I felt different. Scared. But not angry any more. I meditated then."

"Scared of...?"

"This place. Of what's going to happen."

"But not that the government was coming for you?"

"Uh-uh." Something close to a smile moved across his lips. "The government's already got me." He reached down and righted the spilled cup. "Sorry for spilling the water. I'll take the pills if you want me to. What are they?"

"They're called BuSpar. They reduce anxiety, which I'm hoping will keep the paranoia at bay. But only take them if you want to."

Jared looked at Ed, eyes pleading. "Ed, what's wrong with me?"

"I don't have a perfect answer, but we have a direction to investigate. We'll need your help."

His eyes grew guarded. "What kind of help?"

"We'd like your permission, and we need your folks' permission, to do an MRI of your brain. I'm thinking there may be something that's causing the paranoid thoughts."

"A brain tumor." He didn't seem surprised.

Ed hesitated, curious about what looked like Jared's lack of shock. As if he expected it. Much as he wanted to ask about that, he needed to nail down the MRI issue first. "Maybe. It's something we should check out—it could be causing the problems. You willing to have the MRI?"

Jared nodded, smiling sadly. "Yeah. Whatever. Although you're supposed to tell me the risks and benefits." His smile flashed full for a moment, lighting up his face.

Ed chuckled, but felt embarrassed. *Forgot that part.* He pulled the consent form from his briefcase, and began reading the risks-and-benefits section. Jared stood up and walked to the cell door, where Ed stood, and looked over Ed's shoulder, grasping the bars with both hands. "I know what it says, Ed. Did you know that only 55% of patients with grade IV brain cancer live five years?"

Ed stopped reading. "No, I didn't. Sounds like you do, though."

Jared turned around and leaned back against the cell door, looking up at the ceiling of his cell. Ed waited, watching Jared's back.

Jared turned and faced him again. His eyes had filled with tears. "My grandpa died of brain cancer when I was twelve." A sob rose in his throat, and he stopped, breathing hard. After a moment, he said, "He lived with us the last couple of years, and I took care of him. Well, we all did." He looked far away, out, beyond the jail walls. "Anyway, while he was dying, I studied brain tumors. I thought I could learn something that could help him." He shook his head. "Stupid. The afternoon he died, I knew I would get a brain tumor someday." He coughed gently. "Looks like I was right." He brushed his eyes. "The Buddha was wrong. There's no end to suffering, is there?"

Ed found his throat full, he couldn't speak.

Jared looked away. "Dumb question, huh?"

"No." Ed found a word. "It's *the* question."

116

Promptly at five, Magnus pushed into Ed's office and sat down boldly, not falling heavily into the chair as before, nor lowering himself gingerly. Ed felt the change. *He's ready to act. I'm behind his curve.* He thought fleetingly of Art's words. *Nobody's savior.* Ed seized the lead.

He said, "I'm done trying to save you, Mack. That's your job."

It got a rise. Magnus's hand flinched on the arm of his chair, but his reaction flickered only briefly in his steady blue eyes. "That so? How do you suggest I save myself?"

Ed shrugged. "Face your real motives."

"I am."

"No, you're not. Father Jerome is only a symbol."

Magnus made a dismissive gesture, but his eyes told Ed he'd made a dent in the rancher's resolve. Magnus was an honest man, even if his darker side, that knot in his spirit, was opaque to him. He looked out the window, as he so often did, and Ed realized why: The valley's open spaces, the far mountains' heights, beckoned. Out there, up on the Coliseum, Mack could lay down his responsibilities. Ed himself had often looked up to the mountains, yearning for release from the duties of compassion.

After a moment, Magnus turned back and growled, "A symbol of what? You're thinking what I really want is to kill my father and sleep with my mother?"

To kill my father. Ed felt a shock that emptied his mind, then cleared it. They'd come finally to the knot in Magnus's spirit. Delicately, now.

Ed framed his question carefully. "What does killing the monk say to the valley people? About who you are?"

Magnus looked disgusted. "Ed, this isn't about what people think or who I am. What's your damn symbol?"

"Humor me. What do you think killing Father Jerome would say to people?"

Magnus shook his head, but he took a moment, then said, "It'll tell them, 'Don't rape Magnus Anderssen.'"

"Right. 'If you hurt an Anderssen, someone dies.'"

Magnus narrowed his eyes, nodded. "Wouldn't have worded it that way myself, but that's right."

"That's the philosophy of which Anderssen men?"

Magnus lowered his head, a bull eyeing the red cape, wary, but also curious. "Explain yourself."

"Is that Anders' philosophy? Günter's? Royal's? Or are we maybe talking your father Daryl, Daryl the violent?"

Magnus's eyes darkened and he turned his head to the side, watching Ed from the corner of his eye. "Tell me what you mean."

"It's the part of you that's like Daryl. If Daryl was hurt, he became violent. You're hurt, so you want to kill. You're going to leave Junior with the same burden Daryl left you."

Ed watched Magnus's face move through wariness to rage. His voice rumbled deep in his throat. "I could kill you for saying that. I *should* kill you for it."

Ed felt calm, assured by Magnus's reaction. *He could kill me, but he won't.*

274

He knew his friend's stronger side, and now he knew he could push. "Yeah, you could kill me, and that would prove what I'm saying: Your father left a piece of himself in you and you haven't faced it."

"Don't provoke me, Ed. I'm too angry to be provoked."

"Or what, Mack? Or you'll kill me? Or you'll put a bullet through your head and leave the mess for Luisa and your son to deal with?" *He's right. I'm provoking him.*

"I'm still in this chair out of respect, but I'd be in my rights to beat you senseless."

"You'd be 'in your rights'?" Ed felt the rising anger in his own chest, took a breath to still it. "Where the hell did you learn that phrase?"

Magnus jerked back in the chair, suddenly breathing too rapidly, and Ed reminded him of the calming words. "Calm yourself, Mack." The big man slowly settled down, but remained furious, face flushed. Ed, waiting, settled himself as well.

"All right," Magnus said, eyes still angry, but calmer. "Daryl said it, before he struck my mother." He took a few long, shaky breaths, and a shadow crossed his face. "For a moment, I felt—" He stopped.

Ed waited.

"Ed, I was on the edge. I really could've killed you." Magnus's hands gripped the edge of the seat, bunching it in his fists.

Ed nodded again. "You could. Or you could face that urge in you. And tame it."

Magnus looked once again out the window at the rain that had begun wetting the glass, at the haze of snow blowing high across the face of the mountains. He pulled his fingers through his hair. "I don't know what to say to that." He remained silent, staring at the mountains. Then, softly, "If Daryl is in me, I should kill myself."

Ed said, "And leave it for your son and your wife to deal with? No, you can tame this. Tame yourself."

Magnus swung to face him, angry again. "Mumbo-jumbo! Say what you mean!"

"I said what I mean, Mack. You tame dogs. How?"

"I'm not here to talk about taming dogs. Say something I can work with, for God's sake." His anger was tinged with fear. He said, "Please, Ed. Help me."

"You tame dogs by getting to know them and working *with* their character, not against it. You use the good aspects of their character to reduce the bad behavior and increase the good. You tame the Daryl part of you the same way. Get to know that part of you, don't bury it. Learn why your rage rises, then find ways to channel the energy into solving whatever set off the rage in the first place. Then use your honesty and your generosity to tame it."

"Nonsense."

"No, it's not. You woke the Daryl-part in you and he's not going back to sleep; you have to work with him, with yourself. To learn him so well you can figure out how to redirect his energy for good. To accept him." He almost didn't say the next words. "Hell, to love him."

"I can never love that man."

"No, not Daryl. The Daryl-part of yourself."

Mack abruptly stood, swung around, snatched open the door. "We're done here." He stepped out into the hall, leaving Ed behind.

Ed extended his hand, offering to shake, but also trying to draw Magnus back.

"Tomorrow, then?"

Magnus looked at Ed's hand, then in his eyes. He did not shake hands. "Perhaps. I will call you."

THURSDAY, DAY ELEVEN

117

Although a fine powdery snow drifted like a veil in the air, breaks in the clouds let the morning's first light drape Hunters' Peak in pink. Ed was on his way into town. In his rearview, snow billowed up like clouds of smoke. The radio predicted one-to-three inches. *No big deal, it'll melt in a day.* As he drove, Ed felt his excitement bubbling. Finally, a day with some joy. Grace was dozing beside him.

He said, keeping a neutral voice, "Grace?"

Grace didn't move, but her voice said, "She's sleeping."

"No, you're not. I need to talk to you. Change of plans, kiddo."

She roused herself and looked at him. "How does my being almost seventeen qualify me for the word 'kiddo'?"

He chuckled. "You're six months away from seventeen."

"Huh." She began tapping on her phone, and after a moment, she showed him the phone's screen. "Look."

He glanced over and saw a calculator screen showing the figure 0.030303. "Which means what?"

"At my age, six months is a mere three percent of my life. I'd call that 'close.'"

He smiled at her. "Fair enough. Anyway, I want you to take my pickup today. Drive yourself home."

"Why?"

Ed let her think about it.

After a moment, she said, "Do you remember, me and my girls are prom-prepping after school? We don't get done till six, and then pizza at Alice's. I can't pick you up till after all that."

"You don't have to."

Grace looked puzzled. "You and Andi—" He eyes flashed. "Omigod, Northrup! You're bringing home my new car!" She darted toward him for an

277

arm-hug, but her seatbelt jerked tight and she didn't reach him. "Omigod! Omigod! Northrup, you're the best."

"Three 'omigods.' Impressive. I'm glad you're pleased. So you'll be home what, seven, seven-fifteen?"

"No way! Now I can't wait. I'm coming home right after prom prep. Some things are better than pizza!" She bounced in her seat. "Tell me all about my car!"

He shook his head. "Surprise doubles the pleasure."

"That's the stupidest thing I've ever heard."

He glanced at her, could see on her face frustration wrestling with excitement.

Excitement won. "Okay, string it out," she said happily. "I've got all day to enjoy this."

118

By the time they reached his office and Grace had driven off, the fine snow had stopped. Blue patches showed over the mountains. *Ah, Montana weather.* Before opening his office, Ed stepped into the sheriff's department. The big clock showed *8:01.*

"Morning, Callie," he said. "The Hansens here yet?"

"Morning, handsome. In the conference room. Lookin' scared as pups at the vet's." Callie squinted at him. "So we're thinking brain tumors now?"

"Privileged information, Callie," he said, putting a big smile he didn't feel on his face.

"Not so privileged when it's written all over this court order. Your girlfriend asked me to give you a copy." Smirking over the counter top, she handed him a document. He scanned it. "The parents already agreed." He handed it back. "Don't need this."

"When was this?"

Last evening, he'd gone to the Hansens' to tell them about his suspicion of a brain tumor, and to get their permission for the MRI. During the entire talk, tears had wet Marie Hansen's cheeks—it had been her father who'd died of brain cancer in their living room. Despite her emotions, her questions had been precise and focused. She must have studied brain disease, as her son had. Perhaps they'd studied together, a shared labor of grief. Phil Hansen had been oddly silent.

"Care for a word of advice?" Callie asked.

He nodded. "Sure."

"You probably know this, so all due respect, but you should tell them to refuse permission."

What the hell? "Why?"

"If they consent, they pay for the MRI. If they refuse, the court order trumps and the county pays."

"I didn't know that."

Ed could see her puffing up just a little. "Glad to be of help to the citizenry." She giggled. "Actually, it was your girlfriend who mentioned that to me."

"Well, it's good thinking, whoever thought it." He took the court order back and went to the conference room. Andi waited outside the door. "Right on time," she said. "They're all waiting inside."

He kissed her. "I need to advise them to rescind consent so the court order will take effect. Give me five minutes?"

She looked at her watch. "That's about all we have. Gotta get on the road."

Phil Hansen was pacing when Ed came in, and they shook hands. Jared sat beside his mother, her fingers making small circles on his forearm. He lifted his eyebrows at Ed; his eyes were red. *He looks calmer than I'd feel*, Ed thought.

Ed nodded to Marie Hansen, and said to Jared, "Holding up?"

He nodded.

"Phil, Marie, I have to talk to you about something. You too, Jared. We have a court order to get this MRI done. I didn't realize this yesterday, but if you folks give formal consent, you'll have to pay for the procedure. If you rescind your consent, though—which is your right—the MRI will still happen, but the county's on the hook for the bill. My advice is to rescind your consent."

Phil shook his head. "Thanks, Ed, but no. Our lawyer already told us about that. Jared's our son, we're the ones to take care of him. We don't need charity."

Ed could see wounded pride in his eyes. "This isn't charity, Phil, it's—"

Marie said, "Ed, we'll pay for Jared's care." Her voice was iron. You could have struck her words with a hammer and not dented them.

Andi knocked, then stuck her head in the door. "We ready in here?"

To Jared's parents, Ed said, "All right, then. I hear you." He waved her in.

Brad Ordrew followed her, looking hard at Ed. He may have caught the Hansens' sudden angry glances, or seen them stiffen when he appeared, but he ignored them. Ed watched Jared for a sign of fear or anger, but his face reflected only sadness. Or maybe composure.

Andi said, "Hey, Jared." He looked at her briefly, nodded.

Ed watched Andi gauge the mood of the room; she gave him an almost imperceptible lift of her eyebrows. Ed said, "No rescission. Their consent stands."

She nodded, then sat and laid her hand, flat, on the table. Everyone but Jared looked at that hand. "You folks realize you'll be billed for the MRI?"

Phil nodded. "We do."

"Good. Any other questions?"

Phil shook his head.

Andi said, "Okay, here's how this goes. Jared's in custody, so Deputy Ordrew and I drive him to Missoula." She offered a small shrug, an apology. "I'm sorry, but you two will have to drive in your own vehicle, but we won't be using lights or sirens, just normal speed so when we get there you three can be together right away." She smiled. "Jared, I'm sorry you'll have to endure a ride in my back seat."

He looked up. "No worries. But do I have to wear handcuffs in the car?"

Ordrew jumped in, "Yes. You're—"

Andi interrupted him. "No, it's too long a ride. Once you're in the car, I'll take them off."

Jared looked quickly at Ordrew, who said nothing. Jared looked surprised, and said, "Thanks." To Ed, his voice sounded resigned, infused with sorrow, but held no tone of paranoia or hostility. *The BuSpar's working*, he thought.

Andi continued the briefing. After discussing what would happen at the hospital, she said, "Except for the drive up and back and during the MRI itself, your mom and dad will be beside you the whole time. Do you understand, Jared?"

Ed tensed. This would be a moment for Jared's paranoia to assert itself. It was the moment he'd dreaded, being cuffed, put in the squad car, and taken away. *The government wants to kill me*. But the boy simply nodded. "Uh-huh." He looked at Andi, then at Ordrew. "Where will you guys be?"

Ordrew jumped on it. "We'll be right there the whole time—in the vehicle for the trip, and just outside your door in the hospital. If you try anything, there'll be trouble."

Jared flinched. Ed tensed again. The young man took a couple of long breaths, his face softening into a smile. "Yeah, deputy. Shit will come down that I can't imagine, right?"

Marie looked shocked, but Phil Hansen smiled. Ordrew, his lips tight, locked eyes with Jared for a moment, but when Jared held his gaze, he said nothing.

"What happens after the MRI?" Phil Hansen asked.

"One of two things. From what I was told by Dr. Keeley, they'll use some sedation during the actual procedure to make Jared comfortable, so we'll wait until that's out of his system. Once the doctors release him, we'll drive back to Jefferson. I understand there's a bail hearing this afternoon, so if that works out, when we get back, Jared can come home."

Marie Hansen said, "What if they don't set bail today?"

"In that case, unfortunately, Jared will have to spend the night here again." She looked at him softly. "I'm sorry, Jared. Let's keep our fingers crossed your lawyer works it out before we get back."

Jared lowered his eyes to the table.

Ed noticed the boy's hands trembling on his lap, and thought, *There's no good end here.*

119

After the caravan to Missoula had gone, Ed went to his office. He finished his morning patients and was jotting notes, trying not to worry about Magnus or Jared. At noon, the waiting room door opened, and Lynn Monroe came in, followed by another woman. *Must be the friend*, he thought. "Hey, Lynn. Right on time."

"Morning, Ed. This is my, uh, friend, Rachel Anders."

After handshakes, he offered coffee, but both women shook their heads. "Okay, then, let's take a look."

Ed grabbed his coat and they went out to the parking lot. The morning's brief snow was gone, leaving only wet pavement. The air already had lost its chill.

Rachel said, "Don't be put off by appearances."

Looking at the car she was pointing at, he knew immediately what she meant. He searched for the word. "Unique."

"It is. But the rest is fantastic." She launched her sales pitch. By the end, Ed was sold, especially because the car was one of the safest in the world.

"A '96 Volvo 380 wagon. It averages about 21 miles to the gallon, but it's fast when it needs to be and safe as hell. Kelly Blue Book rating is 8.6."

He examined the car, stem to stern. "I'm not a professional mechanic, but you learn a lot from guys out here." He lifted the hood. "I've done most of my own maintenance over the years." On the surface, he saw nothing that concerned him. Except that uniqueness.

Rachel said, "I'm flexible on the price too, Ed."

"Which is?"

"I'm asking three thousand dollars."

"You're asking it flexibly." He smiled.

She smiled back. "Flexibly."

"I'd like to have Reggie Hayes—he's our mechanic—look at it. Without my tools, I can't see the guts. He said he'd do it first thing after lunch. Reggie never skips lunch."

Rachel laughed. "Well, if you want the car, I'm here till Lynn's done working tomorrow." She turned to Lynn and said, "Okay if we stay through Saturday, if we need to?"

"Sure," Lynn said.

Ed said, "No need for that. Unless Reggie finds something wrong, I'm going to buy it. I already told my daughter she'd take delivery tonight, and I've made her wait long enough."

Lynn said, "Hell hath no fury like a teenager deprived of her ride."

They all laughed, and Rachel said, "What's your offer?"

"Oh yeah, that. Unless Reggie finds something wrong, this car's easily worth your flexible three-thousand. Minus maybe fifty for the uniqueness. I'll have the check when you come over at five."

Rachel laughed. "You're on. I'll miss her, but I'm sure she's in good hands." She handed him the keys, and they shook hands. He thought, *Her?* "By the way, what's her name?"

Rachel smiled. "Jayne. With a 'y.'"

"Jayne?"

"As in Jayne Mansfield."

Ed decided not to ask.

120

Promptly at five, Lynn and Rachel came into the waiting room. His last patient had just left, and he ushered them into his office. "Reggie says the car's in fabulous shape, inside and out. You've taken good care of it."

"Her," Rachel said, smiling. "Jayne's not an it. And yeah, I've treated her like my baby."

They transferred the title and he wrote out a check. They shook hands. Rachel said, "Mind if I go sit in her one last time?"

"Not at all," Ed said. They went out to the parking lot. After a few moments behind the wheel, Rachel got out. Her eyes were moist. "Silly of me, but I get attached."

Lynn gave her a hug. "Let's go get drunk at—" She turned to Ed. "What's the gay guy's name, owns the Angler?"

"Ted Coldry."

Rachel laughed. "That's perfect. We'll get drunk with a gay fellow." She shrugged to Ed. "Lynn and I are partners."

Lynn smiled. "Lesbian partners."

Ed smiled back. He'd wondered. "Gonna get married?"

Rachel glanced at Lynn, who said, "So far it's a tie: one for, one against. Negotiations continue."

They left on foot; the Angler was directly across the street from Ed's office. As he locked up, his cell phone buzzed. He looked at the screen: *Andi.*

"Hi, lover. How'd the MRI go? Jared all right?"

"Change of plan. We're not coming home tonight. Jared had some problem with the sedation. They're keeping him overnight for observation. Brad and I are taking shifts sitting outside the door. If he's okay, we'll be home sometime tomorrow afternoon." She paused. "If not, God knows."

"Oh, man, I'm sorry. You have to sit up all night by the door?"

"Three-hour shifts." She sighed. "If we get home tomorrow, I'll be ornery as a wet kitten."

Ed decided not to pursue the simile. "How about Ordrew?"

He could almost hear her smile. "Pissed, as usual. He gets to sleep in the doctors' lounge, but it turns out he hates doctors." She chuckled. "By the way, guess who found Jared's room?"

Ed thought about it. "Jack Kollier?"

"The same. He'd heard about the MRI. The man's got to have an inside source. But get this. When Kollier strolled down the hall, Ordrew got antsy and said he had to go outside for a smoke. When he came back, Jack was still there, so Brad hightailed it the other way."

"Meaning?"

"Number one, Brad doesn't smoke. Number two, I think he's Kollier's inside source."

"Whew. If that's true, Ben'll be pissed."

He heard Andi sigh. "I doubt we'll ever know. Kollier's good, and he's a bulldog about protecting his sources."

"Well, we've got a big evening planned. Grace's car is coming home."

"Damn, I hate to miss that."

"Yeah, I wish you'd be here. Call me at ten. I'll be going to bed."

"Don't tempt me, wild man. Fantasies can be fatal at our age."

121

As Ed drove homeward in Grace's Volvo, he tried to imagine a good outcome from Jared's MRI. What was *good*? If he had a tumor, even if it helped his legal situation, how *good* was that? And if there were no tumor? The seed theory was shot, and Ed had nothing to replace it with except tedious searching through databases of external toxins, or maybe re-thinking the schizophrenia option. What else could keep the boy out of prison?

The three-inch snow they'd predicted hadn't materialized; what little had fallen was already in puddles on the road. A typical mountain weather forecast: Wrong. The air was already warming again. He shifted his thinking to this vehicle. He loved its feel—tight, responsive, safe. He could relax about Grace driving it. A fine car, if a bit unique.

Just after six, he'd settled himself in front of a fire in the wood stove and poured himself a glass of wine. A few minutes later, he saw his pickup sweep up the drive. When it stopped, rocking, Grace bounded out of it so fast he wondered if she'd even turned off the engine. He went quickly onto the porch to watch her reaction to her car.

Grace's hands went to her cheeks. She stood statue-still. Ed walked down the porch steps, trying to gauge her response.

Her eyes, wide, fixed on the car. After a long moment, he asked, tentatively, "Whaddya think?"

Grace looked at him. "Northrup, it's *pink*."

He nodded. "It's a Volvo."

Her hand covered her mouth. "Omigod. A pink genital. I can't drive this."

Ed laughed, though he knew it might set her off. "Not vulva, Volvo. Safest cars built."

Grace stared at the pink car. "Yeah? In what century?"

"Well, the last one, but it's in perfect shape." He tossed her the keys; they bounced off her arm onto the ground.

She straightened after retrieving them. A small smile touched her lips. "Wait'll Jen and Dana see this." She turned to Ed. "I'm taking it for a test drive."

"And to show your girls?"

"Whaddya think?"

He laughed at her quoting him. "Sure. Go for it. Home by *9:30?*" He expected a fight.

All he got was, "You bet, kiddo."

Dad-like, Ed began studying his watch a few minutes after nine. He knew that if Andi had been there, she'd have teased him about his worrying. Exactly at nine-twenty-eight Grace drove Jayne into the yard. He could hear Andi's "Told you."

Grace burst in from the porch. "Northrup! I love my car. And me and Jen, sorry, Jen and me named it!"

He decided to skip the grammar lesson. "Great. What's her name?"

"The Pink Vulva." She gave Ed a peck on the cheek and dashed back outside.

Ed could imagine Andi's comment at this moment: *You asked for that.* He went to the window and looked out into the darkening yard. Grace was sitting behind the wheel, interior light on, fiddling with the radio buttons. He thought, *It's a fine car.*

He could hear Andi's reply. "It's a fine *pink* car."

He dialed her cell phone, told her the story, gave her the name.

She said, "The car's pink?"

"Uh-huh. But it's a Volvo. Perfect condition. Safest car in the valley."

"But *pink?*"

"Pink."

There was a silence. Then, "Every now and then, you re-notify us that you have no operative experience with a teenage girl." He heard the laugh in her voice.

"'The Pink Vulva,' though?"

Another chuckle. "It's called, 'Touché, Dad.'"

FRIDAY, DAY TWELVE

122

Long day, Ed thought. He'd had patients every hour except at lunch, which Grace had spoiled by locking her keys inside the PV and calling him to bail her out. He worked the lock tool to open the door, but he didn't mention that he kept that tool at his office because he frequently locked his own keys in the truck. "Make a place for your keys and always put them there," he lectured, omitting the fact that he'd never bothered to do that.

"Thank you, Doctor. I will keep my Alzheimer's under better control."

She was embarrassed, he realized. "Sorry, kiddo. Or rather, Grace. Next time they get locked in, if I'm not around, call Reggie Hayes."

"He'll charge me money."

He said nothing.

She said, "Got it, loud and clear."

When he'd gotten back to the office, Andi had left a message. "Not on the way, yet. Docs say we can get out of here around three, so should be back to Jefferson six-ish. Jared's apparently okay but they want to be sure. The bail hearing went okay—that Donna Ratner's tough, according to Ben. Got bail cut in half and the Hansens are posting it by phone, so he can go home when we get there."

Just after six, Ed was locking his office when the door from the parking lot pushed open. He turned to see who was coming in. Andi and Ordrew, one on each side, escorted Jared into the building, fast-walking him toward the sheriff's department door. Ed saw hands cuffed behind his back and his eyes shiny with fear.

"Hey," Ed greeted him. "How's it going?"

Andi, walking fast, said, "Bail's set and paid. We're a little tense after the long day." She nodded at Jared. "Jared's folks are right behind us, so they can take him home when we sign him out."

287

"Great," Ed said, but saw that Jared's panic looked undiminished. He said, "What's wrong?"

Ordrew shook his head. "Later, shrink. We got paperwork."

Jared swiveled his head to look at Ed.

"Breathe, Jared," Ed hollered through the glass door. The boy disappeared into the back rooms of the department.

Ed followed them in, pondering Jared's apparent terror. Was he slipping back into psychosis? If so, what if he went home, then ran again? The door opened and Phil and Marie Hansen came into the reception area.

"Jared's coming home," Marie said, a big smile on her face.

Ed smiled back. *Don't alarm them yet.* "That's great news. Look, I just saw him and he seemed a little shaky. Mind if I spend a few minutes with him, make sure he's stable?"

Phil deflated. "My God, Ed, it doesn't stop, does it?"

What to say? "I guess not, Phil. I'm sorry."

Marie, whose eyes had teared when he asked for the time, said, "Talk to him, Ed. I want him home with me."

Ed followed Jared into the interrogation room. Andi was removing the cuffs. Ed put his hand on Jared's shoulder. "You okay, man?" Andi finished, and stood off to the side.

Jared shook his head. "On the edge. That MRI was terrible, I thought I was going to die."

"Paranoia?"

"No, claustrophobia, I think. But that plus the drugs they gave me, then staying overnight." He stopped, looked at the wall. "It was terrible."

"How are you now?"

"No crazy thoughts, just...I don't know. Afraid."

"Afraid of something in particular?"

Jared shook his head. "Just afraid. But not crazy."

"Have you taken your BuSpar?"

He shook his head. "Deputy Ordrew took it."

"Damn it!" He contained his anger. Andi said, "I'll get it."

Ed said, "I'm on it. I'll let you know if I need help."

He found Ordrew was at his desk, working on the computer. He said, "Jared needs his medication. Now." Ordrew ignored him.

"Ordrew, I'm speaking to you."

The deputy swiveled toward him. "I don't talk with people who interfere with police work."

He bit back the *Fuck you*, instead said, "Fine. But Jared's physician prescribed that medication and it belongs to him. He needs it now." Ordrew swiveled back to his desk, ignoring him again.

Ed returned to the interrogation room. He said to Andi, "Guess I need your help. He's blowing me off."

She closed her eyes a moment, then nodded. "I'll bring it in."

Ed sat with Jared, who had closed his eyes. "Meditating?" he asked.

Jared nodded. "Trying, anyway."

When she returned, Andi put the pill bottle and a cup of water on the table. "I'm sorry about that, Jared. Here they are." She looked at Ed. "How many?"

"Just one," he said, then turned to Jared. "I'm going to get your folks." He found Marie and Phil in Reception. "Sorry about the delay. Jared's going to be okay in a short while, but if you see him getting angry or paranoid, or even suspicious, don't let him leave and call me right away."

Marie's eyes welled up. "My God, I thought we were past that." Her voice died.

Ed touched her on the shoulder. "I'm probably being alarmist. But the MRI isn't a treatment, it's just diagnostic, so till we get the results and decide on a treatment, if we need one, I'm afraid you need to be alert."

She nodded, touching her eyes with a tissue she'd pulled from her sleeve. "I understand, Ed. I'm just a bit emotional."

"If it were Grace, I'd be a basket case, Marie."

She nodded sadly.

"Be sure he takes his medication." He handed her the pill bottle. "Directions are on the bottle. If he refuses to take it, call me. I'll come right over."

"It seems like it won't end." She reached out toward him.

Ed held her hand a moment. "Hang in there. As soon as we learn the MRI results, we'll see further down the road. Meantime—"

Phil interrupted. "Meantime, hell continues."

123

Outside, walking to his truck, Ed considered Phil's words. *Meanwhile, hell continues.* True. Whatever Jared's future, no road looked good at this moment. He climbed into his truck and sat a moment, gazing at the mountains. Evening sun reddened their peaks; the soft air carried the scent of budding trees. He wondered briefly how Magnus was doing; the last session had been hard on his friend. *I need to call him.* When he dialed the Anderhold, though, there was no answer. He left a message.

Savoring the soft, warm air, on an impulse he drove to Art's Fine Foods and picked up three steaks and baking potatoes. Grace'll want something green. He grabbed a clump of broccoli. At the checkout, Anne Marie wore a black armband.

"We'll miss Art," he said to her.

She continued ringing up his groceries, nodding. "Sucks, Ed. Nothing else to say. He was a good man."

"Any word on who might take over the store?"

"Rumors is all."

"Like what?"

She looked around. "Shouldn't speak out of school, but some say when Art took sick, Magnus Anderssen told him if there aren't no buyers, he'd buy it to keep us all in jobs."

It was a jolt to his midsection. Even amid Mack's trouble, he'd found time to offer help.

Anne Marie looked at him. "You all right? Face went pale."

He nodded. "If that's true, it's sure generous."

She nodded. "You want extra plastic wrap for these steaks?" Without waiting for his answer, she wrapped them in the plastic, and put them in the bag. "Generous is right, Ed. But that's Mr. Anderssen for you, isn't it?"

When Andi finally got home, around seven, he had just fired the coals in the old Weber. They were talking on the porch when Grace, driving the PV, pulled in. Andi turned to look.

"Wow. That's *really* pink."

"Don't rub it in," he said.

"Don't rub what?" she said, arching her eyebrows.

Grace leaped out of her car and waved. "Hi, Andi," she sang when she ran up the steps. "Northrup! The PV's amazing. I can get it up to sixty in twelve seconds!"

Andi gave her the police eye. "The speed limit on the road out here is fifty-five, Grace."

Grace cleared her throat. "Right. I don't drive sixty on that road. Just on the highway. South. Where it's safe."

"Good answer," Andi said, smiling. "Just don't do anything to make us arrest you."

Grace ignored that. "Isn't the PV awesome?"

Andi laughed. "Your dad told me what the initials stand for."

"That's the greatest, isn't it?" She opened the door. "Anyway, I'm tired. I need my beauty sleep." She pretended a long yawn that made Andi laugh.

Ed shrugged. "Not hungry?"

Grace ignored that and started inside, then turned. "Do. Not. Disturb. I'm sleeping eighteen hours." She closed the door firmly. Andi went inside. He stepped down to the grill, checking the coals. Fifteen minutes until he could put the t-bones on.

A half hour later, when he came in with the steaks, he paused near Grace's door and called, "Steaks on the table!"

In a minute, Grace popped out of her room. "Steaks! I'm starving." No yawns this time.

As they ate, Andi told them about her night in the hospital. "It wasn't pleasant. I could come to hate nurses' lounges."

Ed asked, "Ordrew behave himself? He still think you're interested in his hard-on?"

Grace looked up. "Eeeuw."

"Nope, he was pretty low-key. I think he's catching on that he's going to lose this obstruction bullshit and that I'm pissed at him. Hell, the whole department's pissed at him. He offered to take a couple extra shifts so I could sleep. The smell of the nurses' lounge kept me awake, though."

Ed laughed. Grace had resumed chewing rapidly through her steak, but asked, mouth full, "What's 'this obstruction bullshit' mean?"

Ed explained the situation.

Grace swallowed her mouthful. "Did you obstruct justice? I thought you were trying to help Jared."

"I was. Nobody except Ordrew thinks it'll amount to anything."

Grace put her fork down. "That deputy was a jerk when he interviewed me."

"He interviewed you?"

"Yeah, nine, ten days ago."

Ed noticed her eyes going down, avoiding his look.

Grace said to Andi, "Tell me about Jared's MRI."

"In a minute. What happened during that interview?"

Grace whitened. "Well, nothing." She looked toward the ceiling fan, working something out. A moment later, she shrugged and looked at Ed, then at Andi. When she spoke, her voice was casual, but her eyes weren't. "He thinks he caught me saying I was at a drinking party, and he threatened to find out if I did anything illegal unless I said something bad about Jared."

Ed bridled, but Andi spoke first. "He threatened you? To get information?"

Grace looked caught in a hard place. "Uh-huh. I guess."

Ed slammed his fist on the table. "That prick."

Grace looked half-shocked at the word. Andi, calmer, said, "Did he say anything specific?"

Grace looked at her rapidly cooling steak. "Naw, just what I said."

"Jesus!" Ed muttered. "This guy's a piece of work."

Grace looked very uncomfortable. "What if he finds I did some drinking, like at a kegger or something?"

Andi and Ed looked at each other. Finally, Ed managed, "Will he find that?"

"I don't know if he *will*."

Andi half-smiled, but concealed it quickly. "Fair enough, but *could* he find it?"

Grace swallowed. "What do you guys have to do if I admit to something, uh, illegal?"

"Like drinking?"

She nodded. Carefully.

Ed thought, *Could be worse, she's at least talking about it.* "I don't have to do anything. It could make driving the PV doubtful, though."

Andi shook her head. "Ed, you *are* a jerk." But her voice smiled.

"Yeah, Northrup," Grace echoed. To Andi, she said, "But what about you?"

"I suppose I'd have to take you to the station and show you my pictures of teenage corpses killed in drunk-driving accidents."

Grace's eyes widened. "That's all?"

Andi shot her a look. "Trust me, girl, that'll be *more* than enough."

Ed said, "So, *have* you been drinking?"

She looked forlorn. "I *need* the PV, Northrup. For the Meals-on-Wheels.

Please."

"New negotiation then. You can drive the car after you come clean about drinking."

Grace thought for a moment, then brightened. "Does that mean I don't have to work on my grammar?"

124

After they finished the dishes, Grace said, "Northrup, I need to go back into town."

"Why? It's late." Of course, he knew that, to sixteen-year-olds, *late* didn't start until the parents wake up and find them still not home.

"To tell my girls about Jared coming home. They'll be glad."

"You can't text?"

"Northrup!"

He chuckled. "Sure. Have a ball." As she grabbed her coat and opened the door, he called after her, "Drive carefully." A moment later, they heard the spray of gravel. He said to Andi, "Looks like I'll be re-graveling the yard."

She laughed. "Better pave it." She put two glasses on the counter. "Time to relax. I'll pour the wine. You light a fire."

He started to sing. " 'I'll light the fire, you place the flowers in the vase that you bought today.'"

She shook her head. "Sorry. Graham Nash sings better."

"Got that right." When they sat down, he said, "So tell me how Jared held up to the pressure."

Just then, his cell phone rang. He groaned. "Probably a client emergency." It was John Keeley.

"Ed, Doc here. Bad news, I'm afraid. The radiologist called. He said it looks like the boy has an astrocytoma."

"Shit."

Andi looked alarmed. *What?* she mouthed.

He said, "Jared. Brain tumor." To Doc, he said, "Where's it located?"

"It's right between the left amygdala and the hypothalamus."

"Oh, man, that's bad." He rubbed his eyes. "I suppose that could explain the paranoia and the fear, but could it account for his paranoia ebbing and flowing?"

Keeley said, "It could, actually. I asked the neurologist about that. The tumor lies against the amygdala, but hasn't infiltrated it yet. So any change in local conditions inside the cranium could make the tumor press on the amygdala and, which could trigger a panic reaction. I told him about your seeds theory. He doubts the seeds cause the panic, but they're hallucinogenic, so they might add delusional content to the panic. When local conditions change again, the pressure on the amygdala could stop and the panic and the delusions could fade."

Andi had stood up and come over near him. She watched his face.

Ed reached out for her and she moved in under his arm. He said, "So what's next?"

"That's not my call, but given the location and the effects of the tumor, I'm betting they'll want to try to remove it soon."

"That deep in the temporal lobe? Wouldn't it be inoperable?"

"Not necessarily. There are a couple crack neurosurgeons in Missoula; we'll set the boy up with them."

Ed pulled Andi closer to him. "John, you think he'll make it?"

For a moment, Doc was quiet. "That's the question, isn't it? Look, I gotta call the Hansens now. I don't relish that."

"Lousy part of the job, isn't it? I'll call them in a half hour or so, see how they're taking it."

He ended the call. Andi said, "Really bad news, huh?"

"About the worst." He felt his eyes warming. He wanted to cry, but something about that felt too self-absorbed.

Andi moved closer and put her arms around him.

His voice felt barely under control as he told her about the severity of the tumor. "John thinks they'll want to try to remove it soon."

"That sounds bad."

"Yeah. Huge risks in the inner brain." Out of nowhere, Ed felt a jolt of panic. He shook his head roughly.

Andi said, "You really care about Jared."

Maybe that's it. "Yeah, I do." He sighed. "I failed him."

"How'd you fail him? You came up with the idea for the MRI."

"No, Doc brought the tumor idea up. Merwin and I had talked about it, but the morning glory seeds thing sidetracked me. How the delusional thinking came and went threw me a curveball. Tumors usually don't present like that."

"You're being too hard on yourself."

"Maybe."

It hit him like a blow to his gut. Magnus had said he'd call, but two days—two days full of concerns, Jared's MRI, Grace's car—had passed without a call. Ed's heart pounded against his chest. "I need to call Mack," he said, and lifted his phone again. "And after that, I should call the Hansens. You mind waiting a few minutes?"

"Of course not." She went to the couch and sank onto the couch. "Long day all around."

The Anderssen phone rang, then rolled over to voice mail. Ed said, "Mack, Ed here. I'm thinking of you. Hope you're working your way through what we talked about. Give me a call, my friend."

He dialed the Hansens. Phil answered.

Ed said, "Hi, Phil. I spoke with Doc Keeley, and I assume he's called you?"

There was a moment's silence, then Phil said, "Yeah, he called."

"How are you folks doing?"

"Like somebody scooped out my heart." Ed heard a sob, stifled. "Look, Ed, I appreciate your call, but we need to be by ourselves tonight."

"Absolutely, Phil. I'll give a call tomorrow morning, if that's all right?"

"That'd be good, Ed. Appreciate it. We just need some time."

Ed stood for a moment at the kitchen island, looking out at the night. His face in the dark window looked tired, sad. After another moment studying the sorrow in his eyes, he walked out to the living room.

Andi said, "How're the Hansens?"

"Phil said it was like somebody had scooped out his heart."

She shook her head. "I can only guess how bad it is. How's Mack?"

"Didn't answer. I left a message. Hope he calls back tonight."

Andi sipped her wine. "So you're on duty, eh?"

He looked at her. "Not really, but I want to talk to him, make sure he's okay."

She laid her hand on his thigh. *High* on his thigh. He glanced at her. "You're in the mood?"

She rubbed his leg softly, circling slowly higher. He wondered if he was quite in the mood. On the other hand, maybe quiet sex would ease his heart. "Spending the night with Brad Ordrew got you hot, eh?" He grinned.

"No, silly. *Not* spending the night with you got me hot."

After they climbed into bed, Ed realized he'd forgotten to tell her about Loyd Crane being the second novice in Magnus's 1976 class. He told her about the abbot's call last Tuesday.

She sat up and glared at him. "*Loyd Crane?* The bastard that got me shot?"

"One and the same."

"Jesus, Ed, you sure know how to dry a girl's juices. This sucks."

"Thought you'd want to know."

She turned away, lay on her side; her breathing was fast. He rubbed her back a few minutes until she calmed. After a while, he slipped his fingers between her legs. "Uh, your juices aren't dry, by the way."

"That's just leftovers."

But they weren't.

125

Deep shadows layered the high, dark beams of the Great Room of the Anderhold. In the flickering firelight, Magnus sat alone, the lamps off, his right hand resting a tumbler of Scotch on his thigh. His left hand, hanging out of sight beside the left arm of the leather chair, clasped a pistol.

From the archway between the Great Room and the hall, Luisa studied him sadly, quietly. She saw his drink, not the gun, and felt a chill not caused by the night air. Was the drinking upon him again? Decisions swirled in the darkened room, demanding an accounting. One seemed to be Magnus's—the set of his jaw, the fingers around the tumbler, bespoke something coming to a head—but Luisa realized she faced her own decision: Mack's drinking could not continue, not with her in the house. She summoned her resolve and softly cleared her throat.

"Do you wish to be alone, *mi esposo?*" she asked, pitching her voice as intimately as she could remember.

He did not move; he'd felt her watching. After a moment, he said, "No. Please, sit with me."

She approached and sat in the soft leather chair on his right, unaware of the pistol. They watched the fire for many minutes, Magnus sipping occasionally. She ventured, "You are thinking on something important."

He licked a small bead of Scotch from his upper lip. "Yes." He stared into the fire. "Very important."

She let the silent moments pass. This was not her husband, who seldom pondered situations long before taking command of them. When a thing needed harder thought, he always talked with her. She steadied herself against her tension. After another span of time she could not gauge, she asked, "Do you wish to share your thoughts, *mi amor?*"

She felt him lean away from her, to his left, but could not see him resting the pistol on the carpet before standing to lay more wood on the fire; nor could she see, when he returned to his chair, that his left hand retrieved the pistol, that arm hanging beside the chair, out of her sight.

Finally, he spoke. "Ed Northrup says this is happening because I have something of my father working in me."

Looking at the fire, she lifted an eyebrow. "Daryl?"

"Daryl."

"What does he mean?"

Magnus lapsed into another long silence, and Luisa watched him in the firelight. He remained as handsome to her, in his age, as when they'd fallen in love twenty years ago. Until this madness had taken him, she'd seen nothing of his father in him, neither tone, nor glance, nor harshness, nor pain. What had Ed seen that she could not?

Then, abruptly, Magnus said, "To tell you what he means, I need to tell you the rest." As he said it, he lifted the pistol over the arm of his chair and rested it on his lap.

Luisa suppressed her gasp, looked at his shadowed eyes.

His index finger rested on the trigger guard. She mustered a calm she could barely feel, and said gently, "I would like to hear the rest."

The flickering light of the fire softened his features, but his mouth was grim. He did not look at her. "No, you won't."

Luisa unexpectedly recalled that warm afternoon long ago in Mexico. Holding her mother's dying body in her arms, she'd felt the last shuddering breath depart into a stillness that stretched out and out into eternity. In that moment, she'd realized the grief that would overwhelm her father when he returned from the barns and learned of his wife's passing. Her own bereavement transformed into a grim resolve to protect him. Flowing like grace from some high large space, an unexpected strength had poured into her, then. This same resolve filled her now: No matter what pain Magnus's story would bring, she knew she would hear it.

She whispered, "Perhaps I will not like the rest, Magnus, but I want to hear it."

The rancher nodded. Luisa looked at the weapon. Magnus sipped Scotch again. His knuckles whitened around the gun, but his finger lay unmoving alongside the trigger, not upon it. He began speaking.

In a soft voice, he told her the entire tale, and when he finished, his gaze fixed intently on the pistol.

She was electrified. She had expected any story but this. She must speak, must respond, but sorrow closed her throat.

After a long moment, he looked once at her, then nodded, and said, "I disgust you."

She found a word. "No!" She steeled herself. "I have told you before what my uncle Agosto did to me. I cannot know what you suffered with this monk, but the shame you feel, that I remember too well." Suddenly fierce, she reached over the space between them and grabbed his arm. "We did nothing wrong! *You* did nothing wrong."

His grip flinched on the gun. "So you say," he said. "So Ed says. But I don't feel it—what I feel is hate. I can't tell if I hate him or hate myself, but someone must be punished."

Luisa lifted her hand. "Ah. So *this* is the Daryl in you."

He looked sharply at her. The pistol jerked a little in his grip. "Say what you mean." His voice was ragged. Luisa recalled the drawn-out shudder of her mother's final breath.

She held her own breath to steady her voice. She watched her husband's hand. The pistol seemed alive, red firelight dancing on blue steel.

Magnus repeated himself. "Tell me what you mean about Daryl in me." The pistol moved again, upward, toward Magnus's face.

She whispered, "*Mi amor*, give me the gun."

He looked down at it again as if he were seeing it the first time. "I won't harm you," he said.

She forced herself to hold out her hand. "If you harm yourself, you harm me. The gun." She looked into his eyes. "Please."

They both seemed surprised when he grasped the barrel with his right hand and offered her the handle. She laid the gun in her lap and folded her hands over it, as in prayer. She said, "I knew your father only as a crippled, angry old man. Even in his wheelchair, he hated. He punished you—and me, the men, even little MJ—in any small and silly way he could. I watched you bear his cruelty with patience. Your father was a vengeful man. I do not know what wounds life had given him, perhaps it was his stroke, but he punished all of us for them. He would not forgive."

Magnus's jaw rippled. Through clenched teeth, he said, "And you see this in me?"

She hesitated, then straightened in the chair, clasping the pistol firmly. "If for an injury forty years ago you can kill..." She hesitated. "Then, yes. This would be from Daryl." Again, she held her breath, as she had held it that warm afternoon so long ago. And then, exhaled. "But this is not you, my husband. *Mi amor*. It is *not you*."

Magnus turned his face to the fire. "I see," he murmured. His voice seemed to come from a far place, like a faint echo out in the night. "Yes," he sighed, "I see."

SATURDAY, DAY THIRTEEN

126

Ed slept restlessly, waking often, fretting about the morning's interview with the state police. More than once, he told himself the interview didn't count for much compared with Magnus's or Jared's predicaments; it didn't measure against Art's dying. His rationalizing, though, brought little sleep. His worry made him feel selfish, even self-absorbed, but he couldn't banish his fantasy about Grace being left alone if he went to prison. Around five a.m., he gave a small groan and got up. During his run, alone in the dark, he chided himself. *You gave Jared good advice, so follow it—meditate!*

When he got home, he did just that. After twenty minutes of following his breath, he felt worse, even more anxious. If nothing else, his efforts had brought the clock around to six. He dressed casually, moving quietly to not wake Andi. In the mirror, he looked at the jeans he'd put on and decided on more professional dress. *Make a good impression on the interviewer.* He felt self-absorbed again. Andi stirred.

"Your interview isn't till 10. Why don't you come back to bed? We can drive in together when I go in."

"Too nervous. Thought I'd catch up on some paperwork beforehand."

"Suit yourself," she said, rolling over and pulling the covers up to her chin.

Dressed now in work clothes, he left a note for Grace telling her where he was and that he'd be back for lunch. Driving in to town, Ed replayed last Wednesday's phone conversation with Jerry Francis. He'd called Jerry and retained him, and outlined the issue and his own view of it. The lawyer hadn't seemed too concerned about the charge.

"Just tell the truth," he'd counseled. "You've got a good rationale: You didn't obstruct justice, you helped further the investigation into the truth of the case. Stick to that and we'll be fine. Remind me what time the interview is?"

"Ten o'clock Saturday morning."

"Good. I'm free. See you there."

Ed hadn't told Jerry about Ben's or Andi's involvement, and he didn't intend to.

After breakfast at Alice's Village Inn, he strolled along the river where it flowed through town, inspecting the repairs to the damage from the April flood. Still restless, and with time passing too slowly before the interview, he worked on paperwork for an hour, but he got little done. A few minutes before ten, Ed pushed open the heavy door to the sheriff's department; Ben was waiting in the reception area. "Right on the button. You—"

The door opened behind him. Jerry came in. After handshakes, Ben pointed to the waiting room chairs. "Set yourselves down for a minute. She's finishin' up with Ordrew."

"She?"

Ben nodded. "Sergeant Kendall from Helena. Smart gal. We talked before she started with Brad. Did her homework, asked some good questions."

Ed wanted to ask Ben if his own involvement had come up, but didn't want Jerry to know about that. "How'd you think it went?"

"Couldn't say. She's smooth as a mirror. No surprises, though."

"Well, I guess that's something."

Jerry said, "Relax, Ed. Like I said, worst case, you'll get a fine for withholding material information." He patted Ed's arm. "Besides, Ordrew entered your home without a warrant, so we can make noise with that."

"I thought he could do it with probable cause. What do you guys call it, 'exigent circumstances'?"

"The same, and he can. I said we'll make noise, not cause any damage."

Callie, behind the desk where she could see the interior offices, whispered, "Heads-up!" and pointed toward the inner door. A woman came through it, wearing the uniform of the Montana State Police. She looked at Ed and Jerry, and after a brief deliberation, addressed Ed. "Dr. Northrup?"

They did introductions, then she said, "Follow me, please, gentlemen," and led them back to the conference room.

"Before we start," she said, as she closed the door and seated herself across the table, "may I have your permission to record this interview?"

Ed said, "Certainly." Jerry nodded slightly. Ed said, "How'd you know I was, uh..." He hesitated, not sure how to refer to himself.

"My suspect?" She smiled as she said it.

"Huh. No, I didn't mean..."

"That's okay, Doctor. I didn't really know. Just guessed." She smiled again.

He relaxed. A little.

She turned on the recorder, and after the preliminaries, directed herself to Ed. "I want you to know that this interview is informational in nature. As you know, we're investigating the possibility that you obstructed the sheriff's investigation when you sheltered Mr. Jared Hansen from Sunday through Tuesday last week. No charges have been filed, and at this point, you are considered innocent until proven guilty. I've already spoken with Sheriff Stewart and interviewed Deputy Ordrew. You need to be aware that anything you say may be used against you in a court of law, if it comes to that." She smiled at Jerry, then looked at Ed. "I guess I don't need to remind you of your right to have your attorney present. Do you understand all that?"

Ed nodded. She smiled. "How about saying it aloud for the tape?"

He did.

"Okay, then. That's done. Let's start with the basics." She asked a series of questions about his background, training, credentials, about his relationship with Jared prior to the days in question. Finally, she looked up from her notes. "Please tell me how you found Mr. Hansen in the first place."

After Ed told her about the text messages and meeting at the river, Sergeant Kendall asked, "I'll circle back for details in a bit. Let's get the big picture first. What did you actually do with Mr. Hansen while he was in your custody?" She glanced at Jerry Francis, who'd sat forward, and added, quickly, "Ah. Perhaps *custody* is the wrong word, since you're not a police officer. Let's say, while he was *with* you."

Ed related almost everything he'd done with Jared—negotiating by the river, walking and talking near the cabin, taking him to the Anderhold, retrieving the pickup. He left out Andi's presence. Kendall listened steadily, jotting notes without glancing down.

"Let's go back. I believe you said he tried to jump into the river?"

"Yes. He dropped his rifle. He walked fast toward the river and started to throw himself in. I had to tackle him."

Her eyebrows lifted slightly. "Hmm. Did he struggle?"

"He did. I had to grab his belt, and even then, I almost lost him."

She wrote something. " 'Almost lost him'? What did you think he was trying to do?"

Ed hesitated. What *had* he thought Jared was going to do? Why did it matter what he thought?

"Doctor?"

"Sorry. I thought he was trying to drown himself."

She jotted another note. "Did you happen to confirm that at some point?"

He nodded. "Yes. We talked about it. He admitted he was suicidal." He stopped, then added, "At the river. Not later. He agreed not to attempt anything while he was with me."

She looked intently at him. "And you believed him?"

"I did. Trusting a person's word not to act on suicidal thoughts is quite common in psychotherapy situations."

"I see. So you considered this a psychotherapy situation?"

"Potentially, anyway, if it turned out his condition was due to something psychotherapy could address."

She nodded. "Okay. Now, later. You said you took Mr. Hansen with you out to, where was it? A ranch?"

"Yeah. The Anderhold is the main house on the Double-A ranch. I had to meet with the ranch owner, Magnus Anderssen, on a personal matter."

"Can you tell me the nature of your business with Mr. Anderssen?"

Ed hesitated, tense again. Was this where things turn bad? "No, I'm sorry, I can't."

Jerry Francis intervened. "Dr. Northrup has a fiduciary responsibility not to discuss some details of his professional activities."

"May I infer, then, that Mr. Anderssen is a client of yours, Doctor?"

Ed swallowed. "I don't mean to be unhelpful, Sergeant, but..."

Jerry said, "I think you can infer whatever seems reasonable to you, Sergeant. But my client isn't really at liberty..."

She put up her hand. "I understand. Enough said." She jotted something in her notes.

Ed thought, *Not attacking. Well-prepared.* He relaxed a bit. Just a bit.

"Doctor, was Mr. Hansen in your presence the entire time you were with him?" She chuckled gently. "That's redundant, isn't it? Let me rephrase it."

Ed smiled. "That's okay, I understand what you're asking."

"For the tape. Were you ever out of Mr. Hansen's presence during the period in question?"

"Yes, I was, for about two hours, maybe two and a half, an hour or so at the Anderhold, and the other hour while I visited a patient in the hospital."

"During that time, did you leave him alone?"

Ed felt his chest tighten. *Here it is.* "May I ask my attorney a question?"

"Certainly," she said, pressing the *Stop* button. "I'll just step outside."

When the door closed, Ed said, "So far, nobody knows Andi knew I had Jared. I should say, Ordrew hasn't named her, although he probably suspects. Do you think I should mention her?"

"Andi was involved?"

He nodded. "She was there at the cabin when I brought him home."

Jerry frowned. "Never a good idea to hide the truth. Tell her." He stood up, still frowning. Looking down at Ed, he said, "Anything else you haven't told me, Ed?"

Ed looked up at him, avoided answering. "I didn't want Andi to get in trouble."

"Not your call, man. Look, if you lie, it comes back and bites your ass. Always. Ordrew probably knows, remember?"

Ed nodded. "Got it." Despite his tension, he tried to smile. "The truth and nothing but the truth."

"So help you God." Jerry clapped him on the shoulder, strode to the door, opened it, and said, "We're ready, Sergeant."

She came in and pressed the *Record* button. Toward the machine, she said, "Continuing the interview with Dr. Edward Northrup. So Doctor, during the approximately two or two-and-a-half hours you were gone, did you leave Mr. Hansen alone?"

"No. In the first instance, while I was meeting with Mr. Anderssen, Jared was with my daughter, Mr. Anderssen's son, and Mr. Anderssen's wife. To my knowledge, he was never alone." He watched Kendall jot the names on her pad. "As for the second time, when I went in to the hospital, for the first fifteen minutes after I left, he was watched by Deputy Andrea Pelton." Kendall looked up sharply. Ed realized that Ordrew hadn't exposed Andi. *Why not?* He forged on. "But she was called away to accompany Deputy Ordrew on an interview with Jared's parents, so Jared was at home with my daughter, Grace, for about thirty minutes before I came back."

Sergeant Kendall frowned. "I wasn't aware that other department personnel were involved." She jotted another note. Ed thought, *Andi's in this*

304

now. Damn.

Kendall asked, "Do you know why Deputy Pelton accompanied Deputy Ordrew to the interview?"

Ed's tension tightened. "I do," he said, reluctantly.

"How do you know?"

"She told me."

"And what did she tell you?"

Ed looked at Jerry, who nodded his go-ahead. Ed said, "She said that he was threatening to interrogate the Hansens very aggressively, because he assumed they were concealing the boy. She decided she had to be there to, I guess, keep the interview on track."

"On track?"

This time, Ed's glance at Jerry was nervous. His lawyer nodded, *Go ahead.* Ed said, "As I understood it, she thought Deputy Ordrew's..." He paused, searching for the right word. "His preconceptions might cause him to mistreat the parents."

"So, am I correct that Deputy Pelton knew the whereabouts of Jared Hansen during the whole period he was with you?"

"Yes, she did." He took a breath. "I think she assessed the situation and determined Jared was safe. Besides, he was sleeping. I think she chose the lesser of two evils."

Sergeant Kendall looked at him, her eyes narrowing. " 'Two evils,' Doctor? What were the two evils?"

He glanced at Jerry, who again nodded. "Well, I think at this point, she had determined that Jared wasn't going to run—if he ran, that'd be one evil. The other was that Deputy Ordrew was angry and wanted to confront the parents. She saw that as the worse scenario, I think."

"Because?"

"As I said, she knew Deputy Ordrew's preconceptions. He assumed they were hiding the boy, despite the absence of any evidence to that effect, and he intended to wring the information out of them."

Kendall looked at him for a moment. Finally, she nodded. "I understand." She glanced at Jerry, then added, "I believe I'm familiar with Deputy Ordrew's preconceptions." She cleared her throat. "Did Deputy Pelton at any time try to interfere with your plan? For example, did she try to arrest Jared?"

Ed felt his gut tighten again. Would this drag Ben in? "Yes, as a matter of fact, she did. We had a serious argument about it. She reluctantly agreed to let him stay with me for two days."

"Why do you think she agreed? It could be seen as a violation of her duty."

He nodded. "That's exactly how she saw it."

"So then why did she agree?"

Ed squirmed. How could he tell the truth without exposing Ben?

"Doctor?"

"I told her that if Jared went back to the jail at that point, he'd never cooperate, and we wouldn't find out what was causing his paranoia and suicidal thoughts. I was seriously afraid he would kill himself in jail."

"And she accepted that as your professional opinion?"

"Eventually, yes." It wasn't a lie. It just wasn't the whole truth. He squirmed. Jerry had been very plain: the truth. He added, "But she changed her mind and we ended up compromising. I agreed to let Sheriff Stewart make the call. He and I argued, but in the end, he gave me 48 hours."

Sergeant Kendall sat back in her chair. "The sheriff knew about this and approved it?"

Ed nodded.

She glanced at the machine. "Say your answer, please, for the tape."

Ed did. Now, he thought, *the ax falls.*

She jotted some notes, then looked up. "Very well. I believe you've also just told me something else I wanted to ask, namely, what your motive was for sheltering the young man. Do I understand correctly, you felt you could use the time to help him, and that a return to jail would shut down that chance?"

"Yes, ma'am," Ed said. He breathed a bit easier.

"And Sheriff Stewart decided that this was a strong enough reason to let you go forward?"

Jerry Francis laid his hand on Ed's wrist. "Don't speculate about Ben's mind, Ed."

Kendall nodded. "That's right, Doctor. I shouldn't have asked that." She hesitated. "Did Sheriff Stewart give you any indication of why he allowed you to continue with your plan?"

"Yes, he did. He implied that I'd persuaded him that I could help the investigation by spending the time with Jared, diagnosing him."

She waited a moment. "'Implied'? Can you be more specific?"

"Well, I presented just that argument, and Sheriff Stewart said he'd call me back with his decision. When he called, he said, 'You got forty-eight hours.' I took that to mean he accepted my argument."

She jotted a note. "Very well. Let's move on. How did Deputy Ordrew find out you had Jared?"

"It's my understanding that he went to my cabin at some point, and took a picture of Jared's truck beside mine. He also entered the cabin, without my permission."

"How do you know that?"

Ed squirmed. *This can't be good for Andi.* He swallowed. "Well, Deputy Pelton told me Ordrew had confronted her and showed her the picture, and that he'd taken a toothbrush from the bathroom."

Kendall took a page from her file and handed it to Ed. "Is this a copy of the picture?"

It showed Jared's truck with the cabin in the background. Ed said, "Well, I never saw the original picture, but this looks like the one Andi described. She said—"

Jerry touched his arm. "Let Sergeant Kendall ask what she needs to know."

Kendall smiled and nodded to Jerry. "Always wise when you're talking to a cop." She paused. "Or a lawyer." Jerry grinned in return.

She asked, "Do you know exactly when Deputy Ordrew was at your cabin?"

"I think it was Tuesday morning, but I don't know for certain. But Tuesday morning was probably the only time no one would have seen him there."

"What makes you say that?"

Ed thought about the grove in the woods. "There was a period of about an hour when Jared and I were walking in the woods. He was nervous about returning to jail that evening, so I was helping him prepare. My daughter was at school, so the cabin would have been empty. After that, Jared and I went back out to Mr. Anderssen's ranch house for a couple of hours. Other than that stretch, there wasn't any period when he would've been undetected." Something struck him. "May I look at that photo again?"

Sergeant Kendall handed it to him.

"Sergeant, there's a date and time stamp. It shows the photo was taken Tuesday morning." He handed it back.

"Yes, I knew that. I wanted to get at why you and Mr. Hansen weren't at the cabin, but you already answered that." She consulted her notes again. "Let's go back to your time with Mr. Hansen. You're claiming that despite being left alone, or with your daughter, nothing happened to derail the case?"

"Yes, that's my view of it. I learned what I needed and he kept his part of our bargain."

"Your bargain?"

"I'd protect him for two days and he'd cooperate with me. At the end of the time, he'd go back into custody."

"I see. And you completed your evaluation?"

Ed wondered at the change of subject. "I made real progress. I was able to rule out a number of possible problems, and I continued to consult with our local internist and my Minneapolis consultant after Jared came back into custody."

"Who are your consultants?"

He gave her Merwin's and Doc Keeley's names and phone numbers, then added, "We came up with the possibility of a brain tumor when we'd pretty much ruled out everything else. That was after Jared returned to the jail." He looked at Jerry, who shrugged.

"And they discovered a, uh..." She consulted her notes. "A brain tumor."

"Yes, unfortunately."

"And you believe that explains his paranoia, his weaponing up, his threats?"

"I believe it's possible, even likely, but we won't be sure until the cancer's removed. If it can be."

"Why did you decide to keep Jared at your home, rather than returning him to custody?"

Ed tensed. They'd already covered that. Why was she asking again? "I was very concerned about him. For one thing, I wanted to ensure he didn't kill himself. On top of that, I was afraid he would refuse to talk to me, and shut down any chance of diagnosing what was going on."

"Tell me why you thought that."

"His psychotic thinking involved the false belief that we were trying to kill him, and that it could happen in jail. That degree of stress could easily trigger an episode, or at least I was worried about it. If he became psychotic again, he'd be of little use to the evaluation, and there was intense pressure to charge him. I felt the chance of learning what was disturbing him was more important."

"You said there was 'intense pressure to charge him.' What did you mean?"

"From Deputy Ordrew. He believes Jared is a terrorist, and he was pushing hard to charge him that way. I felt we had to learn more before he went back to jail. And as you probably know, when he returned to custody, he did relapse."

"You took a risk in second-guessing police procedure, Doctor. The rules are there for a reason."

"Andi made that abundantly clear to me."

"She did? When?"

"During our argument, which lasted all of Sunday night."

"So if Deputy Pelton was that forceful about procedures, and Sheriff Stewart argued with you as well, tell me again why you took the risk." She raised a hand as Ed started to speak. "I'm sorry, I didn't phrase that well. I understand your belief that Jared would relapse if he returned to custody and your professional interest in evaluating Jared's condition. What I want to know is why you were willing to take such a serious risk with a young man who, for all we know, could have been a potential terrorist or murderer."

Ed sat back, wondering how else to answer. He wanted to ask Jerry what to say, but decided against it. *Just tell the truth.* He took a long breath. "I'm a psychologist, Sergeant. Jared was a young man in terrible trouble, both mentally and legally. There didn't seem to me to be any other path but to spend time with him in a safe environment—I believed my home was safe—and to try to help him. It may have been an error in judgment, but..." He thought about that. "No, it *was* an error. But I also accomplished the bigger thing, ruling out what wasn't wrong with the boy and opening the door to finding out what was. I guess I took the risk because..." He had to pause a moment; his emotion surprised him, forced him to clear his throat. "I cared about him."

"Well, Doctor, you're the psychologist here." She smiled. "I think I have all I need to wrap this up." She paused, then shut off the recorder. "After I interview Deputy Pelton, I'll have my report to the county attorney within three business days. Thank you, Doctor." She nodded to Jerry. "Mr. Francis." After shaking both men's hands, she left. Ed saw her step into Ben's office. He turned to Jerry. "How'd I do?"

Jerry patted his shoulder. "You did fine. I don't think anything you said is going to hurt you."

They filed down the hall and out into the reception area. Ed and Jerry stood talking for a moment; as Jerry turned to leave, Andi stuck her head into reception, glaring. "My turn," she said. "Thanks for throwing me under the bus."

127

In his office an hour later, Ed took a call from Ben. "She's done with your girlfriend. How about poppin' over for a post-mortem?"

"Sure. Be there in a minute." He locked the office, and hoped Grace was still having her weekend beauty sleep.

He met Ben and Andi in the conference room. Ben hit a button on the speakerphone and leaned over the machine. "Hey, Callie, can you get some bottled waters for us?" But it hadn't worked. "Jesus in a sidecar," he muttered. "Andi, show me the damn button again."

She did. Callie picked up. "Darlin', can you bring us in some water?"

"Can Donald Trump do brain surgery? I'm Reception and Dispatch, not a waitress."

Ben chuckled and hit the *End* button. "Just wait," he said to Ed.

While they waited, Ed asked Andi how her interview went.

"Not too bad, I think." She didn't seem angry now. "She seemed a little perturbed that I knew Jared was with you and didn't report it, but when I explained about him being your patient and all, and about your thinking if he was locked up he'd relapse, she seemed to accept it. I said in my judgment it had been the lesser of two evils."

"Nice. I used the same words. She probably thinks we cooked up our stories together." He looked at Ben. "I had to tell her you approved it." He expected anger.

All he got was Ben's shrug. "In a minute."

They heard what sounded like a kick on Ben's door. When Ed opened it, Callie pushed three waters at him. "Just this once," she warned, looking in at Ben.

Ben called from his desk, "Many thanks, sweetness."

"I'm the only darn sweetness around here, Ben." Ed caught the start of her smile, though, as he shut the door. Ben guffawed.

Sitting back down and placing the three bottles on Ben's desk, Ed said,

"In the big city, you'd be up on harassment charges."

"Hell, in the big city, I'd have a damn refrigerator in my office." He laughed again, opening his water. "So, business. First off, I ain't real happy about gettin' outed."

"I'm sorry, Ben. Jerry insisted I tell the truth." He turned to Andi. "Same with you."

She nodded. "I suppose. We'll see what the damage is."

Ben swallowed his water and said, "Best guess, Kendall writes a no-harm, no-foul report, and Irv tosses the whole thing." He frowned. "I'm a tad nervous about what the guys will think when word gets out I knew where the kid was but didn't call off the hunt. Probably shoulda told everybody I approved your stunt." Then his face relaxed, and to Andi, he said, "Me bein' outed means I don't have to do what I woulda had to."

Andi nodded. "I'm good with that." She looked at Ed. "This was the bus I thought you threw me under."

"Whoa. What bus?"

Ben said, "As long as it looked like Andi was breakin' the rules on her own say-so, I'd've had to suspend her for a week, no pay. Otherwise, too much shit'd hit my fan."

Ed frowned. "Wow. I'm glad I ratted you out, then."

Ben took another swig of water, nodding. "You should be. I was goin' to tell her to make you pay her wages for the week."

128

Back in his office, Ed decided to write a few notes summarizing the interview with Sergeant Kendall. Fifteen minutes later, as he was putting on his jacket to head back home for lunch with Grace, his cell phone buzzed in his pocket. The screen read "Magnus Anderssen." Feeling a surge of relief, he wondered which Magnus would this be—the one who could no longer wait for vengeance, or the other who would give Ed time?

He answered. "Ed here, Mack." Outside the window, a spate of small gray clouds like bullets slid down the sky.

"It is Luisa." Her voice was tight, controlled. "Magnus has gone again. I believe he went to kill the monk."

"Shit," he barked, then apologized. "Do you know—?"

"—what the monk did? *Sí*. Magnus told me. He has taken his great-

great-grandfather's rifle. I am going up to the monastery."

"Wait, Luisa. I'll call the abbot and warn him. I'm right at the sheriff's department. I'll pick you up. Ben will probably come with me. Wait for us down at your head-gate in, say, 45 minutes."

"No," Luisa said, firmly. "I can be at the monastery by then."

"And do what? They don't let women inside the monastery itself, only the church, and Mack won't be in the church. I'll call the abbot and he'll keep things under control. Just wait for us."

Her voice was frosty. *"Ahora voy." I'm going now.* She hung up.

He called the abbot, but the monastery message machine answered. He swore under his breath, left a message about the threat, then ran over to the sheriff's office. Andi and Callie were talking in Reception. Ed said to Andi, "Got an emergency. Ben in?"

Both women shook their heads. Andi said, "What's up?"

Ed shook his head, then mouthed, *Magnus.* "Callie, where's Ben?"

"Left right after your meeting. He's on a domestic up at Bern Slattery's nephew's place. Why?"

"I've got an emergency, and I need his help. Can you reach him?"

"Can Mickey Mantle hit homers? I'm Dispatch, ain't I?" She started punching numbers.

She handed him the phone. Ed, keeping his voice low so Callie wouldn't need to hear it was Magnus, told Ben what was up.

Ben said, "Crap on toast. I got this Slattery domestic to handle. I'll get 'er wrapped up and head up ASAP. No, hold on, Andi's in the station. I'll send her up. Give Callie the phone."

"I'm going now, Ben. Luisa's already on her way."

Ben growled. "The hell you are. You said Mack's armed. You two leave it to...Give the damn phone to Callie!"

Ed handed it to her. "He wants you." He turned to go out to his truck.

"Wait!" Callie yelled. "Andi, Ben says you go up."

Andi said, "On it. I'll get my gear."

Ed said, "Meet me at my truck."

But when Andi dashed out onto the parking lot, she pointed to the squad car parked near the door. "Much faster," she called, climbing into the driver's seat and flipping on the light bar.

129

Soft snow filtered from the frozen sky above the monastery, and the distant sound of Gregorian chant drifted through the stained glass windows when Magnus climbed out of his truck parked beneath the monastery walls, at the shore of Lake St. Mary. The monks would be at mid-morning prayer. A grim smile played on his lips. *Good planning.* How had he remembered their schedule after forty years? Slinging *Kött Hitta* over his back, he eased the truck door shut without a sound. Staying close against the monastery wall, he trudged through drifted snow—spring had yet to arrive this high on the mountain. He moved around to the small back door on the forest side of the cloister, used by monks coming in from the barns or workshops. It was where he remembered it, unlocked as always. He stepped quietly inside, listening for footsteps in the stairwell, hearing only the deep silence. He slowly opened the door to the first corridor and looked up and down. No one. *They're all in the church.* He softly closed the door and climbed the stairs to the third floor infirmary. Here, on the side of the monastery farthest from the church, echoes of the chanting came faint and soft, like conversations on a distant porch in the night. He moved quickly, silently, looking into each of the rooms, until he came to the last one in the hall, the room where monks were brought to die. The room's name was embossed beside the door: *Golgotha.* A white card with the name *Jerome* was slipped into a frame, centered in the upper panel of the oaken door.

Inside, Father Jerome's skeletal body lay under gray linen, devoured from within. The white name card was fortunate, because he barely recognized the man in the bed. *Cancer,* Magnus saw. The monk's closed eyelids and gaunt uplifted nose made a death mask. Magnus carefully closed the door. Driving up the mountain, he'd worried that when he saw his once-beloved mentor, his emotion would weaken him. But, no. Here, in the room, he felt only an implacable resolve.

He knew this room. He'd kept the death vigil with an old monk in the spring of his first year. The monastic Rule assigned this task to the youngest monk in the House: *To give the monks a close acquaintance with the reality of death,* the Rule said. Magnus glared at the bed. *Well, you're facing the reality now, old man.* The narrow room was unchanged, arranged exactly as it had been when he'd kept the vigil so long ago. The single chair; the small table holding a pitcher of water, pill bottles, and the same tattered prayer book; the empty cross on the wall at the foot of the narrow cot where fading eyes could find it and take what comfort they could. With the unsentimental plainness of monks, they'd arranged the room so every monk died in the same surroundings, and named the room after the naked hill where Jesus was executed. Jerome indeed lay at the door of death. No doubt, the youngest monk would come to start the vigil, perhaps this morning, when prayers were done. Magnus glared down at Father Jerome. "It'll be soon now, Jerome."

The shallow breaths continued, the only sign of life.

Magnus glanced at his watch. The service would be ending any time now, and there would come the slap of sandals on the polished corridor floor. *Time to go.*

130

High up Mount Adams, beneath the towering Coliseum, Ed and Andi spotted Magnus's pickup truck parked against the gray monastery wall. Luisa's Outback angled recklessly behind it—or perhaps with forethought, to hem Magnus's truck in. Andi swerved the squad car in beside Magnus's truck, blocking it against the wall. They ran into the church. Luisa, visibly angry, had cornered the abbot by the altar.

Timothy was saying, "...could not leave the service, Mrs. Anderssen."

"Your priest may be in danger and you force me to wait!"

"I had no idea—" He jerked around at the sound of Ed running up the aisle, a step ahead of Andi. "What...?"

"No time! Magnus Anderssen is armed. He intends to kill Father Jerome. Take us to him!"

"Armed? My God, Ed. We should call the sheriff."

Andi stepped forward, "I'm Deputy Pelton, sir, and Sheriff Stewart's on his way. We need to move! Please show us where Father Jerome is."

Luisa had already run toward the cloister door. She called back over her shoulder, "Magnus will not harm me. I will go." But one of the monks stood in the cloister door, barring her way.

Puffing, Abbot Timothy caught up. "I'm sorry, Mrs. Anderssen, but our Rule forbids women in the monastery."

Luisa stopped. "In your monastery, your Rule prefers a murder to a woman?"

The abbot blanched. "Let's go," he said, pointing to the cloister door.

The other monk stood aside, frowning at Luisa and Andi.

They took the stairs, Andi leading the way, checking each landing. At the door to the infirmary wing, the abbot pointed to the far end. "The last door's where Jerome is."

Andi said, "Stay here." When she pulled her weapon out, Luisa gasped. "No, no shooting."

Andi was already moving fast down the hallway, gun up. When she reached *Golgotha*, the door stood ajar. She peered in, then holstered and beckoned the others. They hurried down the hall. Inside the bed was rumpled and empty, its blanket gone.

Andi said, "We need to search the monastery."

Ed shook his head. "They're not in the monastery. He took Father Jerome up on the Coliseum."

They all looked up through the big window at the end of the corridor. The massive amphitheater of granite, the Coliseum, loomed 1300 feet above them.

"How do you know?" Andi said.

Not the time for confidentiality. "He told me."

131

Andi led the way up the trail, Luisa, Ed, and a young monk sent by the abbot following. Timothy had remained behind to meet Ben Stewart and send him up after them. Magnus's big boots were easy to track up the snow-packed trail, but they had no snowshoes, and the going was slow. After a quarter mile, Luisa touched Andi's shoulder and stepped around her on the trail; Andi grabbed her arm, whispered, "Stay behind me, Luisa."

Luisa said, "He will not harm me," and pulled her arm free and went past. Andi started after her, trying to stop her, but Ed whispered urgently. "Wait, Andi. Mack won't shoot her. You, I don't know." He could not conceive Magnus shooting anyone, but...

Andi nodded. She closed the gap with Luisa, but stayed close behind.

The trail struggled up a first set of switchbacks, then a second, then leveled and entered a cedar grove. Everyone was breathing hard, puffing white vapor into the cold air.

Under the ancient trees, a blue-shadowed depression in the snow lay beside the trail, surrounded by a trampling of boot marks. "He must've laid

Father Jerome down for a moment. Maybe needed a rest," Ed said to the young monk; they were both breathing hard.

Andi and Luisa hadn't stopped, following the boot prints into the trees on the higher side of the meadow. Ed and the young monk caught up. The trail climbed steadily through the last pines below the tree line, emerging into a high meadow, a long, blue blanket of snow extending to the edge of the Coliseum's cliff.

Magnus knelt on the snow, three feet from the lip of the precipice, cradling the old priest in his arms, rocking slowly back and forth. Luisa called to him and ran. The others followed.

Magnus, his face streaked with tears, never looked up. The priest was dead.

132

With the others, Ed waited in the monastery library, a long room paneled in age-darkened pine, lined floor-to-ceiling with long shelves of old books interrupted occasionally by portraits of saints and faded photographs. Three rows of stacks ran two-thirds the length of the hall. The remaining space was filled with study tables on which rested low, green-shaded lamps. A conversation area, two couches, overstuffed chairs, clustered in a corner. Tall, narrow windows let in northern light, but hardly enough. Late afternoon clouds dampened the sky and darkened the room. Lamps were lit along the walls, yellowing the air. Everyone sat quietly in the conversation area, avoiding each other's eyes. Brother Anselm—the young monk who'd accompanied them up the mountain—had brought coffee.

Magnus had carried the body down the mountain himself, and when they reached the monastery, Abbot Timothy and two monks had taken Father Jerome to prepare the body for monastic burial. Now Magnus, his eyes distant, waited on a long couch under a window, Luisa beside him. He had refused Brother Anselm's coffee with the barest wave of his hand. Ed wondered if he even noticed the others—himself, Luisa, Andi, Ben Stewart—sitting around him. No one spoke.

Anselm stood at the door. "Can I get anyone anything?"

"How long will Abbot Timothy be?" Ed asked softly.

"I'll go check," Anselm said.

A few minutes later, Timothy came into the library, followed by Brother

Anselm. "The brothers will finish up," he said. He looked at the tableau, silent friends, a pall of pain in the room. He sat in the chair next to Ben's, looking steadily at Magnus, who seemed not to notice.

The sheriff shifted in his chair, then sighed. Everyone looked up. "Mack, we need to talk about what happened up there." He turned to the Abbot. "Father, you have a private room where me and Mack can talk?"

Magnus stirred, shook his head. "We'll talk here, Ben."

The sheriff glanced sharply at him. "In that case, I gotta clear the room." He looked around at everyone. "Mind steppin' outside, everybody? Hate to say it, but I gotta consider this a possible, ah, murder investigation..." His voice caught. He'd been Magnus's friend all their lives. "And you folks ain't allowed to be here for that."

"I will stay, Ben," said Luisa.

Ed said, "Me, too. I'll stay."

Abbot Timothy said, "I'm going to stay too, Ben."

"Damn it, people." Ben frowned. "You stay and this thing comes to court, you'll be witnesses for the prosecution. This here's the initial interrogation in a possible murder case, for Christ's sake." He stopped. "Sorry, Abbot."

Timothy waved it off. "Father Jerome was my son in the Order. I want to know what happened to him."

Ben nodded. "Yeah, I get that. But you'll find out in due time. Don't put yourself in jeopardy."

The abbot stood to leave, then rubbed the pink dome of his skull. He turned to Magnus. "Magnus? You were a Catholic and a novice of St. Brendan's. Do you wish to confess?"

Magnus leaned back on the couch, running a hand through his hair. "What I have to say, call it confession. It is, of a sort." Luisa, alarmed, lay her hand on his thigh. But Magnus's face was serene, no longer distant and obscure. Ed studied his friend's eyes. Had he found his vengeance—or his justice—after all?

The abbot turned to Ben. "I am bound by the seal of confession now. I cannot testify."

Ben rubbed his hand roughly through his hair. "Crap on toast." He pointed at Ed. "You. Scram."

Ed shook his head. "Magnus is my patient, Ben. Whatever he says to me about this is part of his therapy, so I won't testify. You and Andi do your job.

I'm doing mine."

Ed caught the swift smile on Andi's face, quickly wiped away.

Ben scowled. "Luisa, I hate to be a hard-ass, but you gotta go."

Luisa shook her head. "They cannot force a wife to testify against her husband."

Ben shook his head, then waved his hand, fed up with the fine points. "Jesus. That ain't exactly the point." He shook his head again. To Brother Anselm, he said, roughly, "You got a freakin' reason to hang around?"

"No, sir."

"Then on your way, son." When the library door clicked shut, Ben turned to Magnus. "Okay, Mack, tell us your story."

133

Magnus gathered himself, as if he were about to lift a great burden. "Jerome weighed nothing. On the trail, he was so still in my arms, I thought he was already dead, but his breath made the smallest puffs of vapor. When we came to that clearing in the cedars above the switchbacks, I laid him down. Jerome opened his eyes and looked bewildered, but all he did was move his lips, then fell asleep again. I wanted to tell him I was leaving him to die, and had he stayed awake, I might have. But when he fell asleep, I decided to carry him to the summit."

Ben frowned. "So you were climbing the Coliseum to kill him?"

"To leave him. But yes, I believed that would kill him." Magnus closed his eyes.

Ben waited a moment, then prompted him. "Mack?"

The big man opened his eyes and went on.

On the summit, lying in snow near the cliff, the priest's eyes, full of confusion, search the rancher's broad red face. After a moment, he relaxes and smiles and his eyes clear. His voice sounds dry as sand blown against a window. "Magnus. My son."

"I'm no man's son! I'm your whore."

The old eyes widen, then soften. "There were many whores, my son. So many." He sighs, looking across the meadow at the trees, the gray sky, then toward the edge of the Coliseum a few feet away. For a moment he stares out into the void, then looks at Magnus. "But not you, Magnus. You were my beloved."

Magnus, stiffens. "Beloved? You took me against my will." He swings Kött Hitta off his back and presses the barrel hard against the old man's privates. "I should destroy them!"

The shock of the rifle startles the priest fully awake, but dry lips crack in a tight smile. "My boy, those have been dead for years. The cancer started in the prostate, you know. But it was a blessing—release from the body's urges."

Magnus roars, "Your urges destroyed me!" His roar echoes down the Coliseum, so close are they to the edge. Magnus could roll the old man off with a toe.

"I destroyed you?" The old voice sounds confused. "How did I do that?"

Magnus becomes agitated, fingering Kött Hitta's trigger shield. "Don't play with me, Jerome. You're dying of cancer, not senility."

The priest waves feebly, then his hand drifts feebly onto the snow. "My time is short; I don't play. Tell me, please. How did I destroy you?" He lapses a moment, then opens his eyes. "You know, I have watched you from the monastery. I watched you caring for your father. When you married Luisa, my heart broke, but I tried to be happy for you when your fine son came."

Enraged at his mentioning Junior, Magnus lifts Kött Hitta to club him, but the monk's eyes gaze into his. "You had success, Magnus," he says. "You won honor, you gave much to the valley people. You are a good man, Magnus, and I watched you and waited and longed for you to come back to me. But you never came." The rheumy eyes fill. "How did I destroy you?"

Magnus thrusts the rifle barrel hard into Jerome's ribs. He pitched his voice low, controlling his anger. "You raped me."

The old head jerks up toward Magnus looming over him. "Raped? Never! My son, I loved you."

"Loved? No, you never loved me, Jerome. You raped me." He presses the barrel harder into the old man's body.

The monk's fragile hand flutters, searches, finds the cold steel barrel where it thrusts into him. The hand taps it feebly. "It hurts, my son."

Inexplicably, Magnus pulls the rifle back.

The priest's eyes dart back and forth, probing Magnus's. "You felt raped?"

"Not felt raped, damn you. Raped. I never wanted sex. I wanted your love."

The gaunt face grimaces, bewildered. "But you had my love, boy. For the whole year before, I loved you, your energy, your will, your skillfulness. You listened to me, you tried anything I suggested, you appreciated everything. You breathed in my teaching like air, my words were food to you. I loved you with all my heart."

Magnus's mind empties, befogged by the truth of the monk's words. It had been

319

a magical year of wooded walks and evening conversations that opened new worlds. For all that year, when Jerome entered the room, Magnus's heart had soared.

And then his pain rips into him again, the stabbing anal agony, and Magnus's rage snaps into focus. "But it was painful, priest! I never agreed to it. I never wanted that!"

"But..." The monk's body sags back into the snow, his filmy red eyes filling.

Magnus, enraged by his pain, cannot fathom the old man's tears. "Why? Why are you weeping?"

"Magnus, why did you have pain? I gave you the drug to relax you. The first times often hurt until one learns, but the drug spared you that."

Magnus remembers the drug-numbed fog, remembers how he forgot for so many years. "The drugs numbed me then. The pain is now."

Jerome nods. "So, it's this pain now you are calling rape?"

Magnus, enraged again, needs to breathe deeply to calm himself before he can speak. He remembers Ed's calming words, uses them. "Damn you, no. It was rape then."

"But you wanted me."

"Never. Not like that."

And the mountain air is pierced by a wail rising up from the monk's whole body, the keening of one who learns, here at its end, that his life's suffering has been a mistake, and when this howl falls to a long moan, and then dies away on the cold air, the monk whispers, "But Loyd Crane told me!"

Stunned, Magnus forces out, "Loyd Crane told you what?"

Jerome, emptied, can barely whisper. "He came to me. He told me you wanted to...wanted to...something." The whisper fades like evening light. Jerome is moving beyond memory.

134

Magnus had paled and his eyes had closed as he described Jerome's wail, and now he opened them and looked over their heads at the shelves of books. He had not lost the eerie calm they'd found in him on the mountain, but he shook his head sadly. "This next will be more difficult."

Ed said, "Need a break?"

Magnus looked at Ed gratefully, but shook his head. "No. Let me talk through." He fell silent again, then began again. "It was early September, just after we'd been accepted as novices. Loyd and I were in the library." He looked up, startled, then peered momentarily around the room. "This room." He pointed at one of the study tables. "There. We were looking at a book about Heloise and Abelard."

Ben interrupted. "Who are who, exactly?"

Abbot Timothy said, "A medieval monk and nun who fell in love and ended tragically."

Ben's eyebrow lifted.

Magnus nodded. "Crane said to me, *monastic love is sweetest. Not crass and lustful, like in the world.* I agreed, but I reminded him there weren't any women here. Crane laughed at me. *I'm talking about the love between you and Jerome,* he said, and I was shocked that he knew. He said it was *virilis.*"

An audible gasp came from Abbot Timothy. Magnus glanced at him, and Timothy apologized. "Pardon me. It has a double meaning. *Virilis* means *manly,* but also can mean *homosexual.* I'm sorry." He motioned Magnus on.

A cloud passed across Magnus's face. "I didn't know that.' He took a moment to compose himself. "I told Crane, 'Yes, I do love him. He's a father to me.' And Loyd patted my arm and said, 'And you'd do anything to please him, wouldn't you?' And as embarrassed as I felt, I told him, 'I'd give my life to serve him.' And I meant it."

Andi asked, "What did the priest say Crane told him?"

Magnus again pulled his fingers through his hair, then rubbed one eye hard. To Ed, he no longer looked calm. His breath was ragged. His eyes were pools of sorrow.

Jerome's body is nearly still but for ragged, sporadic breaths. Magnus leans down and touches the chest; the closeness of bone shocks him. He cannot find a pulse.

"Jerome," he says softly. The dim eyes open, still moist, adrift, but after an unfocused moment, they find Magnus's eyes and lock on to them, a lost child finding his father's face.

"Jerome. What did Loyd tell you?"

Incomprehension.

"About me. What did he say about Magnus?"

"Magnus?" The monk repeats it, and slowly his confusion lifts like fog. "Magnus, yes." He nods once and closes his eyes again.

Magnus touches his shoulder, touches it again, harder. "Jerome? Did Loyd Crane tell you I wanted to serve you?"

Jerome, breathing almost too lightly to lift his chest, moves his head weakly side to side. "No, a different word."

Magnus touches him again. The priest opens his eyes. Magnus asks, "What word?"

"He said...you...wanted...to service me."

Magnus Anderssen falls to his knees in the snow beside Jerome. Kött Hitta drops from his hand.

Jerome trembles as he reaches to pat the big man's hand, but he is too weak, and his hand falls short. "I loved you, boy. Crane told me...you were ready. That you wanted me."

Magnus, confused, overcome, can only roughly shake his head.

Jerome whispers, nearly inaudibly, "I thought you were...ready, but you say...I...I hurt you." He looks up into Magnus's eyes. "Forgive me."

Tears shine on Magnus's red cheeks. The priest's withered hand finds Magnus's, pats weakly, insistently. "I will not live many more minutes, my son. When you left me, I was heart-broken. Did you hate me so?"

Magnus wipes his face. "I loved you. You were my father, until...until the rape. I hated you from then until this minute. Now I am, I..."

The priest, barely with him, suddenly grips Magnus's hand fiercely. "I loved you, boy, and I die loving you." His grip weakened, the fingers falling on the snow. "Forgive...me."

"I loved you, old man. You were wrong to do what you did."

Magnus feels the old hand quivering, slackening its grasp. The old monk's lips move, a syllable, barely a sound.

Magnus thinks it sounds like a yes. Tears re-gather in his eyes. "Still, Father, for what you gave me, I forgive you."

And then, Magnus Anderssen gently kisses the old monk's forehead, and whispers, "And I love you."

But the old man is gone.

Magnus, finishing, fell into a well of sorrow, blinking, his eyes brimming. Luisa enfolded him. The others waited. Ed closed his eyes, his own heart full. For thirty years, he had counted Magnus his friend; at this moment, he loved the man.

When Magnus was calm, Ben said, "There ain't no words about how sorry we are, Mack. That was one hell of a sad, sad thing." He looked around. Ed knew Ben was about to lighten the mood, hoped he wouldn't. As if he'd felt Ed's wish, Ben sat quietly for a long time. When the abbot had wiped away his own tears and looked at him expectantly, Ben said, "Any more of that good monks' coffee, Abbot?"

Timothy at first simply nodded, looking vaguely surprised, then rang a bell; a couple minutes passed before another pot was brought. Luisa had moved to the floor beside her husband's legs, her arm resting on his thigh, her chin on her arm. His fingers twined quietly in her hair. For the entire time, no one spoke.

135

At last, Ben made a small noise in his throat, as if something unpleasant lodged there. "Look, Mack, I know that rifle of yours ain't been fired, but it ain't quite clear how Father Jerome actually died. We have to investigate that, you know. Hate to say it."

"While we awaited your arrival, I washed the body, Sheriff," the abbot said. "There were no wounds or bruises, or at least no new bruises."

" 'New bruises'? Meanin'?"

"Father Jerome was dying of cancer, all through his body. He was a mass of bruising."

Ben scratched his head. "Well, I guess Doc Runge'll have to get here and do his examination."

"Who's Doc Runge?" asked the abbot, who knew only Doc Keeley.

"He's retired, but he does our coroner work. He'll decide whether the bruises are consistent with cancer." Ben looked around, and seeing the eyes watching him, held up his hands, palms out. "It ain't up to me, folks." He put his hands down. "I gotta investigate this kind of death, especially if there's a chance takin' him up there on that mountain hastened the end."

The abbot broke in again, "Wait, Sheriff. Father Jerome was dying, today or tomorrow most likely. Doctor Keeley was up to see him last Wednesday and said he doubted he'd last to Friday, so it's already past that. Maybe Magnus hastened the end by a few hours, we'll never know, but I would say that Father Jerome experienced redemption up there, and it sounds like Magnus did too." He looked quickly at the rancher, who nodded slightly. "He may have climbed the Coliseum intending to kill, but he came down free. Let it rest there."

"I appreciate the input, Padre." He looked at the others, finally resting his eyes on Magnus. "Your thoughts, my friend."

Magnus smiled sadly. "He loved me and I forgave him at the end. My need to kill him left me. The abbot's right, I'm free. Whatever the law requires of you, Ben, do it. I'm free of it now."

Ben vigorously rubbed his face, then stood and paced the length of the library. "Crap on toast," he growled when he got back to the sitting area. He collected himself and sat down. "Okay. Here's how she'll go. Magnus, pending investigation of the death of Jerome—" He glanced at the abbot. "Last name?"

"O'Brien, Jerome O'Brien."

"Like I'm sayin', Mack, pending the investigation of Father O'Brien's death, if you agree to stay in the valley and make yourself available to my office, I am willin' to release you OR."

Luisa looked up. "Oh Are?"

"Own recognizance."

Luisa looked confused.

Ed said to her, "It means on his word of honor he won't flee." To Ben, he said, "Is this necessary, Ben? Mack told us what happened. I don't think—"

Ben slammed his hand on the table. "Damn it, people. I'm bendin' all the damn the rules here. Again." He glared directly at Ed. "Mack carries a fucking dead man—sorry, Abbot—down that mountain and tells me he planned to kill him and...and I'm lettin' his ass go!" Ben leaped up suddenly, his big, sad eyes wide. Ed had never seen tears in those eyes before.

Ben strode toward the door, then turned and looked at Magnus. "And I'm doin' it because you're my friend, and that ain't the way the law works!"

He barged out through the door.

And just as suddenly, he barged back in.

"Mack," he said, sharply.

"Ben?" Magnus smiled, calm.

"You believed he *raped* you. What the hell changed your mind?"

Magnus smiled faintly. "Does the name Loyd Crane ring a bell?"

SUNDAY, DAY FOURTEEN

136

Luisa Anderssen met Ed at the big front door of the Anderhold. Her eyes widened, smiling. "Ed! This is a surprise."

"I thought I'd drive down and see how Mack's doing." He saw the redness of her eyes. "And how *you're* doing. You all right?"

"*Sí.* I am *muy triste* for him. Very sad. He weeps, but I believe he will be well soon. He is more like himself."

Ed felt his shoulders relax. "Good. Is he home?"

Luisa, nodding, stepped aside from the doorway. "Come in. I will call him."

Ed waited in the dim light of the great room; a small fire flickered in the tall hearth. A book was open, face down on her leather chair. Perhaps Luisa had been reading. After a few minutes, Magnus came into the room. "My friend," he said, extending his hand.

Ed shook it. "How are you, Mack?"

"I'm free, Ed. I slept all night, no dreams."

"No words, no anal pain?" He glanced at Luisa, who briefly closed her eyes.

"None of that." His tone, though, implied something else.

Apprehension tickled Ed's neck. "But what?"

"Grief, I suppose you'd call it. I find myself weeping unexpectedly."

"Ah." Ed waited, apprehension lessening. Grief was good.

Magnus stared into the low fire, nodding slowly. "It breaks my heart that I buried Jerome so deep in my mind. Buried him before he died. All those years I could have known him, visited him." He paused, eyes full of emotion, but after a moment, he forged on, his voice the sound of a soft breeze passing through pines. "All the years I could've forgiven him, and my son could've known him."

After a moment, he gathered himself, said, "Luisa tells me Art Masters passed."

"Yeah, Wednesday."

"A good man, Art. I knew he was dying, but got so tied up in my own anger I didn't realize he'd gone." He shook his head. "Many things to regret, I guess."

"There's a rumor you offered to buy Art's Fine Foods if no one else did. To keep people working."

Magnus looked at the fire. "Art died. No use letting his employees' lives end too."

Ed stood, stepped toward his friend, stopped. He had never embraced Mack before, not in all their years, and had no idea how the big rancher would respond. He put his arms out. "You're a good man, Mack," he said, and moved slightly forward.

Magnus squared his shoulders, smiled. He opened his own arms and the two men moved into an embrace. Ed said nothing. After a moment, he opened his eyes. Luisa stood in the archway, her fingers to her lips. Tears had formed in the corners of her eyes.

Magnus stepped back and walked to the fireplace and laid another log in the flames. "So you'll join us for dinner this time?"

Ed chuckled. "What're we having?"

137

Driving back from the Anderhold, pleasantly full of Luisa's elk roast and spring asparagus, Ed tried to avoid thinking about Jared, but failed. When he got home, he dialed Lynn Monroe's number in Missoula.

"Hey, Ed. This is a nice surprise. What's up?"

"Sorry to bother you at home, but Jared Hansen's got a pretty high mountain to climb, and I've been thinking about how to help him. Got a minute?"

"Sure. What's happening with him?"

Ed's stomach tightened. He'd failed to call the Hansens yesterday as he'd promised; he'd call after he hung up. "I'd like this to be confidential. That all right?"

"Of course."

"He's got an astrocytoma, near his left amygdala."

"Astro-what?"

"Astrocytoma. Brain tumor. He'll probably be having surgery soon."

"Which means he won't be coming back to school this term."

"Yep. That's the first thing I wanted to run by you. Think we could talk Monica into letting him graduate without finishing the year? He might not be..." He hated to say it. "...able to come back in September."

Lynn was quiet for a moment. "Of course. I'll talk to her first thing when I get over there tomorrow." She paused. "How serious do you think this is?"

"Astrocytomas in young people don't grow as fast as in adults, but they're serious. Doc Keeley said the neurosurgeon thinks surgery's worth trying. After that, they'll probably do radiation and maybe chemotherapy."

"You said this is the first thing. What's next?"

"Let's assume Jared comes through the surgery and eventually comes home for recovery. He'll need his friends and a lot of support from the community. As things stand now, too many rumors and bad feelings are swirling around for that to happen." Ed felt a rush of sorrow.

Lynn said, "People are afraid, Ed. Nobody feels safe. They're reacting like people do—blame somebody. They're just—"

Ed felt a spike of irritation, stifled it, but still cut her off. "I understand that, Lynn. But I want to do something to change that fear into support."

"That's a tall order."

"Uh-huh. But Jared needs me to try." He paused. "No, I need to try. For him."

"Okay, what do you want to do?"

"I want to give a speech to the whole student body, tell them what's really going on with Jared, try to get them back on his side."

Lynn gasped. "Wow. That's maybe a good idea, but you're going to be telling everybody some very personal stuff about Jared. Is that wise?"

"There'll be gossip, but there already is. At least it'll be gossip about what's actually going on."

Lynn was quiet for a moment. "Okay, let me talk to Monica tomorrow. I'll go to bat for your idea. Doing something positive for Jared instead of just reacting to the fear—that appeals to me."

"Great. When do you think—"

"Friday's all-school assembly, the day before prom. It's the last one of the year. That work for you?"

"I'll make it work. Thanks, Lynn. That's why I called you first."

138

Loretta Tweedy sat on her sun porch and watched the pink car roll slowly up the street and pull against the curb in front of her house. "Ardyss, come quick," she called. "There's the ugliest car out front."

Ardyss came out from the kitchen, wiping her hands. She stooped and peered out. "Oh my goodness," she clucked. "I'd go blind driving a car that pink."

As she spoke, Grace climbed out of the PV and started up the walk. Ardyss smiled. "Ah, I see." She opened the front door and met Grace. "You have your car!"

"I do, and I love it. Did you know Volvos are the safest cars in the world?"

From inside, Loretta harrumphed. "My Oliver said Mercedes Benz was the safest."

Grace lifted her eyebrows. "Don't tell Northrup. He likes to think mine is."

Ardyss patted her arm. "Fathers are like that, dear."

"Tell me about it. Anyway, I wanted to show you the PV and talk about Meals-on-Wheels."

"What does PV stand for?" Ardyss said, again stooping to look out at the car.

Grace gulped. "Uh, it means, um, the 'Pink *Volvo*.'"

Loretta snorted. Ardyss tilted her head. "Did I hear correctly? The Pink Vulva?"

Grace's face went white. "Ardy! How do *you* know that word?"

Ardyss glanced at Loretta, and the two old ladies giggled. "Goodness, my dear, it's a word I've always been fond of." Her wrinkled fingers brushed her lips, turning a giggle into a smile. "And I've always liked how it works."

Loretta snorted again. "Or how it *used* to work."

Grace reddened. "Omigod," she whispered. "Do you think Northrup knows what it means?"

FRIDAY, DAY NINETEEN

139

At eight-twenty in the morning, as Ed was driving into town, his cell phone buzzed on the seat beside him. The screen read *Stewart, Ben*. He pulled onto the shoulder and took the call.

"Ed, we got good news and bad news." He coughed. "The DA got the report from Sergeant Kendall. She decided it was no-harm, no-foul, just like I figured, but noted the statute don't give us no wiggle room for considerin' outcomes, or motives, neither. So Irv and me talked it over and he says since I've got the authority to 'direct the investigation in all its aspects,' his words, and since I approved what you were doin', he ain't chargin' you."

Ed felt a surge of relief. "That's welcome." He hesitated, unsure if he wanted the rest. "What's the bad news?"

"He wants me to issue a press release taking responsibility for approving the 'change in the investigative procedures.' And you know what that means."

A rain of remorse drenched his relief. "It means some folks'll call for you to resign."

"Maybe, maybe not. What it means, it makes the TV news everywhere in Montana and north Idaho."

"Ben, I'm sorry. I—"

"Whoa, there, bucko. I ain't fishin' for apologies. I knew the odds when I okayed your stunt, so I ain't pissed at you. What happens, happens. And a public shamin' ain't nothin' compared to a brain tumor or gettin' raped, so let's move on." He coughed into the phone. "Besides..."

"Besides what?"

"Your girlfriend told me she's thinkin' Ordrew might be Jack Kollier's source in the department. You put that together with two other things, about how he treated Gracie and the Hansens, and about him enterin' your place without permission, I'm thinkin' Brad and me are gonna have us a little

329

negotiation."

"What's to negotiate?"

"Irv says when Ordrew took that toothbrush, he didn't have no search warrant. Goin' into your place is one thing—he saw the boy's truck, so he had a reason. But searchin' is somethin' else. The kid couldn't be hidin' in your bathroom trash. So I'm givin' Brad a choice: He can take a two-week suspension without pay for that and the other things or go find him another job. Hopin' he'll get mad and go away."

"If he takes the suspension and stays?"

"Then I put him on notice, due process and all that. He goofs two more times, I give him thirty days notice."

Ed smiled. "Something tells me he's not going away just yet."

Ben grunted. "Probably right on that." Ed heard him take a hefty sigh, then he coughed again. "Well, I gotta write me a press release." A third cough.

"Are you all right, Ben? You're coughing."

"Pay no mind. Ain't nothin' to worry about."

"You holding a press conference or just sending it to the media?"

"Naw. I'll offer an exclusive interview with our pal Jack Kollier, if he tells me his source. He names Ordrew, Bradley's only got one more strike."

"My god, Ben. You're good at this."

"Bet your sweet butt I am. Problem is, Jack's the genuine article. He'll never tell me his source. I'll give him the exclusive anyway."

"Well, I still am sorry I pulled you into my, as you call it, stunt."

"Word to the wise, buddy: Next time, don't call me."

Ed heard Ben laughing as he ended the call.

140

Ed, sitting on the stage set up in front of the basketball net in the gym, looked over the audience. He hadn't felt this nervous since those dreadful piano recitals for the parents of Mr. Case's piano students. While the principal, Monica Sergeant, went through the regular news and announcements about prom, graduation in two weeks, and the end of the year, he thought back to yesterday's conversation with Jared.

"Whatever you think they need to know, Ed." Jared had been subdued, his eyes haunted. "You can tell them everything."

"You're sure? You want all the kids at school to know what's wrong?"

Jared smiled faintly. "They already know. They just don't know why. Or how it ends." His eyes teared briefly, but he wiped them quickly. "I had a dream about my grandpa last night. He told me dying wasn't so bad."

Ed had felt his own eyes moistening. "You scared?"

"Sure, but it's funny. I'm not the same kind of scared as when I have my paranoid spells."

"They're still happening, I suppose."

Jared nodded. "Now and then, but the BuSpar helps in between. My mom or my dad just stay with me when I get bad."

Ed felt a thickness in his throat, thinking of how stricken he would be if Grace got sick. He wondered where the Hanson's got the strength. He stood up. "We're in this together, pal. Every step of the way."

Jared had nodded. "Yeah. And thanks for talking to my school." He looked shyly at Ed. "Will you tell everyone I'm sorry? And that I love my friends?"

Now, as Ed's gaze swept over the faces, most of them stony and veiled, he knew it wouldn't be the facts that would touch them. Too much, he realized, was at stake here. Somehow, a flood of fear and rumor had to be turned into a tide of compassion, or Jared's eventual return to the valley would be a nightmare. If he *could* return. Surgery was scheduled for Monday morning. By Tuesday, maybe Wednesday, they'd discover whatever future awaited him. This speech had to be the memorial Jared might never, otherwise, receive. Mere facts couldn't carry that weight.

As the principal, Monica Sergeant, introduced him, Ed glanced at his notes, then folded them and, when he stood, left them on the chair. He stepped up to the podium. No applause. He breathed deep, swallowed, began.

"You've all lost a friend in Jared Hansen. He was someone you respected, even looked up to. Some of you were close to him. Some of you admired him. Some of you wanted to be like him. Some of you were jealous of him. Whatever you felt about him, Jared Hansen was someone to contend with, either a model to live up to, or a rival to compete with. But he was a real person, right?"

He paused, waiting, praying someone would respond. A few guarded faces nodded.

It's a start. "Three weeks ago, all that changed, didn't it?" He paused again, and maybe a tenth of the crowd nodded. "He was found hoarding rifles and ammunition. He had a pressure cooker. Nobody could figure it out. 'This can't be Jared,' you guys thought. Well, we grownups thought so too. And when we couldn't figure it out, we all got scared. He said he wanted to kill the senior class. He thought the government wanted to kill him. This wasn't the Jared we all knew, was it?"

He looked out at the kids, waiting, challenging them to answer. More heads were shaking. More eyes were on him, some not so stony now. He was manipulating them, sure. Manipulating them emotionally, manipulating them with the truth—*for Jared's sake*, he thought. And maybe for their own.

"You guys know me, right? I'm the psychologist here in the valley." Many heads nodded. "And you know Sheriff Stewart and Deputy Pelton—the one who got shot a couple years ago?" More nods. Inwardly, he smiled. *The old used-car-sales trick: Get them saying 'Yes.'* "We really tried to find out what was going on. We couldn't believe what we were hearing from Jared either, any more than you guys could." He caught Grace's eye, sitting with her girls in a far back row. She nodded hard.

"Psychologists like me know a few things about people's minds," he said, smiling. Some faces smiled back. "We know how people get mentally ill, most of the time. We're supposed to know that, right?"

More nods. "And none of the things we know about school shooters fit Jared. He wasn't bullied—most of you liked him a lot. He wasn't abused, he involved himself in the community, he was a leader, a serious kid. Not a loner, not angry. He made people proud, not afraid. Then all of a sudden, he went crazy. Stark, raving nuts."

Somewhere in the crowd, somebody snickered. *Good sign.*

Ed decided to push the humor. "Here's the scientific term for it: Completely bonkers." Outright laughs. "And we couldn't figure it out, not with all our psychology, not with all the police investigation. Nothing. A mystery." He looked out. There were nods.

Time to turn the corner. "What you guys don't know is that Jared wasn't mentally ill all the time. Some of the time, he was normal, and he felt guilty and ashamed about the threats he'd made. He didn't want to hurt anybody, but then those spells would come over him."

Ed studied the faces. Nearly everyone was looking hard at him, waiting—he hoped—for the mystery to be revealed.

"When I talked to him during the times he was normal, he was as scared of his feelings as all of you were. Are. He was terrified of himself. And he wanted to kill himself to stop it all."

There were a few gasps. One girl in a front row put her hand against her mouth, eyes wide. Despite having gotten Jared's permission to say all this, he felt the burden of betrayal. Jared would come back to a community that knew it all. Would they forgive him? Could he move them enough to save Jared?

Art's last words came back. *You're nobody's savior.* Just do what you can.

He gathered himself. "That's right, he wanted to die. He said, 'Doctor, I need to protect my friends. The only way I can do it is to die. I'm evil.'" He paused. "He wondered if he had a demon in him. Well, he wasn't far wrong."

All the faces lifted to him, open now. Some heads tilted, questions in their eyes. Demons? He could feel the energy changing.

"It wasn't a demon, though." He paused again, looked around at all the faces. "Jared has a tumor in his brain, right near the fear center." More gasps, whispers. One girl began to cry, quietly, about ten rows back. "The tumor causes him to become paranoid—that's the real scientific word. And the reason he gets paranoid is that this growth makes him so terrified he can't bear it. Becoming paranoid is your brain desperately trying to explain the terror it feels but can't figure out. It's like, 'If I'm this scared, the only thing that makes sense is the government wants to kill me.' You guys get that?"

There were a few puzzled looks, but a wider wave of nodding flowed across the young faces.

"Of course you get it. There's nobody here who hasn't experienced their fear center acting up, making you think things you'd never think if it wasn't in the driver seat. 'If I don't pass this test, my Dad'll kill me!' 'If I don't kiss him on this date, he'll never go out with me again!' 'If I don't get elected to school council, I'll never get into a good college.' None of those things are true, but when your fear center's working overtime, they feel as solid as the Coliseum. Anybody ever think thoughts like that? Raise your hand."

Hands started rising, some fast, some tentative, but a wave spread across the whole gym. "Sure you have." He raised his own hand. "Me, too. Know what? I felt that sort of fear when I couldn't figure out what was wrong with Jared. I thought, 'What if I fail? What if he dies because of me? What if I can't save him and he kills somebody? I'll be disgraced. I'll have to leave the valley.'" He thought of Art Masters, sitting his horse patiently, watching.

There was a rustle of whispering. He had them.

"Crazy thoughts. I was stark, raving nuts!"

Everyone laughed, but the laughter quickly sputtered out.

"Okay. Next Monday morning, Jared will have surgery to take the cancer out. If the operation's successful, we hope he'll be the Jared all of you have known all along, with the same normal, crazy fears we all have, and the same great personality. And sometime this summer, he'll come home to recover."

He let that hang in the air, thinking, *I hope to God*. The smiles faded as what he'd said began sinking in.

He waited the span of a long breath. This was it. "Between now and then, though, you're going to hear lots of opinions—most of them based on rumors, on so-called facts that aren't true at all. People will tell you he's violent. That he's evil. You know the kind of thing they'll say." Nods. "Some people will say that this talk of a tumor is just an excuse, and they won't know how much like you and me Jared was, only worse because of his tumor."

He paused. "Unless you guys spread the word and fight the rumors that aren't true with the facts that *are* true."

He watched them a second, willing his point to reach them. "You know the kind of rumors you'll hear, don't you?"

Again, nods flowed across the crowd like ripples across water.

"Do you want me to show you what you can do about those rumors and lies?"

Nods now, vigorous, rapid. He steeled himself. What he was about to say went beyond facts. Perhaps he was telling them the truth, but it was a truth about what he *hoped*. Which might not be true at all.

"Okay, listen hard to me. There are two things you all can do. The first one is, when you hear somebody say something stupid or pass along a rumor, stand up to it and tell the truth. Tell 'em, 'My friend's got a brain tumor and they're going to take it out and that's all this is.'" He looked out. Some of the kids were scribbling in their notebooks.

"Okay," he said. "Here's the second thing. I want you all to close your eyes, and imagine something." He waited while eyes closed. "Okay, just take a few deep breaths." He waited, a few moments, watching faces relaxing. "Okay, now, imagine that *you* are Jared Hansen. Imagine that *you* were the one who made those horrible threats, who did those horrible things. That you're the one with the brain tumor pressing against your fear center.

Imagine *you are the one*. Are you imagining it?" Many heads nodded, eyes closed.

"Good. Now, imagine that you are coming back to Jefferson, the cancer in your brain taken out, trying to be normal again. Imagine what it will feel like to face your friends, knowing they know all this about you. All the horrible things you said, the horrible things you did, because of that damn tumor. Can you imagine facing your friends? It'll be awful, won't it?"

A tide of nods.

"Okay, now imagine this: You're Jared Hansen. You're back in the valley, facing your friends, and you're scared of how they'll react to you. Now imagine how you *want* them to react when you first meet. What do you *want* your friends to say? How do you *want* them to look at you? When you say, 'Let's go to Alice's for pizza,' how do you *want* your friends to respond?"

"Is it, 'Uh, well, I gotta go do my homework'? or do you want them to go, 'Yeah! Let's do it!' Can you imagine what you'd want, if you were Jared?"

Nods all across the room.

"Okay, open your eyes. I want you to look at me."

Everyone did.

"You are who you are. Every one of you is a good human being. Every one of you has fears, has problems. None of us is perfect, and nobody *really* expects us to be. Every now and then in our lives, though, we get a chance to be better. To be compassionate. We get a chance to care about somebody outside ourselves." He looked across the gym, pausing a moment. Then he gave it: "People say teenagers can't do that, they're too self-centered."

Frowns spread across the gym. He paused, waited, then said, "I say, bullshit."

Titters rippled through the room.

"I believe you guys can be compassionate. I want you to prove what people say about you guys is nonsense. When you hear someone spreading rumors about Jared, and when he comes back, I want you to show the folks who say kids can't be compassionate, just how goddamn wrong they are."

The gasp at that *goddamn* cemented its message. In the back of the hall, Lynn Monroe raised her thumb, smiling.

He finished. "You guys want to know what Jared told me when I asked him if I could tell you all this?"

Nods, all across the room. Ed felt his throat thicken. He had to clear it before he could speak.

"He said to me, 'Tell everyone I'm sorry.' " He paused a moment, his own emotion filling his chest. He coughed. "And he said, 'Tell them I love my friends.' "

The tears he saw on some faces surprised him. As did the tears he felt on his own.

141

"Heard you gave a hell of a speech," Andi said. They were sitting on the porch swing, watching the light grow dim above the mountains, and enjoying one of the warmest evenings in a month of warm evenings. Grace was in town, putting up the last decorations for tomorrow night's prom. The spring air felt sweet and easy and dry.

She nudged him. "So, was it a good speech?"

He didn't want to talk about the speech. "Fabulous weather, isn't it?"

"Come on. Tell me about your speech."

He knew she'd probably already heard the finer points. He gave a barebones summary.

"Doesn't sound inspiring to me."

"You're getting leftovers."

Andi laughed. "Leftovers, eh?" She put her hand on his lap. "Little Eddie doesn't feel very, shall I say, attentive."

"It's been an emotional day." He chuckled. "Hell, it's been an emotional month."

The PV pulled into the yard, too fast, crunching gravel as Grace braked. When she jumped out of the car, Andi quickly withdrew her hand from Ed's lap. Grace, who saw the movement and frowned, ignored it, bubbled, "Northrup, me and my girls, we're über proud of you."

He smiled, then said, "Thanks. And that would be, my girls and I are über proud."

"That's what I said."

"I've got one word for you: *Grammar*."

Grace rolled her eyes. "I've got one word for you: *Obsessive*."

Andi laughed, and Ed smiled. "It's my job. So tell me, what's happening after the prom?"

"Geez, Northrup. We're having a party. What'd you do after prom? Read a book?"

Andi laughed again.

"Will there be drinking?"

"That's not fair, Northrup. It's *prom.*"

"A simple 'yes' or 'no' answers the question."

"Okay. No."

Andi made a disbelieving sound, but said nothing.

Grace looked sheepish. "Okay, everybody, like, drinks a little after prom. So, yes, drinking in moderation."

This time, Andi laughed. " 'Moderation' is a mythical country where drinkers say they live."

Ed chuckled. "I want you to call me after the party and I'll pick you up."

Grace shook her head. "Uh, Mr. Demented? I already told you, the party's at Jen's, and we're staying overnight."

Ed nodded, remembering. "Right. You did tell me. Good plan."

Grace made an exaggerated bow. "Thank you, Master." She turned and went inside, and they heard her bedroom door close.

Ed looked at the lines of bare dirt, the gravel scraped away by her tires. "Looks like you're right about paving the yard."

"You comfortable with her drinking after prom?"

"I guess so. I called Jen's dad and he said they'd supervise closely. I trust him." He took her hand and laid it back on his lap. "You were saying?"

"I believe we were discussing *leftovers*. It's a warm night. What say we grab a blanket and a bottle of pinot and head over to the river?"

"You ever hear about the Baptist preacher?"

"No. What about him?"

"Gave a passionate sermon. 'We'll throw the booze in the river, throw the dice in the river, throw the condoms in the river!' The piano started playing and the choir broke into the hymn. 'Let us gather at the river.'"

"What I had in mind."

142

Lying on the new spring grass beside the river, watching the sea of stars flowing over them, they murmured, pointing out satellites gliding down the star-washed sky. The river burbled, at last confined within its banks, though still running high from snowmelt in the mountains, brimming over rocks, tamed. On the far shore, sprouts of grass and weed pushed up through the flood-spread mud.

Andi turned on her side, facing away from Ed. "It's been a rocky month," she said, her voice velvety. Ed's hand circled slowly on her lower back. "First the flood, then Jared. Nobody's felt safe here for a long time."

"Add Mack into that equation." He shifted gears, rubbing her shoulders and down her spine. "Plus Ordrew's obstruction crap." He slowly massaged her lower back. "Think Ben's press release will cause trouble?"

"Ben'll be fine. He's an old bull in a field of calves."

"Ordrew's a calf?"

"No, he's a calf's fart."

Ed started laughing. Andi turned and lay back, pulled him down, and kissed him softly, which stifled the laughter. After the kiss, she rolled again onto her stomach. "Rub my back some more."

He leaned across her and took his cup, sipped the wine, placed it carefully in the new grass, then resumed his gentle circular massage. He drifted his fingers across the seat of her jeans.

She turned, leaning on her elbow, smiling. "You're getting fresh."

"Sorry. A guy's gotta do what a guy's gotta do."

She rolled onto her back again. He slipped his fingers under her belt buckle. "Mind if I loosen the reins?"

"You're still getting fresh."

"We came down here to get stale?" With his free hand, he took another sip of wine, while the fingers of his other hand worked her buckle looser.

Andi smiled. "Nope. Fresh is good." She giggled. "Bet you can't undo it one-handed."

"Easy as pie. I'm a one-hander with bras, too. Number one on every guy's bucket list, the old one-hander."

She laughed again. "Know what's number one on my bucket list?"

"No, tell me." The belt came open. "Ta-da!" He started working on the top button of her jeans, one-handed.

"Number one is finding a guy who can figure out a terrorist's brain tumor, stick with his friend when he threatens murder, buy his daughter a safe car, and..." She caught her breath as he undid the button and pulled down her zipper. "And undress her one-handed. Irresistible combination."

His fingers, freed to fondle, found what they were looking for, and she sighed. "Yep, you make a working girl feel nice and safe." She pressed herself up against his fingers.

They lay together, arousing each other slowly, gentled by the bubbling of the water over the rocks a few feet away. Ed leaned closer against her and kissed her neck.

He thought about Andi feeling safe here. His fingers continued their work.

"Jesus," she purred.

"No, just Ed," he whispered into her soft hair.

The End

View other Black Rose Writing titles at www.blackrosewriting.com/books

and use promo code PRINT to receive a 20% discount when purchasing.

BLACK ROSE writing™

CPSIA information can be obtained
at www.ICGtesting.com
Printed in the USA
LVOW03s0703130418
573034LV00001B/54/P